CHALLENGE

"You are Lord of the Trees," Julian said, as evenly as he could, "and your people's roots spread through the land. I must know where the Earthstone came to rest after the explosion on the Red Mountain. And you must accept my right to call on you for aid."

"That is more than your father ever dared," responded the Guardian.

"That may well be." Julian thought of what he had heard of the dead King. "But my father had the four Jewels. My father did not have to fight a sorcerer. And now your young trees root in his bones," he added brutally. "As my father's flesh has fed your young, and as someday mine shall do the same, *I call on you to aid my father's son!*"

A shudder swept through the trees around them; and even Silverhair stared at him in shock.

TOR Books by Diana L. Paxson

SILVERHAIR THE WANDERER
THE EARTHSTONE

DIANA L. PAXSON

CAN PRINCE JULIAN SAVE
WESTRIA FROM THE INHUMAN
POWER OF THE BLOOD LORD?

THE EARTHSTONE

THE FOURTH BOOK OF WESTRIA

A TOM DOHERTY ASSOCIATES BOOK

THE EARTHSTONE

Copyright © 1987 by Diana L. Paxson

First printing: September 1987

A TOR Book

Published by Tom Doherty Associates, Inc.
49 West 24 Street
New York, N.Y. 10010

Cover art by Tom Kidd

ISBN: 0-812-54862-0
CAN. ED.: 0-812-54863-9

Printed in the United States of America

0 9 8 7 6 5 4 3 2 1

To Ian—

Grow strong as the bedrock,
Fertile as the soil,
Upright as the growing things that seek the sun!

CONTENTS:

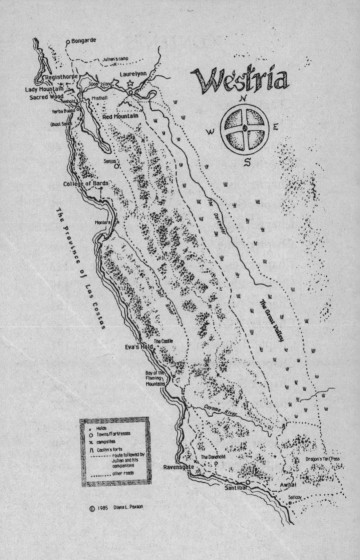

Westria

Holds •
Towns/Fortresses ○
campsites ✕
Caolin's forts ∧
------- route followed by Julian and his companions
.... other roads

© 1985 Diana L. Paxson

❦❦ ONE ❦❦

Beyond the western hills the sky glowed amber. But the hillsides had faded to a patchwork of olive and ocher, as if the sky were distilling all the splendor of the June day. Soon, only the undulating line of the ridges lifted black against the afterglow. Southward across the river, the Red Mountain dulled from rose to garnet and then to a dim bulk among its attendant hills.

Julian shifted position uncomfortably. For a moment he had seen not the rounded slopes of the hills, but a woman's breast and the long, sweet curve of her thigh. Then he became aware of his body's response and grinned ruefully. The mountains of his childhood were palisaded with pine and buttressed with stone. He was not accustomed to the naked femininity of these coastal hills.

The plucked carcasses of two quail sizzled over his little fire. Julian turned them carefully. He had been lucky to get them, he thought, for his weapons were the ax and the sword, not the bow or snare. At least he would eat well, even if he must sleep alone. Then the water in his battered pan began to boil and he dropped in a few pinches of chamomile tea, breathing in appreciatively as the fresh scent of the herbs mingled with the savor of quail rubbed and stuffed with wild onion. Tubers of the nutgrass he had found near the spring were roasting among the coals. He would fare well enough tonight, though this little hollow near the empty road through the hills above the Great Bay had to supply both dinner and lodging. He had fared far worse on campaign.

Julian lifted the pot from the fire and blew away the steam. The live oak trees around him stretched a black net of leaf and branch between him and the rapidly dimming

1

sky. Already one star winked through them like a distant
eye. On the earth, the only light was the flicker of his little
fire, the only light he had seen since he passed the last
holding, busy with its preparations for the Midsummer
Festival.

Perhaps he should have accepted their invitation—it
seemed strange to be alone when all over Westria men
would be drinking and dancing the shortest night away. But
the Feast, and the recovery afterward, would have lost him
at least a day on the road.

His lips twitched, mocking his own urgency. The messages he was carrying from the Lord Commander of the
Ramparts to the Regent of Westria would not suffer from a
day's delay, and as for his other errand—he had lived for
eighteen years without knowing his parents' names. Why
was it so important to him to learn them from the Master of
the Junipers now?

But foolish or not, here he was, and there was no profit in
wondering. Julian shrugged his heavy shoulders, poured out
a little tea for the earth offering, and drank. All around him
the crickets were tuning up for their nightly concert, accom-
panied by the juicy tearing of grass as his bay mare grazed
near the spring. But somehow these friendly sounds only
intensified the deepening silence of the land.

Julian swallowed and gazed unseeing into the night. It
had been a long time since he had been so alone. In camp
with the border guards or with Lord Philip at Rivered there
had always been laughter and the echo of song. Even the
inns where he had stayed as he crossed the Great Valley had
been islands of human sound in the immensity of a world in
which men, since the Cataclysm, had been only tenants of
the land. He had forgotten what it was like to be alone with
the hills.

A flare of light in the sky to the south caught his eye—at
first he thought it a star, but it burned too low. Then he
remembered the Red Mountain, and realized that someone
had lighted the beacon fire there. It should have comforted
him, but it seemed to glitter like the eye of some great beast
crouching in the dark. Gooseflesh pebbled his skin as the
silence deepened. He lifted the pan to his lips again.

"Tea! Is there enough of it to warm an old woman's
bones?"

Julian coughed and spluttered, scalding his chin. His head came up and he focused on the figure at the edge of the firelight.

"I didn't hear you!" Astonishment slipped the words past his lips' guard. His hand moved to the worn hilt of his sword and to the pouch where his messages lay. The old woman cackled, her features revealed and veiled as the fire flared and fell. Julian grimaced, disgusted at the ease with which this gentle land disarmed defenses trained into him by two hard years with the border patrol.

Even his pony had ceased munching and lifted her head, gazing at the newcomer with liquid eyes. Then the woman laughed again; the mare blew gustily and returned to the grass. The animal's placid reaction was reassuring, and Julian realized that he had been wondering if this old creature with her stained and broken smile was real.

"I'll be happy to share with you if you don't mind drinking from the pan—" He held out the tea, trying to smile. The old woman sidled around the fire, wheezing, and maneuvered herself down at his side.

Julian's nostrils flared at the sour smell of her, but he controlled his expression and continued to offer the pan of tea. Her brown fingers curled around the handle like Ancient tree-roots at the edge of a stream.

"Mind? No indeed—how should I mind setting my lips where a young man's mouth has been?" Her quick glance snared his, and at his reaction she began to cackle again. Then she applied herself to the tea. Fascinated, he watched the muscles in her scrawny throat constricting as the hot liquid went down.

"Now that was just what an old lady needed; that, and a moment's warmth from your bit of a fire. . . ." She sighed in satisfaction and handed Julian the pan. He peered into it and his eyes widened—she had swallowed the tea and the chamomile flowerets as well!

"The fire, and that lovely smell of roasting bird—" she went on. She leaned forward, eyes slitting in ecstasy as she breathed in the rich aroma of the cooking quail. The fringes of her tattered shawl fluttered dangerously close to the flames.

It's not her age—thought Julian, tensing to pull her away from the fire, *it's her smell. . . .* He could not quite bring himself to grasp her arm. Half the earth of Westria seemed to be caked on her thin neck or ground into the hands that reached for the quail. With a sigh he lifted one of the spits from the forked sticks that held it over the flames and handed it to her.

She tore at it eagerly. "A real gentleman!" She paused, jaws still working, and her beady eyes fixed his. "Not like some, that would as soon rape a poor old body as look at her!" She made some sound halfway between choking and laughter, and Julian flinched as a bony forefinger stabbed at him. "What is your name?"

"Julian—Julian of Stanesvale," he added. As he spoke, for a moment he saw the forested ridges above his home, blue with summer haze, and smelled the aromatic scent of sun-warmed pine. He saw again the sun-browned smile of the woman who had raised him and the blunt features of his foster father, powdered with granite dust. Perhaps he should have stayed with them, but a mound of earth where the mariposa lilies bloomed every spring was the only part of Stanesvale that really belonged to him. His mother was buried there, but he did not even know her name.

"More tea, lad—unless you have some wine to help me wash this down!"

Julian stared at her. She was still gnawing at the quail carcass, and it took him a moment to understand her. Quick anger reddened his skin, but he suppressed it. With her tattered grey shawl and the scrap of quail in her mouth she reminded him of a wolf bitch he had once nursed back from starvation in the snow.

He sighed and reached for his water bottle and the little packet of tea. Gold glinted from the hag's skirts as she leaned forward to watch him. The layers of clothing that swathed her had been good cloth once, but now the rich green of her skirt had faded to the color of drought-dried leaves; the saffron petticoat grimed until it was the color of earth baked to clay by the sun. The gold thread that edged it was tarnished and frayed.

I can afford pity, Julian thought grimly as the water began to boil. *I have the health and the strength to make my way. It must be worse to fear one's ending than to be ignorant of where one's life began.*

The old woman smacked her lips and tossed the quail's

polished bones into the fire, then wiped her mouth on the muddy blue of her sleeve and reached for the tea. Half hoping it would burn her mouth, Julian handed her the pan. She stopped suddenly, looking at the badge on his shoulder.

"Stanesvale lies in the Snowy Mountains— I've been there!" she said accusingly. "But that's the Lord Commander's badge. Why would a good lad like you leave your home and go to Rivered?"

Julian shook his dark head and smiled. If it really had been his home, he thought, perhaps he would not have been so eager to leave.

"Doesn't a young man usually want to see the world?" he asked. "Lord Philip's younger brother Robert was in the group of initiates when I took my name. We became friends. Afterward, the Lord Commander took me into his household, and when I had learned something of the sword, Robert and I went out with the border patrol."

His right arm twitched with memory of the endless hours of practice with the heavy wooden sword and the shock of surprise when he had used an edged weapon on a man's flesh for the first time. His neck ached still with the strain of learning to do a soldier's job without hating your enemy, though it was hard when you saw what was left of the mountain villages when the raiders from the Barren Lands had passed by. He shook his head to dislodge the memory and saw that the old woman was gobbling down the second quail.

Julian poked among the coals, speared one of the nutgrass tubers and popped it into his mouth, blowing and cursing as it burned his tongue. *Fool!* he told himself, but now his unwelcome guest was turning the coals over too and he speared another, suddenly frantic lest he get nothing to eat at all.

"And what of you, Grandmother?" he asked, swallowing the last bite of tuber. "You're far from home—why do your children let you wander the world?"

She sagged where she sat, shapeless as a bundle of rags. "I have borne so many babes. . . ." She sighed mournfully. "My children dwell the length and breadth of Westria, but there's scarcely a one of them still cares for me! They don't remember the womb that bore them, or the breasts that fed them—no!" She began to rock, keening softly. "My children are gone and I am cast out to wander. Where will I go and who will care for me?"

Appalled, Julian pushed some of his carefully hoarded dried fruit toward her. She still rocked, but at least that stopped her moaning. Even her gibes were better than this grief.

He should not have asked about her family. He had seen bereavement often enough on the border and even as he crossed Westria. In the mountains the danger was the raiders who were becoming bolder with every year. But even in the Great Valley there were abandoned villages and tattered bands of refugees. Landholders were beginning to fight each other now, and though the lords who commanded each Province tried to keep the peace, the authority of the Regent was not sufficient to judge between them, now that there was no King. He knew that other systems worked well in other lands, some places electing their rulers, others ruled by an Emperor with absolute power. But though the sovereign of Westria held authority over Province and holding loosely, it seemed that he had to be there.

Without a King, the fabric of Westria was tearing as a garment will tear when the thread that binds its seams decays. Now it was only the borders of the Provinces, but Julian could see the rot spreading until every little holding armed against its neighbor.

His fingers went to his message pouch, but there was no comfort there. Lord Philip had told him its contents—a request for Lord Eric to punish a man of Las Costas who had raided into Lord Philip's lands. Once more he saw the trouble in the Lord Commander's eyes. The twenty years of Regency agreed upon when the Queen and her child had disappeared would be over soon. Philip of the Ramparts and his young brother, Robert, were the last of the royal kin, and neither one of them wanted to rule.

"It was not so in the old days!" the old woman mumbled, "in the old days when a King ruled in Laurelynn!"

The echo of Julian's thoughts startled him. It was true. Westria must have a ruler soon, but he feared that even if Philip took the throne, peace would be hard to find. Philip was Lord of the Ramparts just as Eric the Regent was also Lord of Seagate. The other Provinces would resent any of their number who rose to rule. *If he asks, I will serve*

Philip to the end, thought Julian, *but it will take a master weaver to make Westria whole again!*

"Ah—I am so hungry, and it has been so long!" the old woman moaned. Still distracted by his own thoughts, Julian gave her the rest of the dried fruit. She snatched it from his fingers, her eyes brightening.

"Ah, you're a generous lad and a strong one. Perhaps now I'll be satisfied." She popped a chunk of fruit into her mouth and began to chew on it, still talking. "And you're a fighter too—" She gestured toward the use-smoothed hilt of his sword. "Are you a good one? You should be, with those shoulders!" She smacked her lips, her sorrows for the moment forgotten.

Julian shrugged, acutely conscious of the development that a boyhood spent helping his foster father quarry stone had given to his shoulders and arms. They had teased him about it at Philip's court, and next to his friend Robert's classic beauty he was always aware of the weight of his straight dark hair and the uncompromising line of his brows. But it was true that when he struck a blow his opponent did not rise again.

"And you have seen battle, too, I'll wager!" The old woman nodded with a broken grin. "Tell me—I never knew a young man yet who would not boast of his deeds!"

Julian began to shake his head. There had been songs made about him already, but he did not sing them. Yet without his willing it he found that his lips were moving and he *was* telling her.

"Do you think that fighting is glorious?" he asked. "Haven't you suffered enough, old woman, to know that isn't true? They sent me and Robert out with the border guard, just to season us, Lord Philip said. But when we came to the third village—Bear Valley, they called it—we found the raiders we had been tracking wintering there. And they were waiting for us. An unlucky arrow took out our captain and then they were all over us. I saw an opening and went for it, and suddenly the rest of our men were following me." Words rushed from his lips as the blur of events that had been the battle replayed themselves in his memory.

"And when it was over, the men that survived came to me for orders—and the villagers, too, when the storms came and we were snowed in." Julian shook his head, still confused when he remembered the commands he had given and the decisions he had made. But at the time it had seemed the natural thing to do.

"It was like that all winter, until the roads cleared and Lord Philip came. . . ." Julian's stomach rumbled and he looked up at the woman on the other side of the fire. There were only coals left now and her face was in shadow. Its contours changed with every moment that passed.

"Ungrateful man— He should have knighted you!" The familiar cackle startled him.

"He wanted to," Julian said simply. "He wants to make me a lord and a leader, and *that* makes me afraid. I don't know why I took command, or why the people followed me. I don't know who I am!"

"Don't snivel, boy—" came the tart rejoinder. "You just told me your name!"

Julian forced a laugh. "The ridiculous scruples of youth? That's what Lord Philip says! But knowing that no one else cares who my parents were doesn't help. I have to know!"

There was a short bark of laughter from the other side of the fire. "Because you won't be a leader without a title to your name?" she asked.

"No . . ." Julian answered slowly. "Because I will be. It's happened often enough now. When something goes wrong I start making decisions and people do as I say. I never intend it, but—" He shrugged his heavy shoulders.

"Perhaps it doesn't matter, after all," he went on. "But I would feel easier if I knew more of my heritage than the bare fact that my mother died on the way to the Sacred Valley of Awahna. There's a man called the Master of the Junipers—an adept of the College of the Wise. He was with her when she died, and he left me to be fostered by the folk at Stanesvale. His home is in Seagate, and when I've delivered my messages to the Regent I intend to find him. The Master is the only man in Westria who knows the truth about my mother and me!"

The fire had dimmed so that now he could see only the glitter of the woman's eyes. "And if you are the child of rape or incest," she asked, "do you really want to know?"

Julian hugged his knees as a chill wind lifted fine ash into the air. "Yes—" He found his voice at last. "*Especially* if there is shame in my heritage. It would not matter if I lived for myself alone, but I am afraid to take responsibility for others without knowing the mettle of which I am made!"

The shadowy huddle beyond the dying fire shifted, and it seemed to Julian that she nodded, though he could not be sure. "Self-knowledge—yes, you must have that, but do you think you will find it nesting in your family tree? To know yourself you must climb a different sort of tree; you must put your roots into the land. . . . I could tell you . . ." Her voice faded and Julian leaned forward, trying to see her through the shadows.

The woman shook her head and her sudden cackle shocked him into full awareness once more. "It's late. I'm weary. Time enough for talking when the sun warms old bones! I'm weary—" she repeated querulously, "and the wind is very cold!"

Julian suppressed a groan. He had been imagining things when he suspected her of hiding secrets. How could he have forgotten her wretchedness? Now the darkness covered her with its kind veil, but he remembered too vividly her torn garments and how the skin of her wrist stretched over sharp bones, and he knew his duty. Swearing softly, he got to his feet and picked up the saddle blanket upon which he had intended to sleep.

"Here—" he said roughly. "This will keep you from the cold." He thrust it at her and stumped back to his side of the fire. As he pulled his cloak around him he could hear her grunting softly and the rustle of cloth as she tried to find a comfortable position in which to lie. He suppressed the impulse to offer help and curled up on his side with his back to the fire.

Julian had thought that his own weariness would claim him quickly. But whether it was the cold, or the hard ground beneath him, or only his awareness of the creature on the other side of the fire, the best he could manage was an uneasy doze. And some time past midnight, when a haze of thin high clouds had begun to veil the stars, he heard the old woman moan and was abruptly fully awake, knowing that he had half expected this all along.

He lay still, wondering what to do. The woman whimpered. He could hear her teeth chattering and the rustle as she tried to curl up in a way that would keep out the cold. He was cold too, and he had shared his blankets with other men on campaign often enough to know that two bodies together slept warmer than one—though he doubted that there would be much heat in this old creature's frame.

He remembered the smell of her then and swallowed painfully, but he also knew that the nose would become immune to any stench in time. *Come on,* he told himself, *the night will be over in a few hours!* Stumbling with stiffness, he stepped around the dead fire and with a sigh knelt next to the dark shape huddled there.

He spread his cloak over them both and curved his body around the old woman's, finding it surprisingly substantial. He waited until first her whimpering ceased, then her shivering. He felt her turn.

"Lie still, or do you want to freeze?"

She made a stifled sound, and after a moment Julian realized it was laughter. "It's been a long time since I lay in a young man's arms; let me savor it. . . . His name was Julian too. . . ."

Julian stiffened, then realized that her wits must still be wandering in the land of sleep, and held still. She stirred again, and hair like dry straw rasped his neck.

"Give an old woman a kiss then," she said, "to warm me!" She was not laughing now. Her voice held the echo of a song sung many years ago and miles away.

What harm can it do me? he asked himself. *I'm like a girl afraid to lose her maidenhead!* His heart wrenched with pity and an odd surge of protectiveness, Julian took a deep breath, held it, and bent his head to kiss her dry cheek.

But it was the parchment of her lips that he found. He began to pull away, but she was holding on to him and he did not want to hurt her. And then it seemed to him that her mouth was softening, her lips growing smooth, and shock held him still.

Her lips were as full as a girl's. Julian felt dizzy, for surely her hair was still as coarse as a horse's tail— His grip tightened, and his hand slid easily across silky strands that smelled of wild thyme.

"Love me—" she whispered as he fought for breath. "Love me and I will live again!"

There had been an earthquake in the mountains the year Julian was ten. He remembered how the ground had danced beneath him, the twisting of perception until he did not know whether it was he or the world that had gone mad. It was like that now.

He pushed against her, trying to break free, but wherever his hand passed the flesh grew firm and smooth. He was caressing skin like the petals of a flower. His hands shaped breasts as round and sweet as river melons, whose nipples hardened as he touched them. He did not know where her clothing had gone. Skin touched skin and he did not know what had happened to his own.

Julian knew only the urgency that fired his body, and the splendor of that other body that ripened beneath him in curves as smooth and welcoming as the slopes of the hills. He explored those hills, and the valleys below them, until he found the forest they sheltered, and the sweet waters within. And then her arms tightened around him and he moved upon her with all the power that was in him, all that was potential in his body and spirit seeking to fill the depths of hers.

Morning light shone through Julian's closed eyelids, and he stretched lazily. Then rough wool scraped his bare skin. He frowned. He felt warm and rested—he must be in his bed in Rivered, but there he had sheets beneath his blankets, and how could there be so much light in the dormitory? He moved again, and chill, moist air drove him back under the blanket. He heard someone moving nearby, and then the crackle of a new fire.

Memory lashed through him, impossible, glorious, and he opened his eyes.

The woman beside the fire rose to her feet, looking down at him. Dawn light shone full upon her, and Julian's eyes moved unbelieving from hair the color of ripe wheat down a lush body imperfectly concealed by rich robes of green and saffron velvet embroidered in gold, and a mantle the color of the summer sky.

"Do I look now as I did when first you lay down with me?" She smiled, and the words died in Julian's throat. He swallowed and tried again.

"Who are you?"

She shook her head. "That is not the right question. When you know who *you* are, then perhaps you may find a name for me."

He felt dizzy. Still staring at her, he managed to sit up, not noticing the chill of the air on his bare skin. She waited, watching him.

Painfully he fitted together the scattered puzzle pieces of memory. Throat muscles strained out the words. "You are one of the Guardians, surely, but why have you come to me?"

He blinked as she grew suddenly luminous, not knowing if the change was in her, or if the morning sun had lifted over the mountains far away. She grew brighter, and still he stared. Who was She? Not the Lady of Earth, for men said She was dark and did not wear blue. This Lady's colors encompassed earth and sky and sea.

She spoke, and he felt the words resonate through the air, the ground, his very bones.

"To test you, and to claim you . . ."

He reached out for her, his fingers closed on rich fabric, then passed through it as Her radiance flared outward, Her colors diffusing into the deep tones of the hills and sky and the triumphant splendor of the sun.

"Stay!" he cried. "When will I see you again?"

The answer came faint as if spoken by the wind, but it reverberated through his awareness.

"When you come to your Crown . . ."

For a moment Her image remained transparent against the blaze of the morning sky. Her lips rounded in a kiss of farewell. Then She disappeared into the glory of Midsummer Day.

The grass where the Lady had stood trembled, though Julian could feel no wind. As he lay back against his blankets, the tremor was already spreading invisibly through the uptilted faces of rock that began the coastal hills down through the soil and sedimentary rock of the Great Valley. Swiftly the vibration traveled through the mafic underlayer, northwest and southeast along the myriad fault lines, and east and west between them, carrying their news the length and breadth of Westria—

The lord has given himself to the land. . . .

From rootlet to root the grasses spread it across the Great Valley, from needlegrass to wild rye, from mustard and filaree to wild oat and turkey mullein, from the late poppies still glowing in the damp hollows to the clover and fragrant chamomile the message ran, until it met the barriers of the eastern mountains and the gentler coastal hills.

To the west the green grasses and tangled laurels and madrones by the drying streams transmitted the word to the golden ridges where the scattered stands of live oak grew. From the dry inland hills it spread until it reached the lushly forested hillsides that sloped down to the sea.

In the Sacred Wood, the redwoods drew the knowledge up the towering columns of their trunks until it flickered in every leaf that brushed the sky, and the Great Redwood, who was also the Lord of all Trees, shifted into human form, for this matter was between the land and men.

Will he come to me? the Redwood wondered, and wondered also what advice he could give.

In the east the message passed through the vivid red earth of the foothills to manzanita and chaparral and scattered strands of yellow pine. And still the knowledge spread, traveling up slopes that grew steadily steeper as the trees changed to Douglas fir and white pine, black oak and hemlock. Now it quivered through the granite bones of the earth to the holy valley of Awahna that ice had once carved out of the living stone.

And the Powers who had made Awahna their temporal habitation were aware of its meaning, and took counsel.

The message passed along the fault lines northward to the Father of Mountains, and the Mistress of the College of the Wise stirred on her hard bed and half opened her eyes. Something had changed; not in the weather of the tangible world, but on some inner level whose gates had been closed to her for twenty years. Heart beating with an excitement whose source she could not name, she sat up. Suddenly the frailties of her eighty years no longer weighed upon her. She remembered faces and emotions she had shut away; she wondered if the Master of the Junipers lived still, and wondering, got up to look for paper and pen to write to him.

And far to the south, where beyond the arid mountains the hosts of Elaya snapped at the borders of Westria, a last fading impulse carried the news to a secret fold in the chaparral-covered hills. Within the cavern it hid, something that had been inherent in every plant fiber and particle of soil solidified into the form of a woman in earth-brown robes whose black eyes flashed beneath waves of shining dark hair.

"*Wait—*" she told the priestesses who served her.

"Watch, and wait for the one who will seek Me here. . . ."

But when the magnetic currents strove to carry the word to the Red Mountain at the center of the Kingdom, they were repelled by the aura of blood and fire. Another power held the peak now, which had no ears for the revelation that was stirring in the land. Thus the awareness sank instead of rising, deep to the roots of the mountain. And so the blood-cloaked man who gazed out across the land from its peak had no knowledge of it, just as he knew nothing of the secret that lay hidden in the passages at the Red Mountain's heart.

⇒ TWO ⇐

On the peak of the Red Mountain a wisp of smoke still curled from the embers of the Midsummer Fire, wavering like a ghost in the pale morning light. Perhaps it was a ghost, thought the man in the crimson robe who stood watching it, for the charred bones of the beacon-keeper lay among the coals. In life and in death his service had been the same.

Wind stirred the ashes and dissipated the smoke, and the man in crimson turned, gazing out across the tumble of golden foothills, still veiled by morning mist, to the pale shine of the river that flowed into the Great Bay. There had been strange powers abroad during the hours of darkness, but now everything was still.

To the west he could see the coastal lands of Seagate, where Eric the Regent struggled ineptly to uphold an empty throne. To the north lay the Corona, where the man in red had once had enemies. But he had brought down Lord Theodor at last, as an old tree long past its prime is felled by a great storm. Now there were only the indolent Sandremun and his chit of a daughter to deal with. In the east, Lord

Philip of the Ramparts was to be reckoned with, but he had troubles of his own—the watcher smiled thinly—and one great handicap: he did not want the throne. To the south, Lady Alessia of Las Costas still kept one hand on the reins of power she had given into her son's uncomprehending grasp—a dangerous bitch, but growing old now.

From south, to east, to north and west again the man in crimson turned, claiming with his eye all that his eyes could see. And that was most of Westria, for the Red Mountain rose at its heart.

And I hold the Red Mountain, he thought triumphantly. *They do not know it, but I am the Lord of Westria now!*

His old enemies were dead or dying, leaving children with no knowledge of the past to try and fill their shoes. At last, the land of Westria was ripe for the plucking—he had only to stretch out his hand.

Footsteps crunched on the loose stone behind him. He turned, and the man stopped short, mouth tightening as he saw the veil of shadow with which his master had covered his scars. His hand came up to the salute. Despite the early hour he was fully dressed and freshly shaved. The red badge with its grey wolf's head glowed like a patch of blood on the cordovan leather of his metal-studded gambeson.

"My lord Sangrado—" said the officer.

The man in red nodded. To his face that was what his men called him, but he knew of the other names they had for him—Wolfmaster, or the Blood Lord—when they thought he did not hear.

"The wagons are unloaded, my lord. The workmen wish to know where to begin."

The Blood Lord looked across the notch in the mountain that separated the beacon from the other peak, squinting into the sun.

"There—" One long finger indicated the masses of tumbled stone that were strewn and shattered as if a star had exploded there. "Let them sort and pile those pieces that are large enough for building, and heap up the smaller fragments for filling later on. I will make the foundation there, on the other peak, when the ground is clear." Once, he had felt the touch of the spirit at the Red Mountain's core. He would call up that spirit again, and bind it into the foundations of a fortress that no power of man or nature could destroy.

Looking at the ruins that had been his temple eighteen years before, nothing seemed to have changed. But everything was different. He had both power and the knowledge to use it, now. And soon the Red Mountain would become the outward manifestation of his impregnable soul.

"Have the scouts returned?" he asked. For a moment he sent his awareness questing outward, touching the life-energies of the men who had come with him, knowing the answer even as the soldier spoke again. Their main camp was a little ways down the slope of the mountain—nearly a hundred men from Elaya, from the Barren Lands, even from Westria, who were bound by his will. It was only a crude circle of tents now, with picket lines for the horses and mules, but in his mind's eye the Blood Lord saw the fortress that he would build here, with stabling for scores of animals, and barracks of stone.

"Those you sent down the western road are returned," the officer was saying, "leaving two on guard according to your command. The party you sent toward Laurelynn should be back soon."

The Blood Lord nodded. With men on the old roads to east and west he could not be surprised, and he had already stationed guards on the new, secret road they had made along the spine of the coastal hills. The only danger had been the Red Mountain itself, for there was no way to come at its peak unobserved. But by the time the beacon-keeper had seen them, the Midsummer Fire was already blazing, and there was no other warning he could give to Westria. For long enough the Blood Lord had worried at the edges of the land, setting outlaw against village, and neighbor against neighbor as well. It was time to act openly now.

The men thought it was a good trick, but there had been more than strategy in the sorcerer's choice of this day. It was on a Midsummer's Eve that he had made his first temple here, and at Midsummer that his temple had been destroyed. It was fitting that this day see the foundation of his resurrected power.

"Is there anything else, my lord?"

He turned, seeing with satisfaction how the man stiffened as he felt his master's gaze. He nodded.

"A message for Ordrey. There is a man—a white-headed harper called Silverhair. He is on his way to the Regent at Bongarde. Tell Ordrey to make contact with our informant there. I want to know when Silverhair reaches Bongarde and when he leaves again. When he goes, Ordrey and his patrol are to take him and bring him to me." He smiled, and the man paled beneath his tan and looked away. "Ordrey will understand why."

He slipped his scarred hands back into the sleeves of his scarlet robe. For a moment the steady beat of his heart had quickened. He controlled it, became still again. His other enemies were all from the past, but the harper had crossed him once too often, the last time only a month ago. He was a distraction, best removed now, before the real struggle began.

The officer was still waiting.

"That is all, Esteban. You may go."

Esteban stepped back a pace and saluted stiffly. "Yes, my lord Sangrado." His step quickened and grew easier as he made his way back down the hill.

The man he had called Lord Sangrado waited, like a splash of blood beside the ashes of the dead fire, watching his workmen on the other peak struggle with the jagged fragments of rock. The sun rose higher, until heat shimmered from every stone. But he did not stir. The men wiped sweat from their eyes and watched him with furtive glances as they worked, muttering uneasily and making the sign against evil that had no power over him anymore. Some of them had come willingly, brought by promises of Westrian gold; others had been picked up from scattered steadings in the hills and carried along. Their origins did not matter now.

Then at last he glanced at the sun. It was almost overhead. The men stilled as he began to move down the slope of the watch-peak and up the rough path to the mountain's other hump, following a faint track that his feet had once known very well.

There was a cleared space, roughly circular, on the second peak now. It was not large—the fortress would use the slope of the mountain. But once he had consecrated it, this spot would be the foundation of its highest tower. He paced its circumference, internalizing its dimensions and orientation.

He could sense the echoes of power left by the four Jewels of Westria when they had been scattered in the same explosion that had nearly destroyed him so long ago. For a moment remembered lust for their strength that was the strength of the four elements from which the world was made stirred in him. But the Jewels were gone, and there was no use in wondering how he could have used them now, when he had paid the price for full mastery of his own considerable powers.

Around the cleared space he moved, and around it again. He began to hum softly, and the men who had been watching found themselves drawn forward until they stood crowded around the circumference of the circle he was drawing, mesmerized by the crimson figure and the motions he made. The air grew heavier, as if his movements were creating a vortex that drew everything to the center of his sphere.

"I name this place Blood Gard," his voice held them, "and it shall be the foundation of my power."

Now the Blood Lord began to slowly turn. His humming vibrated through the naked stone like a deep bell. This was no ritual memorized from the manuscripts of the College of the Wise, but something deeper—a direct communion of power with power. Hoarding his own strength, he drew upon the energy of the men surrounding him. They would be good for nothing else for the rest of the day, but that did not matter—this was the most important part of the building, the unseen part upon which all that was built would stand. The watchers stood, and swayed, and from their throats came a distorted humming that echoed his own. Faces that had been tense with fear or creased with curiosity were blank now. They had no will but his. . . .

The man they called Lord Sangrado looked up at the sun, triumphant in the glaring splendor of noon. He grew still, and the silence built and built until it hammered at their ears.

Then he spoke. He pointed. "Come—"

There was a man—the Blood Lord had marked him a long time ago—the fairest in a company of wolf's heads

and human scavengings. The others had noted it as well,
and in that company without women it gained him certain
advantages. He was better fed than the others; glistening
with sweat, his muscles rippled smoothly beneath brown
skin; he had deep blue eyes and shining dark hair. He came
forward slowly, moving with grace even as the terror in his
eyes fought the movements his body made.

So beautiful—the sorcerer's eyes noted it without emotion. He had wondered sometimes if the man might be a
bastard of the dead King's. But he had not himself touched
him. He touched nobody now. His power's price, and its
protection, was invulnerability to the needs of body and
soul—to desire, to pleasure, to love.

"Come to me . . . ," he spoke softly, and the man took
the last few steps to stand before him.

"Take off your clothes."

The man had already stripped off his shirt because of the
heat. Now he let fall breeches and clout, stepped out of his
shoes as well. There was a wordless exhalation of sound
from the watchers, but they did not stir. The man's muscles
jumped beneath his skin like those of a frightened horse as
his master looked him up and down. He was the most
physically perfect—the best they had—a fitting sacrifice.

The Blood Lord gazed into the man's eyes, those blue
eyes that should have awakened painful memories. But
those memories had been part of his own sacrifice. He saw
the young man's pupils expand until the blue eyes became
black mirrors for the veiled face of the sorcerer.

"You know you have no will but mine," he said softly. He
let the illusion of shadow with which he had obscured his
ruined features dissipate. For a moment the man's face
showed sick understanding. Then the sorcerer's features
changed again, into a dark mirror image of the man's own.

"Do you see yourself?" he asked. "What I will, what you
will, your body will be. Earth to earth, and water and air
and fire—man is a synthesis of the elements, a microcosm
of the world. It is merely a matter of understanding how
they are bound to know how to unbind them again."

The Blood Lord's robes hung like frozen fire. Then
suddenly he reached out and without quite touching the
young man began to stroke the air around him, shaping his
sloping shoulders, the rippling muscles of his belly, his

genitals, his strong thighs. The victim's lips twitched, his throat quivered, and though his body shook with denial, the chant flowed out of it, louder than the voice of the sorcerer.

> *"Bones of the earth to earth return,*
> *And flesh dissolves into the sea;*
> *Within the blood life's fires will burn,*
> *By wind unbound the breath goes free. . . ."*

Red sleeves flapped like bloody wings as the sorcerer lifted his arms, focusing the pulses of power that shuddered through the man's strong body ever more swiftly now. He sensed the waiting strength of the mountain beneath him.

Here is a life for you, he thought, *to seal our union anew.*

His hands closed on the glistening shoulders. His lips fastened on those of his victim in a parody of an embrace. He breathed the breath of the other man in, sent his own breath into the other's lungs again, shaping silently the syllables of his own true name.

Then he stepped back. The man swayed and pitched forward to lie with jerking limbs outflung against the mountain's unyielding breast. The sorcerer stooped over him and traced a line the length of his spine to his brain.

"By wind unbound the breath goes free—" He touched a spot at the base of the fallen man's neck and the untidy twitchings ceased.

"Within the blood life's fires will burn—" Again he pressed, a little lower down, and smoke rose from the still body, though there was no visible flame. Its outlines shimmered in the heated air.

"Flesh dissolves into the sea—" Another touch, in the small of the back, and the flesh sagged, its outlines running as substance dissolved and blood spread around the body in a bright pool, sinking quickly into the thirsty stone.

Now only the skeleton remained.

Once more the sorcerer bent, and his fingertip brushed the base of the exposed spine. "Bones of the earth to earth return—" he hissed, and then even the skeleton crumbled into a white powder that clung for a moment to the bloodwet rock, dissolved, and was gone. A tremor ran through the mountain, a myriad of tiny cracks opened to receive the sacrifice. Then all was still.

The Blood Lord straightened, took a deep breath, then another, while the soul energy of the man he had slain sang in his veins. He was preternaturally aware of the throbbing power of the mountain beneath his feet, and an exultation for which he had thought the capacity gone fountained within. The stone to which he had bound himself vibrated with the syllables of his name.

"Caolin . . . Caolin . . . Caolin . . ."

Deep within the mountain, the echoes reached passage-ways long forgotten, where in the time of the Ancients men had delved for coal and sand and cinnabar. Other powers dwelt there now—the spirits the men of a far-off land had brought with them when they dug their mine, and the elementals who were native to this earth and stone.

"I smell blood; it troubles me." The Gnome-King shifted on his cold throne. *"What is this name that echoes through our halls?"*

"Do not let it disturb you," came the thought of the pisky who served him. *"Another name is already written here. Let the sorcerer lord it on the surface of the mountain. We still rule the roots."*

"Do you think he will covet our treasure?"

"He would if he knew of it," came the answer. *"He possessed it once, if only for a little while. But how shall he learn of it? If he sends his servants here, here they will stay. . . ."*

The laugh of the Gnome-King was like grinding rocks. He nodded.

"What we have we will hold!"

The Master of the Junipers glanced sideways at Julian, and then turned back to hang the teakettle on the bracket over his little fire.

"Your mother was running from Caolin, the Seneschal of Westria," he said. "She sought safety in Awahna, but her strength was not sufficient for the road."

Julian stared at him. He had arrived at Bongarde scarcely an hour ago, and since Lord Eric was away and the Master was here, it made sense to go see him first. After the expected greetings, he had begun with a question that seemed innocent enough—how had his mother come to die in an obscure valley near the Pilgrim's Road?

But this answer made no sense to him.

As he looked at the old man, it seemed to him that the Master's face was like a familiar landscape gone strange in mist or moonlight. Since Julian's childhood, those deep eyes, the nose that seemed too large among features that had been weathered by time like the rocks of the Ramparts, the familiar face of the Master, had been a landmark of certainty. But the answers he had come to demand were only revealing greater mysteries, and the Master's face was like a foreign country now.

"But why should the Seneschal pursue her?" he asked carefully. "Who was she?" His unvoiced question echoed between them—*Who am I?*

"Your mother was Faris, the Queen of Westria," the Master said gently. "She fled with you from Laurelynn because Caolin would have made you both pawns in his game of power. You are King Jehan's son, Julian, and the heir of Westria. . . ."

The Master's voice, like harsh bran bread soaked in honey, was lost in remembered echoes of a voice like distilled sunlight that had promised him reunion *"when you come to your Crown!"* For four days those words had haunted him. He had thought of a thousand things that they might mean. But *that* crown? By birthright?

It was impossible.

The Master must be reading his mind and playing on his fantasies. Julian could hear children shouting, the bark of a dog, the sharp *rat-tat* of someone hammering. A bee buzzed through the window and out again, seeking the roses in the garden below. That was reality. Julian unclenched his fingers and forced his lips to move.

"It doesn't make sense. If you knew where the Queen's child was, why would you leave him in the hills?" He used the third person deliberately, as if that "him" could protect him from the "me" that would doom him to this identity. The heir of Westria was Lord Philip, or maybe Robert, or some dim, amorphous figure out of a harper's tale. Not Julian . . .

For four days he had thought about the Lady's words, thought his way from the glamour of kingship to a dim apprehension of how awful a burden it might be. He could rage against the troubles that beset Westria—oh, he was full of fine words when it was someone else's responsibility. But just because he had spent so much time thinking about what was wrong in the land, the idea that he might be the one who must set things right terrified him.

The music of that harper who had shared his camp last night had almost comforted him—without Silverhair, Julian might not have had the courage to ride the last few miles to Bongarde. But there was no comfort now. He heard the Master's reply with the same feeling he had in sword-play when a stronger opponent began to batter down his guard.

"When your mother knew she was dying she told me to keep you hidden in the mountains. Remember, the King was dead, and Faris was afraid that Caolin, or some other, would try to use you as he had used her." The folds of the Master's grey robe seemed carved from granite; his face was as implacable.

Julian found that he was trembling. "But look what has happened to the Kingdom! How could you dare to leave Westria so long without a lord?"

"You are not thinking," the Master sighed. "Even if you had been bred up in Laurelynn a Regent would have ruled until you were grown."

Julian was shaking visibly now. He gripped the arms of his chair, raging at the pity he saw in the Master's eyes.

"At least you could have told me—" he muttered, feeling his defenses faltering. "It seems to me that you left a great deal to chance." He did not know whether he was angry for Westria's sake or his own.

"Do you think it has been easy for me?" exclaimed the Master. "Do you remember when you ran away from Stanesvale, the summer you were ten years old? That time I was able to go after you, but when raiders carried you and the others off from your Initiation I could do nothing but pray. Each month that you were cut off in the mountains last winter was like a year to me. I had to let you find the strength that was in you, as a tree grows strong by resisting the wind. I had to trust to the Maker of All Things that your mother's suffering, and mine, and even yours, would not be in vain!"

He poured tea into an earthenware mug and held it out. Mechanically, Julian took it, his eyes fixed on the Master's cragged face. Perhaps one day he would be able to understand, but not now, while this new knowledge lay in his belly like a lump of porridge four days old. The resistance went out of him then, and he set down the mug and hid his face in his hands.

"How can I do it? I have no desire to wear a crown. Even Lord Philip does not want the Kingship, and he was raised to rule!"

"Oh, Julian—" the Master's voice softened. "You chose a King's name at your Initiation because when your companions cry out for aid you cannot help but respond to them. You may reject the Crown, but the staff of the people's guardian comes readily to your hand. If I thought you *wanted* this, I would never have told you who you are! But look into your heart, Julian—this time it is Westria who calls out to you, and will you say her nay?"

Julian jerked as if the old man had struck him, putting finally a name to the Lady who had lain in his arms. Even then, not knowing, he had not been able to deny the Lady of Westria. But he still could not speak of that—not even to the Master. His temples throbbed as if they already bore the weight of the Crown. He felt hot tears start in his eyes.

"Let me go!" he whispered desperately. "I will try—to be what the land needs, to do what you want me to—but for just one moment more—let me be alone!"

The Master nodded. "It will not be easy for any of us—not for you, or for Lord Eric, the Regent, or for that harper you rode in with. He told you his name was Silverhair, did he? I know him as Sir Farin Harper of Hawkrest Hold. Your mother was his twin. . . .

"But surely you can have a little time before it all begins. At the bottom of that stair is my herb garden. No one will disturb you there."

Julian got to his feet. More by feel than by sight he found the doorway and stumbled down the stairs. But as he heard the garden door swing shut behind him the strength left him. He took a deep breath, smelled sweet basil and sage and the deep scent of roses. He sank to the earth then and let the salt tears fall.

He did not know how long it had been when self-awareness returned and with it the strength to stand up again. He began to walk along the pebbled path that separated the herbs in their raised beds. He recognized comfrey and aloe vera among them, for his foster mother had grown them in her kitchen garden to treat the household's inner and outer ills, but there were others whose names he did not know. Suddenly he was conscious of a desire to learn them, to know everything about his land! He was acutely aware of the scent of the herbs and the solidity of the ground under his feet; he spread his arms in a surge of fierce protectiveness.

And presently he began to hear music from the top of the tower, at first tentative, then stronger and more sure. He looked up and saw the harper sitting there. The fire of the setting sun flared from the harp's bronze strings.

Silverhair is my uncle—he thought in dim wonder, *and neither of us knew. Something is beginning—I can feel it in the music, and in myself, now!*

Above the wall of the garden he could see the tawny slopes of the hills that backed Bongarde, and the deepening glow of the sunset sky. He had seen these hills, this sky, when he rode in. But now everything was changed. He knew that he was not what he had been—stirring within him he felt the first fragile movements of the thing that he would be.

Julian felt the beauty of sky and hills and garden and the triumphant music that precipitated from the air as if they were a part of him. All these things seemed suddenly unbearably precious, and fragile. "I will guard you. I will serve you." His whisper of assent seemed to him a shout that the whole land must hear—

"When I come to my Crown!"

⇛ THREE ⇚

The sword was a brown blur against the blue sky. Julian's shield arm came up in automatic response, and the blow jarred all along his arm as his opponent's blade smacked his shield. But he was already pulling back to absorb the force of the blow. Over the rim of the shield he glimpsed walls of timber and warm, cream-colored stone and the curve of the Master of the Junipers' tower.

He heard, rather than saw, the next blow, and as he swerved, the tip of the wooden sword grazed his hip.

"That would have drawn blood if this sword was real!" The words came on a gust of laughter, and Julian forced himself to focus on the blue gaze of his opponent, Frederic —the Regent's son and heir—who despite his golden hair and sweet smile had been well trained in the art of the sword.

They probably gave him his first blade at two and set him to fighting practice at three, Julian thought sourly. *If I had been brought up in a royal fortress instead of a stone quarry I would probably fight like that too. How in the names of all the Guardians do they expect me to make a King?*

He lifted his own blade in acknowledgment and settled back into a defensive crouch. *Think of the blade,* he told himself, remembering the words of Lord Philip's armsmaster, a man who had no other name but Sword. *No, don't think about it, become it! Do not think at all!*

And without thinking he found that he was already moving, his sword sweeping out and around in a smooth arc, which Frederic avoided only by an awkward twist. Smiling with sour satisfaction, Julian paused to let him find his balance again. Someone gave a grunt of approval from the benches above the ring.

Julian looked up and saw the Regent himself, Eric of

Seagate, as tall and stout as one of the great timbers of his hall. Then he had to make a hasty recovery as Frederic, laughing, came after him again.

It's all very well not to think about my swordplay—his blade swept up in a quick feint, then around to slash at Frederic's thigh—*if my other worries would only leave me alone.* The sight of the Master's tower set echoes ringing in his memory.

"You are the heir, but that does not mean that they will give you the crown of Westria on a platter," the Master had told him. *"Even when the child of a King has been raised in full sight of the people, he must be formally elected by the Council in order to reign. You will have to win the approval of those who now govern Westria."*

After the emotional upheaval that had brought him to accept the idea of Kingship, hearing that was like being doused with cold water. Julian had felt a strong impulse to resign his rights then and there. He was not even sure he wanted the throne. How could he fight for it?

But he was fighting Frederic now, and the other boy was beating him backward with quick jabs of his blade. Julian shook his head to clear it and forced himself to concentrate on his shieldwork. One part of his mind babbled that this play was madness when there was so much else to do, while another remembered his training and reminded him sternly that this was the *only* thing that mattered, as long as your opponent had a blade in his hand.

But he could not forget that the Regent was watching him. . . .

Frederic came in with a beautifully executed double feint; Julian blocked the first and felt the second blow numb his left shoulder. Frederic stepped back politely as Julian let his shield slide to the ground, then, with a little flourish, cast his own shield away.

Wonderful! thought Julian. *Why should Lord Eric back an unknown bumpkin who can't even defeat a boy a year younger than he? And the harper Silverhair, my uncle, is up there with the Regent too. The two of them should find a great deal to criticize!*

There's no hope for it anyway, his internal dialogue went on. *Let's see if I can at least wipe this fellow's eternal smile away before we end the game!*

Finally, Julian was able to let his awareness flow down through his arm and into his sword. He saw the other's blade flicker toward him. With a precise turn he curved his body away while his own blade swung up. The blades kissed lightly, but the weight of Julian's own blow kept his sword on target while Frederic's spun aside. Julian felt the jar as he struck Frederic's shoulder, and the other boy's weapon, released from suddenly nerveless fingers, wheeled through the air.

Frederic's eyes widened, and for a moment he swayed. Julian took a quick step forward, but the Regent's son put one hand to his shoulder and managed a rather twisted grin.

"Did I hurt you?" asked Julian helplessly.

"Not permanently," said Frederic a little breathlessly. "We'll both have bruises, but my mother makes an excellent liniment."

Julian nodded. He supposed that with three sons and a husband who had been the most notable fighter of his day, Lady Rosemary must have a fair knowledge of healing. And she alone had made him feel truly welcome here. She told him stories from the days when she and his mother had been girls together in the north. She was making a new cloak for him to wear.

Limping from a blow he had not noticed before, Julian went after Frederic across the worn turf of the practice ground. The stone walls of Bongarde glowed golden as the sun sank, and some shift in the wind brought him the smell of baking bread. The dark green banner of Seagate fluttered from the tallest tower, and above it, a brighter green pennon that bore a circled cross in gold. *The emblem of Westria* . . . Julian gazed up at it, tasting the knowledge that one day that banner might fly for him.

Then Frederic called to him, and he followed the other boy through the door to the changing room.

"I've had them prepare the sweat lodge for us," said Frederic. He pointed through the other door to a little garden, where Julian could see a low turtle-shaped building of deerskins draped over a framework of saplings. "Do you mind? It's the best thing for loosening up and cleansing after a bout like that one."

Julian shrugged and began to pull off his sweat-soaked

practice gear. He had done a ceremonial sweat when he was initiated, and the men at Bear Valley had a sweat lodge they used before they went hunting. It seemed to him that Frederic's tone had held just the faintest hint of challenge, but he was not likely to be intimidated by a little steam.

Frederic was already stripped. His pale hair had been darkened by sweat to the color of autumn honey, and there was a red mark on his shoulder. He was going to have a nasty bruise there soon. Julian looked down at his own body, naturally brown-skinned, and already marred by old scars.

Frederic's eyes widened as he saw the livid line that twisted across Julian's thigh. Afraid of pity, Julian ducked into the dark entrance to the sweat lodge and sat down on a grass mat on the damp floor.

"It's not as bad as it looks," he said as Frederic joined him. "It healed oddly because we had no surgeon in the hills."

"You have seen real fighting—I should have remembered that," said Frederic. "They knighted me last year, but I've never used my sword."

"You will," said Julian grimly. Frederic's fighting had not suggested a bloodthirsty turn of mind, but you never knew.

Frederic stuck his head out of the door and called for someone to bring the hot rocks in. Then he sat back on his own mat and sighed.

"Yes, that's what I'm afraid of—I trained as a warrior because of my father, but I don't want—what I want is to follow the Master of the Junipers and finish my studies at the College of the Wise."

The light that came through the door of the low hut modeled Frederic's smoothly muscled shoulders and supple hands. Julian remembered his grace with a sword, and sighed in turn. How he envied the Regent's son those years of training! And yet he too had once longed to take the road to Awahna and learn the secrets of the soul.

He heard the sound of something being dragged, looked out, and saw a servant sliding a glowing rock toward them on the tines of a pitchfork. As he pushed it through the sweat lodge door, Frederic grasped it between two sets of deer antlers and maneuvered it into the pit. A second man came with another stone, and then two more. Then Frederic signaled enough and pulled the flap of the lodge-covering down.

Darkness engulfed them, as if the Earth Mother had taken them back into Her womb. Julian blinked. As his eyes adjusted, he saw the rocks glowing in the firepit like giant coals, netted with grey where their rough surfaces had cooled.

Frederic cast sweet herbs on the stones and then sat back and gave a commanding shake to the rattle that had been lying beside him.

"Spirits of the East and the sun's rising," he chanted. "Grandfather Wind Lord, Guardian of the sky! Hear us and bless us. May we be purified by the air we breathe! Ho!"

As Julian echoed him, he felt moisture on his legs and the rocks hissed as Frederic splashed them with a dipperful of springwater. Julian took a deep breath of steam, then another, as Frederic doused the rocks again.

"Spirits of our ancestors, bless us, and all you Guardians. Cleanse our hearts as we cleanse our bodies, in the name of the Maker of All Things!"

For a little while they simply sat, breathing the steam and letting the moist heat penetrate their bodies. Then Frederic thrust open the door flap, and Julian took a deep breath of cool air. The servant brought them more hot rocks, and the sweat lodge was closed again. This time, Frederic invoked the powers of the south, and Julian felt the air grow hot with something more than steam.

After the third load of rocks and the invocation to the western waters, Frederic poured most of his remaining water onto them, and for a moment the rush of steam made it almost impossible to breathe. Julian gasped, then remembered the dried sage beside him, crushed a handful and held it to his nostrils, letting the aromatic vapors filter the steam. He considered leaving the lodge when Frederic opened the door once more; then it occurred to him that the other boy was testing him, more subtly than he had on the practice field, but more seriously.

And so when Frederic passed him the water jar, he drank deeply, and held the cool liquid in his mouth as long as he could. Then the closing door brought darkness down upon them again, and a heat that was suffocating. Sweat poured

from his body. Almost at his strength's end, but determined
not to be beaten in endurance, Julian finally remembered
that it was cooler near the floor.

He sank down upon the bare earth gratefully. And after
his first relief at being able to breathe had passed, he
became acutely conscious of the ground beneath him,
almost as he had felt the body of the Lady of Westria with
whom he had lain. But this sensation had nothing sexual
about it. It was more like the feeling of a child who seeks the
comfort of its mother's breast. He clung to the earth,
drawing up strength and an obscure sense of reassurance.

Earth is the ground of our being. He remembered fragments of the teaching from his Initiation. *If you stay
connected to Her, She will lend you Her power. And that was
as true for a King as for any other man,* he thought dimly,
glimpsing for the first time where he might find the strength
to do what they were asking of him.

Frederic still sat upright, shaking his rattle and chanting
an invocation to the Lady of Earth to support them and
strengthen them and help them to walk in harmony with all
Her children. He spoke without any self-consciousness, but
when he fell silent, Julian's opened awareness felt his
emotion, a leashed longing like a caged bird's dream of the
skies.

And then, finally, Frederic thrust the flap of the sweat
lodge open. Feeling like a dish cloth that has been boiled
and wrung out again, Julian crawled after him through the
door into day.

Next to the lodge, water had been brought down from
one of the cisterns to fill a little pool. Frederic was half-
submerged, and with more eagerness than grace, Julian slid
in after him. For the first few moments he could do nothing
but breathe as the water brought the glow in his skin back to
a more bearable temperature. Then he tipped back his
head. His dark hair swirled around him and the mud his
sweaty skin had picked up from the sweat lodge floor
floated away.

"Ouf!" sighed Frederic. "It's hard to find words for how
good this feels. I added more rocks than is usual, and kept
us in longer—at least it felt longer!" he added. "I think I
was trying to test you. . . ."

"I wondered about that," said Julian peaceably. Bathed

in this glorious coolness, he was incapable of resentment.

"I don't think I've done such a punishing sweat since I left the College of the Wise—" Frederic went on.

Julian remembered the longing he had sensed in the other boy and turned to him.

"I'll speak to your father if you like, and ask him to let you go back there," he said then.

"What?"

Frederic's response startled Julian upright, water swirling around him. Why had he said that?

"That is, I would, if there was any chance Lord Eric would listen to me!" he added lamely.

Frederic's bony features warmed in a surprisingly sweet smile. "I'll hold you to that one day. But you should be asking for *my* loyalty. You have it, you know. . . . "

Julian felt his heartbeat slow. The air seemed to thicken, as if something that had been looming on the horizon were suddenly near. This had happened to him before—trust given unasked, a life laid in his hand. It was a gift he did not know how to refuse. But this sense of impending crisis was new. It went with the promise of the Lady of Westria, and the burden the Master of the Junipers had laid upon his soul.

Almost angrily, Julian pushed sopping strands of hair out of his eyes and hunched forward, crossed arms resting on his knees.

"Then speak to your father for *me!* Is he going to send me back to Philip or offer me a crown? When will he make up his mind?"

Frederic's frown reminded Julian of the Master. "Papa never decides anything quickly, but when he has decided, he doesn't change." His eyes held Julian's. "What do *you* want him to do?"

Julian felt his own muscles knotting beneath his hands and took a deep breath, then another, willing his trembling to ease. To be King—to bear the whole weight of Westria upon his soul? How could *anyone* desire it? If the Master of the Junipers spoke truly, that burden had crushed his mother, and perhaps his father too. And yet—unconnected images swirled in his memory—a stand of oaks still smouldering when the work of a raider's torch was done, the body of a little girl flung into a snowbank like an abandoned doll. . . .

He could not speak. *Westria! Westria* . . . there was no decision to make, only the need to see clearly what must be done. He had thought he had chosen to accept Kingship the day before, and here he was doing it again. He had a sudden sinking suspicion that it was going to be like that until they put him on the throne in Laurelynn, and maybe after—not a single commitment that would bind him, but a perpetual choosing with every day that dawned, and every decision he made.

The cheerful clamor of a gong came muffled through stone. Frederic swore and heaved himself out of the water. "We've got to dress—that's the warning bell, and we don't dare to be late for this dinner. If you're hungry, come on!"

Julian's stomach rumbled and he realized how empty he was. A full belly made everything look brighter—no wonder he found it hard to think now! He clambered out of the pool after Frederic and reached for one of the rough towels, mouth already curving in anticipation of the feast to come.

"Earth our Mother, we thank Thee, and all you spirits of plant and animal who have given your substance to make this meal—" The Master of the Junipers lifted his arms in invocation, beauty shining through his weathered features like lamplight through a shade.

I must believe he was right to let me grow up in ignorance, thought Julian, watching him. Now, when the Master's face glowed as the stones of Awahna were said to reflect the light of the Overworld, he forgot the bent, harsh-voiced shape that the adept usually wore and remembered the power within. Recalling the few times during his childhood when he had seen that radiance unveiled, Julian realized that perhaps there had been nothing haphazard about the Master's irregular visits to Stanesvale. He had not grown up without knowledge, only without knowing his heritage.

"In joy your lives were given, in joy we receive them, and as your many bodies, consumed, will become part of our own, let us serve the land and the Maker of All Things!" The Master brought down his hands, passing them reverently over the bread and meat and pitchers of chilled wine.

"The Blessing of Earth and Water, Air, and Fire, upon you, and through you upon us all!" The focused movements of his hands compelled the attention as he traced the equal arms of the cross of the elements and surrounded it with the circle of unity.

For a moment Julian thought he saw lines of power glowing in the air like the trail of a falling star, but he had not the gift of such vision. He glanced at Frederic's rapt face and knew that the other boy had *seen*. For a moment an old envy stirred in him. He stilled, and let it go, remembering what Frederic had told him that afternoon. Was it not worse to hear the call and be prevented from answering?

The deep echoes of the Master's voice faded. He stepped back, arms falling to his sides, illuminated now only by the ordinary light of the dying day. Lady Rosemary, solid as the hills behind Bongarde and splendid in a blue gown with interlaced golden ears of wheat embroidered around the neck and hem, rose to her feet and motioned to the servers to begin distributing.

First came finely woven baskets filled with loaves of the bread Julian had smelled baking that afternoon, and earthenware platters upon which sculptured radishes, curled slivers of carrot and sunchoke, sliced fresh beans and cucumber rounds encircled by rings of white onion had been arranged with slices of cheese and a variety of sauces ranging from incandescent mustard to a minty cream as smooth as snow. That was the first course.

The bread was substantial without heaviness. It had a flavor that Julian could not quite identify, as if nuts had been ground in with the flour. He chewed slowly, his awareness focused on its taste and texture. Was it because of the Master's blessing? Perhaps, yet he had noticed a new awareness of food ever since he had shared his meal with the old woman on the road. Certainly there was enough here to satisfy even *her!*

Once the edge was off his hunger, Julian looked around him, for the first time really seeing the hall. It was the oldest part of the fortress—indeed, one wall was a smooth slab of poured concrete from Ancient times. The others were of local stone. Not that one could see much of them, covered as they were with painted panels and woven hangings of varying age and state of repair. Not that one could fault

Lady Rosemary's housekeeping—worn wood shone with oiling and new yarn stood out where frayed edges had been bound.

His eyes fixed on a Seagate banner whose dark green had faded to olive-grey. One of the white wave-horses that danced across it was stained with brown. Old blood—he realized suddenly. Frederic saw where he was looking and grimaced.

"My father's—from the Battle of the Dragon Waste, where he nearly died."

Julian nodded. "My foster father still limps from the wound he got there."

"Your uncle, Farin Silverhair, made a song about that battle. Have you ever heard it sung?" Frederic shook his head. "He was about a year older than we are now."

They looked toward the head of the table where the harper sat beside Frederic's father. Worn and silvered like driftwood by years on the road, he sat listening to Lady Rosemary, dark eyes veiled, agile fingers playing with the stem of his silver goblet. As they watched, he put it to his lips, drank deep, and set it down again. He did not look like a legend, thought Julian, trying to visualize the ardent boy this man must have been eighteen years ago. To Julian's eyes, it seemed that hardship had made him old before his time.

"He plays the harp like a legend, though—" Julian said finally. "He played all that night when we camped together on the way here. But we didn't talk."

Silverhair drank again. Rosemary frowned, then said something and they saw the harper's eyes light in a brief smile.

"It's a hard life, though, being a legend. Here's to sunny skies!" Frederic grinned and lifted his own pewter goblet in mock salute.

Julian shook his head. The Battle of the Dragon Waste had been fought while he was being born. He and Frederic were both the children of legends—the past sent its chill over them as the shadow of the western hills stretched across the Great Valley when the sun went down. For him to come seeking his heritage at the same time that Silverhair returned from his long exile made a pattern too plain to be ignored. The story might be as old as one of the tapestries, but he was being woven into it now.

Into the silence a phrase from Silverhair's conversation with Eric fell like a stone into a still pool.

"Caolin is behind the woodsrats who have been giving you so much trouble in the north."

The rest of his words were lost as the servers came around with deep pottery dishes steaming with brown rice cooked with tomatoes and zucchini and liberally seasoned with oregano and basil and dill. They were followed by baskets full of ears of fresh corn. Julian let them serve him, still thinking about Silverhair's words.

A pattern, he thought. *There are raiders in the Ramparts too. . . .* He looked up, met the Regent's troubled grey gaze, and knew with a tightening of the gut that Eric was coming to a decision. He would tell them soon.

"What do you want him to say?" Frederic had asked not long ago, and Julian still did not know.

Course followed course: roasted chicken basted with garlic butter, three-foot whole baked sea bass from the Bay, a ragout of venison and stewed fruit and onions, and great slices of beef smoking from the spit with no seasoning but a little pepper and its own savory juices. The progress of the feasting could have been calculated from the changing aromas and the ebb and flow of conversation as the arrival of each new dish silenced the feasters again.

Julian caught Lady Rosemary's eye and saw her smile, and knew that although the festival was officially in honor of Silverhair, she had meant it to welcome him as well. For a moment her golden hair reminded him of his Lady of the road, and in a peculiar, detached sort of way he felt himself in love with her. Somehow, he did not think she would mind.

He leaned back to give his belly more room and his eyes fixed on the single timbers of redwood that beamed the ceiling. It was rare that the cutting of such large trees was allowed.

"A gift of the Sacred Wood," said Frederic, following his gaze. One of the servers whispered in his ear and he nodded, then turned back to Julian. "We're summoned to a family conclave on the terrace after the sweets have been served. I guess Papa doesn't want to risk any serious discussion with this lot standing around."

Julian nodded and pushed his plate away. The six other tables set up in the hall were packed with officers from the fortress and their families and some of the more notable citizens from the town below. He considered their flushed faces.

How would they look at me if they knew I might be their King? he wondered then. But he could not even imagine it.

Jasmine curtained the curving wall behind the terrace; with the fall of darkness, the little waxy white flowers were releasing their heavy scent into the still air. Julian reached the top of the stair and paused to catch his breath, wishing that he had not stuffed himself quite so thoroughly. The peaked expanse of the hall roof projected from below the balustrade, and beyond it he could make out the dim gap of the practice ground and the pale stone of the western tower. The fortress was a collection of buildings that seemed to grow one from the other in no particular order until one came to the gate in the inner wall. Beyond it lay the ring of stables and workshops, and the outer palisade.

One by one, slotted windows were transformed from black holes in the walls to rectangles of gold as feasters returned to their chambers and lit their lamps. As darkness deepened, the stars winked into visibility above, as if there had been a feast in the heavens as well. But the terrace was lightless. Julian squinted, trying to identify the dim shapes around him. His gut was cramping as it did sometimes before battle. He jumped as he felt Lady Rosemary's encouraging squeeze on his arm.

"First of all, I wish to welcome Julian here—" Eric's voice rumbled out of the darkness. Julian turned and saw the Regent standing like one of the hills behind the fortress, featureless and immovable. "It heals an old wound in my heart to know that something of your parents remains. . . . But you must understand," he added suddenly, "the Crown of Westria is not mine to bestow."

"You are the Regent, Papa!" burst out Frederic. "Who else *can* decide?"

"The Provinces and the Estates of Westria in full Council," his mother answered him.

"Especially now," Eric added painfully, "when they are squabbling over the body of Westria like carrion crows. I have to be neutral to retain any authority at all! I do not know whether my support would help or harm you, and I do not know *you*, Julian, or whether you have the makings of a King!"

Frederic began to protest, but Julian's deeper voice overrode his.

"My lord, neither do I. And if even I doubt my fitness, why should the rest of you scurry for a cushion on which to present me with the Crown?" The challenge in his own voice astonished him, but he could not stop now. He had waited for Eric to answer his questions, but now something within him was answering for them all.

"Would you take a sword into battle without having tested it? You have to test *me*. Then we will all know if I am fit to bear the Jewels!" Julian stopped short. They had been talking about the Crown—why had he used the older paraphrase for sovereignty?

There was a change in the charged darkness around him. Then the Master of the Junipers spoke for the first time.

"Then let your test be to find and master them. . . ."

There were small shocked sounds from Frederic, and, he thought, from Silverhair, but Julian's own astonishment held him motionless as the Master went on.

"The peak of the Red Mountain was blasted when your mother and father stopped Caolin from using the Jewels of Power to destroy Westria. He took them off before they destroyed him, but the explosion of forces scattered them beyond the knowledge of men."

"I always assumed that *you* had them," said Lord Eric in a shaken voice. "And of course there was no need for them, with no King. . . . Have you searched for them?"

The Master's answer was tinged with a bitter amusement. "Why else do you think I spent so much time wandering, those first few years after the Queen disappeared? I can assure you that they are not lying like pebbles on the beach for any child to find!"

Julian took a deep breath of perfumed darkness. "What makes you think I can succeed where you have failed?"

"You are your father's and your mother's son, Julian," said Lady Rosemary gently. "You are a child of the Great Marriage, and you bore the Jewels yourself, however briefly, at your first Naming, when you were three months old! The

Crown of Westria is in the gift of those who speak for her people, but the Jewels were made by the founder of your line, and they are your inheritance."

Julian groped for the rough stone of the balustrade. The thought of the Jewels held a terror that was different from the threat of the Crown. Once, he had longed for the powers of the spirit, and when they were denied him, accepted the discipline of the sword. Now they were asking him to master the primal elements, a power which the greatest of the Wise might desire in vain. There had been too many revelations, given too quickly. It was like the moment when he had felt the flesh of the old woman growing young beneath his hands. Dizzied, he held on to the harsh stone.

"A quest!" said Frederic brightly into the silence. "Let me come with you, my lord!"

His offer was in its way a rebuke to his father, but though the Regent stirred compulsively, he made no reply.

"And I." Silverhair's smooth voice grew more ironic as he went on. "I am surely no stranger to hopeless quests and hard living, and I have searched too long for this boy to let him leave me behind now."

Julian stared, trying to read the shadowed features beneath the harper's faintly shining hair. *The night we met on the road he spoke to me with his music,* he thought, *but we have not exchanged three words since we got here. Why does he want to come with me?*

"The Sacred Wood lies two days' ride from here. Let the search begin with the Lord of the Trees. . . ." The Master's quiet voice focused Julian's confused emotions.

"And what about you?" he said harshly, accepting the pain he had suppressed until now. "I would not know what to do with the Earthstone if I stubbed my toe on it. Will you be coming with us, or must I once more just struggle along on my own?" Appalled, he listened to his own bitterness. But the Master had known who and what he was and never told him—the Master could have prepared him for this day!

The old man's voice, answering, held no emotion, and Julian could not see his face in the dark. "I will come with you and teach you what I can. But I am not the only one from whom you will learn."

Once, the Master of the Junipers had had the answers to

everything, had been able to put right all the wrongs a child could see. Julian was aware of an irrational anger. What use to have a Master of the College at your side if he could not magic all obstacles away? Shaking, he turned and stared out into the darkness, but he found no answers there.

❧ FOUR ❧

It was a brilliant day. The hills glowed golden beneath a sky like the turquoise of Aztlan, and Silverhair found himself wondering why he had ever left Westria. They had ridden out from Bongarde in the morning, making their way through the chain of linked valleys toward the north end of the Great Bay, but despite the glow of the sky and the pure curve of the hills, the harper was growing tired. Perhaps it was a natural reaction after the first joy of finding Julian, but understanding that did not make it go away.

I thought I had come home for good, and now I am sworn to more wandering, he realized with a rare moment of wry humor. *Perhaps I am not very good at happiness. I should have let the children wear themselves out upon the road while I stayed with Eric and Rosemary. What possessed me to insist on coming along?* His dun horse missed a step, trying to snatch a mouthful of yerba santa from the side of the road, and he wrenched its head up and kicked the animal to hurry it along.

The horse leaped ahead and he had to pull it up to keep from running into the rump of Julian's bay mare. The boy looked around, but Silverhair could see that it was only an instinctive movement—his dark eyes seemed to look though the harper. He had been silent all day.

That's why I came, thought Silverhair, *for that boy. . . .* But they had hardly exchanged two words since that night they had met upon the road. He saw nothing in Julian to remind him of Faris or Jehan, nothing to compel his love.

His mouth was dry and he reached for his canteen, took a long swallow of tepid water, and hung it back on his saddlebow, wishing it was ale or the cool white wine they made in the valleys east of Bongarde.

Beyond Julian, the Master of the Junipers plodded along on a flea-bitten white gelding as imperturbable as he. Frederic rode beside him, struggling to hold his flighty grey mare to the gelding's slower pace but managing to talk at the same time. It seemed to Silverhair that Eric's eldest son had done nothing but talk since the day began, as if he were trying to fill the others' silences.

"Are we going to the Sacred Wood first because it is the closest of the shrines," he was asking now, "or is there some other reason to look for the Earthstone first?"

Julian straightened in his saddle, appearing to pay attention for the first time that day. "At Initiation, they taught us that the Wind Crystal was the first of the four Jewels."

"Yes," said the Master. "The Crystal focused and vibrated the Word by which all things are made."

Silverhair shivered remembering how the Lord of the Winds had come to him. *And I promised to serve him,* he thought. *Will I do it by serving this boy?* Once more his eyes sought Julian's unresponsive back. *He will have to show me how—he will have to make me feel the bond. . . .*

"Earth is the first of the elements and the last and nearest sphere of power," the Master was continuing. "The sphere of manifestation, where we must begin in order to learn the Way."

Frederic laughed ruefully. "I should have understood that, after spending my whole first year at the College of the Wise studying it!"

"There was a time when I wanted to go there," said Julian. "A friend of mine from Initiation did go—a tall, fair boy that I called Pine. Did you know him?"

"The one who talked to the trees? Oh yes, he came the second year I was there. Everyone liked him, when you could get him to look at you. He said he couldn't hear us; the trees were making too much noise." Frederic grinned.

"When I knew him he was just beginning . . . to be able to hear." Julian looked around him, as if seeing his surroundings for the first time that day. They had crested the last hill; through the branches of the live oaks they glimpsed the blue glitter of the Bay. Cicadas were singing in the grass. Silverhair barely heard Julian's whisper, "I envied him. . . ."

"My father summoned me home when I finished my fourth year. It is as much training as a Lord Commander's child usually gets." Frederic sighed. "I might persuade him to allow me the priest's initiation, but what I really want is to go . . ." The words died in his throat and he shot a quick glance at the Master of the Junipers, but the name he had not spoken echoed through all their minds. *Awahna . . .* Frederic wanted to make the pilgrimage to the Sacred Valley. Those who set out on that journey returned as adepts like the Master of the Junipers, without name or family, if they returned at all. *Small wonder,* thought Silverhair, *that Eric did not want his son to take that road.*

Faris had been trying to reach Awahna when she died. . . .

"I have dreamed of that valley," said Julian softly. "I grew up a stone's throw from the Pilgrim's Road."

They all looked at the Master, who alone of them all had seen Awahna with mortal eyes. Slowly he smiled, and they saw in his face a brightness, like sunlight reflected by moving water into shade.

"Perhaps one day you will both come there . . ." he said at last.

The road sloped downward and the horses quickened their steps. The color of the sky had deepened, and the trees cast bars of shadow across the road as the sun sank into the west. On the Bay, the little fishing boats were turning homeward, the long rays gilding their sails. The flat, oar-driven hulk of a ferry drove among them like a beetle among butterflies, crawling purposefully toward the shore.

They were approaching a small holding—a single timber and adobe house with a corral, and children and chickens busy around the door.

"We cannot enter the Sacred Wood after sundown"—the Master drew rein—"and we still have some hours' riding to get there. We can continue on the Bay road and camp in the meadow outside the Wood, or we can turn inland now, stay overnight at Registhorpe, and go on in the morning."

Silverhair was still watching the ferry, fascinated by its inexorable progress. His horse broke into a half trot under the stimulus of an involuntarily applied heel. Silverhair swore and reined him down again, forcing his gaze back to his companions.

"It's no contest to weigh Sir Randal's hospitality against the hard ground!" said Frederic. "He's been like an uncle to me."

Silverhair frowned. "Sir Randal of Registhorpe?" He remembered a dark shape looming out of the fog, mist sparkling on a jutting auburn beard. "I fought beside him at the Battle of the Dragon Waste. It would be good to see him again."

The Master nodded and reined his white gelding off the road to the right, where a rutted track wound into the hills. Frederic waved to the children at the house they were passing, calling them by name, but Silverhair looked back at the Bay. The ferry had passed behind the point and was hidden by its mane of trees; he found himself obscurely relieved not to be able to see it anymore.

"You were the one who found my father after that battle, weren't you," asked Frederic, "when you and Sir Randal searched the field. Mother says he would have died there if it hadn't been for you!"

Silverhair grimaced, remembering the wreckage of the battlefield, and carrion birds black against a sunset sky. He wondered if those days were going to begin again. Twenty years ago he had gone into battle singing. He did not feel like singing now. War was for the young, who did not know the price they would have to pay. But if battles were coming now it would be old men who planned them, though the young might be the ones to die. Old men, or one old man—the same who had engineered the carnage of the Dragon Waste—Caolin . . .

Silverhair shivered as if a cold wind were blowing at his back, though the air was warm and still. The sun was already low in the west. Nervously he peered into the deep shadows, where eucalyptus trees overhung the road. The dry grass on the slopes above them still shone golden in the sun, but beyond the hills he could see the first billows of incoming fog. Soon it would roll over the crests like a white wave and flow across the Bay. Perhaps he was only anticipating its cold breath.

The grade grew steeper and the horses slowed. Silverhair

heard the thudding of his heart—no, it was some other beat that throbbed in the earth beneath them—irregular, thunderous, the sound of horses being pushed to speed over stone. Silverhair's nerves prickled; an instinct for danger honed by years of wandering clamored. He wrenched his pony's head around and saw Julian already doing the same, his hand on the hilt of his sword.

And then the riders were upon them. Silverhair had a swift impression of dark jerkins glittering with rivets of steel, the flicker of drawn swords. Then they were surrounded. Two of their pursuers held cocked crossbows, but they all looked alike. On their shoulders, he saw the bloodspot of a red badge from which a grey wolf's head snarled.

"Farin Harper! What a pleasure to find you here!"

Even as Silverhair's stomach was clenching in sick recognition of the badge, that voice jerked him around. He saw a piebald horse and a bald pate surrounded by thinning, gingery hair.

"Ordrey!" The word was a snarl, but he could not control it. Ordrey and the wolf badge both meant Caolin! He struggled to understand what they were doing here!

"Did you think you could evade my master forever?" asked Ordrey sweetly. "You have crossed him once too often. There will be no other time."

Silverhair felt the muscles of his face congeal. Frederic's horse half reared, as if a heel had been driven involuntarily into her side. One of the crossbows gestured grimly and Frederic forced the animal down, face reddening, gaze going from the Master of the Junipers, whose white gelding stood calmly, to Silverhair.

"Has the wolf lost his teeth that he must send dogs to hunt for him?" Silverhair found his voice at last. "Do you think you can kill me when your master has failed?"

"Kill you?" echoed Ordrey in sweet surprise. "Oh no —that would be too kind."

"We will take you to the lord Sangrado," said one of the others, a tall man with empty eyes. "You are meat for the Blood Lord now."

"How dare you!" Frederic's voice cracked, and he fought to control it again. "How dare you threaten my father's guests on my father's land!" He did not hear the Master's warning murmur, but his mare began to prance again and for a moment he was kept busy stilling her.

Ordrey grinned nastily. "Be quiet, buttercup! We are soldiers, not bandits, and there is a greater power than your father in Westria now. My lord gave me no orders regarding you, but it would be amusing to deprive Eric the Ox of his heir. Do not tempt me!"

From red, Frederic's fair cheeks had gone pale, as if for the first time he had realized his own danger. Silverhair's eyes went back to Ordrey's followers, assessing them. There were eleven of them—competent, intent, with well-worn and well-kept weapons and gear.

"That's the way of it, boy—" crowed Ordrey. "You just keep still, and you too, old man!" His bright glance pinned the Master of the Junipers, whose eyes were half-closed, almost as if he were going to sleep. "Don't you try any of your tricks on me! Oh, you'll soon learn the meaning of real mastery, all of you! The good days are coming again, when this land will lie beneath my lord's heel."

Silverhair's glance swept the circle again, and he schooled his face to keep from showing his despair. They were too many, and what could a weary harper do against them with a force consisting of one old man and two boys? Even if they could break free, their horses were too tired by the long day's ride to outrun their enemies. He took a deep breath, thinking of the music he had never played, the words he should have said. But he had never expected to make old bones.

The harper tensed, allowing himself one last glance at Julian, who was sitting his horse with a watchful stillness that almost equaled the Master's. *I have wasted this chance to know him,* he thought. *Perhaps if I fight well enough he can break away.*

"Enough chatter," said Ordrey. "Throw down your weapons now. That's it, unbuckle your swordbelts and toss them on the ground."

Obscurely disappointed, Silverhair saw Julian's hands go to the clasp of his worn swordbelt, and realized that he had expected Jehan's son to put up at least a token resistance, even while he feared to see him slain. Cold mist swirled around them; the harper's hand crept toward the hilt of his sword.

A sudden gust of wind sent twigs and eucalyptus leaves showering across the road. For an instant the eyes of their captors flickered after the motion, Julian's horse flung up its head, and in that moment of distraction the boy's sword was in his hand. The bay mare leaped forward, Julian's blade sliced the string of one of the crossbows, continued through its owner's throat and out again before he could move.

After a moment's astonishment, Silverhair jerked his own blade free. With a yell he spurred his mount, leaned away from the blow the nearest foe aimed at him, and struck with all his strength. The Master kicked his mount into motion, away from the lashing swords. The old man put his hands to his lips and the ground beneath them seemed to vibrate to his deep call.

The struggle was too mixed for the remaining crossbow to be any use now, but the wolves still outnumbered their prey. Silverhair saw Julian trading blow for blow with the outlaw leader, his movements economical but effective. Once Frederic had recovered from his first surprise, he had drawn his sword swiftly and was struggling to make his horse stay within range of his enemies.

Ordrey, almost incoherent with fury, pulled his piebald back. Silverhair wrenched his pony's head toward him, but two of the other men came after him and his awareness narrowed to the reach of their hungry blades. He laughed, knowing that they were still outnumbered, but the battle-madness pulsed through him and he did not care anymore. Dimly he heard Julian's deep cry—

"For Westria!"

Silverhair's sword slammed into hardened leather, checked, then thrust more easily through the flesh beneath it. He jerked the blade free and whirled it upward to guard. His head was ringing. Even the trees seemed to be shouting Julian's battlecry.

Then he realized that it was not the trees but other men that were shouting. He heard a confusion of cries— "A - Regis," and "Westria!" The air throbbed with the insistent lowing of a hunting horn. The man Silverhair was fighting pulled back and the harper kicked his horse to follow, but already the fellow was reining around and clattering down the road after Ordrey.

Horsemen surged around him. Silverhair glimpsed an auburn beard and put up his sword. His breath came in harsh gasps. As the world steadied around him, past memory joined with present reality. He was not at the Dragon Waste, but here on a road in Seagate with Sir Randal drawing rein before him, his teeth white against the conflagration of his beard. A young man with a windburned face and sun-bleached hair pulled up behind him. Beyond them he glimpsed a girl of about sixteen, with hair like a poppy field, holding a bow.

"Sir Randal—there could be no more welcome way to meet you again!"

Sir Randal's laugh rumbled over the sound of retreating hoofbeats as the rest of the newcomers swept down the road after Ordrey and his men. Two of those who had borne the wolf badge lay still in the road. Frederic was gazing with sick eyes at his bloody sword. Julian wiped his blade, slid it into its sheath, and looked from Silverhair to Sir Randal. He was still breathing rather quickly, but there was no emotion on his face.

Silverhair frowned, wondering if the killing had meant nothing to this boy.

Sir Randal urged his horse forward. "Farin, is it really you?"

The harper looked back at his old friend and grinned. "Thanks to your rescue! Give us houseroom for the night and you shall have the full tale!"

"Gladly! Arn and my men will deal with that rabble. Registhorpe is just around the curve of the road—" He turned in the saddle, gesturing, and saw the girl, who was trying to back her pony into the protection of the trees. His face darkened.

"Rana! I told you to stay within walls! Get back to your mother—I'll deal with you when we get home!"

The brightness of the girl's hair seemed to fade. Her lips tightened, but she did not reply as the pony, obedient at last, reversed direction. She slapped its neck with the reins and disappeared among the trees.

Rana sat with her back against the chimney, plaiting and unplaiting the end of her long braid of copper hair. From here she could see through the railings of the little balcony while remaining hidden from those in the hall below. If her father had remembered about the balcony, she thought morosely, he would probably have confined her to her room.

And it was not fair! They had all heard the Master's summons—some, in words, some in a call that stirred their hearts like a battle horn. Her father had been first into the saddle, quivering with eagerness like a hunting dog who sees his master pick up the bow, although only that morning he had been complaining of a crick in his back that kept him from the fields.

Rana had gone for the bow she used to hunt the wild birds that rested on the sloughs near the Bay each fall, kilted up her gown, and scrambled onto her pony with the rest of them. And had been ordered to stay home. . . .

She heard her father's bark of laughter and peered through a knothole. The harper, Silverhair, said something in a low voice, and Sir Randal laughed again.

"Well, here's a song you may not have heard—" His deep voice vibrated in the wood against her cheek as he launched into a ballad of two heroes forced into combat, though they were really on the same side. Silverhair listened attentively, eyes half-closed, his hand unconsciously caressing the golden interlace on the frame of his harp.

When he finished, everyone applauded, even Rana's older sister, Isabella, although the way she and her new husband, Arn, were cuddling, Rana doubted she even knew what had been in the song.

I should be down there with the rest of them! Rana thought angrily. *It wasn't because I'm a female—Marla followed him with the sword she used at the Battle of the Dragon Waste. Father thinks I am still a child. There were too many trees for shooting, and my bow is light, but it might have been useful if we'd had to follow them. I've taken my adult name! I should have been allowed to decide! And now they're all down there enjoying themselves, and I haven't even been introduced to our guests!*

Frederic she knew. The children of Registhorpe and Bongarde had grown up like cousins. The Master of the Junipers had a cottage on the slopes of the Lady Mountain and had served as priest to their holding whenever there was need; a fixture in her life, almost as familiar as the weathered grey stones of the hearth. But that harper, Silverhair, was obviously someone important, and no one would tell her why. She did not even know the name of the other one, the dark young man who had fought so well.

"It's my turn now, Papa, isn't it?" She heard her little brother's squeak and sat back with a groan. They were going to run it like a Bardic Circle, as they often did at Registhorpe, to make the harper feel more at home. He did not seem to mind, but perhaps he did not realize how much patience he would need to sit through one of Cub's performances.

"I'm going to tell you a story!" The boy took a sip of juice from his mug with exactly the same air with which his father had swallowed his mead, cleared his throat, and began.

"You know that after the Maker of All Things created the world, the First People were made to live in it, and that was the First Age. They looked like human beings, but some had the spirits of plants, and some of animals, or stones, or earth or fire. After a long time, the Maker decided to create men, and they were the Second People, and they were all told to live together at peace."

The harper was gazing into the fire, his thoughts obviously far away. But the Master of the Junipers watched the child with a smile, and Frederic and his friend, after exchanging rueful grins, were applying themselves to the mead.

"Everyone was very happy until the Father of the Coyotes, who was always getting into trouble, decided that men were too favored, because the Creator had made them last, and they got all the help and advice," Cub went on. "So he went to all the other First People to make them stop helping men, and told them that men were going to take over all the earth and leave the First People with nothing.

"And then he went to the men and told them that though they had everything else, they could not truly love. They were immortal, you see, and so they could not grieve at death, or rejoice at the birth of a child. The other First People agreed with Coyote, and they told men the same."

Rana let the words wash over her. A restless wind was whispering in the trees outside, and she pressed closer to the warm stones of the chimney. She thought she had heard some tale of a wandering harper with silver hair, but he could do magic with his harp. This man, thin and wearied, seemed quite content to just sit by the fire.

"So the next time the Maker of All Things came to visit, the men asked for the gift of death. The Creator knew where that idea came from, but they insisted. So the gift was given, but the Maker said that now everything would die, the children of Father Coyote, as well as the children of men. After that, Coyote was sorry, and he was very angry with the Creator and tried to lead all the other First People in a revolt. Of course this made the Maker angry too, and a great flood came to carry away all that had been made. Only one mountain was left in the center of the world, and those creatures that could climbed up it and were saved."

The wind was sighing more loudly now. For a moment it sounded like rushing waters, and Rana shivered. The Master lifted his head as if listening, then the sound faded and the priest relaxed again.

"When it was over, only a few people were left. The Maker of All Things took the First People and gave them the forms they wear today. He told the men that now *they* would be lords of the earth, but they must take good care of it, for all the other creatures had once been people too. A few of the First People who had not joined the revolt were made the Guardians of their kinds. The People of the Wood are the Guardians of the Trees, and the Lord of the Redwoods rules them."

Papa should stop him now, thought Rana, *and make him save the rest of the tale for another round.* But perhaps she was impatient because the story of how men had abused their trust and the earth had finally avenged its wrongs always made her uncomfortable. The stories of the Cataclysm, the Covenant, and the Making of the four Jewels were the primary myths of Westria. Even now, an earthquake or a landslip would sometimes uncover one of the buildings the Ancients had made—a great source of profit to the neighborhood until the glass and metal had all been chiseled out and the rubble sorted for crockery or jewels. Sometimes there were books as well, though most of them crumbled at a touch. Sometimes there were bones.

She found it hard to believe that so many people had lived here—that so many people could live together anywhere, although they said there were several thousand in the Royal City of Laurelynn. How could the surrounding land produce enough food for all of them? Where did their garbage go?

Her brother was finishing up at last. "And when the earthquakes and fires and floods were ended, in all the places where there had been cities there was wilderness," he said gleefully. "The tree and grass and bush people rushed in to take back the land, and they would not give their fruits to the men who survived, and the men were starving.

"Then some of them who knew about the Maker of All Things cried out, and the Maker said, 'Where are the tribesmen to whom I gave this land to be its lords?' And they answered, 'We do not know what you mean,' for only a few of the Second People—the tribes—were left. And the Maker of All Things sighed, and was silent a long time.

"And then at last the Maker said, 'Well, you are still here, and so you may remain, and the First People shall be commanded not to harm you. But you will live henceforward as tenants of the land, not as its lords, and the powers of the First People shall be restored, lest you disobey.' And so a Covenant was made between them, and it has been kept by the people of Westria to this day!"

Clapping covered the noise of the rising wind. Frederic passed the mead horn to the other young man and grinned. "Your turn, now, Julian!"

But the stranger shook his head. "You wouldn't ask if you had ever heard me sing, and I don't know any tales. Maybe the next time around I'll be able to think of something. . . ."

Rana thought that Silverhair looked displeased, though she could not imagine why it should matter to him. But now it was Frederic's turn, and he tipped back his fair head and quite unself-consciously began to sing:

There is a valley they say, fairer than any,
Fresh with the flowers of May, divers and many.
The river makes sweet music there, trickling so merry,
And sweet songs of birds fill the air, trilling so fairly.
The noblest of trees guard the ways, boughs swaying
    slightly,
Gay in the branches the jays, flicker blue-brightly.

High are the walls of that place, guarding the valley,
Veiled by its falls, white as lace. There would I dally,
Free from all fear and all care, peace welling through
    me.
Oh, when will those who dwell there show the Way to
    me?"

It was a song of Awahna—Rana should not have been
surprised. Everyone knew that Frederic wanted to go there,
and his father had forbidden it. Maybe that was why
Frederic wore his rank so lightly. The high table at Bongarde meant nothing when what he really wanted was a
campfire in the wilderness.

The note of a harp caught her attention. She bent
forward, ceasing to worry about being seen, for without
preamble or explanation, Silverhair had passed from tuning
his harp to the first exploring chords that picked up
Frederic's melody and developed it into a deep music that
soared and sank and lifted the heart again.

Listening, she saw a valley carved from living stone. The
peaks around it were eternally snowcapped, but the valley
floor was verdant with groves of trees. It was Frederic's
song, and Frederic's longing, translated into music with
such purity that the same desire awoke in everyone who
heard. For a moment Rana saw the face of the Master of the
Junipers transfigured by memory, then her own eyes misted
with quick tears.

Deep in his music, Silverhair was the first to become
aware of the other sound. For a moment he thought that one
of Swangold's strings was slipping, although the temperature had not changed, and it was rare for the harp to need
retuning before the end of a song. He moved his hands
higher on the strings to compensate, but that only made it
worse. He shifted back, plucked louder to try and hear
where the problem lay.

The strings sang true. It was not the harp. Silverhair shut
his eyes, trying to isolate the pure thread of music within.
But that made it worse, as if the disharmony were his own.
Panic stirred in his belly; he forced himself to shut out the
inner music, to concentrate on the movements his trained
fingers made.

"What is wrong?"

The touch on his mind was familiar and friendly. Silverhair looked up quickly and met the Master's deep gaze. Then he realized that if the Master could reach his mind, so could someone else. He glanced around the room, seeing eyes beginning to lose their tranced look as the power of the music faltered, but nowhere that sense of wrongness that was torturing him.

He had not felt anything like this since—abruptly he remembered thunderclouds building above the Lake of Sorcerers, and a red-clad figure singing madness upon the men who struggled on the island there.

Silverhair looked back at the Master. His mind formed the name—

"Caolin . . ."

Carefully, watching his own fingers upon the strings, the harper modulated his melody to a conclusion. For a few moments the strings shimmered with an echo of the final chord, then were still. The Master sat motionless, eyes closed, listening.

Frederic was staring at him. Sir Randal looked from the Master to Silverhair and back again, and very gradually, like water draining from a pool, the joy left his face.

"What is it?"

Silverhair drew a deep breath and gently set the harp on the floor.

"I should leave you," he said steadily. "Ordrey has had time to find his master—he must be closer than we knew. Caolin wants me. . . ."

Sir Randal shook his head. "I would not give up a man who has eaten at my board, even if you were not my old companion-in-arms. You stay here." His wife, Leonie, swallowed and pulled her son to her side.

Silverhair grimaced. "I have fought him before—" *With the help of the Wind Lord,* he remembered. *Will he help me now?* "If I remain I may bring down his wrath upon you all."

The Master sighed deeply and opened his eyes, for the first time looking his age. "No. He knows you are here, and his attention is fixed on Registhorpe. I am not sure he will know if you leave. His men are probably waiting to attack you if you get away, but that will not change the direction of

Caolin's blow. He wants you to run, Farin, so that he can take you. What happens to the others here will simply be their punishment for helping us this afternoon! He will strike here whatever you do."

The harper groaned and covered his face with his hands, aware of the gathering attention of the household, of the stillness that spread through the hall, and above all, of the increasing pressure on his mind, like the heaviness of the air before a thundershower.

"I should never have come back."

He felt another presence beside him, steady and obscurely comforting. He looked up and was surprised to see that it was Julian.

"It will be better to meet it all together—" Julian managed a small smile. He turned to the Master. "What must we do?"

The old priest straightened, the lines of his face hardening as if he had put on an invisible armor. His gaze fixed Sir Randal. "How recent are the wards around this hall?"

Randal frowned. "We replaced them as usual at the Feast of the New Light last year. But I don't understand. We defeated that rabble you were fighting this afternoon easily, and our palisade is strong. What can the man do?"

"Is Caolin a man anymore?" murmured Silverhair. "I'm not so sure."

But the Master was already answering. "The man you knew as Caolin the Seneschal is dead, Randal—he is the Blood Lord now, and his weapon is fear. . . ."

⇛ FIVE ⇚

The people of Registhorpe sat in two concentric circles with linked hands. The Master of the Junipers had taken his seat in the midst of them. Silverhair sat with his harp across from him, flanked by Frederic and Julian. Sir Randal had claimed the place of the doorkeeper, facing the entrance, with his drawn sword laid across his knees.

"We are the children of the Light. . . . Darkness has no part in us. . . ."

Rana forced her attention back to the Master's words, trying to visualize the golden sphere of protection that was supposed to surround them. The face of the priest was calm, intent—the face of a man driving a team of half-trained horses across difficult ground, with every sense extended and focused on his task. She looked from him to her father.

Sir Randal had not forbidden her to participate in this battle, but she was uncomfortably aware that it did not mean there was less danger, for everyone who dwelt at Registhorpe was here in the hall, from old Hawken, the herder, to the baby in Catalina's arms. There had not been enough time for them to scatter sufficiently to avoid Caolin's blow, and if they could not escape it, it was better to meet it with united strength. Dimly, Rana sensed the difference between a skirmish in which her lack of skill might have made her a liability and a battle of the spirit in which they were all at risk equally, and the only protection was a disciplined will.

That uneasy feeling crawled along her nerves once more. The expressions of those around her showed that they were aware of it too. Curiosity about the Red Sorcerer, who had been only a legend, stirred in her, and her discomfort increased. She forced herself to stop speculating, knowing it made her more vulnerable. She could wonder about Caolin later, when he was not attacking them! *Concentrate!* she told herself. *Think only of the Master's words. . . .*

> "*We are the Children of Love, we may not be touched by hate;*
> *We are the Children of Victory, we may not be governed by fear. . . ."*

The Master continued to chant until the affirmation was finished. When he paused, Silverhair began to play a hymn and their voices united in its melody.

Rana clung to the music, feeling the hairs on the back of her neck rise as a chill wind gusted through the room.

> "*O Thou who wert before the days, before the circling years,*
> *O Thou who art, deliver us from all our transient fears . . . ,"*

they sang. Rana fought to maintain her focus, to sense the strength of the people around her—family, and those who had raised her, and these newcomers who were the cause of their danger, and, she hoped, their defense as well.

Hour by hour the strange battle went on. Like the driver of many horses, the Master captured the wandering wills of those gathered around him, held them, bound them to his own, directed them in the one purpose, spiraling upward to the source of all strength, negating and denying the evil that attacked them and affirming the Rampart that was their protection.

The Master's voice faded as he finished a prayer. Rana lifted her head, aware of the absence of pressure for the first time since the attack had begun. Had the sorcerer given up?

Her nose wrinkled, and then all of them were coughing at the stench that had invaded the room. Rana held her nose and looked around her. Nothing in the hall had changed. Timber and stone still retained their integrity. Then she heard a long howl that increased in intensity until she covered her ears in pain. It seemed to come from everywhere at once, but the grunt that followed it originated directly beyond the door.

The floor trembled, and they heard the padding of heavy feet outside. The thing was pacing, around the building and then back again. Now Rana understood why the Master had not wanted anyone to leave the hall.

"The Hunter . . . ," whispered Hawken, sweat running down his face.

It was still pacing, but now and again it would sit down, and the timber walls groaned as it leaned against them. And all the time it kept up a constant undertone of sound —grunting, gobbling, whining in eagerness or giving an anticipatory slobber. Even the sound of its heavy panting brought terror as it went on and on.

"If that is Caolin's kitty cat, he'll have to feed it himself. It will not enter here!" Silverhair forced a grin.

The harp began to sing again, at first hesitating, then gaining strength. The music covered the breathing of the beast that waited outside, but even Silverhair's singing could not drown out the rasp as it scraped a huge paw along the wall. Carlos jumped up with an oath and tried to run out the door. Rana's sister Isabella whimpered and clung to her husband. Their sobbing mingled with the other sounds.

"Power of Earth—power to endure, to nourish, to grow, bone of our bone . . ." The Master began the litany.

"We claim thee as our own tonight!" Frederic responded.

"Power of Water—retreating only to return, patient conqueror, bearer of nourishment and blood of life . . ."

"We claim thee as our own tonight!"

"Power of Air—power of inspiration, of force invisible, the breath of life . . ."

"We claim thee as our own tonight!"

"Power of Fire—sustaining warmth, revealing light, purifying, transmuting, spark of life . . ."

"We claim thee as our own tonight!" the litany went on.

The beast outside was quiet now, but the walls rattled in a rising wind. It whistled through the cracks, whispered in corners and sent stray drafts to brush faces and lift locks of hair. It was as cold as the grave, and there were words in it.

"Nobody cares about you . . . ," it said to Rana. *"Your father doesn't love you—you are not a son like Cub or an*

obedient daughter like Isabella. Why try to protect them? They will never understand you. Listen to me . . . Listen to me. . . ."

She shook her head, trying to shut the words out, aware that the full-throated response to the litany was wavering. What did the others hear?

"Do not listen to it!" the Master cried. "He will try to tempt you—think only of what you are saying—grasp each other's hands and sing!"

They sang. But Rana could see the strain of the battle in the Master's face. Hourly he had grown paler, and the beads of sweat stood out on his brow. How could he endure it? And if he did not, how could they? Rana's head ached from holding the fear at bay.

"Why are you doing this? Let go and there will be nothing to fear. There is no sorcerer, only the wind. Why have you let them frighten you with this child's tale?"

The Voice promised peace and understanding, an end to the stress that stretched every nerve like her own bowstring.

I will not give in—I will not! Rana repeated to herself, though she no longer really knew why. Her mother motioned to her to help add oil to the lamps. The men heaped more wood on the fire so that the flickering light could drive the shadows away.

Yet still the Voice whispered. The air was becoming oppressive now, and from time to time a face would pale, or someone would moan. Even the Master was slumping now.

Rana looked at him, and in her quick rush of sympathy her strained barriers went down and she was aware of his thoughts and of the thoughts of the one with whom he strove.

"Pride, little man, pride! You could not protect the King from me before, and you will not be able to protect the harper now. Why do you struggle? His punishment was only an example, a demonstration to show my power, and I have not yet put forth a tithe of the strength I have now! See, already these sheep begin to fail you. Soon they will run, blind with fear, and Ordrey and his men can take what revenge they please. As for you, I have an old account to settle with you, and your doom is sure."

"To all of us comes the doom appointed," came the Master's calm answer. *"But your victory is not yet."*

But even the Master flinched before the blast of hatred with which the sorcerer responded, and Rana, shocked out of contact, nearly fell.

The wind shrieked blasphemies as it tore at the stout timbers of the hall. Silverhair was playing like one possessed, plucking from his instrument the notes to answer each convulsion of the air.

The Master turned to Frederic and Julian. "You must hold the people for me—gather the power and channel it to me so that I can mirror Caolin's attack back again."

"But I can't do that!" whispered Julian.

"I think the strength for it is in you." The Master's face was as implacable as stone. "If it is not, better we should know it now. If you fail, the burden of their sacrifice will be upon your soul. . . ." His glance encompassed the people around them, who were beginning to stir uneasily as the focus of the Master's leadership faltered.

Frederic had already moved to the outer circle, found a place to sit down, and extended his hands. "Grip hands, everyone," he told them. "Feel the power of the earth beneath you and let it rise up your spine as you breathe in. When you can feel it, let it flow out through your right hand to the person next to you and receive the power the person on your left is sending to you."

Julian glared at the Master. "Why do you lay this upon me?"

The Master looked at him, and Rana thought she saw pity in his gaze. "Because you are who you are . . . ," he said.

As if that were an answer, Julian nodded and with set jaw took his place in the inner circle next to Rana and held out his hands. Rana felt the strength of his grip, a palm hardened by ax handle and the hilt of a sword.

"We'll send the power around and around until this place glows like a beacon, and then I'll focus it toward the Master—" Frederic's voice was calm, friendly, as if he were explaining the rules to some new game. "Come now, breathe in . . . and out . . . in . . . and out. . . ."

Rana straightened and closed her eyes. She had received some training in this at her Initiation—she wished now that she had practiced it more. She forced herself to breathe regularly, four beats in, four beats to exhale again, acutely conscious of the stranger's hand that gripped her own.

Relax, she told herself. *Give yourself to the power.* And surely she could feel it now, rising and falling with every breath, beginning to move through her as the energy started to flow. And as her barriers thinned she recognized the personalities of her mother and brother, as one might note the flavor of herbs in a stew, and less clearly, the essences of the others in her circle. But overpowering them all was the sense of this man, Julian, a force that despite his diffidence was strong enough to stamp the energy of the entire circle with his own identity.

He was like stone, she thought, and like something softer as well, perhaps the scent of a rose. Complexities and contradictions within him teased at her understanding, but that was not what she was supposed to be doing now. Surely she felt the power building, swirling around the circle as it built to sufficient intensity.

There was a heavy pounding outside, a throbbing in the earth as if the greatest of all beasts drew near. The flames of fire and lamp flickered madly. The Master sat like an image in the midst of them all and did not move.

The air shivered to a howl that sounded as if all the hunting packs of Westria were at the door. Silverhair struck one great chord to counter it, a sound that hung in the room like the reverberation of a great bell. Then another Sound tolled from outside, equally clear, and of so precisely tuned a vibration that the two notes mingled in a cry of exquisite agony. With a sound like a breaking heart the golden harpstrings snapped. The harper gave a great cry and collapsed over the cracked frame, bleeding from face and hands where the broken wires had sliced him, and then was still.

Suddenly the Master leaped to his feet. "The power —pass it to me now!" He lifted his hands, and Rana felt something flowing from her like a great sigh, saw Julian's face brighten, the air brighten, saw the Master's open hands trailing a luminous haze.

He stepped over their linked hands and began to pace clockwise around the hall. And where he trod there was a swirling, as if a million dust motes had been set in motion there. Now they could *see* the wall they had been trying to imagine, growing, glowing more brightly with each circuit the magician made. It was a sphere of gold, radiating around them, expanding until Rana could no longer see the paneled walls and painted timbers of the hall.

The Master returned to the center and stood, turning slowly as he continued to receive the influx of power. The people of Registhorpe sat in a golden dream while outside the heavens wheeled relentlessly toward dawn. Somewhere far away a cock crowed.

The golden wall shimmered and started to thin. The Master stiffened and stood still, facing east with arms outstretched, palms up as if he held an invisible foe at bay.

"As thou hast given so shalt thou receive! Mirror, show my enemy his soul!" he whispered hoarsely. "Frederic, Julian, give me all you can!"

Abruptly the golden sphere around them silvered. Rana swayed, dizzied by the rush of sensation as her whole life seemed to flow out through her hand. The sphere flared around them, and the Master shone as if his body had become a lantern to hold the light. The earth trembled beneath Rana, and she fell over, blinded, or perhaps it was only the shock of sudden darkness, for after a little she perceived the pallid illumination of dawn.

As painfully as if she were waking after having spent herself on some unaccustomed labor the day before, Rana pulled herself up from the crouch into which she had fallen—how long ago? All around her, crumpled bodies were straightening, inert forms beginning to stir. Somewhere, scattered bird-voices announced the advent of the day.

Only Frederic and Julian still sat upright, their faces remote as if they dreamed. And the Master still stood in the midst of them like an icon of protection. A first ray of sunlight made its way through one of the high windows of the hall.

The Master looked at it, sighed, and then, with the deliberate inevitable unfolding motion of a falling tower, he crumpled to the floor.

Up and down the long fault lines that broke the bedrock of Westria the tremors traveled, branching faults carrying the vibration through the ranges between them until all the land knew of the battle that had taken place at dawn. But it had only been a minor earthquake. Plants and animals were hardly shaken, and soon returned to their normal early morning activity. Only those who understood that this was more than the Earth Mother's normal turning in her sleep remained thoughtful. And in the Sacred Wood, so close to one of the two poles of power, the Lord of the Trees began to call his people to Council.

On the Red Mountain, men huddled in terror until it was full day. Some had been driven mad by the backlash of the battle. The others waited apprehensively for their master to appear. The sun rose higher, but the Blood Lord did not come out of the chambers that were the first thing he had ordered built for him. That building was untouched, but a great crack had opened in the foundation they had laid for the main part of the fortress. When Esteban saw it, he immediately set the men to working, hoping to repair it before Caolin could see.

"Is he dead?"

Julian looked down at the still face of the Master of the Junipers, then back to Frederic. It was so quiet there in the little corner room, he was not sure whether he was breathing himself.

"No. Not yet, anyway," said Frederic. "But he hasn't moved. At the College they taught us how a Master can leave his body in trance. I've been in the guarding circle once or twice when it was done. The Master looked like this when he was . . . away, but that was voluntary, totally under control. I don't know what happens when someone has to channel so much power."

Frederic looked weary too. His hair was lank, and there were marks like old bruises beneath his eyes. He eased back in the chair, and Julian saw dried blood around a tear in the green wool of his breeches.

He pointed. "Did you get that in the fight?"

Frederic looked down. "That—I suppose so—I didn't notice it before."

Julian grinned. "If we keep on like this you'll end up with as many scars as me. But you should get that taken care of. Go on—you've been with the Master all morning. I'll watch beside him for a while."

"All right." Frederic got to his feet, swayed a little and put out his hand to the wall. "I didn't realize I was so tired.

They've sent for my mother to come nurse him, you know," he went on. "She learned healing from the Master himself, and—"

"Frederic, go get some rest!" Julian took his arm and pushed him toward the door. "I'll call you if there is need."

When the other boy was gone Julian sat down in the empty chair. Now there was no sound but his own breathing and the faintest of whispers from the man on the bed. Indeed, all Registhorpe was unusually quiet for this time of day, with half its population asleep or too exhausted to move.

Sir Randal and Julian had gone out that morning with a few of the stronger men to look for Ordrey, but there was no sign of the wolf's heads nearby. At least they need not fear physical attack, and as the day wore on with no sense of evil, it began to seem as if that final confrontation had knocked out the sorcerer as well as the priest, at least for a while.

Julian's own muscles complained as he moved, as if he had been beaten with clubs all night instead of just sitting still. But it had been an active sort of stillness, with his muscles straining against each other as he strove to resist Caolin. And if the battle had wracked Julian, who was relatively oblivious to such things, no wonder that the more sensitive Frederic looked like the victim of some particularly talented torturer. *His father should let him go back to the College,* thought Julian. *He will make a good priest someday.*

Sunlight slanting through a chink in the shutters crept across the floor. It was hard to believe that there was still life in the man who lay in the narrow bed. But it had been hard to believe in the transfigured being who had led them in that last hour before the dawn.

How can I hate him? Julian leaned over the still figure to adjust the coverlet. *It was only my anger speaking, because I loved him all through my childhood, and I thought he was playing with me.* But one could no more resent the man whose radiant spirit had shone through his flesh last night than one could resent the ordered movements of the sun.

He laid his hand across that other hand that lay so still, gnarled with use and age. "You must not die—" he whispered. "I won't know what to do."

But there was no answer. He was free to consider the Master's face, so familiar and yet so strange, as he had never dared to do before. At intervals throughout Julian's childhood the Master of the Junipers had come to Stanesvale and stayed awhile before going away. Julian's foster mother had assumed he was coming or going to the Sacred Valley, but Julian knew now that the journey to Awahna was not often repeated in one lifetime. So the Master must have come to Stanesvale because of him. . . .

His hair was all silver now. On top it was gone completely —strange how Julian had not noticed that before. The old man's weathered skin seemed ageless, and his nose, which always seemed too large for his other features, would never change. And then, of course, there was the spirit that glowed in his eyes. But now the Master's eyes were closed.

Sunlight moved inexorably across the floor, marking out the hours. Hanks of yarn hung from the ceiling, and a spinning wheel had been shoved out of the way against the wall to make room for the bed here, in the quietest corner of the house. It hardly seemed worth the trouble, for the Master could hear nothing as he was now.

"Do you remember how you came after me the time I tried to run away to Awahna?" Julian spoke softly, as if his old teacher's insensibility gave him freedom to say things he had hardly dared voice to himself before.

"My foster brothers had been teasing me, and I thought that if my mother had wanted to go to the Valley, I could go too. But I got wet and chilled, and I was tossing with fever by the time you found me, and nursed me, and began to teach me the secrets of the hills. . . ."

Julian frowned. He had forgotten that teaching, with all the fighting and fellowship and fear. But for a while he had gone about with the feeling that each tree he saw was about to speak to him. When had he lost that, and why?

For certain he had not felt it at his Initiation, wrapped up in his first passion for a woman and his rivalry with Lord Philip's brother Robert, who was now his friend.

"I am glad you were there to receive my oath and conduct the ritual," he said to the still face, and realized that this, also, had probably not been chance.

"But even if I was not completely abandoned as a child,

what about the future? I don't have the skills or the training to be a King, even if I do have a right to the throne!" He gripped the Master's hands, leaning over him as if he could make him hear.

A tremor shook the limp body; Julian heard a breath of sound. Startled, Julian let go of the Master's hands and stiffened, listening. The old man's head turned a little on the pillow and his lips moved, but in a moment Julian realized that this was no waking—the old man's spirit still wandered, and this was only the echo of a dream.

But still he listened, as if even these ramblings might somehow hold answers to his questioning.

"Faris . . . Faris—"

Julian stared, for the Master was calling his own dead mother's name.

"I have done what you asked of me. The boy is grown. My lady, my lord, now let me follow you . . ." The Master's voice failed, he frowned a little in his strange sleep, as if he were listening.

And Julian, hearing him, felt as if he were eavesdropping, but he could not draw away. Outside the light was growing deeper with the ending of another day.

"No—but he is ready, he will . . ."

"I am *not* ready!" Julian exclaimed in spite of himself, in spite of a sudden amazed suspicion that the Master was neither remembering nor dreaming, but taking part in an actual conversation with those spirits who had been his parents when they walked the earth of Westria.

"Perhaps the road remaining is a short one, but it will be hard. Caolin has become . . ."

Julian strained to hear the whispered words. The Master's face was not peaceful now, and his breath came painfully.

"I remember the promise," the Master said then. "But I cannot offer forgiveness to Caolin. Yes . . ." The words came slower. "I will . . ."

The Master spoke no more, but he was breathing more easily now, and small movements of his body spoke of normal sleep instead of the deathlike trance in which he had lain before.

And as if the Master's sleep had released him, all the

accumulated fatigue of the last twenty-four hours fell upon Julian like an army from ambush, and before he could resist it, he slept as well.

Perhaps an hour had passed when he came to abrupt awareness again. A voice, so faint it might have been his spirit's whisper, was calling his name.

"Julian . . ."

His eyes flew open. He saw the sunlight glowing like fire through the western window, edging the Master's folded hands with light and glowing in his deep eyes. Julian started out of the chair, then sank back again.

"Thanks be to the Maker of All! I thought—we were afraid—" He could not finish, for despite the life in his eyes, the Master looked so frail, surely any breath of harsh air would be enough to finish him after all.

One side of the Master's face twisted in an attempt to smile.

"Caolin has . . . more power than I thought. Almost too much . . . for me to handle. Even . . . with your help."

"But you reflected it back at him, didn't you?" protested Julian. "It must have blasted him!"

"Perhaps . . ." There was the suggestion of a shrug, still only on the right side. "For a while. Julian, you must go . . . with Silverhair. If the Blood Lord learns you live he will seek to destroy you."

Julian stared at him. He had not thought about Caolin. It had never occurred to him that he might inherit his father's enemy with his Crown. He had fought to protect Silverhair and the Master. With a cold churning at the pit of his stomach he assimilated the realization that perhaps the greatest danger might be to *him*.

"But what about you?" Words came at last, though he could not have said whether he feared most for the Master without him, or for himself without the Master.

"My left side . . . is stricken—" The words confirmed Julian's growing apprehension. "I don't know if it . . . will heal. *He* will discount me. You are the one in danger. Go to the Lord of the Trees. He will know what to do. . . ."

The final words came out in a gasp. Breathing with difficulty, the Master lay very still.

I am tiring him, thought Julian. *I have only just found him again, but I see that I cannot lean on him anymore.*

"I understand," he said aloud. "Frederic will have a chance to show how much he has learned from you. But when I come back, please be here—I was surly to you because I was afraid. I need so much to know that you are still here!"

The Master's fingers twitched, and Julian reached out to grip them in his own strong hand. He felt something flow between them like an affirmation.

"I have promised . . . ," said the old man after a little while, "my son . . ."

And then the door swung open and Lady Rosemary swept into the room. The late sunlight blazed on the tiered braids of her golden hair, haloed now with wisps from hard riding. Her face was grimed from the dust of the road, and grim with worry. But as she saw that the Master was conscious, and smiling, the tension in her shoulders eased and she sighed.

"From Frederic's message, I would have thought you were at death's door!" she said tartly. "Well, we'll see how you like being on the receiving end of what you have taught me." She looked around, saw Julian still standing there, and frowned. "You've been making him talk, haven't you? You get out of here and leave him alone!"

Julian's expression must have betrayed him, for as he began to move her grim look softened and she patted his arm.

"Go on, lad, and don't be afraid. I'll take care of him for you. I've been waiting for a chance to order that man around for twenty years!"

➤➤ SIX ➤➤

The five slashed furrows seemed very white against the weathered boards of Registhorpe's great hall. Julian looked back at them and shuddered. Close up, he had not realized what they were. It was only now, looking back down the hill at the holding, that he recognized the mark of a giant claw. Morning mist lay heavily in the folds of the hills, making everything seem insubstantial and unreal—everything but that new scar, which showed far too clearly that they had not dreamed what they had endured the night before.

It had been two nights, really, thought Julian as he kicked his mare after the others. But between preparation for their journey, Sir Randal's endless advice, and their early start, he had gotten hardly enough sleep for last night to be counted. At the same time he felt as if that strange bloodless battle with the sorcerer had taken place a century ago.

The road passed beneath a stand of pines that cut off what little light there was, and Julian shuddered, suppressing an irrational spurt of fear. Sir Randal would never have let that redheaded daughter of his guide them to the Sacred Wood if he had expected there to be any danger, and Rana was hardly likely to lose her way—she had grown up in these hills.

Now that the worst of his anxiety about the Master of the Junipers was over, Julian was realizing that something had happened to him, too, a kind of soreness of the spirit, and a perturbation of the senses that left him wondering whether it was the fog that made everything look so ghostly, or whether he was only now beginning to see the reality behind the appearance of things. He had felt something similar after he met the Lady of Westria, but then he had staggered beneath the weight of glory. Now he saw shadows everywhere.

It's lack of rest that is making me feel this way, he told himself. *A good night's sleep will set me right again.* But it did not look as if he was going to get much rest—not for a while.

He tried to remember how he had longed for an adept's vision and resigned himself to living without it as a man blinded might grow accustomed to the loss of light. *And if the darkness should be suddenly lifted, would not that man hide his dazzled eyes and cry out in pain?* he thought. *That's me—whimpering because my dream is coming to life around me, and I am afraid. . . .*

And maybe I am right to fear it, his thought went on. He remembered the Master's ravaged face, closed in sleep as he had seen it just before they left Registhorpe. And there was Frederic, riding just ahead of him with his eyes like two holes in a blanket and his hands shaking with fatigue. Even Silverhair, who had only the magic of his music, looked as if the sorcerer's curse had shattered his arm instead of the harp whose pieces were tenderly shrouded in the case slung across his back.

Then from up ahead he heard a tune—Rana was whistling the song Frederic had sung about Awahna. Julian saw Frederic's back straighten and knew that his friend had recognized it too. At the same moment they passed out from the darkness beneath the trees into the pearly light of early morning once more.

The mist had begun to lift, but it still veiled the treetops, and moisture beaded the leathery foliage of the chaparral. Julian, used to the thick ground fogs of the Great Valley, found it very strange, but Frederic had assured him that in the winter and spring, when vapors rose from the marshy ground of the Great Valley and spread a damp pall over the land, the skies along the coast were relatively clear. But the hotter the rest of Westria got, the cooler the coast would be, and many of its plants used the fog's insubstantial moisture to get through the dry season of the year. It seemed to Julian that there was a kind of beauty in these sea mists, almost a coquetry, which hinted of secrets invisible in the full light of day.

The road rounded the base of the Lady Mountain, and then began to wind down a long fold in the hills that led toward the sea. Here, slopes of bleached grass broken by scattered clumps of brush fell away to one side while a forest deeper and greener than anything on the Lady Mountain filled the folds and hollows of the hills like a lake of trees.

Rana pulled up to rest the horses, and Julian took advantage of the pause to look around him. Julian could see no sign of habitation nearby, yet for such a remote place the path seemed surprisingly well-worn. But a closer look showed grass beginning to grow in the wheel ruts—whoever had made this road had not used it for some time.

"Do you see down there?" Frederic pointed toward a level area across the ravine, where an irregular black circle marred the grass. "At Midsummer we build a huge bonfire there. People come from all over the Province and dance through the night."

"They say that the People of the Wood come out sometimes and join the revelers," said Rana, "but no one enters the Wood itself without the approval of the Guardian. . . ."

Julian thought of Midsummer Revels, and beings that took human form in order to mingle with men, and he repressed another shiver. In the arms of the Lady of Westria he had known a fulfillment he doubted any mortal woman could ever bestow, but she had laid upon him a burden he was not sure a mortal man could bear. And who, or what, was he on his way to meet in the Sacred Wood now?

Rana kicked her pony and they began to descend the trail. At the edge of the trees before them Julian saw a little house of grey stone.

"Who does the Guardian allow to enter here?" asked Julian. He was riding beside Rana now.

She gave him a quick sideways look and smiled. "People who love the trees and would learn how to care for them."

"And those who come to bury the Kings of Westria—" said Silverhair harshly. It was the first thing he had said since they set out that morning. The other three turned, for a moment so startled to hear him speak that they did not comprehend his words.

The harper looked at Julian with eyes like dead coals. "The last time I was here I followed your father's bier."

Rana suppressed a shocked exclamation, but Julian met his uncle's stare, giving nothing away. Behind his stony mask his thoughts were in turmoil—was Silverhair making a threat, or offering a warning, or did the harper's grief for the loss of his instrument make him see shadows everywhere?

He was still trying to think of some reply when Frederic tapped his arm and pointed. A young man in a green robe was standing at the edge of the forest, as still as one of the trees. His face was in shadow, but there was something familiar about him. Julian opened his mouth to greet him; then, afraid he might be wrong, he shut it again. He turned to Frederic.

"Ask him if he will let us in."

Frederic rode forward. They saw him gesture and the young priest's nod. Frederic waved and they reined their mounts after him.

"I am the Warden of the Wood," the young man in the green robe said gravely. "The Guardian knows already who you are, and why you have come. Unsaddle your animals and leave them here—they will not stray—and take off your boots. We have slippers of soft leather for you that will not bruise the ground, or if you wish you may taste the earth with feet bare."

Julian swung down from his mare, dropped her reins, and took a quick step toward the Warden. The sun was burning through the mists, and now he could see clearly the browned features beneath the young priest's sun-bleached hair.

"Pine?" he asked softly. "Is it you?"

The other's gravity broke abruptly and he grinned. "I was wondering if you would remember me. . . ."

Julian thought of those nights of anguish on the trail when they had both been prisoners of slave-raiders from the Barren Lands and shook his head. "There are some things that one does not forget easily. . . ."

Pine smiled, stepped forward, and hugged him. Julian felt arms with the whipcord power of a tree-root close around him and put out just enough of his strength to make the other boy give way. Then they separated, grinning.

"Are they really expecting us?" asked Julian. "How did the Guardian know we were on our way here?"

"The People of the Wood have their own ways of talking —roots send messages through the earth, and when leaves flutter, it is not always the work of the wind. My master has been expecting *something* since Midsummer; we all felt the earthquake two nights ago, and now you are here. Now you tell me—why should the Lord of the Trees be in such a flutter over a visit from you?"

Julian felt the expression leave his features, and Pine laughed.

"I remember that stone face of yours, and I see that it's no use questioning. I suppose that in his own good time my lord will tell me whatever he thinks I should know!"

Julian tried to smile, envying Pine's cheerful serenity. It reminded him a little of Frederic's manner, and he wondered if it was something they learned at the College of the Wise. Then he remembered that Caolin had been to the College. . . . It must be some gift of the spirit, then—one more thing he lacked, and he had a feeling that in the days ahead he was going to need some source of cheer.

"And it will not do to keep him waiting—" Pine went on. "Take your shoes off quickly, and I will show you the way."

Julian blinked as he walked, wondering if his eyes were tricking him. The forest seemed to be moving, as if some of the trees were constantly slipping in and out of visibility. The sunlight poured down like a river of green gold, and strange sparkles of light flickered among the leaves. Even without being told he would have known that this was a place of power.

As they moved farther into the Wood that feeling of pressure increased, until the air throbbed with an almost painful tension. And still they went on, until they came to a clearing deep in a fold of the hills, where a carpet of green moss covered the ground. A circle of matched redwoods encircled it like a guard of honor for what looked like the forefather of all redwood trees. Pine led them to face the central giant on the hard and flattened space within.

Then they waited. Julian took a deep breath of spiced air and felt a pang of longing for his own mountains. The Sequoias of the Ramparts were stouter than these trees, though not so tall, but their fragrance was much the same. He should have been impatient, waiting here, or afraid. But it was impossible to fidget in an atmosphere of such concentrated calm. Even Silverhair's set face had relaxed a little, as if he had found a momentary release from his pain.

And why should he be impatient? It was not as if there was anywhere he needed to go. There was good air here in the shelter of the hills; good soil, and water enough. It would be a good place to take root and grow. . . .

From some deeper part of his consciousness came a jangle of alarm, and just as he became aware of what he was thinking Julian realized that it was not his changing vision but the tree before him that was altering, shimmering, dislimning and forming again in the shape of a giant robed in russet and cloaked in dark green. Slowly the form solidified and shrank until it was nearer human size, but the afterimage of the tree remained like an aura around it.

Frederic and the Warden bowed low, and after a moment Julian pulled himself together enough to imitate them. Silverhair was standing by himself, as still as any tree, but Julian heard a sound behind him and realized that the girl, Rana, had stepped into his shadow, as if it could shelter her from the full impact of what she saw.

"You are welcome," came a deep voice that seemed to come at once from the earth they stood on and from above. "But it is hard enough for me to peer down at you when you are on your feet. You will have to stand up if you wish to speak to me!"

Julian scrambled to his feet again and looked up to meet a gaze as limpid as a forest pool. Abruptly much of his tension left him, and his mouth twitched with an involuntary smile. The Warden had spoken of the Lord of the Trees with reverence, but surely no one with his friend's sunny disposition could serve a being who lived by inspiring fear. It was not until some time later that he remembered the difference between the Lady of Westria by night and by day, and it occurred to him that all of the Guardians must be able to cloak their power in order to deal with men, and that perhaps his first instinct had been the right one.

There was an awkward silence. Then Frederic cast a quick look at Julian and cleared his throat.

"My lord, the Master of the Junipers told us to come to you, and the Warden of the Wood said that you were expecting us. Can you tell us what to do?"

"Softly, softly, sprout!" said the Redwood. "You must

plant the seed before the tree can grow. The knowledge that guides me may or may not be appropriate for you. After the earthquake, it was inevitable that I should set my people to watch Registhorpe, and that they should tell me who came this way. But they cannot tell me what happens within walls. I do not see the Master of the Junipers among you, yet surely I would have felt his passing. Why is he not here to speak for you?"

Julian stared up at the gnarled features of the Lord of the Trees and found himself growing angry. If the Guardian had felt the earthquake, then surely he must know that there was an evil in the land that could threaten trees as well as men.

"He is alive, but barely, and that alone should tell you how much we need your counsel," he broke in.

"It is Caolin—" echoed Silverhair harshly. "Caolin, who tried once to destroy Westria and lost the Jewels of Power. Once more he holds the Red Mountain. He tried to destroy us two nights ago. Do you think he will be any more tender toward you if you stand in his way?"

Foliage rustled around them as if the trees were trying to shrink away from the power of the harper's pain.

"Then perhaps I should send you on your way now, and avoid his wrath . . . ," said the Redwood softly.

Julian heard Rana gasp behind him, but his own mind was working furiously on several levels. One set of perceptions told him that the Guardian was only testing them, and he must not let that provocation anger him. But another trembled because he realized suddenly that the Lord of the Trees had committed himself simply by allowing them to enter the Sacred Wood. He recoiled from visions of blighted leaves, logs lying on the earth like scattered bones, a forest writhing in the agony of fire.

"You cannot—" he exclaimed involuntarily. "We have brought the danger upon you by coming here!"

He felt the full force of the Tree Lord's attention upon him suddenly.

"That may or may not be so—we have our own defenses, which even the Blood Lord might find difficult to get through. What is important is that you realized what you have done—" said the Redwood in a deep voice. "Perhaps the message I received regarding you was true after all."

Julian stiffened. He had meant to stay quiet and let Frederic speak for them all, and instead he had betrayed himself again. *"Since Midsummer he has been expecting something—"* Pine had said. Julian had an uneasy certainty that he knew from whom the message the Guardian was referring to had come. Frederic was beginning to smile triumphantly, but Julian felt Rana's bewilderment even without looking at her. Well, she would just have to wonder. He realized now that it had been foolish to think he could put off facing this. If he was to be King, his duty would be to the People of the Wood no less than to the people of Westria.

"If you believe that, then you must accept my right to call on you for aid," he said as evenly as he could.

"That is more than your father ever dared to do—" responded the Guardian.

"That may well be." Julian thought of what he had heard of the dead King. A fine fighter and a winner of hearts, he had been, but as far as anyone remembered, not much interested in the world of the spirit or the strange powers which the four elemental Jewels conferred on a sovereign of Westria. Julian did not judge him, but neither did he feel any necessity to emulate him.

"But your young trees are rooted in his bones," he added brutally. "As my father's flesh has fed your young, and as someday mine shall do the same, I call upon you to aid my father's son!" Another shudder swept through the trees around them, and Julian wondered if he had gone too far. Even Silverhair was staring at him.

He wanted to shudder, himself, thinking of meat and bones decomposing in that moist earth, of flowers growing through the eye sockets of his empty skull. But that was the price that all men paid for walking upon the land and consuming its bounty—not only the sovereigns of Westria.

"My father had the four Jewels, and my father did not have to fight a sorcerer," he went on. "I do not ask you to send your people to fight for me, only for your counsel. You are the Lord of the Trees, and your people's roots spread through the land—can you tell me where the Earthstone came to rest when the explosion on the Red Mountain whirled the Jewels away?"

He stared at the Lord of the Trees, and saw the Guardian's clear gaze grow troubled. After what seemed a very long time the Tree Lord sighed.

"Deep as our roots go, they have not touched the Earthstone anywhere . . . ," he said slowly.

"But it can't have been destroyed!" broke in Frederic. "Surely something drastic would have happened to the land, instead—" He gestured his frustration, unable to find words.

"Instead of this slow unraveling of the web of the Covenant because there has been no King to perform the ceremonies!" Julian finished for him. It was something he had thought about often, standing watch on the border, or during the long ride across the Valley to Bongarde, but this was the first time he had been able to put it into words.

He met the Guardian's deep gaze, knowing that if, beyond all odds, he succeeded in the quest the Master of the Junipers had laid upon him, it would be his responsibility to conduct those rituals and set things right again. If ever he became King, he and the Lord of the Trees were going to know each other very well indeed, so he might as well begin boldly.

"Like you, I believe that the Earthstone still exists in the world of manifestation," said the Guardian. "You are right—even humans would not have been able to ignore the effects of its destruction, and the People of the Wood would have felt the first tremors of it through every leaf and rootlet, as we did when Caolin first put on and claimed the Jewels. But it is not buried in the soil. You must seek the Earthstone in the deep places of the earth, where other powers rule. I have no jurisdiction over the elementals. If you want to question them you must look to the Lady of Earth for authority."

Julian felt a sinking in the pit of his stomach. The Master of the Junipers had told them to come here, and he had assumed that if he asked the right questions, the Lord of the Trees would have the answers. And so he did, but the answers only pointed the way to a new search, and what he had expected to be a conclusion was just the beginning. For a moment disappointment held him silent.

"Well, then, we will have to go to the Lady of Earth and ask Her." Frederic, more resilient, grimaced and added, "But if they know at the College of the Wise where She dwells, I was not advanced enough to be told. If you cannot tell us where the Earthstone has gotten to, surely you must know where the Lady is—"

"In one sense," the Redwood began, "the Lady of Earth is everywhere, and you can invoke Her anytime you stand upon the soil. . . ."

Julian frowned, but the Guardian went on before he could speak again.

"But if She has the Earthstone, it will be at one of the shrines where she speaks face to face with men. At this season you will find Her in the south, at a place called Awhai."

Frederic looked blank and turned to Julian. "I've never heard of it. I don't think it's even in Westria. . . ."

"I have—" Silverhair said grimly. "And whether it's in Westria or not is a matter of opinion. I heard of it when I was in the town of Saticoy on my way through Elaya. They spoke of it as being in the mountains a little south and east of Santibar."

"What's wrong with it?" asked Julian, responding to the harper's manner more than to his words.

"To be fair, I'm not certain that the whole place is evil," Silverhair frowned. "But I have heard some odd stories about it. The way is guarded, they say. . . ."

Julian blinked. To have to deal with Caolin was bad enough. He did not feel ready to cope with even the thought of other powers.

"Well, if we've never heard of them, then perhaps they have no interest in Westria, and will let us pass!" said Frederic stoutly. "And there's one thing—if Caolin comes after us, the road south is the last place he'll think to try!"

"That's a great comfort, Frederic!" exclaimed Rana. "You're talking about going nearly to Elaya! If you want to stay secret you can't take the main roads, and when you get there, how are you going to find your way into the hills?"

They all turned to look at her. Her eyes were sparkling, and there was more color in her cheeks than was likely to have come from the sun. Julian did not think she looked frightened. He thought she looked excited, and he reminded himself to squelch firmly any notions she might have that they were all a lot of romantic heroes going off on a quest.

"As you pointed out, you were expected," the Lord of the Trees said then. "And my people and I took counsel regarding ways in which we might help you without straining the Covenant, or making ourselves too vulnerable to the sorcerer. You have said that my people are everywhere, and surely they could be of great help to you—"

"If we could only communicate with them . . . ," Julian began dubiously. It was too tempting an idea—his old dream of being able to talk to the trees reborn.

"If you could speak to them they would be your allies—" the Redwood echoed. "And so that you may do so, we offer you one of our own people as an interpreter."

"One of *your* people?" asked Frederic in awe.

The Lord of the Trees nodded. Then he gestured with a rustling of soft bark. The trees at the edge of the clearing parted, and someone came through—a girl, at least it looked like a girl, with smooth red-brown skin that whitened to pale curls on her head, dressed in a short garment of shiny green leaves.

"Daughter, these are the children of men we spoke of in Council. They must go on a journey. It will be dangerous, both for them and for any who go with them, but greater evil will follow for all our Peoples if they do not succeed. If our People are to help them they will need an interpreter. Will you go with them for the sake of the People of the Wood?"

"Yes, my lord." Her voice was like the whisper of leaves in the wind. Her eyes were large and dark, as the eyes of a doe, but when she turned the sun caught them and Julian saw that they were the deep green of a forest pool. He was still trying to think of ways to describe her when the Redwood spoke again.

"This is their leader." He pointed at Julian. "He is the one we have awaited, and you must obey him as you would me."

She turned and came toward Julian with a movement that looked like walking, but it was more fluid than any

motion he had ever seen made by human limbs. Too
stunned by the Redwood's words to stop her, he stood
speechless as she bent before him in a graceful obeisance.

"One day all will bow before you," he heard a still voice
say. Julian did not know if the words came from outside of
him or were his own. *Perhaps,* he thought numbly, *but she is
the first, and she is not even one of my own people, but a
Guardian of one of the other kindreds! The gift is too great
for me. . . .*

"This is Lady Madrone."

The voice of the Lord of the Trees broke his paralysis.
Julian reached out and accepted the smooth, unhuman grip
of her hand.

⋙ SEVEN ⋘

It was cramped inside the boat-chest, and damp too, and
Rana could hear men quarreling outside. The chest smelled
strongly of moldy grain—she had been afraid that when the
ferry got underway the stink would make her ill, but
fortunately her stomach was exceptionally strong. She had
never been sick at sea, but that was almost the only positive
thing about the situation she was in now.

She twisted her body around in the chest, trying without
success to find a more comfortable position, and began
seriously considering the possibility that she had made a
mistake in stowing away. It wasn't too late to change her
mind about going on the search for the Earthstone, even
though the boatman she had bribed to conceal her and her
pony on the ferry that went from Seahold to Yerba Buena
would probably laugh at her if she insisted on returning. If
Frederic and the others discovered what she had tried to do
they would be furious.

But they were going to be furious anyway, and for much

longer, if she succeeded in following them. . . .

The plunging motion of the ferry told her it was breasting
the strong current that flowed through the Gateway into the
Bay. She did not have much time to make up her mind.
Soon they would reach the slatternly village that clung to
the sand spits below the ruined city, and Frederic, Silverhair, and Julian would be following the tree-woman south.

Rana tried not to think what they would say when she
joined them. They had been willing enough to have her
guide them by a shortcut she knew from the Sacred Wood
to the ferryslip near Seahold. Since her sister Bella had
married the Lord of Seahold's son, there had been a lot of
coming and going between the two holdings, and her
father's boast was true—Rana knew every path through
these hills.

She bit her lip, remembering how he had hugged her
when they set off from Registhorpe that morning. Had it
been only that morning? It seemed like a week ago. What
would Sir Randal do when she didn't return? She supposed
he would shout and make everyone's life a misery, trying to
hide his anxiety—the thought of his worry set treacherous
tears pricking beneath her eyelids. Then she remembered
how he had punished her for joining the fight, and the tears
dried.

She was not going to allow her resolve to be weakened by
any fear of *him!* She suppressed awareness of her mother's
grief without letting it come to full consciousness, tightening her grip on the little bag of necessities she had brought
with her. She had not been able to pack much, or someone
would have suspected, but Frederic and the others had
known they might be away for some time and were well
provisioned. She hoped they had enough to spare.

Yet even Frederic had not expected the journey to lead so
far. Almost to Elaya, they had said, into a land of sorcerers.
And one of the People of the Wood was to guide them! It
was a wonder beyond anything in the tales her little brother
loved so. And if she had understood rightly, there was a
greater wonder. If the mysterious young man Julian was
really the Prince of Westria who had been lost so long ago,
wouldn't it be worth any hardship to ride at the side of the
future King?

A gust of wind heeled the ferry over, throwing Rana painfully against the side of the chest. She suppressed a cry. She heard the drumming hooves of frightened horses; the captain shouted an order, and bare feet pattered on the deck. Someone laughed bitterly. Even muffled by the wood she recognized the voice of Silverhair, and Julian's quieter tones as he tried to calm him.

And that, more than any fear of unknown terrors or her father's too familiar wrath, was what was making her wonder if this had been such a good idea after all. While she had been finding the man on the crew of the ferry who owed her a favor, the harper had somehow managed to find a wineskin, and by the time the others were ready to board his tongue was well-oiled. She could not hear clearly what he was complaining about, but she could feel the force of his pain. Julian seemed pretty stolid, and she supposed that Lady Madrone was armored against human emotions, but Frederic was obviously still exhausted from the battle with the sorcerer. How could he bear it?

Without thinking, she shook her head, bumped it against the chest lid and winced. Julian might be heir to Westria, but he was an unknown, and she didn't want to know any more about Silverhair. That left only Frederic, whom she loved like a brother, while privately doubting that he was any more fit to travel alone than Cub was.

And that decided her. Her father might never forgive her for running away, but Lady Rosemary would surely not forgive her for abandoning her favorite son to such untrustworthy company.

The ruins that rose from the sand dunes were an uncanny place to spend a night, but Julian could not see that they had any choice. They had sworn the ferrymen to secrecy and gotten past the little settlement of Yerba Buena without attracting any attention, but Frederic was so exhausted he swayed in the saddle, and as for Silverhair, Julian almost wished the harper would fail off his horse and be done with it. If he had dreamed that the man was so vulnerable to wine he would never have agreed to travel with him. He wondered if the Master knew.

Across the Bay the moon was rising, haloed by clouds,

silhouetting the low eastern hills. Quiet waters lapped
gently at the shoreline, for here they were on the Bay side of
the peninsula. Soon enough their road would lead them
beside the sea, and they might look back with longing to
even such shelter as they could find among the dunes.
Ghost-sands, they had called them, but Julian felt no
inimical presence here. He peered at the skeletal pillars that
had once supported one of the Ancients' towers—twisted
pieces of metal too tough or rusted to interest the metal
miners—and thought that the place felt lonely, but friendli-
er than the little town. The contorted girders looked like
dead tree branches against the dimming sky.

"We'll camp here—" he called softly, turning his mare
off the road. "Frederic, take the harper's rein. . . ."

"The road is dark before my feet . . . ," Silverhair half
sang, "there is no way that I can go . . . where we goin'?
Hey, let go my rein, I can ride all right. I can outride you,
damn interfering puppy . . ." His protests died away into
muttering as Frederic led him after Julian without bothering to reply. Sand crunched under the hooves of the horses
as they wound between two dunes into the dubious shelter
of what had once been the foundation of the tower.

As Julian had hoped, parts of the concrete walls were still
standing, dividing the place into two sections. He swung
down from the mare's back, unsaddled her, and turned her
into one of them. Wincing, Frederic did the same for
himself, and then for Silverhair. The harper had collapsed
untidily against one of the old walls. He was still mumbling,
but at least the argumentative phase of his drunkenness had
passed.

Julian stretched stiff muscles and crunched back over the
sand to the path. There was a new tree beside it—he
stopped short, thinking of ghosts, then realized it was not a
tree. He took a deep breath, peering through the shadows in
which tree shape and woman shape seemed to flicker in and
out of vision.

"My Lady Madrone—we need to rest. Will you stay with
us here?"

The figure before him brightened; Julian could see faint
sparkles of light running beneath her smooth skin, and it
occurred to him suddenly that perhaps neither her tree
form nor the woman shape she wore now was her true body,

but he did not ask. He had had enough of wonders for one day.

"The water is brackish, and I have tasted better soil, but at least it stays still." Foliage rustled as she laughed. "I was not meant to travel upon the sea. I will root here for the night, and do very well."

Julian nodded. "I'm going to look for firewood now —dead wood," he added quickly. "I'll be back soon." He went on, and when he looked back he saw only the silhouette of a living madrone tree below the tracery the metal pillars of the ruins made against the sky.

Not much that was burnable grew in this sandy soil, but with some searching, Julian collected enough brush to fill his cloak, and the rotting timbers of an old shack provided more substantial fuel. Dry and powdery as the wood was, he doubted it would burn for long, but they should be able to heat some soup, and after such a day, they needed the comfort of a little fire.

He was just straightening to haul the wood back to their shelter when someone sneezed nearby. Julian stiffened and turned around. For a moment he had felt the touch of fear, but ghosts did not sneeze.

"Frederic, is that you?" he called softly. There was no reply, but he heard a horse whicker, and testing the direction of the wind, he knew that it could not be one of their own. Julian's practiced eye searched the shadows, sifting the darkness until he distinguished among the bushes a mass darker and solider than they.

Then he dropped his load of wood and took a swift step sideways. His hands closed on the rough fabric of a cloak, and then on the shoulder beneath it. A quick pull brought the struggling body against him while his arm vised its throat. For a moment the prisoner fought him. Julian grabbed with his other arm, and at the same moment, as the panting captive sagged against him, he recognized the shape and feel of the flesh beneath his hands and realized that he was holding a girl. He stilled with a sudden awful suspicion, moved his hand, and touched silky hair.

"Rana, what are you doing here?" he asked helplessly.

She squirmed; he realized that his arm was crushing her breast, and abruptly let go. He thought of her as a child, but it had been a woman's body in his arms. The momentary

quickening of his pulse was swamped by a tide of anger as
he began to realize what she had done.

Rana shook herself and straightened her cloak. "Isn't that
obvious?" she answered a little shakily. "I'm coming with
you."

"Oh, no, you're not. Your father gave you permission to
guide us to the Sacred Wood, not to follow us all over
Westria. A fine return for his hospitality that would be!"
Wind whispered in the brush as if the spirits of the Ancients
were laughing, peppering his face with sand.

"What does my father have to do with it?" she exclaimed.
Her face was a dim oval in the moonlight, but he caught the
glitter of anger in her eyes. "I've been initiated—I've taken
my name! When you were my age you were helping your
friends escape from the Barren Lands. Master Pine told me
so!"

"We didn't *choose* to be taken captive," Julian began,
though he could not help remembering how miserable he
had been at sixteen, only two years ago. If the slavers had
not taken him, he might very well have run away too. . . .
"And we aren't making this journey for the sake of adventure. Believe me, you will be much more comfortable at
home," he added as repressively as he could.

"Speaking of comfort, don't you think we should continue this discussion around your fire—when you have taken
that wood back and built it, that is!" she said reasonably.
He stared at the sturdy silhouette before him, but could find
no hint of yielding. It was true that the others would be
wondering what had happened to him, and Frederic had
known Rana from childhood. Maybe he could explain to
her why she must go home.

Silverhair appeared to have passed out at last, but
Frederic had unpacked his own gear and even managed to
get a bit of fire going with leaves and sticks he had found
drifted up against the walls. He looked up eagerly as Julian
came back, then he saw the girl and his eyes widened.

"Rana, what are you doing here?" His question echoed
Julian's. Rana made a small, exasperated noise, and Julian
began to grin.

"She followed us—" he explained. "She wants to have an
adventure." He dropped the wood and brush beside the fire

and began to arrange his own gear near Frederic's. In the firelight he could see faded remnants of color on the pitted concrete walls, as if something had once been written there. He wondered what this place had been.

Frederic whistled. "Does your father know?"

Rana took a piece of wood from the pile Julian had dropped and carefully edged it into the fire. "Of course not, silly—you know he never lets me do anything!"

"Well, considering some of the things you've tried in the past—" Frederic threw up an arm in mock defense as she lifted a stick. "Yes, Rana, I know that's not fair—but this is serious!"

Rana flushed, but continued to feed the fire. As the dry wood caught, the flames leaped up, throwing the ragged walls into bright relief against the misty stars. Frederic took out a pan and the little sacks of dried vegetables and started measuring them into it. But his hands shook, and when half a cup of rice went into the fire instead of the pan, Rana took it away from him, and with swift, competent movements added water and balanced the pan on three stones over the fire.

As the smell of boiling soup began to drift through the air the harper stirred and pushed himself to a sitting position with a groan. He pulled his cloak back up around him, then focused on the girl by the fire and looked from her to Julian and back again. "What is *she*—" he began.

Julian and Frederic chorused, "She wants to go with us, but of course it's impossible," in answer.

"Impossible—" echoed Silverhair. "Two half-fledged boys are bad enough, but I won't be responsible for a girl! Sir Randal would never forgive me if I let anything happen to his child."

This was exactly what Julian had told Rana, but hearing it from the harper angered him. Nobody had asked Silverhair to come along either, as he recalled. But he mastered his temper and turned back to the girl.

"You see? In the morning you'll have to go back."

Rana looked up at him with a sweet smile. "How? The ferry has gone. It only crosses the Gateway once a week unless someone charters it specially. The men who crew it go out fishing the rest of the time. You're all so worried about my safety—do you want me to hang about for a week in that stinking town with not a copper to rent a bed?"

"Then we'll wait and take you back—" Silverhair began.

"Why?" she interrupted him, and turned to the other two. "Why is it so impossible for me to go along? I can tend horses. I can ride as well and as long as any of you. I can set a snare and I'm a good shot with the bow. I don't have a sword, but with only three of you, you'll want to avoid any serious fighting. What could a boy do that I cannot?"

Julian suppressed a smile. Certainly she looked like a boy, dressed in high boots and breeches with a baggy belted tunic. From a distance, the only thing that would give her away was the red flag of her hair. And though people might gossip if they heard of a girl her age traveling with three men, there was nothing in her manner to inspire lust in him, even if his passions had not been still focused on the Lady of Westria.

"You may be a boy in Westria, but we're going too near Elaya to take a woman along," said Silverhair grimly. "How would you like to spend the rest of your life in Prince Ali's harem? I cannot allow—"

"Oh come now—" said Frederic suddenly. "You may be the Queen's brother and the most famous harper in Westria, but you are not the leader here. If we were voting, I would say yes—let her come!"

Silverhair jerked as if Frederic had struck him, but Rana gave him a quick smile.

"I've known Rana since she could walk," Frederic went on. "She was always getting the rest of us into trouble, but she usually managed to get us out again! I think she would be good company on the road—better than you have been! But it's Julian who has to make the decision, thank the Guardians, not you, and not me!"

"We are all tired," said Julian slowly. "In the morning I'll decide."

Silverhair shook his head. "You can't put it off, boy. You must tell her now."

Julian turned on him. "As Frederic pointed out, I am the one who has to make the decisions. Well, I have just made one!"

"The Lord of the Trees has spoken to you, and you think

you are already King? I have knocked about the world for twenty years and—"

"And where has it gotten you?" asked Julian brutally, knowing he was too tired to guard his tongue but unable to stop himself now. "You are my uncle, and I must honor you, but I won't be governed by a man who cannot even hold his wine!" He had put drunken comrades to bed often enough after a festival, but the harper's search for oblivion in alcohol frightened him.

There was a long, shocked silence. Then Silverhair straightened, and Julian realized abruptly that whatever had been wrong with the harper earlier that evening, he was not drunk now.

"Ah, yes—" said Silverhair bitterly, "how well I remember the invulnerability of youth, that knows nothing of loss, or failure, or time! You tell me not to advise *you*—don't you dare judge *me!* I can see you thinking—'he is weak to be so upset by a broken harp. It was only an instrument, after all.'" He sighed and went on. "Only an instrument? Perhaps it was, and your sword is only a piece of metal, Julian—and the staff that Frederic hopes to carry someday will be only a piece of wood. If someone cut off your manhood would you shrug and say it was only a piece of meat?" he shouted suddenly. "A good harp takes fifty years to mature and then grows steadily mellower. It will outlast the man who made it and the man who played it. Swangold should have outlasted me!

"Swangold was more than wood and bronze, Julian. Your father gave her to me just before he knighted me, and I played for him as he lay dying at Misthall! More than once Swangold saved me and others from Caolin's sorcery; for twenty years she was my livelihood and my reason for living! I am only just now beginning to understand what I have lost. You may say that she was only a harp, but I say she was my soul!" Silverhair leaned forward, eyes blazing, and it was Julian's turn to recoil.

"If I have hurt you, uncle, I apologize," he said finally, wondering what he would do if he ever suffered such a loss, "but still, I must decide. . . ."

The harper gave a short laugh. "Decide then, if you can, and explain yourself to Sir Randal when, or if, we return. It is no longer anything to do with me!" He pulled his cloak more tightly around him and lay down again with his back to the fire.

Frederic took the pan off the flame and got out the spoons and bowls. They ate in silence, and afterward spread cloaks and blankets as comfortably as they could on the sand. Rana went off to retrieve her pony from its hiding place down the road while Julian made a last check on the horses. They had been watered at Yerba Buena, but they could not let them graze until it was light again. He leaned against the ruined wall, patting his bay mare, until Rana led her pony up and turned him in with the others.

"I'm sorry to have caused a quarrel," she said quietly, "but Silverhair was right in one thing. This isn't really your decision. You dare not risk being discussed by all the gossiping tongues of Yerba Buena while you wait to take me back to Registhorpe. Unless you imprison me, all you can do is forbid me to ride with you, and what's to prevent me from following your tracks from here to Awhai? Surely I will be safer in your company than alone."

Julian worked his heavy shoulders back and forth to relieve their tension and sighed. "I'll decide in the morning," he said tiredly.

But both of them knew already that she had won.

The half-built walls of Blood Gard made a ragged bulwark against the stars. Caolin watched the firelight play on the faces of the men gathered before him, letting his own silence still them, waiting for their expectation to develop into the subliminal anxiety that was the prelude to fear. It was cold at night on the mountaintop, even with the great fire. Caolin felt the chill through the stiff folds of the red cloak in which he had wrapped himself, but he did not allow himself to respond to it. There had been a day or two, after the attack on Registhorpe, when he had almost remembered he had a body, but that weakness was now past.

The stillness became absolute. Esteban got to his feet and bowed.

"My lord, we are ready to hear your will. . . ."

Caolin remained motionless as an image in his bloodcolored robes. But when he spoke, a trick of projection bounced his voice off the rough walls so that it seemed to come from behind, around the men—from everywhere. One or two started; he marked them for watching. He needed men who would model themselves on him, who would be unmoved even by their fear.

"Report—"

The lieutenant motioned to the chief of construction, a heavily-built, florid-faced man Caolin had taken out of Elaya's desert mines. He nodded, got to his feet with the deliberation of a block of stone being tipped on end, and began to speak.

"The foundations for the outer walls of the fortress have been laid, and the walls of the inner keep are rising steadily. We have begun to quarry stone from the south side of the mountain—but we are having some difficulty finding suitable timber for scaffolding and beams."

Caolin nodded. "You will need to seek farther south, in the mountains near the pillars of stone. Choose a work party and calculate what beasts you will need." A shift in his voice directed his next words to his lieutenant. "Esteban, make up an armed party to support them."

"What shall we do if anyone sees us?"

"Capture and dispose of them. If you need more labor, find an isolated holding and impress the men you require." He did not have to tell the lieutenant how to deal with those who were no use to him. "The security of the hill-road to the south is essential to our purposes. As you go, I wish you to identify positions for watchtowers, to be built at intervals of one or two days' ride. Construction on these must begin as soon as the major work on the walls of this fortress has been accomplished. Until then, small parties of soldiers will be sent to hold the selected spots and to make the surrounding area secure. By the Turning of Autumn nothing should move on that road except by my command. . . ."

There was a satisfying murmur of approval from the men, and Caolin relaxed fractionally. He knew that after the earthquake there had been talk among them. They had speculated on whether the quake had been caused by the Blood Lord, whether it had affected him, even wondered if there was some other sorcerer who was his equal. This was the first general meeting of the leaders to be held since it had happened, and there were reasons beyond the obvious need for coordination and planning for having it now.

And until now, Caolin had not been quite sure that he was ready to preside, but he saw that he had been foolish to doubt his power over himself, and over them. It was going very well.

"What is the word from the borders?" he asked then.

"Wolf Agrimun is gathering more men in the north," said Esteban. "His last message stated that he should be able to start raiding again in a month or so. I have no recent communications from the Barren Lands, but if the band operating in the Ramparts is carrying out your orders they have probably been too busy to send word." Esteban allowed himself a faint smile, and the other men laughed maliciously.

Then he gestured toward a big, dark-skinned man with a full black beard, dressed in the flowing trousers and sash of an Elayan seaman.

"Zoltan will report directly on progress with the sea wolves."

Zoltan got to his feet, smiling a trifle insolently. *He will have to be watched,* thought Caolin, but there was a kind of twisted strength in the man that he liked. A man not to trust then, but certainly a man to use.

"We have one ship fully manned now, and are negotiating for a second one—a royal war galley that has been declared unfit for service."

"But it can be repaired?" asked Esteban.

"Fairly easily—" Zoltan's teeth flashed white against the black beard as he grinned. "The fitness report was a little harsher than necessary. . . ."

"And the Lady of Las Palisadas?" Caolin kept his voice even, cool.

"She listens to me. I think she will agree to join us, and she already has a ship of her own."

"Remember, when she does, she is to have the name of leader," said Caolin. "She is Prince Ali's cousin, and once this is known, suspicion will lead toward him."

"And the reality?" said Zoltan hungrily.

"The reality is unchanged," said Caolin coldly. "You will take your orders from me." He dismissed the man with a glance and shifted the focus of his attention to Ordrey, who had been waiting with uncharacteristic diffidence behind Esteban.

"What have you done about the situation at Registhorpe?" he asked silkily.

Perspiring as if he had been sitting too near the bonfire, Ordrey took a step forward and ducked his head.

"We have had watchers in position since this morning. The Lady of Bongarde arrived there last night and is nursing the Master of the Junipers. Rumor among the folk at the holding is that he is seriously ill, and no one knows whether he will live."

Caolin permitted himself a very small smile of satisfaction, and Ordrey relaxed visibly. At least he had struck down one of his enemies, and that one the most dangerous. With the Master out of the way, there was really no one in Westria with the knowledge to understand what the Blood Lord was doing, much less to oppose him.

He suppressed memory of that moment when the Master's passive resistance had exploded back at him in a pulse of blinding power and he had had to reabsorb the creature he had sent to destroy his enemies. For a confused instant he had seemed to recognize a touch he had not felt since he lost the Jewels in that long ago battle with the King and Queen. But that was impossible—they were dead, both of them, while he lived, and grew in power!

"And the harper?" he asked then. Ordrey grew pale once more.

"He was there in the hall with them, but he has gone. There was some talk that he was injured too, but they say he left with young Frederic and another man."

Caolin sat silent, watching Ordrey's pallor turn to grey. Then he nodded.

"Very well. He cannot hide forever, and when he surfaces once more we will kill him. Keep Registhorpe under observation, and instruct our spy in Bongarde to stay alert."

He watched the defeated line of Ordrey's shoulders with pleasure as the little man hurried away. With the news of the Master's illness to buoy him, even Silverhair's escape could not disturb Caolin now. Ordrey had been thoroughly frightened, and would not fail him a second time, but Ordrey was not sufficient to this task.

The sorcerer turned, and a flicker of his fingers summoned another man who had been standing, a shadow among the shadows, throughout the conclave.

"Malin Scar . . ." His whisper distilled the night air. The man's head lifted, and his hood fell back, torchlight limning cruelly the tortured flesh that had given him his name. Caolin nodded in satisfaction. This man could not veil his disfigurement as did the sorcerer, perhaps did not even know of this bond between them. Like Caolin, Malin Scar had used his pain to forge body and spirit into a weapon of pitiless power, whose use was the only ease for his torment. He was a Shadower, whose vocation was to hunt men down. But unlike the Blood Lord, Malin Scar needed a master, and he belonged to Caolin.

"You heard—" said the sorcerer. "Ordrey can do nothing here. Pick up the harper's trail in Registhorpe and follow him."

"I will follow him like death's dark wing—" Malin's face twisted in what was meant to be a smile.

⇛ EIGHT ⇚

Silverhair took a deep breath and straightened in the saddle as the breeze brought him the scent of sun-warmed redwood. For a moment the past eight years fell away, and he was riding up this road for the first time, worn with wandering but quivering like an unhooded hawk with eagerness.

"Is the College of Bards near?" As Julian brought his horse level with Silverhair's his words jerked the harper roughly back to the present, and the riders behind him —this stolid young man who was his nephew, and Rosemary's son, the tree-woman, and the redheaded girl. He had almost forgotten they were there.

"A little ways up the road——" he answered with difficulty.

The first time he had come here he had been alone, but not lonely, for he had had Swangold. The harp's name vibrated painfully through his awareness once more. For twenty years scarcely a day had gone by when he had not held her and touched the sweet music from her gold-bronze strings. How could the Lord of the Winds have given him such joy, only to wrest it away again? The contrast between this loss and his former exaltation made it all the more terrible. He had believed he knew grief when the King died, and when Faris disappeared, but this was more like losing his soul. It would have been better if Caolin had killed him when he attacked Registhorpe, or earlier. He would rather have died on his wanderings.

He realized that he had let his pony lag, and he kicked it to catch up with Julian. The young man looked back at him and smiled bracingly.

"They will be able to fix the harp—stop worrying!"

Silverhair gave him a quick look and then shifted his gaze back to the road, realizing that was why he had unconsciously let the horse slow. What if Swangold could not be repaired?

It had been Frederic's suggestion to stop at the College of Bards, since their road would take them that way. The harper remembered waking in the foggy dawn near Yerba Buena with the poison of the wine he had drunk hammering in his skull. He would have agreed to anything then, just to make them let him be. Denied the anesthesia of alcohol, he had managed to retreat into a kind of trance for the week and a half it had taken to get here. But now they were almost to the College, and it was time to return to life or the final death of despair.

For a moment his gut twisted with longing for a swallow of wine, and he knew with sick certainty that if Swangold could not be restored, that need would overwhelm him. The others could go on without him, and he would join the drunkards on the waterfront of Montera until he found the courage to walk out into the sea.

It would have been better if Caolin had killed him.

* * *

"Tell me again who we are likely to meet here—I don't want to insult anyone by getting a name wrong," said Julian with a quick glance toward the harper. He could see Silverhair's thin fingers trembling, and dimly guessed his tension. At least there was life in the harper's eyes again, but he did not want to think what would happen if the craftsmen of the College could not fix the harp.

"You said that Master Andreas was still heading the school? Do you think he will welcome us?"

Fractionally, the tense line of the harper's mouth eased. "Yes. He is a man of great kindness, very gentle, but obeyed all the better because no one could wish to cause him pain. He can still a roomful of quarreling musicians simply by entering it and sitting down."

"A valuable talent indeed—" exclaimed Frederic. "The musicians I have met have been as touchy as a maid before her wedding, as if playing in tune had exhausted all their gift for harmony."

The twist in the harper's lips became something that was almost a smile. "I suppose you are right. Mistress Huldah has a tongue you could scale fish with, and Master Sebastian could give lessons in sarcasm along with his counterpoint. But most of the others are decent enough—Mistress Siaran—" He stopped abruptly, his face changing, and Julian remembered that Mistress Siaran had been Silverhair's harp teacher here.

Julian sighed. Then through the veil of green he saw something solid and pointed. "Is that it ahead?" He kicked the mare forward and saw a crosspiece above stout pillars of redwood upon which two harps had been carved. Their gilding was almost weathered away, but the path beyond had been freshly raked, and the sprawling buildings it led to seemed to be in good repair.

As Julian pulled up, the sound of voices in close harmony answered his question. For a moment he held still, listening. Then the music was abruptly interrupted by a woman's scolding, and he turned back to the others.

Silverhair was listening too. "Apparently Mistress Huldah is still here. . . . The stables are around to the right. If we take the horses there first, we can enter through the courtyard."

Julian turned and gestured hesitantly to Lady Madrone, still a little unnerved by her silence and the effortless stride that had kept her beside them all the way down the coast from Yerba Buena. Without appearing to hurry, she moved up beside them, and Julian made himself meet her clear green gaze.

"We must go into the buildings—do you wish to come with us? I do not know just how long we will stay . . ." His voice trailed off, and she shook her head.

"I will enjoy a time of rest. This is a new forest to me, and I will be happy to taste its soil and to talk to its trees. You need not concern yourself about me."

Julian looked at her and nodded, conscious of a faint relief. No one could have asked for an easier traveling companion—between Silverhair's despair, Frederic's exhaustion, and the exasperation of having that girl Rana along, the Lady had been the least of his worries. But though she wore a human form, that smooth-skinned, lovely face neither frowned nor smiled. As he tried to think of something to say, the Lady inclined slightly in agreement, and moved back down the road. In a moment she had disappeared among the trees.

They found the stables and arranged for the care of the horses while a skinny student dashed off to the main building to announce them. When they came into the school's dining hall, a tall, greying man whom Silverhair introduced as Master Andreas welcomed them, but Julian saw that the harper was still tense, waiting. Then a buxom woman with dark hair just on the edge of auburn came running into the room.

"Silverhair—you've come back to us at last! I knew you would one day!" Before he could answer, she embraced him, then stood back, staring. "What is it? Have you been injured?" Quickly she took first one of his hands, then the other, examining it.

"Not me—" he said hoarsely, "it's my harp. Siaran, can you repair it? The frame is cracked! Siaran—my music is gone!"

For a moment longer she looked at him, then gathered him against her again, and this time he shuddered and let her hold him. Embarrassed, Julian looked away and met Master Andreas's compassionate gaze.

"Come, my friend. We'll go to my workshop and see," Mistress Siaran said after a moment had passed. She released Silverhair, and he followed her out of the room. Julian looked after them, feeling as if he had just set a heavy burden down.

"You must all be tired from your traveling—" Master Andreas's gentle voice recalled his attention. "I will ask one of the students to show you where you are to stay."

"Yes, I have seen worse," Mistress Siaran said calmly as Silverhair gently lifted the fragments of his shattered instrument from their wrappings. "But I have never heard of a harp being injured in just this way—" She bent over to examine the pieces more closely, and Silverhair stepped back. She was the expert, the doctor for sick harps. He had seen her perform miracles upon mistreated instruments more than once while he was a student here.

"It was Caolin—" he said hoarsely. "Do you remember the road from Santibar when he would have killed me because my information had cost him the lordship of the town? I gave him cause to hate me then, and now he has taken his revenge—"

"Yes, but your music defeated him then—" she said. Her eyes were shining with remembered wonder.

"That was before he gave himself wholly to sorcery," Silverhair answered her. "We met a second time in Normontaine, and he sang a power song that was the distortion of every dream of music you have known. In his own way he is a master, Siaran, but it is a mastery that I hope will never be taught here!" He stared through her, seeing once more the unbelievable blue of the lake in the mountain, hearing the dreadful harmonies of Caolin's song. After a moment, Siaran touched his arm, and he sighed.

"Only the mercy of the Lord of the Winds saved us. I thought I had escaped, but now Caolin will never rest until he sees me dead." He laid one hand on the pieces of the harp frame, and stilled suddenly. "She told me this would happen—" he added in a shocked whisper.

"Who?" Siaran began to lay the pieces out on the worktable.

"A girl-child I met in the Barren Lands, who made a

prophecy—" Silverhair's thoughts were running back to it even as he answered her.

"Your enemy will break your harp and the hands that made it sing. . . ." He could almost hear the Willa's clear voice saying those words. Silverhair flexed his long fingers as if they already pained him. The harp was broken, and he had found the child he had been searching for. When would the rest of the prophecy be fulfilled?

"What else did she say?" asked Siaran. She picked up the snippers and began to cut the tangle of bronze harpstrings away.

"What?" With a shock Silverhair realized what he had told her. He gave Siaran a quick look, but she was intent on her work. Good—if he was doomed, there was no need for all the world to know.

"She said I would come home again," he lied, shivering.

"Well, she should have told you that the broken harp would be repaired!" Siaran said briskly. "See—the cracks are along the grain of the curve, and when I have glued it and braced it with straps of brass, it should be stronger than it was before."

"And the sound box?" asked the harper, leaning over to see.

"I think a little glue will take care of that—perhaps I can inset more wire, though it will change the design. It looks worse than it is because the pillar has been loosened. When all the pieces are fitted back together and it is strung, it will hold quite well—you will see."

Silverhair tried to speak, swallowed, and then tried again. "How long?" With a distant flicker of humor he remembered watching a man pace while his wife labored to give birth to their child. He had pitied him. An observer might well laugh at the harper's anxiety now, but Swangold was all the wife and child that he would ever know.

"I do have classes to teach too, you know, so it will take me a day or two to repair the frame—" Siaran looked up at him with a smile. "And after that, we should allow a week for the glue to dry. Then it will be time to restring, and we will see how well it holds. Two weeks, perhaps, until it is done."

Silverhair nodded. Without strings, the harp looked

naked. Siaran straightened the frame and then began to
pick out the twisted gold wire from the surface of the sound
box. Her hands were broad, with short, strong fingers that
manipulated tools with the same sure delicacy with which
she plucked her instrument's strings.

"Do you think I am a fool to take on so?" he asked. "It's
only an instrument—a thing of wood and wire. At least for
the past week that is what Julian has been telling me. . . ."
He sat down on the bench, suddenly aware of his fatigue.

"What kind of a question is that to ask another musician?
Especially a harper?" Siaran reached for the stoneware pot
of glue.

Silverhair could hear the amusement in her voice, though
she did not turn, and suddenly he was filled with a sense of
warmth, of ease he had not known since he parted from the
Queen of Normontaine. Afternoon light glowed through the
upper window and aureoled Siaran's dark hair with amber
fire. She had coiled it loosely at the nape of her neck; the
line of her back below it was as graceful as a harp's sweet
curve. Watching her, he felt something quicken within him
that he had feared forever gone.

For a time the only sound in the workroom was the sound
of creaking wood as Mistress Siaran fitted the twisted pieces
of the instrument back into position, dribbled glue into the
remaining cracks, clamped, wiped, and glued again. Silverhair sat still, his thoughts an odd jumble of melodies and
memories. In the years since he had left the College he had
never dared to remember how much happiness he had
found here.

Finally the harpmistress gave a final turn to the clamps
that held the mended sound box in position and straightened, rubbing at the small of her back.

"That will hold it, and tomorrow we will decide what to
do about the wire. It should be left now to dry, and I
suppose that we should join your friends before the bell for
dinner rings." She turned, smiling.

Silverhair took her hand and gripped it, trying to read her
eyes. "How can I thank you? You are restoring life to me!"
Unable to say more, he turned the hand he held and bent
his head to kiss her smooth palm.

For a moment she stood very still. Then he felt her other

hand stroking his hair. She moved closer, and with a grateful sigh he let his head rest against her thigh. Her hand held him there.

"The harp's wounds are easy to diagnose, and to cure—" Siaran said softly, "but I think that you have been wounded too, where no one can see."

Mutely he nodded, and her fingers lifted the hair from his neck and moved softly along the tender skin there. He began to tremble, and did not know whether it was with self-pity or desire. Students did not sleep with the Masters at the College of Bards, even if they were of an age. And Siaran had been his teacher—respect was a great suppressor of passion—he had never thought of the harpmistress as a woman when he was here.

But now her body was soft against him, and he could smell the faint, spicy scent she wore. One of her hands slipped beneath the collar of his tunic, and his grip tightened on the other.

"When Caolin caught us on that road he accused me of being your mistress," she said a little tremulously. "He meant it for an insult, but I have wished ever since that it had been true. . . ."

With exquisite care Mistress Siaran tightened the last peg, tested the string, tightened it once more, and set the tuning key down. Silverhair gazed hungrily at the harp. His eyes blurred, and the lamplight glittering on the strings and the bracing and the golden interlace that ornamented the sound box fused into a golden aureole. For a moment its unsullied beauty was the same as he had seen it when King Jehan first placed the harp in his arms.

Then his vision cleared, and he saw the scars, the distortion in the interlace, the warping of the pillar, which no bracing could ever bring quite back to true. *It's like me*— he thought then. *Battered, but still whole. And for both of us the question is the same— "Is this a husk only, or is the music still there?"*

"Yes—you can play it now," said Siaran very calmly, "though you must remember that it will take time for the new strings to get used to being stretched and hold their tone. You will have to retune every few minutes for a while, and after that several times each day."

"I know," he said hoarsely. His fingers were tingling —with anticipation or with fear? And then something insufficiently suppressed in her tone penetrated his awareness and he turned and saw that her eyes were bright with unshed tears. Quickly he reached out to her.

"Siaran, Siaran, there are no words to thank you—" he murmured into her hair. "Do you know what you have done for me?" Holding her, he realized that he had lost himself in her during the past two weeks as he would have drowned himself in wine, not in love so much as in pure, naked need.

"It is my life you have given me, and not just by mending the harp. I do not deserve it, and I have so little to give you in return!" His hands tightened on her shoulders, and she twisted in his arms to look up at him.

"Did it seem to you that I was getting nothing from the exchange?" She managed a smile. "My friend, it did not feel that way to me! I think we are even as far as the nights are concerned, and as for the days—don't you think it hurt me to see a harp in such condition too? And now I want to know how well my work has been done. Take her up, Silverhair, and let's hear how she sings!"

He let Siaran go and looked back at the harp in anguished realization—the form was the same, but had the fragile relationship of parts that made the music been destroyed? It could happen, and he would smash the pieces into kindling with his own hands rather than let Swangold's husk continue to exist when her music was gone!

Trembling, Silverhair lifted the instrument, sat down on the bench, and cradled her in his arms. At least the feel of her had not changed. Tentatively he plucked one of the new strings. The tone was different—trying to define the change, he plucked its neighbor, then began to move down the scale. Several strings had gone flat already. Automatically he picked up the tuning key to adjust them, then went on. Yes—the tone quality had changed, but as he strained to listen he realized that the alteration was, if anything, for the better. There was a resonance to the sound that he did not remember, a depth that reminded him somehow of Siaran's smile. It had the poignant loveliness that can come to a mature woman who has known grief as well as joy—that beauty which is so much more moving than the prettiness of an untried girl.

Aware only of the need to explore and understand this new music, he played on, tuning and retuning, moving from scales to chords and then to snatches of melody until he found that he was playing the noble chords of the Wind Lord's song. Note upon note the mighty music built, until the room throbbed with pure sound. And for just a moment the veil parted, and he was back in that timeless communion that had satisfied his soul.

The echoes died away to silence. Silverhair looked up again, remembering who he was, and where, and wondering how long it had been.

Mistress Siaran was still standing beside the workbench, and the tears in her eyes were not hidden anymore. Silverhair's fingers caressed the satiny wood of the harp as they had moved over Siaran's smooth flesh. He wanted to go to her, but he could not bring himself to put Swangold down.

"Yes, you are a Master Harper, and to hear you is my reward," she said finally. "But you need feel no guilt in leaving me. Don't you understand? Even if you wanted to stay, this would be all that I could give to you; we both chose our paths long ago. We serve the Maker of All Music, and that love will always take precedence over any human bond."

"Is that the truth of it?" Silverhair said softly. "Perhaps it is so. If I had any gift for making another human creature happy I suppose I would have stayed with Mara of Normontaine. But the path I tread now is not of my choosing, and like it or not, I am bound to follow that young man Julian."

"Why?" She had not blinked when he spoke of the Queen of Normontaine. "Why not stay here for a time and recover your health? I have some promising students you could help train, and I'm sure that Master Sebastian will want to take down all your new songs!"

For a moment the seduction of that offer shook him. He was still tired, and it was very peaceful here. *And how well would I rest, wondering what dangers those children were running into without me?* He shook his head.

"I don't love Julian—half the time I don't even *like* him, but he is my nephew, Siaran, and I cannot desert him. Everything else I could escape from, but I have to somehow come to terms with Julian. . . ."

"Your nephew?" Siaran frowned.

Silverhair could see calculation and confusion in the dark
eyes and realized that Master Andreas must have told her
his real name.

"Your sister Berisa married Sandremun of the Corona,
didn't she? But I thought they had only girls—" she went
on.

"Julian is the son of my other sister," Silverhair said very
quietly. "If our quest succeeds, Julian will be King."

Julian lifted his pewter mug and took a long swallow of
the honey-flavored drink they called "bardmead" here.
They had assured him that it was only honey, lemon, and
springwater with an infusion of special herbs. But he
wondered, for even without alcohol each swallow tingled all
the way down and left behind it a kind of inebriating
clarity. Or perhaps he was picking up the atmosphere of
festivity in the hall, for the senior students who had been
invited to join the Masters at this party for their guests were
making the most of the break in their routine.

Or maybe he was only relieved because Silverhair's harp
was finally ready, and tomorrow they would be on their way
once more.

He heard a burst of laughter from the dais at the other
end of the hall, and beneath the faded purple banner with
its great golden harp he saw Silverhair, eyes alight and thin
hand gesturing expressively, telling some story to a group of
students. There was a mug at the harper's elbow, but even
though the side table bore an assortment of wine bottles
and casks of mead and beer, as far as Julian could tell, the
harper had drunk nothing but bardmead since the party
began.

Someone paused beside him, and Julian turned to meet
Mistress Siaran's smile.

"He looks like he's enjoying himself—" He nodded
toward Silverhair.

She smiled again. "He's a legend to them."

"Yes, I suppose he is," Julian answered slowly, "and
that's one more reason to thank you for repairing the harp. I
was afraid—" He stopped short, unwilling to put his fears

into words, but the harpmistress seemed to understand.

"Do you care about him?" she asked then.

Julian frowned. "I have not known him very long, and the circumstances have been—unfortunate—" he said carefully. "But I am *responsible* for him."

Mistress Siaran laughed and sat down on the bench beside him. "He said much the same thing about you. Farin Silverhair is a difficult man to love, but he is terribly vulnerable—more than ever now. Yet you must not underestimate him, Julian."

"I wish I had the training to appreciate his talent more. Before the harp was broken I heard him play, and it was beautiful."

"It is not only his harping—" She moved closer to him, and he saw a memory of wonder in her dark eyes. "I know that at least one of the legends about him is true, for I was there. He may depend upon your strength during your journey, but if you are in danger, you will be glad to have him at your side. No, not just as a fighter," she answered his look, "but because in such moments he is able to make contact with the thing that gives music its power. He has a great gift—you must learn to use him."

"Yes, I know. Not only Silverhair but all of them, everyone, has some unique ability. I am beginning to understand that it does not matter so much what I can do myself as whether or not I can weld all those powers into something that will serve Westria." Julian stopped again, startled to find himself speaking so freely, but Mistress Siaran's smile told him that she had understood.

He heard a trill of music, and saw that two of the students had brought out silver flutes and were adjusting them to keep tune. Beyond them instrument cases were being opened to reveal dulcimers, viols, pipes of various kinds, and drums. A recorder joined the flutists, and someone began to tune a gitarra. Then the swift beat of a knuckledrum drew the assorted instruments into unity, and music, sudden as a storm in the desert, rippled and cascaded through the room. He saw Rana and Frederic beating out time by banging their mugs upon the table—from the dents in his own mug, he guessed that this was the common fate of the College pewter. Julian grinned, feeling his pulsebeat quicken to the rhythm. Two weeks here had demonstrated the compulsion that was on these people to fill every spare moment with music—he was only surprised they had waited so long.

"It is good to see everyone enjoying themselves," said a quiet voice at his elbow. Julian looked up, saw Master Andreas, and started to rise.

"No, no—I was just going to sit down." Master Andreas reached for another bench and Mistress Siaran put out her hand to stop him.

"Take my place—my flagon is empty and there are two of my students over there who are too nervous during lessons to play as well as I think they can. I want to hear how they sound when they're playing for fun." Smiling, she got to her feet and the Master of the College of Bards took the seat she had left.

"The musicians in Rivered are very competent," said Julian, "but your students have so much energy. It makes me wish I had the gift of making music."

"You have the gift for listening to it, which is just as important from the musician's point of view!" The Master's grave features were transformed by his grin. "But it is true that we have an exceptionally good group here this year. It will be hard to decide which of them to take on the annual tour."

Julian shot him a quick glance, realizing that the Master was speaking to him as an equal, even though many of the students here were older than he. But he supposed he should have expected it. Frederic and Rana had made themselves at home in the student dormitory immediately, but perhaps just because these students were so talented, Julian had found their interests narrow even for musicians. Who among them could share his burdens and his fears? But the Master bore responsibility for all of them—they were equals, not perhaps in authority, but in concern.

"Where will you be going this year?" he asked quietly.

"I have not decided," said Master Andreas. "It might be a good time to go to the Corona—things are quiet there now and we ought to establish relations with the new Lord Commander. On the other hand, it has been a long time since we visited the Ramparts."

"I don't know if Lord Philip has much time for music just now," said Julian. "The raiders from the Barren Lands have been keeping him busy." He wondered if the Regent had written to Philip yet and told him what had happened. He was beginning to accept Silverhair as his uncle, but it was not yet possible for him to think of Philip and Robert as his cousins, or to believe that the Lord Commander of the Ramparts could ever accept his former squire as his King.

Master Andreas nodded. "The students would like to go to Laurelynn, and it would certainly be a good experience for them, but talented as they are, I doubt they have much that would be new to the capital. Master Ras has done an excellent job with the city orchestra there. I thought of taking them south, instead," he went on. "What do you think of the plan?"

Julian looked up quickly. He had not discussed his intentions in so many words, but it was clear that the Master of the College of Bards had some idea of where they were going, if not why.

"I don't know much about the south," he said ingenuously. "Is there much population off of the main highway?"

"There is another road that follows the coast," said Master Andreas. "No good for wheeled traffic, but passable by horses. By this time of the year any slides or washouts from last winter will have been repaired. It's a wild shore, where the cliffs rise straight from the surf and there are few harbors, but there are holdings here and there in the hills.

"But I would not take my students that way—they need the experience in performance, and in that wild country hardly a soul would notice they had passed," he went on. "I'd do better to go straight down the Salt River Valley from Montera and over the pass to the Bay of the Flaming Mountains."

"I'm sure you are right; perhaps I will see that country someday," said Julian gravely. No one seemed to be listening, but you never knew, and he had been trying to leave the impression that once Silverhair's harp was repaired they would be returning to Bongarde.

The musicians' first burst of energy had run its course, and now the brisk dance tunes were being followed by slower pieces that showed off a soloist's virtuosity, and an occasional song.

In a pause between pieces Julian heard Silverhair asking if they still learned the "Song of the Stones" at the College, and when the chorus of affirmation had died away, he struck a chord on the harp that brought silence, and he began to sing.

> *"The folk who roam the hidden hills*
> *Stalk where the circled stones still lie,*
> *But none among the race of men*
> *Can say who set them there, or why."*

He modulated into the chorus, and students and Masters together all joined in.

> *"Oh, wind and water know no time, the flowers know*
> *spring and fall,*
> *The oldest trees count centuries, but stone remembers*
> *all.*
> *And men may come and men may go, their kingdoms*
> *rise and fall,*
> *Through hopes and fears and circling years—the stones*
> *remember all."*

"That's one I have not heard before—" whispered Julian. "It's beautiful."

"It is also true," said the Master. "The circle lies in the hills a little north of here, and no one knows how old it is or by whom it was made. But it marks one of the lines of force that run to the sea, and according to legend, it is a gateway between the worlds."

> *"When tribesmen wandered to this shore*
> *The stones were waiting for them then—*
> *They thought the First Folk put them there,*
> *In elder days when they were men."*

The chorus filled the hall; then Silverhair continued.

> *"The Ancients came and ruled the land,*
> *Their cities rose in crystal towers,*

> *But sheltered by the shadowed wood,*
> *The stones preserved their hoarded powers."*

Julian shivered, trying to imagine such antiquity. How could the Ancients have had such a place in their backyards, and never known? He supposed it was the same kind of ignorance that had caused the Cataclysm.

> *"But in the Day of Wrath the earth*
> *Shook off the works of men like rain,*
> *And then the force the stones had bound*
> *Broke free—the Old Gods ruled again!"*

Julian shivered once more, realizing that the people of Westria might sing of the circle as a legend, but their King would be bound to them as he was to everything, living and inanimate, in the land. *Someday,* he thought, *someday I will have to master those stones!*

> *"And still the secret circle stands—*
> *The ageless stones that guard the Gates*
> *Between the worlds remain unmoved*
> *By men—the Ancient power still waits."*

The students drew out the last chorus in a low, soft wail that blended into the wind in the branches outside. But it was long before the echoes faded in Julian's inner ear, and his pulse beat slow and heavy as if his limbs had turned to stone.

⫸ NINE ⫷

For three days Julian and his companions followed the moon-curve of the big bay, waking in the silver-veiled morning and riding until the sun burned through the mists and sparkled on the blue sea. Then they would stop to eat and rest the horses, and continue riding until the sun blazed across the western sky and sank in an ocean of fire. It was hard to remember their danger or the hard journey ahead of them, for Silverhair carried his harp on the saddlebow more often than in its case, and their ponies' hooves beat out the rhythms of his songs.

When they neared Montera, they camped among the dunes and waited while Julian rode into the town to replenish their supplies, for this was the last town of any size they would pass until they reached the Bay of the Flaming Mountains. There might come a time when Julian's features would be recognized throughout Westria, but at present he was the least likely to be remarked of any of them, and it was essential to leave no trail for Caolin. When darkness fell, they used its friendly cover to skirt the town and continued onward until the last lights were behind them, and they could take shelter in a friendly grove of cypress trees.

Southward, the country grew wilder, as land and sea resumed their eternal enmity. Here the road dwindled to a precipitous track that clung to the cliffs between the ragged mountain crests and the snarling sea. The road had been carved into the cliffs in the time of Julian's grandfather to supply watchtowers against the pirates from the Kingdom of the Isles. A new dynasty in the islands had destroyed the pirates, and the towers were no longer manned, but the upkeep of the trail was still one of the yearly duties of the Lord Commander of Las Costas. Fortunately the weather maintained a late summer brilliance that was probably stifling everyone inland, and even in the height of the drytime, springs from the heart of the mountains sent trickles of fresh water gurgling down the precipitous ravines.

This was a land that had resisted the hand of man even during the time of the Ancients, and though there were a few even now who had sought here a hermitage, the other kindreds had made it their domain. Hawks and buzzards circled regally above the rugged crests, and seabirds squawked protest as these intruders wound single file along cliff edges or over swaying suspension bridges. By night coyotes sang back and forth across the ridges, and seals dove blithely through the lacy explosions of surf at the foot of the cliffs by day. Deer were plentiful, and Julian and Rana were able to hunt enough meat so that they hardly touched their supplies.

With both Silverhair and the weather in good humor, Julian found the dread that had dogged him gradually lifting. The fate of Westria might rest on his shoulders, but for the moment all he had to do was to get a few people and their mounts through the difficult miles they must cover each glorious day. It was much easier to solve the problems of clearing the trail and persuading the horses to cross bridges than to worry about Caolin.

Frederic displayed an unsuspected talent for camp cooking—Silverhair had more experience, but the harper seemed to view food as something whose purpose was simply to keep him alive so that he could play, and like music, cooking was something that Julian appreciated but had no talent for.

And the girl, Rana, turned out to have some kind of intuitive communion with horses that surpassed the skill Julian had learned by hard experience, as Pine's feeling for trees surpassed his forestry. By the time Julian realized that he could have left the girl safely at the College of Bards, he had become used to her cheerful chatter, and both danger and her father's wrath seemed very far away.

He even found himself becoming accustomed to the silent presence of Lady Madrone. In this land where the powers of nature ruled, he was the intruder, not she, and he was grateful for all that she could tell him about the land through which they passed. Only Frederic worried him sometimes, for he had never recovered his full vigor after the fight at Registhorpe. After being snarled at for trying to find out if anything was wrong, Julian had stopped asking. He wondered if perhaps Frederic was one of those people who are good for sudden bursts of energy but not much use on the long haul.

For three weeks they picked their way down the coast. It seemed to Julian that the summer, and the journey, would never end. And then at last the terrain began to grow gentler. The hillsides sloped less precipitously, and now and again the rocks on the shore would give way for a little crescent of white sand. Julian saw ax marks on the trees beside the road and knew they must be approaching some holding, and did not know whether to feel anticipation or regret.

Rana pointed to the hanging gate and the empty field beyond it. "Careless folk down here—" she commented. "My father would blister my bottom for leaving a gate open that way."

Julian reined in, following her gesture, and frowned. "My foster father would have done the same." He looked at the ground before the gate, but the earth was too hard to show tracks. Rana saw him exchange worried glances with Silverhair, then he beckoned to Lady Madrone.

"Lady—what do the grass and the trees tell you? Is there any trouble here?"

She came toward him with that graceful swaying stride that seemed to cover the ground without actual movement, the bright sunlight glinting on her tunic of leaves. Then she stood still, and her great eyes went unfocused, as if she were listening.

"No trouble," she said. "The grass is happy, with no cattle to trample and bite it; the trees are happy, with no one to cut them. It is all very peaceful here."

"No one—" Julian began. "What happened to the people, then?"

"Four settings of the sun have passed since the great burning. By now the ashes are cold. . . ."

"Raiders!" exclaimed Silverhair, pulling back on his

reins as his heels dug into his pony's sides so that the animal half reared. Frederic straightened in his saddle and fumbled for his sword, and Rana pulled out her knife.

"Are they all dead, or gone?" Julian bent over Lady Madrone, who continued to stand in the road as if rooted there.

"One, no—two of the human kind remain—"

"Come on!" Julian's exclamation cut off her answer. He slapped his mare's neck with the reins and she exploded forward, followed by others with the packhorse bucketing along behind.

There won't be anything we can do—whoever's survived won't die in the next five minutes, so why are we racing —Rana's pony stumbled, and she became too busy getting him under control to think any more, and then they were sliding to a halt in front of what had once been a snug little holding where the hills curved down to the sea.

All that remained of the main building and barns were charred timbers, though some of the doorless sheds had escaped the flames. A faint acrid scent hung about the place still. Household goods rejected by the raiders lay strewn about, some of them dappled with bloodstains, but there were no bodies to be seen.

"Do you always approach dangerous territory this way?" Rana asked a little shakily, dropping her reins on the pony's sweating neck and blowing on her leather-burned fingers to ease their stinging. "What if the survivor is one of the raiders?"

Flushing, Julian looked around him, as if wondering how he had gotten there. "I felt an urgency suddenly—I don't understand. . . ."

"Not one of the raiders," murmured Frederic. His eyes were closed and he was hanging on to the peak of his saddle with both hands. "It's a woman, I think, and close by. She was calling someone—not us—and now she's afraid. . . ." He grimaced, and added, "Oh, damn . . ." very softly. Rana saw his grip on the saddle loosen, and even as she opened her lips to ask him what was wrong, he swayed and slid slowly from the horse to the ground.

"Rana, see to him! Silverhair, you come with me!" Julian swung out of the saddle, and almost in the same movement, drew his sword. As Rana scrambled off her pony and ran to Frederic she glimpsed him and Silverhair stalking toward the sheds with drawn swords. Lady Madrone had planted herself rather incongruously before the gate to the empty corral and with a shimmer was transforming herself back into a tree.

Frederic appeared to be unconscious. He had fallen so slowly and limply—Rana thought it would be safe to move him without worrying about disturbing broken bones. She straightened head and arms, swearing as she felt the heat in his skin. Then she started to move his right leg and he screamed.

Rana dropped the leg as if it had burned her, and sat back, shaking. Frederic's eyes were open and he had gone very pale.

"Sweet Lady, Frederic, is it broken?" she whispered. His breeches were not torn and she could see no distortion in the limb.

"Not the bone—" he whispered. "An infected wound from the fight on the way to Registhorpe. Something burst inside during that last dash."

"Well, let me at least straighten you out—you can't be doing it any good lying that way."

He bit his lip and closed his eyes while she worked, and when she had finished, gave a long, shuddering sigh. Beads of sweat glistened on his brow. Rana pulled off her scarf and tried to wipe his face clean, her gut tightening with fear as she felt the heat under his skin once more.

"I could light a fire from your forehead." The fear made her voice harsh. "Why didn't you say something?"

"I thought it was healing, even though it was still sore," he said weakly. "The wound had closed. I thought if I was patient it would go away. And we were in the wilderness anyway. What could any of you have done?"

Perhaps he was right, but Rana still wanted to shake him for suffering in silence like a penitent of some Ancient religion. As a shelter this ruined holding was better than a niche in the cliffs along the road, but not much. Now she wished desperately that the Master of the Junipers had been able to come, even though she suspected he would have found a way to send her home. Frederic's life was not an acceptable exchange for her adventure, and she realized with a sick dread that he could die.

Frederic licked his lips and closed his eyes again. *Water, you idiot!* Rana thought furiously, feeling her own throat dry. *Maybe you can at least cool him down!* She got to her feet, looking anxiously around her. The raiders couldn't have burned the well!

She had taken her water bottle from her saddle and was on her way around the ruins when she met Julian and Silverhair returning with an old woman between them. They had sheathed their swords. Well, perhaps the woman was not truly old, Rana thought as she noted her full figure and dark hair streaked with grey, but she was older than Rana's mother. It was her torn clothing and the deep shadows around her eyes that had made her look ancient.

"Where's Frederic?" asked Julian quickly.

"I pulled him into the shade of the gatepost." Rana gestured back the way she had come. "He's got a fever you could cook dinner with—a wound that went bad, he says. I was looking for water. Oh, Julian, what are we going to do?"

"Give me the bottle," said Silverhair. "There's a spring down the hill. I think Julian can handle our prisoner without any help from me!" His lips twisted bitterly. The woman stared at the dust with her arms clasped as if she was cold, and made no reply.

Julian's big hands clenched and unclenched helplessly. "I can bind a fresh wound or splint a bone, but a warrior's heal-craft is all I know. We can try to make him comfortable, but—" His heavy shoulders lifted in a shrug, and something in Rana's heart wrenched at the pain she saw in his dark eyes. "May the Guardians have mercy, Rana, I don't know what to do!"

"But I do," another voice echoed his, harsh as if scraped raw by screaming, but loud. Both Rana and Julian jerked around, staring. The woman had straightened. Her dull eyes met theirs, she licked her lips, and spoke again. "A bargain, warrior—my grandson's life for that of your friend. My herb garden is the only thing those sea wolves left me. You find my boy and I'll use all my skill to heal your man."

Julian stared at her for a long moment and then nodded.

"Don't call me warrior—my name is Julian."

She looked at him, and Rana could see animation returning unwillingly to her features. Rana read the lines in that
strong face and thought that before her world went up in
flames this had been a woman of humor, and considerable
power.

"That may be, but warrior is what you are—and other
things." She paused, her gaze went inward for a moment,
and then she met his eyes, her face revealing a piteous
vulnerability. "I am Eva," she said, and Rana understood
that her name was the only possession the raiders had not
been able to foul. "Before *they* came, I was the holder
here."

The sun beat down on Rana's back, sending rivulets of
sweat trickling down beneath her tunic. But she sat still
with the big basket in her arms, watching Eva select herbs
and breathing deeply of the aromatic air.

"In the big house I had a stillroom, with drying racks and
little shelves to store the herbs—there now, my sister, come
up nicely, for there's a lad with hair as bright as your
blossoms who has need of you—

> *"Herb come, sickness go; soon more flowers grow.*
> *Fellow-child of the land, come quick to my hand.*
> *Cure the one who lies ill; sister, listen to my will!"*

Eva made a swift symbol over the flower, twisted the
knife blade in the hard earth and waggled it, and the
dandelion came free in her hand, root intact, as if it had
released its hold on the ground in answer to her plea.

Eva gestured to Rana, who held out the basket. "Why
dandelion?" the girl asked softly. "I thought they were only
good in the spring, for greens."

"True enough, but the roots make a tea that is a powerful
systemic cleanser. Once we get your lad's fever down, we
must help his body fight the poison the wound is sending
into it." She sat back on her haunches, looking around her.
"Did your mother teach you nothing, girl?"

Rana grimaced. "She tried, but I was better at gathering
the plants than learning what to do with them. When I was

sick I just drank what she gave me without asking what it was, and, of course, the Master of the Junipers came when any of us were really ill. . . . " She sighed, wondering how the Master was doing.

If I had Eva's gift for mind-calling, she thought, *I would be yelling for the Master now!* It was not an uncommon talent in Westria—people said the dead Queen Faris had been very gifted, more so than the King, and that Caolin had no sensitivity at all—but almost anyone could touch the minds of others when exalted by ritual, or when there was great need. And for many the ability was amplified until they could call or compel whoever was in range, as Eva had done the day before.

Rana had shown signs of such abilities when she was a child, but as usual, all psychic faculties had closed down when she reached adolescence, as if the body's transformations took up all its energies, and talents which manifested during those years were usually haphazard and uncontrolled. It remained to be seen whether the ability would return when she was grown—she had not thought much about it until now.

"My daughter could tell you the name and use of every herb within a day's walk of here by the time she was twelve years old," said Eva with a bitter pride.

"Your daughter?" asked Rana automatically.

"She is dead, like the rest of them, now. The men were in the pastures, but when the raiders came Deira tried to defend herself with her father's sword. They grabbed her boy, and struck her down in the yard, and raped her, holding him so that he could see. When they let him go, he ran off to the hills."

Rana swallowed sickly, wishing she had not asked. While Eva sponged Frederic to reduce the fever and tried to make him more comfortable, the rest of them had labored to shovel more earth over the shallow graves Eva had made for her dead. There had been four men and two women —except for the boy who was hiding in the hills, all the family Eva had had. Rana was glad that the bodies had been already covered by the time they came.

"What will you put in the tea beside dandelion root?" she asked, desperate to change the subject.

"Borage and melissa." Eva pointed across the garden,
where a few blue flowers drooped above furry leaves next to
a clump of foot-high stalks with light green, crinkled leaves.
"They've done well this summer, with all the sun, and you
too, my lovely—" she added in the same even tone, picking
a chamomile daisy from the mat of greenery that divided
the herb beds and murmuring another charm. Rana had
been brought up to honor all living things and to take
nothing from the land without giving thanks, but Eva's
insistence on using the proper charm for each action
seemed superstitious. Still, the woman certainly seemed to
know herb lore!

Rana suppressed a shudder. How could Eva move from
the deaths of her family to a discussion of herbs so calmly?
Especially when the older woman had been raped along
with her daughter, knocked out, and left for dead? Compulsively, Rana picked chamomile flower heads and dropped
them into the basket. She was familiar enough with the
breeding of animals, but human sex was still a dark
territory that she was not yet ready to explore, and having
seen the terror of its perversion, she was not sure she ever
would be.

"Oh, they've all done well, my herbs, flourishing like
children—" Eva's voice cracked suddenly, and Rana understood that her apparent control was only a veneer. She
felt her own eyes prickling with unshed tears.

"I'm sure that Julian will find your grandson," she said
quickly. "He's very good at tracking and very dependable!"
After over a month on the trail she felt as if she had known
him forever, a presence as quiet and steady as the earth
beneath her hand. "Shall I go pick the borage and melissa?
What else will we need?"

"Take two stalks of melissa, and three, maybe four twigs
from the borage plant—good leafy ones, mind you. In my
stillroom, I had willow bark, for fever the best herb of all,
but that's all gone now, and there are no willow trees near
here. We must just use what we have, and poultice the
wound, and pray."

Rana swallowed the sick feeling in her throat at the
thought that perhaps Julian would not catch the boy, that
Eva might not be able to make Frederic well, that there was

nothing there to answer their prayers, and got up to pick the herbs.

Julian thrust aside the old quilt that hung across the open side of the shed and stepped inside. The flickering fire cast dancing shadows, lending it a deceptively homelike familiarity. Rana was cutting up herbs while the woman Eva stirred something over the fire. Some kind of stew was already steaming there and beginning to send a mouth-watering scent through the air.

He cast a swift look toward the still figure on the bed by the wall. With a mattress of sweet-smelling dry grass covered by another quilt and Julian's cloak to cushion him, Frederic seemed to be comfortable; but the sight of those flushed features was like a knife to the heart. Julian had grown so used to Frederic's cheerful support—he should have noticed—he should have known that something was seriously wrong!

If Frederic died, how could he face Lady Rosemary or the Regent? Julian bit his lip, realizing abruptly that if that happened, his own grief would be a heavier burden than any fear of what others would say. Frederic had all the gifts that Julian lacked, and his friendship had been an assurance of Julian's own worthiness.

Eva looked up, and Julian remembered his other failure, and his shoulders sagged. "I saw him, up by the riven oak tree on the hill. But he runs like a rabbit! By the time I got there, he was gone. When it gets light in the morning I'll see if I can pick up the trail."

"It doesn't surprise me," Eva said quietly. "Piper was always a little wild, even before, and he knows every foot of these hills. Deira named him after the sandpiper that flits back and forth along the shore. . . ." There was a short silence, then she added, "I'll put out some food in a little while. Perhaps he will come down when he thinks we sleep."

Julian sat down heavily, unable to think of any reply. He was out of practice for scrambling about the hills, and his feet hurt.

"I think Frederic is a little better—" said Rana. "We got him to drink some of the fever tea. Eva is steeping herbs for a poultice now. With the tea to fight the fever and the poultice to draw the poison from the wound, he should improve soon."

It seemed to Julian that her voice was a little too bright, but he caught the quaver in it, and forced himself to smile as if he believed her. The curtain rustled again and Silverhair came in, carrying his harp.

"The horses are settled for the night—" He looked at Julian, bit off his next question, and looked around for a place to sit down. "I made sure there was enough fodder for them. Is that stew almost ready? It's been a hard day."

Rana passed her basket of herbs to Eva, leaned over to give the stewpot a stir, and sat back again. "Just about," she answered him. "Get out your bowls."

For a time they were too busy eating for speech. Even Frederic woke up enough to drink some broth, which was encouraging, and Julian felt strength flowing back into him as the hot stew went down.

"Thank you," he said when he could eat no more. "That was wonderful."

"It's the herbs—" said Rana. "They make everything taste better."

"My thanks to you, then, Mistress Eva," he said politely. "And for more than flavoring the stew . . . I wish—"

"No, you do not need to apologize." The woman lifted her head and Julian saw that she looked physically stronger, but the fierce light had left her eyes. "When I made my bargain with you this afternoon I was still afraid. My herbs can do much, but not everything. I have hopes of saving your friend, but my grandson is wounded in his spirit, and none of my medicines can reach him there. Perhaps I should not have sent you after him, for he may think you are one of the raiders, and then he will retreat farther into his fear."

Julian nodded. "I understand. But what I do not understand is why you were attacked! I have fought raiders in the Ramparts, and I would not have thought a holding of this size would interest them."

"And I have fought them in the north," said Silverhair. "What could they find to carry off here?"

"Little enough," said Eva. "They took some of our

animals, but I don't think it was food they were after, for they let most of the beasts run free. They were seeking the Castle, and they thought we might have some treasures from it here."

"A fortress?" asked Silverhair. "I did not know there was any stronghold here."

Eva shook her head with a faint smile. "Not a fortress —at least I don't think it was ever fortified. But it was called the Castle even in the ancient times, and according to the tales it was full of wonders."

Silverhair almost visibly pricked his ears, and Julian repressed a smile. Even if there had been no songs about this mysterious castle before, he suspected there would be soon.

"The walls tumbled down during the Cataclysm, and any treasures that could be dug out easily were carried off long ago. Now and again you can find a bit of tile or carven stone, but there is no silver or gold." She fumbled behind her and brought out a fragment of pottery whose cracked glaze showed a dim pattern of vine leaves.

"I picked this out of the ashes—it was set into our mantelpiece. Take it!" She brandished it and Julian held out his hand. "Do you lust after it?" her voice cracked. "Do you see anything in this fragment to justify the deaths of four people and the destruction of a child's mind?"

"There is nothing that can justify it!" Julian exclaimed, a sudden fury making his voice louder than he had intended. Startled, the others all looked at him, but his vision was full of images of the desolation he had seen, here and elsewhere, and anger spoke through him, as if he had become a conduit for all the anguish of his land. "And I swear by my life and my name that it will end!"

Eva's harsh laughter crossed his words. "It will end? Are *you* going to end it? It will take more than a young man's indignation to right all the wrongs in this world."

And that was undoubtedly true, thought Julian, which was why he was looking for the Earthstone.

"Believe him—" A whisper brought all their attention back to Frederic. His eyes were open and he was trying to smile. "If anyone can set things right, it will be Julian!"

Julian nearly knocked over the stewpot, getting around

the fire. He knelt awkwardly beside the pallet and took Frederic's hand.

"You idiot!" he exclaimed softly. "I told you to have that wound seen to. How do you feel?"

"I feel like a sword blank that's just been put into the fire," Frederic said faintly. "The air pulses, and light blazes around me, and then it all goes dark again."

"Then come out stronger from the forging!" exclaimed Julian, squeezing his hand. "Blessed Guardians, Frederic, don't you know how much I need you?"

Frederic tried to nod. "Yes, my lord, I'll try."

"You wouldn't desert me in battle, would you?" Julian seized Frederic's other hand and bent over him, trying to will some of his own strength through their linked hands. "You keep fighting as long as you're conscious, and after. You swore you would serve me, and I'm not going to let you go!"

He closed his eyes and thought he felt the fire Frederic had described around him, and he summoned up all his memories of coldness to blast it away. After a time he realized that Frederic's hands had gone slack in his own, and looked down. Frederic appeared to be sleeping, but it was a restless slumber, not like the stupor in which he had lain before, as if he were indeed struggling with some unseen foe.

Julian let go of Frederic's hands and sat back, shaking. Eva was staring at him. Her eyes were like pools of shadow in the firelight; he could not read them. He reached for his mug of tea and drank thirstily, unable to think of anything to say.

"Perhaps you are the one to end it, after all," the woman said finally. "I sense power about you, and great forces stirring. But you're not using it, except when you're startled into it, as you were just now. Why?"

Julian's gaze flinched away from hers, and met first the sardonic gleam in the harper's eyes and then Rana's confident stare. His heavy shoulders hunched in his habitual gesture of frustration or uncertainty.

"I'm trying to learn," he answered her at last. "I have to. Now let me be." He was willing to endure this kind of probing from the Master of the Junipers, but he would take no more from this old woman who had never even seen the College of the Wise.

Her shrug echoed his own, then she laid one strong hand, brown and veined as old wood, on Frederic's forehead, swore under her breath, and reached for the compresses.

The night was a bad one. Frederic's period of lucidity had been only a breather between phases of the battle, and for hours he struggled in and out of delirium. Finally Silverhair played the sleep-spell on his harp, and that brought a measure of peace to all of them.

Frederic's fever broke a little before dawn and he fell into a normal sleep at last. Silverhair lifted his hands from the harpstrings and began to rub them, smiling crookedly. In the silence that followed the ending of the music, Julian thought he heard a patter of light footfalls.

When he went out to relieve himself in the morning, Julian saw the marks near the shed where someone had sat listening, and the food that Eva had set out for her grandson was gone. And it seemed to him then that for the child, Piper, as well as for Frederic, the healing had begun.

Five days passed, and as Eva fought Frederic's infection with her herbs, Silverhair found himself fighting a different kind of battle for the soul of the child. Since its restoration Swangold's tone had changed. The crystalline clarity of sound he had known as well as the sound of his own voice had deepened to something at once rougher and more mellow, as if the instrument retained the memory of pain. And perhaps it was the pain, as well as the sweetness in the music, that spoke to the boy Piper and brought him closer and closer to the fire.

Then came the crisis in Frederic's fever, and all other concerns were forgotten as they struggled to cool him with wet cloths, and to keep him from hurting himself in his delirium. His broken words revealed more of his longing for Awahna than he would ever have consciously let them know, and Silverhair, remembering the agony of being without his music, felt his heart wrenched in unwilling sympathy. Each in his own way, they were after the same thing.

> *"Earth support and water flow,*
> *Spirit's fire burn steadily,*
> *Body's breath in balance blow,*
> *Maintain this life in harmony."*

Eva chanted desperately. As she had a charm for the picking of each herb and the preparation of each medicine, she had also this chant for the moment when all her herb lore was exhausted and one could only pray. And the others summoned strength for a ragged chorus—

> *"Radiant sun send down your power*
> *For healing in this sacred hour!"*

Silverhair took up the harp again to support the singing. Sound throbbed in the air; he felt it resonate in his bones and took a deep breath, drawing up energy from his solar plexus to carry his chant and the force of its meaning to the invisible powers. Driven by his sudden feeling for Frederic, he dared to reach out as he had not done since the night when he first played the resurrected harp, and he felt his voice deepen, its vibration increasing until his vision blurred and he no longer knew if he was singing sound or waves of light that throbbed in the air.

Again and again they repeated the simple words, focused by desperation until the chanting was their only reality. The harper felt sound scrape through a throat that was going raw, but still he kept singing. And when, despite all will, strength flagged and the sound ebbed, he heard another voice, pure and clear, descanting the melody.

Very slowly, he turned his head. The boy he had glimpsed only as a shadow was standing in the doorway, grimy and gangling, with a tattered blanket clutched around him. Eva had said he was ten, but he looked younger, his face emptied of all emotion as he sang.

Then there was a sound from Frederic. Eva leaned over him, work-roughened hand gentle on his forehead, then straightened, an incredulous relief shining in her eyes.

"He's cool—and look, he's sweating at last!"

Almost too exhausted for emotion, they stared at him and then back to her. Eva's gaze went from one to another, and finally to the boy in the doorway, silent now. She stilled. For a moment Frederic's gentle breathing seemed to be the only movement in the room. Then Silverhair's hand moved involuntarily and drew a shimmer of sound from the harp.

Expression leaped suddenly in the boy's face; he moved like a startled rabbit, but this time he came forward, frantically burrowing into Eva's welcoming arms. She was murmuring broken endearments, but since the singing had stopped, Piper had made no sound. Silverhair stroked Swangold's strings once more, and the boy straightened, turned, and with one grimed finger reached out to touch the harp.

⇒ TEN ⇐

There was no question of leaving Eva and Piper at the ruined holding. By the time the second week of Frederic's recovery was ending and he could walk and sit on a horse again, it had somehow been agreed that when the companions left they would take the old woman and her grandchild with them, and see them safe to some town. Only when they came to the bay where the humped cores of six Ancient volcanoes marched into the sea to join the new cone that had exploded from the waters during the Cataclysm, there was sickness in the village; they paused just long enough to trade for a horse for Eva and a pony for Piper, and went on.

They could have left them at the Danehold, but Silverhair's face was still too well known there. He insisted on taking the longer road across the mountains where the point men called Ravensgate jutted into the sea, and Julian was glad enough to put off facing the world of men a little longer, and did not argue with him. Only Eva seemed unhappy about their choice of a road, but Piper was like Silverhair's shadow, and the old woman was becoming annoyingly conciliating, as if she feared any objections would lose the support of the one person with whom her boy showed any desire to communicate. Julian wondered if they would have trouble getting rid of her when they finally did come to a safe town—but that was something else he did not want to think about now.

"Is that Ravensgate?" asked Rana, pointing to the jutting tooth of rock where the long slope of the next ridge ended in the sea. They had made camp at the top of the pass, ostensibly to rest the winded horses, but perhaps in truth because the sudden, spectacular sight of the frothing waves far below compelled some kind of homage. Late afternoon sunlight shimmered on the blue water and lent a soft glow to the chaparral-furred folds of the hills.

"The point, and all this bulge of land," said Eva gravely. "I have been here to make the offerings three times before —when my father died, and my mother, and then for my husband. I am not likely to forget this road."

"Do you wish to perform some ritual for those who died at the holding?" asked Frederic softly. "I will be happy to assist you."

She looked at him, and for a moment her tired eyes glittered with tears. Then she blinked them away. "What do I have to pay their way with now? Perhaps the demons that guard the gateway will understand why they came unready, and grant them safe passage to the Land of the Blessed across the sea. I will pray for their spirits tonight as I do always, and hope it is so. . . ."

"That is something we can all do—" said Julian quickly. He saw her tears welling in earnest now and looked away. Suddenly the peace of this place seemed more sinister than soothing, like the serenity of the dead who know neither joy nor pain. He shivered and got up to look for more dry wood for the fire.

When he came back, Frederic had set up a little altar of the elements as he did whenever there was time at the end of a day of traveling. The sight of the salt in its tiny earthen cup, the silver thimble of water, the burning votive light and smouldering incense, all laid out on a bit of embroidered silk were familiar and comforting. Eva was telling the tale of the journey the dead make over the sea, and Silverhair was underscoring it with soft, minor chords.

Piper sat still, watching him, tousled bronze hair flopping

over his brown eyes. Cleaned up, the boy could have been any lad from Julian's own hills, except for the look in his eyes, like a wild bird that would take flight if you stepped too near. He had not run away again since the night Frederic's fever broke, but neither had he spoken, except occasionally to hum wordlessly with a song. Could even Silverhair's music break that silence?

Julian sighed, realizing he was coming all too close to accepting Eva and the child as permanent members of their party, and that would be madness. Rana's bright hair glinted in the firelight as she leaned over to dip up another bowlful of soup, and Julian's lips tightened. The girl should be sent to safety too, and Frederic was hardly fit for a long journey. Even Silverhair—with the healing of his harp the harper seemed to have recovered his serenity, but why should he be dragged along on this quest? Julian fought the impulse to ride out of the camp and leave them all, for the first time understanding what had driven his uncle to a life of wandering. But running away would not help Julian, for he was the one who had brought them all here. He could not abandon them now.

His sleep was haunted by dreams of pursuit by faceless men whose cloaks flapped behind them like black wings. When he woke in the grey dawn he saw a dark shape on the branch of the dead tree at the edge of their campsite. As he stared, it shifted position and he realized it was a raven watching him with eyes that glistened like bits of coal.

"Be gone—get away! There's nothing for you here!" Still half-asleep, Julian struggled to his feet and shook his blanket at the bird. The raven gave an affronted croak and flapped awkwardly to a higher branch, then disappeared into the mists so quickly that Julian wondered if it had really been there.

Eva sat up in her blankets, making the sign against evil. "You should not have done that, my lord— The ravens are the Guardians of the gateway. . . ."

"I owe my bones to the Sacred Wood and my spirit to the Maker of All Things, not to *them!*" Julian said harshly, rubbing his arms to still gooseflesh that was not entirely caused by the early morning chill. He had been raised in a kinder faith, but Eva's conviction was disturbing. "And if I can help it, none of those in my care will go that way."

"Woman, be still!" said Silverhair. "Mortal enemies are likely to keep us busy enough—don't wish on us foes from the spirit world!"

Julian looked at him with gratitude, feeling suddenly closer to the older man than he had ever expected to be. Then the first rays of the sun broke through the glittering veils of fog, and he straightened with a sudden urgency.

"Get up, all of you, and take something to eat on the trail. We have delayed too long already—" He could not explain why he was pushing them so suddenly. He had heard nothing, seen nothing but the shadowy pursuers in his dream. But the interchange with Eva had sobered them all, and no one gave him any argument.

Later that morning, as they paused to breathe the horses, Lady Madrone, who had spent the night in a canyon below the pass where there was water, caught up with him.

"You do well to hurry, Lord—" she said softly. She swayed gently as she halted, though there was no wind. "Strange messages come to me through the roots and the leaves. There is an evil thought behind us, a cold thought, like the glacier grinding down from the peak. The image of the music maker is in it, and it travels faster than we. . . ."

The Blood Lord sat alone in the square, windowless room at the heart of his tower. The sound of pick and shovel came faintly through the rock walls as the men labored on swaying platforms above it, laying course upon course of reddish stone; but this room was floored by the naked rock of the Red Mountain, and it was warded by Caolin's word and his will. No one would dare to disturb him here.

He sat motionless in a chair also hewn of that red stone, facing the cubical altar where pale fire flickered in a golden bowl. The pallid light glinted fitfully on the rich furnishings of the elemental altars in the four corners of the room. Caolin took a deep breath, then another, focusing his awareness inward. Consciousness of his surroundings receded, disappeared, and his spirit, freed from the bondage of the senses, turned inward and out again through a doorway that only the adepts know. Like a shark trailing the taste of blood through the sea, through the currents of the spirit world he sought the consciousness of Malin Scar, the Shadower.

"My lord . . ." There was a sense of cessation of movement, as if the Shadower had reined in beside some trail.

"Report—" came the thought of Caolin.

"The harper went south from Yerba Buena along the coast with Lord Frederic and the other man. They took the road by the sea's edge, but all the coast roads join above the Dane-hold. I went inland to cut them off, but there had been plague in the villages and they had gone on. Men said they had a redheaded boy with them, and an old woman and a child."

Caolin's thought wavered in confusion, and for a moment the contact was almost lost. Silverhair had always traveled alone—how had he acquired such an assortment of hangers-on? And why was he going south? Caolin had expected him to seek Eric's illusory protection. The harper must know that Caolin had even greater power in Elaya than he did in Westria. He could hardly expect to find safety there.

"They have taken the coast road again—" Malin Scar's thought refocused him. *"Shall I follow them?"*

"Go straight to Santibar." This answer, at least, was obvious. *"As you have pointed out, all roads must rejoin the main road sometime, and they will have to pass that way. Wait for them. Seize Silverhair."*

"And when I have found him?" There was a quiet certainty in the Shadower's thought that was very reassuring.

"Kill him. Any way you like—any way you can."

The answering surge of emotion destroyed the contact before Caolin could add a request to find out the name of the third man with whom Silverhair had been traveling, and for the moment he could not make the connection again.

Still, he was curious. Stretching his awareness, he sought the harper's, like a scent, or a taste, or the memory of a song. There—he almost had it—and then the barrier of another will slammed down. Frederic? But he knew only too well that this skill was not taught at the College of the Wise. Besides, there was a curious unformed quality about what he sensed here—this was not training, but a clumsy focusing of sheer power. And yet there was something familiar about it, almost like—

As the name trembled at the edge of Caolin's awareness, somewhere far above him a stone's weight broke the flimsy scaffolding, and the agony of the man beneath it, dying as his lifeblood fed the thirsty rock below, sent a shock of pure sensation through the temple that brought the Blood Lord back to climaxing consciousness again.

> *"The foaming beer of Santibar*
> *Is full and rich and brown.*
> *The wonder is that anyone*
> *Gets work done in this town—"*

Rana could hear Silverhair's voice even through the open door of the Papagayo Inn. She paused in the doorway, eyeing him nervously as he lifted his mug in salutation to the stout woman who kept the place. He seemed no more than mildly cheerful, but she could not help but remember how the wine had taken him when he lost the harp. They had all agreed that Swangold should be hidden when they came to Santibar, but what good would that do if people could hear Silverhair's singing all over town? She was glad there were no other guests in the big room.

> *"But the very best drink that I have drunk—*
> *And I have tried them all—*
> *Is the drink the barmaid's bringing now*
> *To fill my flagon tall!"*

It was a mug, not a flagon, but it was empty, and the innwife seemed happy to fill it for him again before she went back to her kitchen. Eva was nursing her own mug beside him, glad of the liquid and the cool darkness of the inn after the heat outside. Julian and Frederic were nowhere to be seen.

Rana flushed as she met Eva's gaze, for the two men were not the only other members of the party who should have been here.

"Piper's still at the bird market—" she said unhappily as she neared the table. "I'm sorry, I couldn't get him to come away, and we'd agreed to meet here by the third hour, so I thought I should come and tell you . . ." Her voice trailed off.

"I suppose we should have expected it." Julian came in from the yard with Eva's saddlepack slung over his shoulder. Frederic was close behind him. "Eva, you'll have to fetch him. I'll come with you—"

Eva looked at the pack, and her mouth set. The question of whether she and Piper should stay here had been the subject of a controlled but bitter argument all the way from Ravensgate. With some effort, Rana had kept her own mouth closed. She would miss the old woman, but her own place in this party was too precarious to dare objection.

"That child, that child—" murmured Eva. "He always did like the birds, and I'm loath to deny him anything that gives him pleasure now. But he hears well enough, even if he won't reply, and he must learn to obey!" Shaking her head, she set her hands on the rough table to push herself upright. "But look—I won't have to go out in the heat again after all!"

There was a blur of motion at the doorway as Piper darted through, slipped past his grandmother, and tugged frantically at Silverhair's sleeve, pulling and pushing at him at the same time. With a furious look the harper started to thrust him away, but Frederic gripped his arm.

"No—he's trying to tell us something! Piper, what's wrong?" Frederic forced the child to look at him. The boy's throat worked as he struggled to speak, and tears of frustration welled in his eyes. Alert as a watchdog that scents a foe, Julian sprang to the door and peered outside. Rana followed him, but whatever had frightened Piper had not yet followed him here.

"Where were you? What could the boy have seen?" Julian asked urgently.

"I took him down to the bird market near the north gate—you remember we passed it as we came in and it was all we could do to keep Piper on his pony then. . . . "

Julian nodded. "The city guard has a station there, and if somebody with influence alerted them—" He did not need to finish. Both of them were remembering Lady Madrone's warning.

Frederic and Eva were trying to calm the child, who seemed on the verge of hysterics. Suddenly Silverhair leaned forward and took Piper's chin in his hand.

"Listen, boy—can you think of a song? Think of a song about what you're trying to say. You don't have to sing it—just hum a few notes of the melody—"

Piper shuddered, and Frederic placed both hands alongside the boy's head, closing his own eyes as if he were willing calm into the child. Rana moved back toward them, leaving Julian at the door.

Straining, she heard the first breath of sound. Piper gasped, and it came again, a boy's sweet treble, lifting softly in a melody that Rana had never heard before. But Silverhair's face grew grim.

"It's the ballad of Orain Long-Bow and the Shadower who hunted him down." His gaze sought Julian's. "I told you before—I'm a danger to you. Get the others to safety. Before I let him take me I'll give this Shadower a good run. At least I have some knowledge of the town!"

Rana did not have to look to know that Julian was shaking his head.

"And what would I say to the Master when I come home?" His voice had gone very gentle, and Rana shivered. "We will defend you—"

"No!" said Eva. "They'll kill you all. But there may be a way—they will be looking for a harper, won't they? A man! My extra gown is in there—" She pointed at the pack Julian was still holding. "We can disguise him!"

"If they've followed you this far they must have descriptions of the rest of us too," added Rana. "We'll have to separate. I'll take off my cap, put on the only skirt I brought with me, and go with you—they won't be expecting two old women and a lass and a boy!"

Julian looked at her with sudden respect. "Do it! And get through the south gate and down the Elayan road! They may know our mounts as well, so Frederic and I will take all of the horses and follow you as soon as we can. Swangold is still packed safely—" he said to Silverhair. "I'll take good care of her."

"Will you be wanting your rooms now?"

Startled, they all turned as the innwife came back from the kitchen, rosy-cheeked and smiling expansively, balancing a tray of tortillas and a dish of creamy guacamole from the avocado trees that flourished here.

"Your two best chambers—" said Frederic with his most lordly air. "One for me and my cousin and another for my old servants here." He tossed a leather bag onto the table that clinked enticingly as it fell. "They're tired and will go up now with the boys, but my cousin and I would like to sample some more of your beer!" He stretched out his long legs along the bench and reached for a tortilla, and Julian, trying hard to look equally casual, lounged down beside him.

"Oh certainly, my lord—" Santibar had not belonged to Elaya long enough for the woman to forget what was due Westrian nobility, and Frederic's tunic and breeches, though travel-worn, had been made of fine cloth, exquisitely embroidered by Lady Rosemary's women around the neck and hem. She motioned to Eva. "If you and your good man will come with me, I'll show you the way."

A sidelong glance revealed a conflict of emotions in Silverhair's face that almost broke Rana's gravity. Schooling her face with an effort, she picked up her own pack and followed them up the stairs to watch the harper's metamorphosis.

Curious, Julian watched Frederic's careful sunwise progress around the room. At each of the four directions he paused, eyes closed and frowning, and his fingers flickered in the warding sign. When he came to the door, he looked quickly to make sure that the innwife was not on her way with yet another delicacy to tempt her noble guest, drew his sword, and sketched an invisible line across the sill.

"I'm just realizing how much I would rather use my sword this way than on the flesh of men," Frederic said ruefully as he sheathed his blade. "Maybe the shock of feeling the man I killed in the fight at Registhorpe die was what made my wound go so bad. I can still use weapons to defend, but I don't know if I can kill again. . . ." He looked at Julian helplessly.

"Do you think that will hold them?" Julian said after a long moment. He didn't like killing either, but he thanked the Guardians that he had never *felt* a soul depart under his sword. There was something to be said for a lack of sensitivity after all!

Frederic brightened, shrugged, and sat down again. "Maybe. For a little while. If they're not too interested. If I had some incense and salt water I could do it better; the Master of the Junipers could do it with nothing but his will. But if this Shadower of Silverhair's has any training, I don't know—"

He bit off the words they were both thinking— *If this man comes from Caolin . . .*

Julian sighed and took a rationed sip from his mug of beer. Silverhair and the others had left almost half an hour before. The harper's disguise would have been comical if the danger had not been so pressing, but it had been a shock to see Rana dressed as a girl. He hoped they had already passed unnoticed through the town. In his memory he reviewed Frederic's conversation with the innwife, searching for anything that might give them away.

"Why did you call me your cousin?" he said suddenly. "Your armsman would be more believable, surely!"

Frederic surveyed Julian's worn leather vest and the faded green of the homespun shirt he wore, and grinned. "A poor relation, maybe? I wasn't really thinking—anyway, I wanted to say *something* that was true!"

Julian stared at him.

"We're cousins by marriage, anyway. Hadn't you realized it?" asked Frederic. "Your mother's older sister Berisa is still married to my uncle Sandremun, so that makes us relations somehow. By marriage, Silverhair is my uncle too!"

Julian found his own face creasing in an answering grin. He hadn't thought about it. He had been too shocked by the discovery of who his parents were to think about what other relatives their marriage might have given him. Looking at Frederic, he thought he was happier to acknowledge their relationship than he had been to find out that he was heir to Westria. He had been worried about Frederic's health, but his friend had been growing steadily stronger, and his quick thinking might have just saved them all.

In fact it was everyone's quick thinking that had saved them, he realized as he reviewed what they had done. Rana had built on Eva's original idea, and Frederic had supported it. It was only he and Silverhair, supposedly the most experienced members of the party, who had stood tongue-tied while the people they should have been protecting arranged their own salvation. He began to laugh, glimpsing for a moment some kind of purpose here. He did not understand it, but he was beginning to believe that a pattern existed, and it eased, just a little, the burden he was learning to bear.

Frederic started to make some reply, then stopped, listening. Julian stiffened as he heard the sound of many voices outside. They sounded confused. He lifted an inquiring eyebrow at Frederic, who was staring in awe at the invisible line he had drawn before the door. Then a different voice ended the babble like cold water thrown on a flame, and just at that moment the innwife came bustling into the room.

"What was that noise? Why is the front door shut? Was someone wanting to come in?" she asked without waiting for answers, sailed across the room, and opened the door. Julian glanced at Frederic's face and found laughter warring with his chagrin—now his friend would never know if his warding would have held.

In a moment the room seemed to be full of men. Someone barked an order; a dark-skinned man with grizzled wiry hair and a cuirass of boiled leather over his blue and silver tunic pushed through the jam.

"Oh, Captain!" The innwife fell back, twisting the folds of her apron in her hands. "Is there trouble? I never dreamed it was you out there!" She cast an accusing glance at Frederic.

"Was it wrong to shut the door? The street was noisy, and I like to do my drinking in peace—" Frederic shrugged his shoulders in such an excellent imitation of the fops Julian used to despise at Philip's court that he had to suppress laughter again.

"We're looking for a foreign harper—he's wanted for questioning in the Campos del Mar—" the captain said sternly.

"Well, there's no harper here!" The innwife straightened, visibly relieved, and several of the guardsmen traded long-suffering glances.

"He was seen to enter here—" said the same cold voice Julian had heard before.

"My only guests are this gentleman and his servants— The old man sang pretty as a bird, but he had no instrument that I could see." She smiled complacently, but the captain's stance shifted subtly, and Julian found himself surreptitiously feeling for the hilt of his sword.

"That could be our man," the captain began.

Frederic responded with a whinnying laugh. "What, old

Tomas? He only sings when he's drunk—" He winked at
the innwife. "It must have been your beer."

"Your man's name is Tomas?" asked the captain. "And
who might you be?"

Frederic looked taken aback, as if it had never occurred
to him that someone would not know his name, and for a
moment Julian was almost worried.

"I am Alain of Eagle's Rest, where we raise the best sheep
between the Danehold and Seagate, and this is my cousin
Jeremy," he answered haughtily.

The captain colored a little beneath his dark skin, and
looked away.

"Nevertheless, the man must be questioned," came a
voice from behind the guardsmen. Two of them moved
aside and Julian saw the man who had spoken, his dark,
hooded cloak open over a faded black tunic with vest and
breeches of worn black leather, and an equally well-worn
sword.

"And when did you start giving orders here?" asked the
captain, turning. Soft-footed as a shadow, the man in black
came forward and slipped something out of the pouch at his
belt. As the new man held it out to the captain, Julian
glimpsed enameled red and grey and felt the short hairs
rising on his neck, remembering the badges the men who
attacked them on the road to Registhorpe had worn.

The sight of it seemed to be having a similar effect on the
Elayan captain. "Your man is upstairs?" he asked Frederic.

"I suppose—" Frederic looked bored. "He's probably
sleeping off his drink by now, and you'll have a job to get
any sense from him. But you'll have to excuse me from
going up there. My old nurse is with him, and if she singes
your ears for you, don't complain to me!"

The man in black cast one comprehensive glance at
Frederic and Julian, then followed the captain like a shadow up the stairs. But that one look had been enough to send
a shiver down Julian's spine. This man's eyes reminded him
uncomfortably of the raven he had seen, and as he turned
his hood fell back and all down the left side of his face
Julian saw the curdled slick skin of an old scar.

Frederic yawned and got to his feet. "You know, Jeremy,
old Eva will likely follow those two back down, and I don't

want to hear what she'll have to say. What do you say we go out for a little air?"

Julian nodded and pushed back his bench. One or two of the guards seemed suspicious, but most of the men looked as if they would like to do the same. And they had been given no orders to hold the two young men here. Forcing himself to lounge along nonchalantly, Julian followed Frederic from the room.

They had gone out of the front door, but as soon as they were past its line of sight Frederic sprinted around the side of the building with Julian hard on his heels. The horses were saddled already, but Julian wished that Rana were there to quiet them as they led them out of the stableyard and into the back lane. When they reached the street they curbed their impatience, for even at a walk, two mounted men each leading two saddled horses attracted attention among the foot traffic of the town.

It seemed to Julian that every farmer within fifty miles of Santibar must have brought his produce to market that day, and he had small appreciation for the graceful lines of palm trees that shaded the streets, or the sparkle of whitewashed adobe houses against the blue ramparts of the mountains that sheltered the town. Every sense was focused behind him, as if his entire back had become a single ear, but it was not until they were five miles past the south gate that he heard the cry go up behind them, and with one accord he and Frederic lashed the horses into a run.

He could see a little knot of foot travelers ahead. They had stopped, gesturing, at the sound of hoofbeats. Julian took a quick look back—their pursuers were black dots on the road behind them, but it seemed to him that one dot, blacker than the others, was leading them. From ahead came a shout. He turned—he could see the graceful shape of Lady Madrone and Rana's bright hair, and in a moment he recognized the harper, who had already shed his disguise.

In moments they were upon them.

"Get mounted, all of you—" snapped Julian. "The pursuit is close behind us, and your beasts will be fresher than ours. We must be near the limits of the authority of the

Santibar men, and they can't follow us for long. Get going, and we'll catch up with you!"

Horses plunged in the road as the others scrambled into their saddles. After one desperate glance at Julian, Rana whipped her pony's neck with the reins and then slapped the rump of Piper's mount to get it going too. Lady Madrone lengthened her swaying stride. Eva's awkward grey labored along like a rocking horse, but after a few steps Silverhair reined his dun gelding down. Eyes narrowed, he gauged the progress of their pursuers. Then he set his hand to the hilt of his sword.

"Three blades will be better than two—one of those riders is my Shadower. He will not stop at the city line, and we have ten miles to go before we reach the turnoff to Awhai."

Julian nodded, unable to argue anymore. It was taking all his energy to keep his bay mare moving. Their pace had slowed to a canter already, and every stumble told him that she was tiring. But the fervor of their pursuers was flagging as well. Faintly he heard the Santibar captain's barked order, and turning in the saddle, saw all but three of their pursuers wheel back toward the city. Three against three —that was not such bad odds! Frederic and Silverhair had seen it too, and like Julian, straightened and let their mounts slow to the long distance alternation of walk and jog. Looking back, he saw that their pursuers had done the same.

But mile by mile, as they gained on the slower beasts ridden by the old woman and boy and the girl, their pursuers, better mounted or perhaps more ruthless riders, gained on them.

"There's the turning—" muttered Silverhair finally. "I told Rana to lead the others up it, hoping we'd escape pursuit once we left the highway. But there's no hope of that now."

He was right. They were all in plain sight of their pursuers now, and as they turned to check the distance they saw them whipping their mounts to sudden speed. Julian kicked his tired horse into a gallop again and drew his sword, gambling all on a last sprint toward an illusory safety.

"Pull up at that first bend past the turning. On that higher ground we can make a stand." He slapped the mare with the flat of his blade and she put out a last burst of speed. In moments they were lurching up the slope, halting, turning to face the foe. Rana and the others had pulled up a little beyond them. With a flicker of relief Julian saw that Lady Madrone had already transformed herself into a tree. Whatever happened to the rest of them, at least she would be safe now.

"We have you now!" cried the black-clad leader without slackening speed. "Give up the harper and you two young ones may go free."

"Never!" shouted Julian.

"What? Give up my uncle to an Elayan lackey?" Frederic laughed. His own blade, longer and better polished than Julian's work-worn sword, cast flickers of light across the road.

Their opponents swore. Julian saw a blur as the first one swung and twisted in the saddle. His own sword lifted instinctively to block it, then continued around in a back-hand stroke that knocked the man into the road. His mate and Frederic were trading strokes when Frederic's plunging grey allowed him to get in range, but the leader had aimed straight toward Silverhair.

The harper's rough form was effective, but the man in black moved like a snake striking. Julian saw steel flare toward Silverhair's right arm, and reined his horse into his attacker's, knocking him off-stride. Before Julian could draw away that same swift sword was hissing toward him. A desperate parry saved him, but he slid half out of his saddle. Exhausted, the bay mare nearly fell, but Julian pulled himself upright again, skin prickling with the same cold fear that had touched him when he first set eyes on this man, and he brought up his blade to guard once more.

"You're good, boy, but I'll take you, and after you, him—" his opponent snarled. Silverhair was clutching at his arm, where a widening line of red showed through the slashed sleeve.

"Uncle!" Julian fought to keep his mount between them. His sword whipped around, and he nearly dropped it as something struck the blade. Something hissed by his ear, biting earth between the feet of the man in black's dark pony, and the horse spooked and reared.

"Hold!" The word seemed to echo from all around them. Dazed, Julian dared a glance over his shoulder, saw a brown face behind a bent bow with another arrow nocked and ready, and more faces behind him.

He reined in and the bay mare dropped her head and stood trembling, the lather on her neck dripping snowy gobs of foam.

"You are on Awhai land now, and Awhai will choose who to save or slay!"

The dark man's head jerked up as if someone had struck him. Breathing hard, he slowly sheathed his sword. Julian imitated his action, and heard the sound of Frederic and Silverhair sliding home their blades.

"Were you coming here, or have you only turned aside seeking sanctuary?"

Julian frowned, decided that lying to their captors would be more dangerous than anything their pursuers could learn, and cleared his throat.

"We seek sanctuary, but I had also another errand here." Julian felt the dark man's gaze, and realized, too late, that for the first time the Shadower was seeing him as an individual, no matter whether enemy or prey, and not just an obstacle between him and Silverhair.

"We grant it, and we will hear and judge your errand," said the bowman. "You others, go your ways and trouble us no more."

The Shadower's face showed no emotion. But when he spoke his voice had once more chilled and Julian's skin twitched reflexively.

"I will go, but I will be waiting for you to leave this sanctuary. The harper is my meat already, and when the time comes, cockerel, I will have you as well. No man escapes the Shadow of Malin Scar. . . ."

❧ ELEVEN ❧

"Yes, the Shrine of the Earth Mother lies near here—"
Alonzo Lion Claw nodded slowly, but his dark eyes never
left Julian's. The curved claws in the necklace that was at
once the symbol of his chieftainship and his name clicked
gently as he moved. "Momoy, we call Her, knowing that the
Lady answers to many names. But it is now the time of the
Autumn Balancing, and all else must wait until we have
performed the rituals. You may seek the Lady afterward,
when you have been purified. In the meantime, you are
welcome to join in the festival."

Julian bit short his protest. They were only in Awhai on
sufferance, and every day that they were here put off the
time when they must come out to face Malin Scar. He ought
to be grateful. Obviously the man was speaking truth to
him. Even here in the chief's house he could hear the deep
drumming. That beat had been omnipresent ever since they
had entered the valley, as if they could feel the pulse of
earth itself here. There was a compulsion to it that made his
breath come faster and the blood move a little more quickly
through his veins.

But Lion Claw's eyes held a twinkle—Julian was not sure
whether of humor or of malice, but either one was disturbing. Julian took a deep breath and managed a bow.

"We will be honored to be your guests at the ceremony."

They came out onto a broad porch shaded by sycamores.
The adobe house of the chieftain was long and low, set on a
little rise overlooking the slope down to the dancing
ground. Behind it, sheltering southern hills curved eastward
to the friendly bulk of the peak they called the Mother
Mountain. Beyond the dance grounds the steeper escarpments of Topa Topa stood guard. Julian looked up at those
gracious ramparts and sighed. Like Awahna, Awhai was a

sacred valley, though more accessible to men. Surely they
were safe here.

The slopes and hollows around the beaten earth expanse
of the dancing floor were gay with tents and shelters of
woven branches for the folk who had come here for the
festival. Even though it was the third week of September,
the days were still hot and the nights mild enough to make
sleeping outdoors a pleasure. As the wind changed he
caught the tantalizing odors of pit-roasted pork and corn.
The bustle reminded Julian of harvest fairs at home, but he
had only felt this atmosphere of exalted expectation once
before, at the Initiation ceremonies when he had taken his
adult name.

Frederic might have been able to explain it—Julian
found himself turning to ask him, then remembered that
Frederic had gone off with the shamanic priests as soon as
they had reached the valley. Now that he thought about it,
he realized that they had all been separated, kindly, but
with remarkable deftness. Silverhair and the boy Piper were
with the singers, and Eva and Rana had been taken off to
the Women's Lodge. Julian had been flattered when Alonzo
Lion Claw had invited him to the chief's house, but without
the others he felt curiously incomplete.

Unwilling to analyze that feeling, he turned back to Lion
Claw and realized that the chieftain had been watching
him.

"You spoke of purification—" Julian said abruptly.
"What did you mean?"

The chieftain's brown face creased in a smile. Like most
of the folk of the valley, he counted among his ancestors the
last folk of the old Chumash blood and other tribesmen as
well as Anglo and Spanyol refugees from the Cataclysm.
The race descended from this mixing were as staunchly
native to this place as any of the Second People had ever
been.

"You also are partly a child of the People, are you not?"
His smiling gaze rested on Julian's dark eyes and hair. "You
may seek the vision as our young folk do, cleansed and
fasting."

Julian grimaced, remembering the solitary fast that had
preceded his Initiation. But it had been the danger from

which he had had to rescue himself and his friends when they were taken by slavers, not vision, that had revealed to him his name. He shrugged his heavy shoulders uncomfortably.

"I am no mystic. If Momoy wants to speak to me She will have to find some other way—"

"The vision always comes." Lion Claw spoke with absolute conviction. Then his voice chilled. "It came even to Lord Sangrado when he was here. . . ."

Julian had the odd sensation that the boards of the porch were tilting, but the potted vines suspended from the rafters hung motionless. With every hair on the back of his neck quivering, he forced his lips to obedience.

"You are speaking of the one we call the Blood Lord? He was here?" Now he remembered what Silverhair had said about Awhai at the Sacred Wood, but he did not think even the harper knew that Caolin had come *here*.

"A month or two at a time, yes—for several years he was a frequent pilgrim to Awhai."

The chieftain's gaze still held Julian's, but the younger man could not read his eyes. He wondered wildly if they had escaped Caolin's agent only to fall into the hands of his allies! Was that why the companions had been separated so swiftly?

But though vision might be denied him, Julian had always been able to trust his instincts about other men. In Lion Claw he sensed no malice—only a steady patience, like the wariness of the stallion guarding his herd. He took a deep breath, and forced his heartbeat to slow to the steady beat of the drum.

"Lord Sangrado came with honey in his words and gold in his hand, and learned all the secrets of our holy ones," the chieftain said then. "In the end he learned the most from the one whom we most feared. And now you come, fleeing from his men. It makes me wonder, but I do not judge him, or you. Momoy will decide."

Julian shivered, despite the dry heat of the air, understanding that it was sanctuary in its strict sense that they had found here—a sanctuary that would shelter without favoring either the hunted or his enemy. From somewhere down the valley he could hear singing, and instinctively he

found himself trusting the truth of those harmonies. He
bowed to the chieftain.

"I will accept the judgment of Momoy—"

> *"Equality of day and night,*
> *Balanced powers of dark and light;*
> *Between the seasons falls the hour*
> *Between the worlds we seek for power!"*

From beneath the oak trees the voices of the singers came
strong and clear, but the song leader was not satisfied. He
stopped them, correcting some detail of phrasing that
Silverhair had not been close enough to hear. The drummers tipped the big drums level again and straightened,
massaging their hands, but the flute players continued to
practice their odd harmonies. The harper smiled, reminded
of the College of Bards.

"You understand that in so large a gathering your harp
could not be heard, though I hope that you will play for us
later on—" said the woman of the Society of Singers who
had shown him where he was to stay. "But your voice is
strong. Will you participate in the chanting?"

"I will be honored to join you," said Silverhair. "But
what shall we do with the boy?" He gestured toward Piper,
who was standing where they had left him, listening to the
singers as if all his senses had focused in his ears. Looking
at him, the harper felt his frustration return.

In that moment when the boy had first come in from the
wild and touched the harp there had been something in his
face that Silverhair, still unbarriered from his contact with
the Wind Lord, had recognized. He had seen in the child
someone who understood his music, as Julian, for all his
enthusiasm, could never do—someone to whom he might
pass on the songs that were the only thing he had gotten out
of his years of wandering. But it was no good. Piper was as
elusive as a wild thing, and to spend energy in courting him
was only to lay oneself open to pain. Once, long ago, a child
had asked Silverhair for help and he had refused her.
Perhaps it was his punishment to find himself unable to give
now because this child was unable to ask.

"He does not sing?" asked the woman.

"He doesn't use words at all—" said Silverhair bitterly.
Her eyes showed swift pity, as swiftly veiled.

"Well, perhaps he can stand with the other children and clap out the time—" she began uncertainly, then stopped, pointing. Piper was edging his way around the singers, moving purposefully toward a wooden flute that one of the players had left on the grass.

"Look—"

Silverhair was looking, feeling the pulse pound in his throat as he saw that shining in the child's face again, wondering if that was how he himself had looked the first time he saw a harp. Silent, they watched as Piper knelt, drew his forefinger the length of the instrument —delicately, like a child trying to touch a bubble without breaking it—then set it to his lips and blew.

The first sound was like a crow's cawing. Piper's face crumpled painfully, but he did not release the flute. He seemed to have forgotten that anything else existed in the world. His chest expanded as he breathed in, then there was a sudden clear note like the call of a bird, and the radiance in Piper's face was like another sun rising over the hills.

Silverhair felt his heart shaking in his chest. He knew —he *knew* how that moment of discovery could remake the world! But what could this damaged child do with it? It was almost unbearable to realize that not only a young life, but a unique gift, might have been wasted when the sea wolves destroyed Piper's home.

"Let him stay with the flute players—" he said harshly. "If they will have him. Now teach me what it is that I must sing." He had only known Piper for a little while and owed him nothing. Why was he so afraid to hope he might be healed?

In all the years of Silverhair's wandering, the only person who had ever really touched him had been the Queen of Normontaine. But now other bonds were tightening—an uncertain respect for Julian, and some emotion he could not name for this child. When Caolin's magic cracked Swangold's frame, Silverhair had realized that it was possible to destroy a world, and even the harp's reconstruction could not take that knowledge away from him. He had thought to find safety beneath the Wind Lord's mighty wings, but instead, all his protections were being torn away.

The song leader was gathering his chorus together again.

Silverhair let the sound wash over him, losing himself in the
surge of many voices as once he had lost self-awareness in
the orchestra at the College of Bards.

> *"Summer's golden time is done*
> *With the waning of the sun.*
> *After winter's healing rain,*
> *Summer's joy will come again."*

So they sang, but over the deep blending of voices Silverhair could hear the flutes' sweet piping, and his eyes stung
with unshed tears.

"My daughter, you are very welcome here—" The priestess laid her hand upon Rana's shoulder. "I do not remember when any pilgrims have come from so far away to join in
our ceremonies, and I see that you have passed through
danger and will soon face more. Rest with us, and rejoice,
and the Mother's blessing will follow you."

Rana's throat grew tight and she nodded, afraid to trust
her voice to answer. She had not allowed herself to recognize the dangers of their journey until now, when she was
safe, at least for a little while. The women of Awhai looked
at her curiously as they found places against the wall of the
round earth-house, but their faces were kindly. Rana tried
to smile back at them, and found a place to sit beside Eva.
She was realizing that she had missed the company of other
women more than she knew. With a sudden pang, she
thought of her mother, daring to want her now, when their
quest had reached its goal.

"Some say that the name of our valley means 'the
nest'—the nest of the condor who watches over us here
—but the stories handed down from mother to daughter
tell it differently." There was a little murmur of agreement
from the other women, and the priestess smiled. "In the
women's stories, Awhai means 'the Valley of the Moon.'"

Rana returned her smile. With the end of her black shawl
draped over her head, and the moon-blossom ornament
gleaming silver on her breast, the woman reminded the girl
of the priestess who had come down from Bongarde to
preside over her puberty ritual. Rana remembered it vividly now—the excitement of being the center of attention, the

security of being part of a tradition of women stretching back to before the Cataclysm, the dimly felt awareness of mystery. It was through her mother that her inheritance in that tradition came. It felt strange to be here without her.

"We celebrate Earth our Mother today, and praise Her for the harvest, but though the dance begins at the time between day and night, as this day is between the seasons of the world, we will dance until the moon rises over the rim of the valley and blesses us. Women know that the moon rules the fertility of our bodies, and of the earth as well. We will dance robed in black, for the night is holy, and draw down the moon's power into the land."

Her gaze moved slowly around the circle, as she greeted the women, questioning them to make sure they were fit for what would be a strenuous night. Rana slowly realized that though the priestess knew the other women, she did not live among them—she belonged to the Shrine of the Lady of Earth that Julian was looking for. Rana bit back the impulse to ask the woman if the Earthstone was being kept there. She had no right to ask such a question. But she could not help imagining the surprise and pleasure that would fill Julian's face if she could bring the Jewel to him. He would be glad then that he had let her come along!

"And you, child—are you with us of your own will? You were not brought up in our traditions, and you need not join in our ritual just because Lion Claw has told you to!"

With a start Rana realized that the priestess was speaking to her. Quickly she shook her head.

"Nobody forced me," she said clearly. "Your ways are enough like those of my own land so that I feel at home here; if you are willing to have me in your dance I will be honored to join you." From across the room Eva smiled approvingly. The older woman's bones were too stiff for dancing, but she knew the chants, and would be singing with the rest.

"Then there are questions I must ask you," said the priestess briskly. "Are you with child, or in your bleeding time?"

Rana felt her face flushing as red as her hair. How could anyone even ask—was it because she had been traveling with three men? But *they* hardly knew she was female! Fragmented visions of Frederic or Silverhair or Julian trying to court her came and fled before the blush had faded. To Frederic she was like a sister, Silverhair could have been her father, and Julian thought she was a pest. For some reason that thought set her blushing again.

"No! I've never even—" Rana bit off the words. It was no business of these strangers whether she had ever lain with a man. She shook her head again. "I'm not on the rag now," she went on. "We've been traveling steadily for over a month, and when my moon-time came there was hardly any show at all."

"That often happens when a woman's body is worked hard," said the priestess. "A protection from nature to conserve the body's resources and prevent a child from starting which could not be carried to term."

Rana sat back with a sigh. Now that it was explained she realized that missing her moon-time had been worrying her.

"Clearly you are strong and healthy," the priestess went on. "We will be glad to have you among our dancers."

"What must I do?"

"The dance step is simple enough. The others will show you. You will be among those who bring in the offerings." She continued with her instructions, and Rana sat back, took a deep breath, and tried to relax.

The Women's Lodge was perhaps fifty feet across, with a conical thatched roof set on a framework of adobe-plastered woven branches. To gain height the foundation had been dug out, so that one had the sense of being cradled by the Earth Mother half-underground. Here the women of the community held their rites of passage; girls spent the month of their first moon-time being instructed here. But any woman could stay in the Lodge if there was trouble in her family or she needed a little time alone. Rana's mother had a small cabin near Registhorpe that she used for the same purposes, but Rana found herself envying the sense of community she felt here.

She listened carefully to the instructions—how they were to dance, where they were to go—wondering if she should have gotten out of it when she had the chance. What if she did something wrong? Would it spoil the ceremony? But soon she found herself going with the rest of them to bathe in a pool fed by a warm spring, draping and pinning the length of black cotton around her, taking up the basketry platter heaped with acorn meal and finding her place in the line of dancers.

The drums that had throbbed all afternoon were still. Northeastward the red sandstone escarpments of the Topa Topa glowed in the light of the sinking sun, deepening from a soft rust color to vivid rose. Birds called sweetly, flickering across the sky and settling into the trees. The creatures of daylight were seeking their rest, and it was not yet time for the children of night to awaken. The hush that filled the valley became almost a palpable thing. Rana breathed carefully, afraid to disturb it. This was the threshold between night and day, which was also the doorway between the inner and outer worlds. Anything could happen now.

The line of black-clad women moved slowly down the path until they could see the dancing floor, surrounded by the silent crowds who had come for the festival. By this time everyone had turned south, their eyes on the rounded silhouette of So-ui-tup-tup, the Mother Mountain. The sun dropped behind the western hills; for a little while the upper slopes of the mountains glowed like fire. Then their high color faded, and there was only a rosy radiance in the sky that deepened to soft purples and blues as the world lost even the memory of the sun.

And still they waited. Rana's eye followed the gracious curves of the mountain. In silhouette, it could have been a woman indeed, lying on her side at rest. There was the sweet curve of hip and thigh, the swell of a breast, the shape of a head cradled on one arm. A shiver ran through the crowd. Then the woman next to Rana grasped her arm and pointed to the mountain.

Rana squinted—where the figure's "forehead" curved inward something was glimmering. A fire? No, the light was too pale. As she watched, the radiance increased, and she realized it was an early star.

"Behold the Mother wakes and smiles on us!" came the shout from below.

"Let the festival begin!"

The star glowed like a promise in the translucent purple of the evening sky. Julian took a deep breath and let it go, for a moment dizzied by the pungent scents of sage and sycamore diffusing through the cooling air. For a measureless moment there was nothing but beauty in the world.

Then a sudden thunder of drumming shook the air, startling him to full awareness again. Flutes twittered in answer, Julian jerked around, every nerve responding with a rush of energy, and Alonzo Lion Claw, next to him, grinned. The drummers were stationed facing outward in the center of the dancing floor, but the flute players were just now filling in the space beside the platform with the harvest offerings, followed by the singers. Softly at first the strains of the festival song drifted across the cleared ground, growing ever louder as more and more voices joined in.

The singing ended. Immediately the drumming changed to a swift *DUM, dum, dum, DUM, dum, dum,* which set the blood leaping again. The draperies around the platform were flung back and bizarre figures crawled from underneath it. More creatures rushed into the circle from outside, the basic human shape disguised and distorted by masks and costumes into something that was neither human nor animal. Their bronzed bodies were painted with red and yellow and black; oddly cut garments in the same colors were edged with bits of white shell; they were crowned by fantastic headdresses of horn and straw and fur.

Squealing and gobbling in high-pitched voices, they cavorted about the circle, juggling fruit and knives and whatever they could snatch from their audience, leaping and rolling acrobatically, teasing the watchers and each other with gestures so funny that one forgot their obscenity. As the light faded the people had lit torches, and the shadows of the clowns leaped across the packed earth of the dancing floor in antic imitation of their originals. Shrieks of laughter followed their progress around the circle, and it was only gradually that Julian realized they were being followed by other dancers less human—the horse and the stag, the coyote and the great condor of the valley with its mighty protecting wings.

He took a deep breath, recognizing the images of the Guardians, and wondered abruptly where Lady Madrone was now. What would these people do if she came down from whatever hidden ravine she had sheltered in and joined in the dancing? Blinking at the riot of color and shadow in the torchlight, he was not sure that anyone would even realize who she was. For a moment his ears rang with echoes, as if the merriment of the crowd had spread to the hills. Or was the ceremony in the valley only a reflection of the revelry of the other kindreds at this balance point of the year?

When he focused again on the center of the circle there were four new figures there. The chieftain saw the question in his face and pointed to the nearest, a big man enveloped in a bearskin robe.

"They are the leaders of the medicine societies—that's the one we call the Bear doctor, who can take the shape of a bear in war. Beside him is the Rain doctor—" He indicated another man in a garment covered with shells. "He's a weather-worker. The woman beside him is our greatest Curing doctor. She knows the name and use of every herb that ever grew."

"And who is the fourth one?" asked Julian, motioning toward a slim figure beyond the drummers.

"Rattlesnake doctor—" said Alonzo. "You'll see!"

Julian leaned forward to get a better look and was dazzled as someone tossed a torch into the air. He shut his eyes against the glare, but the leaping figures of the clowns seemed etched on his eyelids. He rubbed at his eyes, and after a moment the sensation passed. Then he forgot it entirely, for the drumbeat was changing again.

The clowns crouched down next to the drummers. Torchlight blossomed on the hillside, and Julian saw a procession of dark figures winding toward the dancing floor. As they came closer, he recognized one flame-colored head among the others and understood how Rana had spent her afternoon. Behind the women four men were carrying an image of wood and asphaltum decorated with white shells. As the women circled the dancing floor they carried it to the platform. Now he could see that the form was female, darkly shining in the firelight, with staring eyes. One by one, the women set their baskets before it.

"Momoy!" cried the people, "Momoy!"

Swaying like reeds in the wind, the women began to sing.

> *"Strength of stone, depth of earth,*
> *Mother Momoy gives us birth.*

Fur and feathers, scales and skin,
All Her children are our kin. . . ."

Mother Gaea. Julian hailed Her silently by the name the Master had taught him, *Lady of Earth, bless me!*

"Sup and Momoy!" the crowd echoed him. "Sky Father and Earth Mother keep us safe through the year!"

The women began to move, forming a line that spiraled around the drummers and back upon itself, sinuous, hypnotic, like a dark serpent with shifting scales. Julian found himself beginning to sway, back and forth, to the *DUM, dum, dum, DUM, DUM* of the drumming. He saw Rana go past him in the line, her loose hair flaming like another torch in the uneven light. The spiral broke; she turned and reached out to him; his feet moved without his will and as the line re-formed he was drawn into the dance.

Inward and outward the spiral turned. Caught in that pattern of flickering light and dancing bodies, Julian found the boundaries between his senses thinning—he *saw* the drumbeat, he *heard* the step-together-stepping of his feet, the flaring torchlight burned along every vein. He shook his head, trying to clear it. He had only once or twice in his life drunk enough to affect his thinking—he disliked the sensation of losing control.

But he saw the same glazed look on the faces around him, and there were no vats in the land large enough to intoxicate so many. It was no drug, but the dance and the drumming that had bound them together, excitement feeding excitement until it exploded into ecstasy. He reeled with the inebriation of every man and woman on the dancing floor as if they had all shared one skin.

At some unspoken signal the spiral straightened, pulled back until two concentric circles ringed the floor. They parted to let something emerge from beneath the platform —an odd, humped shape that Julian recognized in a moment as the Rattlesnake doctor, carrying a skin sack that bulged and quivered with the movement of something inside.

The shaman was a woman, he saw now—thin, boneless, ageless, with glittering eyes, clad in a single patchwork garment of snakeskins that left her arms bare. With a curious gliding motion she moved into the center of the circle, turning slowly to show the sack she held. Then she set it on the hard ground and began to make sinuous passes above it with her long arms.

"Hear, Goddess!" she cried harshly, and the people echoed her.

"Near, Goddess!" She fumbled with the sack's closure.

"Fear, Goddess!" Her hand made a swift dart inside the bag; returned grasping something that twisted sluggishly around her arm. It made no sound, but Julian's skin chilled as he recognized the vicious triangular head of the rattlesnake.

"Dear Goddess!"

Again the Snake doctor reached into the bag; again she drew out a serpent. The drumming had dulled to a soft thunder. Matching its beat, the shamaness lifted her two arms, braceleted now with the snakes' sliding coils, and began to dance. A breathy shudder of sound swept the crowd. Julian felt the changed tension, the retuning of shared exaltation to a pitch sharpened by danger, fear pushing consciousness beyond the limits of everyday.

One of the priestesses knelt before the Snake doctor, arms outstretched. The shamaness bent, a serpent flowed from her arm to that of the priestess. An Awhai warrior with glazed unseeing eyes held out his hands to receive the other. The shamaness danced to her bag again. In a moment more rattlesnakes wreathed her arms, and were bestowed on her tranced followers.

The circles had dissolved into whirling knots of dancers now, with snakes or without them; each one stamped and swayed in a private ecstasy. With a little shock that almost brought him out of his own trance, Julian saw Frederic spin by, a snake lying upon his shoulders like a collar of office. Someone laughed softly beside him; he turned and saw Alonzo Lion Claw.

"Now do you understand the power that is here? Does it move you?" The chieftain's eyes were glittering.

Julian took a deep breath, feeling the heart leap in his chest as the drumming grew louder.

"I am flesh and blood—" he gasped. "It moves me. . . ."

"But you have not embraced Momoy's messenger—"

Wordless, Julian stared back at him. It was true, there was some part of him that still could not give itself completely to the trance and accept the unity. Was this a test? He thought he had the courage to grasp the serpent in his hand—but he knew that it would be hard behind the wicked head, as an enemy.

"No, you must not force it—" said Lion Claw, reading him. "The snakes must be touched only in love. But this is the easy way. If you cannot do this, then you must make a greater surrender. And you *will* do it," he went on, "for the mark of the chief is on you. Then you will come into your power. . . ."

Julian was still searching for some answer when the moon lifted above the southern ridges like a silver shield. The focused passion of the dancers exploded in a great shout of triumph. For a moment they stood, arms straining upward in ecstasy, while here and there a snake's weaving head traced a circle in the sky. Then, one by one, they sank down, palms pressed flat against the ground, and the energy they had raised flowed into the earth again.

Earth that had vibrated to dancing feet and drumbeats shook to the rush of power. Then the dance floor steadied, but the energy that had passed through it rippled outward like the wave formed when a stone is thrown into a pool. North and south it passed, east and west, vibrating through the latticed molecules of stone. It passed through the faults and joinings of the bedrock that supported the soil, and where the stress of plate against plate was greatest, the pulse of power shook them free. A million tiny tremors quivered through the land.

And then, all tension eased; there was only the stillness that follows passion, and the sweet night breath of earth at balanced rest.

TWELVE

Julian's nostrils flared and he grimaced as he got his first full breath of sulfur-scented steam. Someone laughed —Julian identified him as one of the lesser priests by the single condor feather in his hair, and he forced his own features to calm again. He had a distinct feeling of being on trial, and was determined to give nothing away. Frederic gave a supportive squeeze to his arm, and they picked their way down the last few rough steps to the flat space by the pool.

On the day after the festival they had taken the trail that wound up the canyon northwest of the valley, camping that night beneath spreading live oak trees in a clearing near the hot spring. Partway up the canyon wall a great slab of granite had broken away, and the fallen sections of stone, abraded to smoothness by centuries of weathering, caught the superheated waters as they gushed from the mountainside. Men had brought more rocks to fill the crevices, so that now a smooth bowl of water steamed beneath the mountain's overhang. Julian was uncomfortably reminded of the great cauldron in which his foster mother used to boil stew. At the thought his stomach growled in sympathy, for he had been fasting since the morning before. He hoped that whatever came out of this experience would be worth all the discomfort!

The overhang was not quite a cave. Beyond the great boulders and the fringe of trees behind them, Julian could see the glowing azure of the afternoon sky. Two birds flew past, in sharp silhouette against the blue, and he envied their freedom.

"This is the sacred pool," said the shaman. Julian thought he had been one of the clowns at the festival, but the man was wholly serious now. "In these waters you will find healing for all ills and purification from all sins."

Julian was not sure just what misdeeds he was supposed to be cleansed from—his life so far had not offered much opportunity for spectacular sinning. The worst evils were those of which he accused himself—his failure to protect his companions from danger, his failure to love Silverhair as he should, his failure to develop the gifts of the spirit that he would need if he was to rule Westria. But that was why he was going through with this, he supposed—not just to earn his way to the Earth Mother's shrine and the Earthstone, but because Lion Claw's talk of visions had revived the old longings for the spiritual world.

"What must I do?" he asked.

"Take off your old clothes," said the shaman. "Both you and they must be cleansed before you wear them again. We will give you another garment to wear at the shrine."

At the other end of the pool was a bench. Julian made his way over to it and, feeling a little self-conscious about stripping in front of so many clothed strangers, fumbled with the clasps of his vest.

"Let me—" Frederic had followed him. Julian started to protest, but the other boy shook his head. "No—they accept me as an apprentice priest. I want them to see that I honor you."

Julian sighed and lowered his arms, turning passively as Frederic deftly undid the clasps and helped him out of the vest.

"When you were with their shamans," he said in a low voice, "did you find out anything about this ceremony?"

"A little . . . Lift your arms. . . ." Frederic pulled Julian's shirt over his head. "The cavern is nearby. When you've bathed they'll take you there—it should be around sunset by then."

"Then what?" Julian sat down on the stone bench and held out one foot so that Frederic could unlace his high boot and pull it off.

"I'm not too sure. All I could find out was that they give you a drink—toloache they called it—and then the vision comes."

Julian stared at him. "I don't like that very much. I don't even like drinking wine, and smoking grass hardly affects me. If seeing the Lady of Earth depends on some herb giving me a vision, I think we've come a long way for nothing at all."

"That should be the least of your worries," Frederic said reluctantly as he tugged at the second boot. "From what some of the younger men said, the drink can be dangerous. Maybe they were only trying to impress me, but they said that if the dose is wrong the vision seeker dies."

Julian swallowed, remembering the ambivalence in Lion Claw's references to Caolin. How easy it would be for them to do the Blood Lord's work for him by giving Julian an overdose of toloache. No one could prove murder, not when he was running the same risk their own young people ran. He lifted his head and met the shaman's level gaze. He sensed no enmity there, as he had sensed none from Lion Claw. Should he trust his judgment or his fears?

"I don't think they want to kill me—" he said in a low voice. "They could have done that any time during the past three days. In fact they could have left us all at the mercy of Malin Scar. Anyway, the one Caolin is after is Silverhair. No one here has any reason to get rid of *me*. . . ."

"As far as we know," said Frederic darkly.

"Well, it's a little late for me to back out now." Julian stood up and began to unlace his breeches. "For someone who spent half the festival dancing around with a rattle-snake draped across his shoulders you're certainly being a pessimist."

Frederic blushed. "Don't remind me. When I woke up the next morning and remembered what I had done I broke out in a cold sweat, just lying there thinking about it." He tugged at first one leg of the breeches, then the other, until Julian could step out of them.

"It's just that at the College of the Wise they scared us with all kinds of warnings about what can happen to people who take spirit herbs without training. It's like sending someone who has never been out of Laurelynn into the forests of the Ramparts without weapons or a map to find his way home," he went on.

"Well, I'll have to take my chances," said Julian. "If they taught you any prayers for this at the College, you can say them for me."

"I can do better than that—" said Frederic. "They say

that often people don't remember what they see in the
vision, so a priest stays in the cavern to listen to what they
describe. I told the shaman that I was your priest, and he
said that I can stay with you." He got to his feet again. "The
Guardians know I would rather serve you this way than
with a sword!"

Julian reached out and took his arm. "Thank the Maker
of All for that. Anyway, it's true—and I think this may be
only the first of many times you will act as priest for me.
Guard my back, Frederic! I need you more now than ever in
battle!" He held Frederic's blue gaze with his own and saw
the trouble in his friend's face change to a bright resolve
that was close to joy. Then he stripped off his clout, strode
to the edge of the pool, and, holding his breath to keep from
crying out as he felt the heat, stepped in.

For a moment the blood roared in his ears, and he
breathed carefully, fighting to keep from passing out. He
had not traveled so far to drown in a mineral spring. After a
few moments, his body began to adjust to the temperature,
and he eased down, resting the back of his head against one
of the stones and letting arms and legs float free. He was
already becoming used to the rotten-egg smell of the water,
and as the steamy air eased throat and lungs, the heated
water began to unknot muscles that had been tensed since
he left Bongarde.

With eyes half-closed, Julian could see the wavering
shape of his own limbs beneath the water, greenish in the
glimmering light. Vision confirmed the feeling that his flesh
was flowing away. He was becoming some amorphous
creature of the deeps; he had returned to the womb of earth
to be reborn! Why bother with a drug, he wondered
vaguely, when simply soaking in this wonderful water was
enough to induce such a transformation?

Above the rush of the water he was dimly aware of the
regular hissing of rattles—he supposed that drumheads
would have lost their tension near all this steam—and soft
chanting. He did not need to understand the words. They
were all one with the voice of the spring and the whisper of
wind in the sycamores, that told him, *"Hush, rest, peace, be
still. . . ."*

Julian eased farther down into the water, tipping his head
back so that his hair floated free. In a cleft in the rock above

him the flowers of a paintbrush plant splashed bright coral against the grey. Sweat rolled off his face and he rinsed it. Licking his lips, he tasted the rank minerals in the waters and swallowed some, making it part of himself as he had become part of the pool. The current caressed him—the heat inhibited an erection, but his skin throbbed all over, as if his entire body had become a sexual organ plunged into earth's passionate womb.

He shuddered with pleasure, and for a moment he was holding the Lady of Westria, and his spirit and the water and rock and sky were all one.

A hand closed on his shoulder. Julian's eyes flew open, and he realized that he had almost slid under. Frederic heaved again, and Julian put out a hand to push himself upright.

"You'd better get out of there before you faint," Frederic said severely.

Unable to speak, Julian nodded, got his feet under him, and stood up. His head spun, and his limbs felt leaden. It was time to get out indeed. But he felt a touch of sadness as Frederic hauled him the rest of the way out of the water, and it occurred to him to wonder, if the ritual bath could produce such a reaction, what the ritual was going to do.

With infinite care, Momoy's priestess poured dark liquid from the earthenware crock into a small pottery cup whose surface had been polished by the touch of many hands. Both the crock and the cup bore the incised outlines of long, trumpet-shaped flowers to which traces of white color still clung.

"Some of our seekers call this the moonflower, the flower of vision," said the woman, tracing the flower shape with a callused finger. "Perhaps this is the true reason why Awhai is called the Valley of the Moon. . . ." She set the cup on the floor of the cave and closed her eyes.

Julian saw the expression drain from the woman's face, and he tensed, knowing that his own test was coming now. The effect of the hot spring had lasted through the ride up the mountain—a drowsy acceptance that had kept him from worrying about what lay ahead of him, until now. . . .

The shamaness lifted her hands. They trembled slightly,

but Julian could not tell whether it was from the passion of her concentration or age.

"O Thou Spirit whose sigh is the air, whose soul is the fire of the sun, whose blood runs through the veins of Thy body, the earth—hear me! May Thy power fill this cup, and as this man drinks of it, may it fill him. O Thou who hast made all things, may this man see the truth of Thy making! May the vision that comes to him be the truth that he needs to see. . . ."

The priestess brought down her hands with sudden force, as if she were physically forcing the power into the cup. Then her eyes opened. Glittering, they fixed Julian's. She held out the cup.

"With a pure heart may you drink. With pure eyes may you see!"

Julian felt a little lurch in his belly as he took the cup, and reminded himself not to confuse the effects of the drug with those of fear. He took a deep, steady breath, then another, as the Master of the Junipers had taught him. Then he bowed to the shamaness and to Frederic, who was watching him with wide, worried eyes, and drank.

The taste was bitter, as he had expected, and acrid enough to suck the moisture from his mouth, liquid though it was. Julian drank the contents of the cup in one long swallow and handed it back to the priestess, meeting her eyes a little defiantly. He knew that the woman would be watching his reactions—the dose must be judged carefully, and might be repeated several times if he had not reached his tolerance.

Through the narrow mouth of the cave he could see the last lovely colors of the sunset ebbing with the heat of the day. Already little lamps were flickering in the crevices of the cavern, casting a fitful illumination on the designs painted in black and white and red on the rock walls. Julian supposed he would have plenty of time to look at them. He licked dry lips and swallowed, then resumed the steady rhythm of his breathing. This one thing at least he was good at—he knew how to be still.

Time passed.

Julian's mouth grew drier and he gulped eagerly at the cup when the shamaness offered it again. But the liquid brought no relief. Only now he did not mind it—he realized suddenly the humor of a drink that made your mouth dry. He ought to share the joke with Frederic; he roused himself enough to say so, and Frederic tried to laugh. That was even funnier. Julian grinned conspiratorially at the priestess and saw the woman's eyes glitter in answer like those of some great bird.

Her flickering shadow was like a bird's too—the movement of her robes in the lamplight was like unfolding wings. Vaguely Julian realized that the opening to the cave was dark now, speckled with the cold gleam of stars, and he wondered how much time had passed. But it did not matter. He smiled benignly upon the priestess and Frederic.

His heart beat slow and steady as the deep pulse of the earth. It seemed to him that he could feel the earth turning beneath him. Time had slowed. The watchful "I" within noted his reactions. His stillness had nothing to do with sleep, for he was capable of infinite attention. That shadow, for instance, was pulsing with a green radiance—he focused upon it and saw it detach itself from the shape of the priestess and slither across the wall. A red wheel like the circled cross of Westria turned slowly. Now green and red flashed alternately upon his retina, blobs and zigzags and loops of color outlined in lines of golden light. One shape gave birth to another—alien forms that nonetheless had meaning—some cell-deep memory recognized the energy patterns of the Guardians who had been danced at the festival. He giggled unexpectedly as the rabbit shape hopped across the floor.

"What do you see?" asked Frederic anxiously.

With effort, Julian focused on his friend, and saw the same lines of light shining within—an entire body of brilliance coexisting with the flesh he knew.

"I see you," he croaked. "Your spirit shines through your skin." With double vision he saw color flush Frederic's cheeks and radiance flare around him. And as he saw and understood, he was aware that he saw himself seeing. Once the blush had faded, Frederic's face showed something close to fear.

"Don't worry—" said that separate observer aloud. "I'm still in control." He had been afraid that the drug would not affect him. So far the effects had been very interesting, but he was still master of his mind.

The priestess raised one eyebrow, poured a precise half cupful of the dark liquid, and held it out to him.

"Your will is very strong," she said to Julian. "Do not fight the drink this time."

Had he been fighting it? Some sense that normal consciousness did not know brought the woman's thought to him— *"No one has ever remained aware for so long! This dose is near the limit, but he must go all the way!"* A remnant of caution held Julian's hand, then the woman repeated her command, and perhaps mind and body were more detached from each other than he had thought, for without willing it, he took the cup and drank again.

This time the effect was immediate. A giant hand ripped consciousness from his control. Julian was still an observer, but now he looked down on his body from a spot near the roof of the cavern. He saw it jerk and mutter incoherently. Frederic grabbed its leg as it staggered upright, but Julian had no time to worry about what might happen to it, for the bright forms were flocking around him and bearing him away.

Julian fought them. But for each glittering image he repulsed, three more fluttered around him, darker shadows that shaped his deepest fears. The black eyes of ravens glittered with malice; a heaving mass of serpents slithered toward him; spiders descended in a suffocating cloud. Panicked, he tried to scream, and never knew what garbled sound tore from the throat of the body he had left below.

"No!" All his being shrieked denial. Like a lark arrowing free of the falcon's clutch, his essence burst free. Far away, a hoarse voice muttered disjointedly, but that had nothing to do with Julian. His awareness cast about for some point of reference and found something that he recognized as Frederic, though it burned like an altar flame. He hovered near it, letting that light chase the shadows away.

"Frederic!"

The light flickered, then increased in radiance. *"Julian —is that you?"*

"I think so. . . . Apparently the priestess got the dose right finally. . . ."

"What do you see?"

Maintaining the contact with Frederic, Julian allowed his consciousness to drift outward. Shapes still stirred around him, but the world through which they moved was composed of lines of jeweled light. The patterns varied in extent and complexity, but they were in essence the same—the same plan of creation repeated with endless variations throughout this world. And if that was so here, then perhaps it was the same in the world of manifestation, for those who had eyes to see.

Julian willed his awareness to extend, sensed more entities he could identify as human, and among them Rana's blue flame and a violet glow that he recognized as Silverhair. He was beginning to understand the nature of this new existence now. To go somewhere, it was only necessary to sense the currents of energy that led toward it and move with them. Consciousness quested beyond the human souls. The chaparral that clothed the mountainside was a glimmer of light, and with a little effort Julian found he could see through it to the crystalline structure of the underlying stone.

The shapes that had harried him had drawn back, but now another form approached him—like one of the tree patterns, yet far more brilliant, with a burning core like that of a human soul. Julian drew back watchfully. The shape extended toward him.

"Don't you know me, Prince of Men?"

Like a tree and like a human— *"Are you one of the Guardians?"* he asked cautiously.

There was a sense of disappointment, then laughter.

"How could you know—" came the thought, *"you are like a cub just learning to see. . . . I am the Madrone, and I can guide you through this wilderness as well as through the wilds of the world."*

Julian moved toward her. *"Show me—"*

He had a sense that they were moving upward, away from earth's surface. A confusion of details resolved into a pattern, which became part of a larger design. Julian saw Westria laid out before him in lines of light. He strained to get farther away, seeking to see the whole earth, for it came to him then that if all patterns were only part of something still larger, then from a sufficient distance, one could see all. . . . His spirit strained for that knowledge beyond knowledge, but Lady Madrone held him.

"*I am a child of earth. I may not go so far, and your time for such knowing is not yet!*"

"*Then show me what you may. . . .*"

"*I am commanded to bring you to the one you are seeking here.*"

Julian allowed himself to be drawn after her, and now he saw the earth below him as a shimmering multicolored glow—amber and russet, green and dark brown and a clear pale gold. Slowly the colors swirled. He felt himself being drawn downward, inward. Sight became sound became taste, distilling at last into a single sense that his consciousness perceived as words.

"*Child of my womb . . . What do you want of me?*"

Julian's awareness twisted painfully with a momentary sharp vision of the mound of earth where the body of his mother had been laid. That was his mother—earth of earth indeed. Then the colors around him shaped a face—dark eyes framed by masses of dark hair. Memories buried too deep for words wrenched from him an anguished protest.

"*Why did you leave me? Why did you go away?*"

"*I have always been with you. From Me your substance came and to Me it will return. What more do you ask of Me?*"

Julian's being vibrated with an agony of loss. In another dimension, his body began to convulse; the shamaness swore and grabbed him, forcing her fingers down Julian's throat to make him vomit the rest of the drug before his lungs failed.

Unknowing, his spirit struggled. After a moment's hesitation, the blaze of energy that was the Lady of the Madrones swirled around him, pattern imposing pattern until consciousness responded to will. With a mighty effort Julian recalled himself and his quest. The question formed and was directed.

"*I seek the Earthstone. . . .*"

"*Take it—you have the right.*"

"*Soil knows nothing of it, nor the roots of trees,*" came the thought of Lady Madrone.

"Is it in one of your shrines?"

"When the power of the Jewels exploded, each element sought its own element again. Deep within Me the Earthstone came to rest."

"If it is buried, how shall I take it?" thought Julian.

"Long ago, men delved beneath the mountains. Those passages remain."

The body in the cavern convulsed again, and a bitter liquid splattered the floor. Julian felt the patterns of light blur around him and fought to retain his focus on the presence below.

"Which mountain?" he demanded frantically.

Faintly the answer came— *"The Earthstone sought its own element by the straightest way. It is in the mines at the roots of the Red Mountain now. . . ."*

Some other power was dragging at him like a fisherman pulling in his line. Julian fought it, exploding outward, seeking the Red Mountain and the stone. Lady Madrone sped after him. A murky glow surrounded the mountain, but he had no time to scout it. Desire carried him forward; red terror engulfed him, he tried to escape, could not, then Lady Madrone extended her last strength and jerked him free.

Skeins of light unraveled around them. Julian fell inward, in an endless screaming spiral that brought him with one last convulsion into his body again.

The taste of terror filled Julian's mouth. Blurred vision showed him the grim face of the priestess. Frederic's eyes were dilated with fear. As pain shuddered through his awakening limbs, Julian forced stiff lips to form words.

"The Red Mountain—the Stone—is in the mines!"

Then a darkness that was wholly of the body crushed him, and he knew no more.

Something had breached his warding.

Caolin struggled up from the depths of sleep, heart pounding, blinking at the shadows his little lamp cast upon the stone wall. Senses that were not physical quested outward, marking the perturbation in the darkly glowing sphere with which he had surrounded his fortress. But already it was steadying, and there was no alien presence within. Whatever had come through had managed to break free of the entrapment spell.

And that was more disturbing than the breakthrough. He had not thought there was any entity strong enough to escape once the trap had closed. The invisible barriers of his warding should hold any spirit, just as the walls of Blood Gard would hold fast any man or beast who came in.

But something had escaped it—no, two somethings, for now he traced the trail of the second presence that had wrenched the first one away. A human male, and a spirit of the forest—the sorcerer read the traces their energies had left in passing as a tracker would interpret a bent blade of grass or an upturned stone.

The tree spirit did not matter—obviously it was some entity the other sorcerer had compelled to his service —what concerned Caolin was the man.

Except for the Master of the Junipers, he knew of no one in Westria who might breach his barriers, and his watchers told him that the Master was slowly recuperating at Juniper Cottage. Besides, this intrusion had come not from the west, but from the south. Caolin felt his skin chill, and reached for his cloak. In the south there was a sorcerer with more than enough power. *Katiz . . .*

But it was impossible.

Shivering, Caolin pushed his feet into slippers and took the lamp from its niche in the wall. He opened the door of his sleeping chamber and made his way down the winding stair to his temple, using the lamp to light the candles there. The reassuring glitter of gold and silver winked from the corners of the room. The western altar was ornamented with silver shells and set with turquoise and amethyst. To the east was an altar of carved crystal. In the north black basalt gleamed, inset with golden sigils, while in the south, red gold had been worked into forms of flame.

The sorcerer went to the southern altar, lit the red candle, and set incense to smoking—a heavy, musky rose. Then he stood back and took a deep breath, another, steadying his breathing, focusing his will.

In the south there had once been a sorcerer, who had taught Caolin all he knew. Katiz had explored the limits of darkness and shown his pupil the way to perfect power. And in the end Caolin had forced his teacher back into that empty kingdom and barred the door. For all he knew, the body of Katiz might live still, but for the spirit there could be no return. And that was why it was impossible.

Could another man have discovered the same secrets? Caolin stilled until his body stood like a statue in red stone, drew inward to a single glowing point of power, then made that turning of the spirit that transcends geometry and sent his will southward, toward Awhai—

—And was repelled by another warding that shimmered like moonlight on pearl. It was not so brilliant as the golden glow that surrounded Awahna, but it was strong enough so that without using more energy than he was prepared to expend, the sorcerer could not get in. Caolin withdrew a little, considering that barrier. He should have expected it, for the Autumn Festival was just passed, and the power it had raised had strengthened the warding. Channeling the energy of sufficient numbers, even lesser magicians could erect an effective protecting sphere.

But this was clearly the work of many, not of a single powerful mind. That conclusion soothed some of Caolin's alarm. When the strength of the barrier faded he would break through and eliminate Katiz. Meanwhile, he must look elsewhere for the mind that had troubled him.

Perhaps, he thought, he could find another use for his human instrument, Malin Scar—the man must have had enough time to celebrate his kill. Caolin cast about in the darkness, seeking the sleeping mind of the Shadower.

In the lee of a hill overlooking the road to Awhai a man stirred restlessly in his blankets, tangling them further.

"Malin Scar . . ." the silent voice repeated, calling his soul from the deeps of sleep to that dreaming consciousness in which the contact of mind to mind was most easily attained.

The Shadower grunted, then stilled again. In his dream, he was standing in the entry to the fortress on the Red Mountain, but it was the completed fortress of the sorcerer's vision that rose around him, brooding and terrible, not the half-built walls he had last seen.

"Malin Scar—" The voice seemed to resonate from the very stones. *"Report!"*

"My lord! Forgive me—I need only a little more time! They must leave the valley soon!"

The walls rippled as if a tremor had shaken the stones, but Caolin's voice remained cool, responding with the one word, *"Explain . . ."*

Defenseless in his dream, Malin Scar's dread was palpable. He stumbled through his story, then waited, drawing up his hood to hide his scar.

"Tell me more about the others who were with Silverhair—"

Clearly, this was not the question the Shadower had expected. He straightened and his hood fell back again.

"And Frederic said this other man was his cousin?" Caolin asked when he was done.

The Shadower nodded, seeming to breathe more easily as the pressure of the sorcerer's mind eased. Caolin was thinking furiously, reviewing the tangled family trees of Seagate and the Corona.

"A good fighter," thought Malin Scar, emboldened by his master's silence. *"In the inn he was silent, but on the road he spoke as if he was in command. In the heat of the fight, he called the harper 'uncle,' as well."*

The vision of the fortress blurred and shivered and disappeared in a swirl of scarlet shot with flame. Caught in the maelstrom, Malin Scar cried out, but Caolin had no attention to spare for his fear. By blood, Farin Silverhair could have only one nephew. But the child was dead—as Faris must be also, or why would she not have returned to claim the Crown for him during all these years?

"Describe him. . . ." The command was like thunder.

Malin Scar strove for control, sought desperately in memory for the image of a young man with a stonecutter's muscled shoulders and dark eyes steady in a browned face beneath a fall of dark hair.

It was not the face of Jehan, which Caolin had feared to see. What he read from the Shadower's mind was the atmosphere, and like a dog scenting an enemy on the wind, he recognized the essence of the young man's power.

It was the power that had breached his warding.

It was the power that had come between him and the

harper when he sought him on the road and earlier, when he had attacked Registhorpe in vain.

Untrained, but with a sense of untapped potential that was terrifying, it bore nonetheless a family resemblance to the power that had been in Faris and Jehan.

The world disintegrated in an explosion of rage and fear. But as Malin Scar's consciousness fled to a refuge from which it would not emerge until late the next day, its last thought came fragmented through the sorcerer's fury.

"His name . . . is . . . Julian. . . ."

THIRTEEN

"And then I said what?" Julian asked for the third time.

"You muttered something about the Earthstone being in the mines underneath the Red Mountain," Frederic replied patiently.

Julian shut his eyes again as Eva laid a wet cloth across his brow. Images chased each other across his closed eyelids. Were they fragments of memory, or dream? From somewhere outside came a ripple of harpsong, as purely melodious as the call of a bird. They had told him this was the afternoon after his all-night vigil at the Shrine of the Earth Mother. He found it hard to believe.

"I don't remember," he said with eyes still closed. "The last thing I remember was riding up the canyon on the morning after the festival. But I feel like I've got the great Guardian of all hangovers!"

"It's only to be expected," said Frederic. "The priestess told me that often people have no memory of their experiences. That's why I stayed with you."

"What's the use of having a vision if you don't remember it?" asked Rana. "Especially if it gives you a headache?"

"I imagine that is one reason they don't use toloache at the College of the Wise!" answered Frederic.

"That, and the fact that it nearly killed him——" Eva added tartly. "As my father always used to say, 'Better to walk than ride a crazy horse!'"

Even with eyes closed, Julian could tell that she had moved back to the table where she had spread out her medicines. He could sense all of them, even Silverhair on the porch of the chief's house, as brighter lights within the general soft glow of their shared concern for him. He had felt something like this a few times at festivals, but never at a time like this, when he was so weak and sick that he should have been feeling nothing at all. He wondered if perhaps it was some effect of the drug he had taken. He hoped it would remain when the sickness wore off. If he could keep from being overwhelmed by other people's emotions, it might be very useful to feel them.

"At least we know it wasn't wishful thinking," added Frederic wryly. "No one in his senses would *want* the object of his quest to be located in the middle of his enemy's territory!"

"I don't know why the Lady couldn't have just handed the thing over to Julian! I thought our quest would end here, and now we have to go all the way home again!" complained Rana.

"It would have been nice, wouldn't it?" agreed Frederic. "I don't much fancy walking into the Blood Lord's den either, you know. I wish we knew more about him—about what he can do. I have a feeling that whatever he knows wasn't covered in the course of studies at the College of the Wise!"

"The sorcerer . . ." said Julian, opening his eyes again and squinting at Frederic's confused face. "Lion Claw told me that Caolin had studied with one of their shamans—the 'one they most feared.' If the man is still alive, maybe he can tell us what we need to know."

Frederic gave a snort of disbelief. "Just how do you intend to make him do that? Oh, all right!" he went on as Julian tried to rise. "Only stay quiet—I'll go find out for you. Please, Julian, I promise, just stay still!"

Julian's head was spinning, and he thought that he could not have made it to his feet even if Frederic had refused him. He closed his eyes and let the darkness take him, but the smile on his lips faded, for as consciousness fled, his inner vision saw the figure of the sorcerer blood-red against a midnight sky.

Caolin leaned back in his stone chair and looked at Ordrey, waiting until the man's high color had paled and returned before he spoke again. The construction of the fortress had progressed sufficiently for him to furnish his office with a certain austere luxury that made a satisfying setting for the terror of the man before him. The walls were paneled with redwood, empty shelves waited for the books he was beginning to collect once more. A thick rug the color of spilled burgundy covered the stone floor.

"You have failed twice, Ordrey—once when you let the harper escape you, once when you did not learn the names of those he traveled with. You will not fail me another time. . . ." His voice lingered over the final phrase, making it at once a threat and an assurance, and he was rewarded by seeing the little man lick his lips as if they had suddenly gone dry.

Caolin took a distant satisfaction in his reaction—a small palliative for his shock at the revelation of Malin Scar. Jehan's child lived! He would certainly try to claim his father's throne. How could all Caolin's calculations have ignored that possibility? The mistake bothered him more than the fact. This cub might have a certain rough talent, but without training, what could he do?

"What is my lord's will?" Ordrey did not try to make excuses. At least he had learned *that* was futility.

"Something that should be to your taste, old friend. I want you to go to Laurelynn. Find out if any of our old associates are still in the chancery there. There should be someone—perhaps several—who will either remember past loyalties or be so frightened at the idea they might be revealed that they will find a way to let you look at the archives. And you will know how to read those records far better than they."

In the steady light of the candles, Caolin could see the subtle relaxations in Ordrey's facial muscles that told him the man was beginning to understand. Now that the Blood Lord knew this enemy existed, he could take steps to deal with him. If Julian survived long enough to claim the Crown, he would find the heart of his Kingdom as hollow as a grub-eaten tree. The Blood Lord took a paper from one of the piles on the polished table and held it out to Ordrey.

"Here is a list of the men and women who are now on the Council of Westria, along with their principal deputies. I want you to search the records, Ordrey. Go back as many years as you must, but find out all you can about each one. Everyone has weaknesses—everyone has made some mistake, however small. Even their successes may be used against them. I want to know their alliances, their families, where they are vulnerable . . ."

"I will try—" began Ordrey, and Caolin knew from a tightening of the lips on words unsaid that the man was remembering the secret records that had been kept in Caolin's offices in Laurelynn long ago—records replete with just the kinds of details the Blood Lord was asking for. But Caolin had burned those records himself, the same night he had been cast out by the Council against which he was plotting once more. He would not give in to such emotions again.

"We are fighting a war, Ordrey," said Caolin very gently. "And we will fight it with the weapons I choose. Like a worm in an apple, like a weevil in a loaf of bread, you will make your way through Laurelynn. This child may bluster as he will, but when the time comes for me to reveal myself, I will hold the secret heart of the Council of Westria in the palm of my hand. . . ."

"Well, my son, you can try, but I tell you truly—Katiz has spoken to no one for almost four years." Lion Claw gestured toward the round, brush-thatched house beneath the oak trees, then turned to Julian again.

"Since Caolin's last visit to him?" Julian saw the chieftain nod and understood why the man had agreed to bring them here. For a moment his sight blurred and he blinked rapidly, willing it to clear. He was still a little shaky, but three days had passed since his vision, and a sense of increasing urgency was troubling him more than whatever weakness remained. He had to know!

An old woman whose features were as worn as the rocks of the canyon opened the door to them. The others peered over Julian's shoulder, trying to see inside. "How is he today, Matilija?" asked Lion Claw.

"As usual. This is the young man your message spoke of?" She looked at Julian appraisingly. He flushed under her scrutiny and nodded respectfully.

"I would like to see the one they call Katiz," he said, then indicated the others with a questioning glance.

The woman shrugged. "Oh yes, if they want to they can come in too. It will not matter to *him*. . . ."

Julian blinked as they passed through the low doorway, trying to accustom his eyes to the shadows. For a moment the room seemed empty, and he started to turn, wondering if Lion Claw had tricked them for some reason of his own. Then his eyes adjusted, and he made out a huddled shape in the far corner. There was a stink of urine from the dirt floor.

"Why do you keep him in the darkness?"

"It was his will, when he could still speak to us," said Matilija. "He was afraid of the light. But I have a lamp, if you want to look at him. . . ."

"I remember how Caolin was afraid to be in darkness, in Elaya when I was there—" came Silverhair's harsh whisper as the old woman fumbled with flint and steel.

Julian muttered some answer. Instinctively all of them had lowered their voices, as if they were in the presence of the dead. And when the lamplight flared on the sorcerer's face, he thought that perhaps they were right. Certainly no human life showed in the man's open eyes. Softly he moved forward to squat before Katiz, and felt the others following him.

"What knowledge could do this?" whispered Rana. "What did he teach that the Blood Lord could use against him this way?"

"I don't know what Caolin learned, but I think we are seeing what he could become," answered Frederic. "I've heard"—he swallowed and started again—"at the College there were stories of Masters who had abused their powers. Some of them were among the sorcerers who opposed Julian Starbairn, the Jewel Lord."

"But they weren't like this—" objected Silverhair.

"The ones who would not accept forgiveness were, after the Jewel Lord had used the Stones to conquer them. I was taught that anyone who sought power for its own sake would destroy himself eventually."

"Eventually!" exclaimed Rana. "But what evil did they do until they succeeded?"

"In the time of the Jewel Lord," said Julian very carefully, "they nearly destroyed the world." He looked back at the man they had come to see, who had given no indication that he was even aware of their presence, much less of their words.

Katiz sat huddled against the wall, thin arms clasped around his bony knees. His skin had the papery texture of great age, but the wrinkles that would have given character to the man's face had all been smoothed out, and the skin clung closely to the bones of the skull. Julian tried to meet his gaze, then looked quickly away, for the eyes of the man who had been Awhai's greatest shaman were open, staring fixedly into some void that only he could see.

"Katiz—" he called softly. "Katiz, listen to me. There was a man called Caolin who came to you. He was your enemy, and he is mine too. You must speak to me—you must tell me what he can do. . . ."

For a moment Julian heard only the heavy beating of his own heart in the silence. Then a cackle of derision came from the old woman behind them.

"You may call him till the year turns again and he will not answer you. His body responds enough to drink a little broth when we force it upon him, but his spirit is gone."

"But there must be some way—" Julian sat back on his heels, looking at the others without really seeing them, as the man he wanted to question looked through everything in the room. Even if he could have brought himself to use it, he doubted that even pain could penetrate a barrier that made the boy Piper's withdrawal seem like the flimsiest of veils.

But there was *something* that could reach Piper. . . . Julian straightened, focusing on Silverhair.

"Uncle, will you take Swangold out of her case? There is a power in music, especially in your music, that may reach where nothing else will."

"You want me to play for him?" The harper's face showed his revulsion. "It would be a desecration!"

"Not if he cannot hear you," answered Julian calmly,

"and if he can, it might bring a measure of healing, besides giving us information we desperately need. I cannot order you in a matter concerning your music, but I ask you to do this thing for me."

Silverhair's weathered face creased in a grimace. "When you were still knocked out by that devil's drink I made the Guardians a number of unwise promises, and I suppose I cannot complain if they call some of them in. I will play for you, and I only hope that Swangold will forgive me for using her this way."

Julian raised one eyebrow, wondering about those promises, as the harper dragged the harpcase forward and began to undo its fastenings with elaborate care. Then he felt abruptly ashamed of his surprise at the idea that his uncle should have been concerned about him.

With what seemed agonizing precision, Silverhair checked the tuning of each bronze string. When all twenty rang true, he tipped the instrument back against his shoulder and a flicker of his fingers sent a ripple of music echoing through the room.

"But what should I play?" he asked helplessly.

"Chants of healing—" suggested Frederic, "or maybe songs that Katiz might know. Surely in your travels you've picked up enough melodies!"

"I know the songs of Westria and Elaya, of Normontaine and Aztlan and the Barren Lands," Silverhair said with a flash of pride, "but I do not know what will reach such a man as this one was in his prime."

"Play the music of Elaya, then," said Julian. "I'm sure they must know it here."

Silverhair closed his eyes, and his hands moved upon the strings. A melancholy little tune like a love-lyric emerged, punctuated by odd harmonies as the harper flicked a sharping lever up or down without losing the rhythm of his song.

"This is a melody I played for Prince Palomon," he said softly, "but I learned it in Westria," he added, as if he were only now remembering. "I heard it played by the Royal Consort of Musicians in Laurelynn, and adapted it for the harp so that I could play it for Faris and Jehan. . . .

"Caolin was still faithful then," the harper added meditatively, and Julian checked the sharp question that had been on his lips. Perhaps this was the right music, if it helped them to understand about Caolin.

"I never liked the man—he seemed too cold, too calculating, except sometimes when he was with the King. But no one ever doubted his devotion. I think the Seneschal was a man who needed a master, but after Jehan met my sister, he had little time for Caolin. Maybe that was the beginning of it—not in evil but simply in lack of care. . . ."

The sweet music slowed, shifted imperceptibly into a minor key that dragged at the heart and brought unwilling tears to the eyes.

"And then came the boar hunt, when Jehan was wounded—" Silverhair's voice was harsh with remembered pain. "We thought he would recover, but while Caolin held the reins alone his manipulations somehow slipped over that line between cleverness and dishonor, and when Jehan found out it killed him. Your father was always a man who put trust above all other things—" Silverhair's dark eyes glittered as he looked at Julian. "I think that when he learned the man he loved had betrayed his honor he did not want to live. . . ."

"The King *loved* Caolin?" Rana's voice held mingled revulsion and awe, and Julian looked at her with some sympathy.

"I could not believe it either, not then—" said Silverhair softly. "But I have had nearly twenty years to wonder, and regret. When Jehan died, it nearly destroyed us all. Faris was like a walking ghost—I knew she had never wanted to be Queen, only to love Jehan. I should have understood and tried to help her, but I failed her as badly as anyone. I blamed her for not somehow easing *my* pain! Certainly she did not know how to command Caolin, and she was the only one who might have gained his loyalty, with Jehan gone."

Julian stared at his uncle with mixed emotions. The tale of the wandering harper's long quest for the lost Queen had left him with the impression of an impossible beauty and a perfect devotion to its memory. It had never occurred to him that weakness might have forced his mother into her flight to the mountains, or that guilt might have been the driving force in Silverhair's search for her. Perhaps he himself had felt a need as great as her brother had to believe in Faris's perfection.

"My mother has said that Caolin came to identify his own good with that of Westria, and so he fell—" said Frederic gravely. "He thought he was the only one who could govern the Kingdom."

"He may have been telling truth there," said Julian wryly. "Nothing has run right in Laurelynn since then, as far as I can tell. . . ."

Silverhair shrugged. "That may be, but it does not excuse what happened. Everyone knew the Seneschal and the Lord of Las Costas hated each other. When Elaya attacked us after Jehan died, perhaps Caolin thought too great a victory would give to Brian too great a power—it is hard to imagine what other reason he could have had for what he did then. . . ." The harper's face contorted with the pain of old memories.

"But what did he do?" said Rana into the silence that followed.

"I can tell you that much—I learned it counting my father's scars—" said Frederic. "Caolin betrayed the army of Westria to Prince Palomon. Brian of Las Costas died. My father nearly bled his life away, and as he recovered, he, and my mother, and Farin Harper, now called Silverhair, gathered the evidence that eventually brought Caolin down."

As he spoke, the melody of mourning had changed imperceptibly to a brisker, more bitter tune. Silverhair's voice came in suddenly with a breath of song—

> *"Oh where are the warriors who battled so bravely?*
> *Their lovers and children await them in vain—*
> *The darkness has cloaked the designs of a traitor,*
> *And Westria's victory is vanquished by pain!"*

"I made a song," said Silverhair, "and the people sang it in the streets of Laurelynn. That was the first reason that Caolin had to hate me. I think he hated everyone, then, and perhaps himself worst of all."

"But you didn't know that he had been studying sorcery,

did you—and nobody knew that he had stolen the four
Jewels of Power as well," added Frederic.

"The Master of the Junipers told me that my mother
faced him in the world of the spirit and stopped him from
using them, and in doing so, died," said Julian in a still
voice.

Silverhair looked at him, and then suddenly began to play
once more, a tender, wandering melody that echoed with
longing and transmuted pain. After what seemed a long
time, he spoke again.

"Caolin nearly died too," he said softly. "He is scarred
terribly beneath the disguises he wears. When I met him in
Elaya he seemed emptied of all passions. He saved my life
there. . . ." His tone held wonder, and Julian could understand his confusion at having received mercy from his
enemy.

"Then what turned him against you again?" asked Rana
finally.

"It was ten years later, after Elaya had finally taken
Santibar. I was there with a group from the College of
Bards, and I recognized Caolin in the guise of the Elayan
general. I was the only one who *could* have recognized him,
then. . . . But I told the Lady of Las Costas, and she agreed
to sign the treaty only on condition that he be denied
lordship of the town. So I was the one who cost Caolin
Santibar, and I still do not entirely know why I did it, or
whether it was a good or bad thing. Since then, he has been
my bitter enemy." He frowned, as if at some other, harsher
memory.

"It must have been after Santibar that Caolin began to
come here—" Julian turned to Lion Claw for confirmation,
and the old chief nodded. "He must have been eaten with
hatred, looking for knowledge that would help him to his
revenge. What he had learned at the College of the Wise had
failed him before, and he no longer had the Jewels. What
power did he find instead?" He stared from the chieftain to
the old woman, trying to read their opaque dark eyes.
"What did he learn here in Awhai?"

There was a long silence, broken only by the sound of
their own breathing, and an almost imperceptible rasp of
breath in the lungs of the empty body before them.

"He learned a shaman's blackest sorcery—" said Silverhair harshly. "He nearly killed me with it in Normontaine. At least one of Caolin's powers I have reason to remember—he can distort the very shape of sound with his chanting, he can pervert the very name of song!"

The harper's groan turned somehow into a kind of humming, as if even the thought of Caolin's chant had forced him to imitate it. Julian could feel the pain in him as the harmonies of his chant grew more dissonant—an odd off-key wrongness of sound that set the hair prickling at the nape of his neck and along his arms. Julian tried to find his voice to stop him, but he could not speak. His eyes met Silverhair's anguished gaze, and he realized in horror that once having allowed the evil melody to surface in his consciousness, the bard was being compelled to sing. The others sat transfixed and staring, only their eyes revealing their gathering fear as they realized that they too had been caught by the spell.

Julian looked down looming vistas of darkness swirling with fragments of memory whose subtle distortion became steadily more horrible, like a fair face seen through rough glass. His mother had been a silly woman who betrayed her trust; Silverhair and the others were only with him because they hoped for a slice of the pie that was Westria. Eric and the Master had sent him on this quest hoping he would be killed. Caught unprepared and unshielded, Julian could not break free, and every moment weakened his grasp on the truth he had known.

Then a sound more horrible but less focused than the singing shattered the spell—

Shaking, Julian stared around him, then realized that the silent man before him had shouted—the statue had moved, was moving, the gaunt head swinging back and forth in agony.

"Katiz!" he cried. "Katiz!" He reached out to capture the old man's trembling hands, felt the futile straining of atrophied muscles that could no longer even test the grip of Julian's strong fingers.

"Don't hurt me. . . ." The voice, harsh from disuse, made something deep in the pit of Julian's stomach clench in pain.

"I taught you—everything you wanted—everything —there was . . . please, let me go—"

Julian barely heard that last whisper. He bit his lip, but his grip on the old sorcerer's fingers tightened, holding his consciousness as he held his hands. He could feel the others' returning awareness as a confused relief from pain, and from Lion Claw and the old woman, shock that was mixed strongly with fear.

"What—" he demanded, "what did you teach Caolin? Tell me!"

"There is nothing . . . ," came the answer in a monotone. "Nothing at the heart of the universe—do what you will—" For a moment the dull eyes focused on Julian's face and seemed to realize they were looking at a stranger. "He tricked me into that place and left me there, and I was wrong. At the end of all things there is fear!"

Julian licked dry lips and swallowed, remembering what he had felt when he heard the sorcerer's song. Was this the knowledge that his body had tried to deny by wiping what he had experienced during his vision from his memory?

"If you know that, none of this world's illusions can move you. You will be invulnerable!" The old man was holding onto him now. He leaned forward with a horrible confidentiality and whispered into Julian's ear. "Men will obey you because they sense that, and deep within they are afraid you will strip the illusion from them, too, and leave them alone with the fear. . . ."

A chance fragment of memory showed Julian mariposa lilies blooming on his mother's grave and he clung to the image desperately.

"Silverhair! Silverhair, play something!" His croak drowned out whatever Katiz was trying to say now. "Give us music before he damns us all!"

The harper's fingers stumbled on the strings, but even struck at random, the clean, clear notes of the harp purified the air of the echoes of the sorcerer's song. With more authority, Silverhair touched the harp again, and a major chord built, was modulated, and built again, throbbing powerfully through the silence.

Julian clung to the sweet sound. *Where there is harmony,*

he thought desperately, *there must be something greater than fear!* He felt the solid earth beneath him—that was not evil—nor was the sweet air he gulped in. He tried to visualize sunlight, but there was only darkness here. With a grunt, he struggled to his feet, picked up the old man, and staggered across the room and through the door.

The sunlight was blinding, beautiful! Julian stopped just outside the door, turning his face to the sky in an ecstasy of affirmation. For a long moment he stood so, breathing deeply of the scented air, and then the wasted body he held convulsed in his arms and Katiz began to scream.

Julian gripped him more tightly, not knowing what else to do.

"Bring him back in, Julian—" came Frederic's shaken voice in his ear. "I think it's the light that he fears!"

Julian nodded and turned back to the dark doorway, kneeling to lay the old man down just inside. Hills and sky shone like a promise through the oblong door frame, but Katiz was in shadow. He whimpered and tried to curl himself into fetal position with his back to the door.

"It's all right, old one—" whispered Julian. "No one will hurt you now. . . ."

"Burning . . . burning . . ." muttered Katiz.

"It's only sunshine. You need to get used to it again." Julian patted him awkwardly, thinking that he had been foolish to panic so. No wonder the old man thought he was burning—he had been sitting in darkness for four years!

"It is a lie," said Katiz more calmly. "There is no light. I *know.*"

His words had a dull certainty that made Julian seek quick reassurance through the doorway. Then he sat back and looked up at the others.

"He doesn't want to see," said Rana wonderingly.

Julian swallowed sickly. She and Frederic were looking at Katiz with simple awe that anyone could choose to know only the darkness, but in Silverhair's eyes he read a guilty awareness that reflected what must be in his own—that the certainty of despair could hold a seduction powerful enough to make a man surrender up his very soul.

He forced his voice to obey him. "There was a man called Caolin—maybe he came here as Lord Sangrado, but you would have known his true name. What tricks did you teach him, Katiz? Where does he get his power?"

Katiz shook his head frantically and tried to burrow into the floor.

"Tell me," said Julian with restrained violence, "or I will take you into the light again. . . ."

"No!" the protest tore from the huddle that had been a man. "No—oh, it hurts to remember!" He gave a shuddering sigh. "I taught him the secret paths along the spine of the hills, and the secrets of all that grows there, but it was not enough for him. I taught him the names of demons and spells to conjure them. And still he wanted more knowledge from me." Katiz paused, gasping, and Julian gripped his shoulder, though he himself could not have said whether it was to comfort or compel.

"So I made him a mirror in which to see his soul," said Katiz, "and forced him to look into it until he had seen all the darkness there. And then he knew the truth, and he laughed, and he made me look into the mirror too. And while I was looking he sang the song that bound me, until you came. . . ."

Julian let him go with a long sigh. "Have I freed you?" he said softly. "Then open your eyes and look upon the day. . . ."

The only answer was a shudder that shook the fragile body before him, and a quickly muffled sob. And this wreck had once been a sorcerer greater than Caolin—or perhaps not so powerful after all, for the vision that had destroyed Katiz had only made the Blood Lord stronger! Julian felt his stomach churn again, and instinctively his hand went to the hilt of his knife. If this had been an animal he would have given it the mercy stroke long ago, and surely Katiz was little more than an animal now.

But Rana's shocked gaze held him motionless. Refusing to meet her eyes, he looked past her to Lion Claw.

"You did not believe Katiz would speak to me. I hope we may not both be sorry that he did," he said harshly.

"If he comes to full consciousness again he may be a danger."

"Shall we kill him?" said Lion Claw. His face was in shadow, and Julian could not tell from his tone whether this was a real question or the chieftain was testing him. He forced himself to his feet again.

"I am not his judge." Julian tried to keep his voice steady, tried to pretend he had not heard Rana's whisper asking Frederic if there was no way the man could be healed. He had looked into Katiz's dark mirror too, and he was not yet certain of his own safety.

"That is true." There was no emotion in the chieftain's reply. "We will continue to care for Katiz as we have done, for evil or not, he is our own. As for you—go where you will. We will neither help nor hinder you. But I think that the question I have asked will go with you, and you will have to answer it one day."

⟫ FOURTEEN ⟪

The coast road was closed to them. Scouts had told Lion Claw that Malin Scar was still waiting with a predator's patience on the Santibar trail, and even if Julian had been willing to take the extra time to loop southward and approach the Great Valley by the Dragon's Tail Pass, chances were that the word had gone out against them in Elaya.

But there was another way. While they were still arguing bad choices in the last hours before they left the valley, Lion Claw had relented from his policy of noninterference sufficiently to tell them about the Matilija trail.

To Julian it was all new, though Frederic assured him this was the road that led to the hot springs and the Earth Mother's shrine. They rode out in a chill dawn when dew lay heavy on the ripened grass, crossing the rising slope of the valley floor to enter a fold of the hills, where the sycamore-shaded trail wound among great boulders beside the chuckling stream.

From behind him he heard a low humming, and then Silverhair's voice raised in song—

> *"The mists of night have left the air*
> *And dawnlight fills the sky.*
> *The deer are feeding on the hill,*
> *'Tis time for you and I*
> *To leave our beds and douse our heads*
> *And eat a bite before*
> *We take the road once more,*
> *We take the road once more!*
> *The soaring red-tailed hawk can see*
> *The many miles of ground*
> *That we must cover step by step*
> *To get where we are bound.*
> *So let's make haste, we must not waste*
> *The bright hours of the day—*
> *We must be on our way,*
> *We must be on our way!"*

But as they went on, the canyon narrowed into a high walled gorge, until Julian wondered whether they were being herded into some dead end in the hills. Perhaps Lady Madrone could have reassured him, but there had been no way to tell her they were leaving Awhai. As the hills grew more rugged he began to realize how her presence had mediated their wildness. He felt oddly disoriented, as if there was something very simple that he should remember, something that would bring her back to them and put everything in perspective again. Silverhair continued to sing.

> *"Our path leads through the misty hills*
> *Through many a hidden vale.*
> *By secret springs, through shadowed woods*
> *We follow still the trail.*
> *Ahead we go, the fields we know*

We freely leave behind.
Who knows what we will find?
Who knows what we will find?"

Rock walls drew inward, imprisoning them, and the harper's verses expressed Julian's feelings only too well. He was ready to lead them all back toward the coast, whatever its dangers, when he saw the black mouth of a tunnel and felt that annoying itch in his memory once more. For a moment a wheel of green fire spiraled against the darkness; Julian blinked, and it disappeared, but he felt sweat break out on his forehead.

"The road goes through the hill?"

Frederic nodded. "Do you want me to lead the way?"

Stiffening his face to hide his discomfort, Julian waved him forward. After a moment's surprise, his bay mare fell in behind Frederic's grey, and Julian was glad enough not to have to guide her, for as the darkness surrounded them his vision blossomed with sparkling shapes that only grew brighter when he closed his eyes. They had told him there might be aftereffects from the drug he had taken, but knowing there was a reason for these visions did not make them easier to bear.

He shuddered with relief when they began to climb out of the gorge, and just as the sun was setting, they emerged into a little valley set like a cup into the hills. They made camp beside a spring. Still shaken by his experiences in the tunnel, Julian found the cheerful chatter of the others exasperating. After a growl from him had set Piper leaping like a rabbit for the protection of his grandmother's skirts, he realized what he was doing and with a muttered apology strode off through the trees.

He could hear Rana's startled question behind him, and the softer murmur as Frederic replied, but to his relief, no one followed him. Suddenly exhausted, he sat down on a boulder. The air had that hush that comes at sunset, and the sky had turned a luminous gold. The leaves of the poplar trees and cottonwoods around the spring were golden too, and the ripe grass seemed to shimmer with its own light.

Gradually, Julian's pulse steadied and his breathing

slowed. Why had he been so afraid? This beauty was the reality of the world.

"*Maker of All Things, help me—*" he said silently. "*Lady of Earth, they say I saw you—speak to me again! Or at least send Lady Madrone back to me, if she is willing to come. . . . The burden is too great for me. I cannot do it alone!*"

Words failed and his spirit strained mutely for some communication his mind could not compass. As if in answer, gold blazed suddenly around him, through him, dazzling the spirit as well as the eyes. He blinked, trying to see, and the moment passed, or perhaps it was only that the sun had dropped below the horizon at last. But whatever had happened, it left a great peace behind it.

When he came back to the campsite, a kettle of rabbit stew was bubbling over the campfire, Frederic had his altar up, and Silverhair was singing again.

> "*And when the sun sinks from the sky*
> *We have the fire for light,*
> *And time for food and fellowship*
> *And singing in the night.*
> *But very soon, beneath the moon,*
> *We close our eyes in rest,*
> *And know that that is best,*
> *And know that that is best. . . .*"

That night Julian lay in a sleep too deep for dreams, and when he woke in the morning, he found that Lady Madrone had rooted herself beside their little fire.

The next two days of travel took them through another valley, where slabbed stone poked through its furring of chaparral as if the bones of the earth had been exposed, to a high plateau where stands of spruce and alder rose from the golden grass. And still the trail wound upward, until suddenly the world fell away before them, and they reined in, gazing silently at vistas of rose-colored sandstone that stretched northward toward hazy hills. The black speck-lings of brush seemed to be the only vegetation, and Julian licked dry lips, wondering if even Lady Madrone could find water in this arid land. But they had to pass through it, and the Great Valley would not be much better at this time of year. The nights were growing colder as autumn advanced, but this far south it was still hot during the day.

It took them the rest of that day to make the steep descent and cross the red valley. The folds of the distant mountains seemed carved in sharp relief against an empty sky. They camped beside what appeared to be a dry riverbed, but Silverhair drew upon his experience in the desert to show them how to dig down to the sweet water below. Rana asked if all the rivers in this part of the country ran upside down, and the laughter that followed was almost as welcome as the water.

The next morning's riding brought them into a land of rolling, golden-furred hills studded with single live oak trees. The trail scratched a winding white line across gentle slopes like a rumpled bedspread, so that they could see neither where they were going nor where they had been, and the world seemed to end at each clean curve of hill.

"Silverhair—you've been this way before—" said Julian. "How far do you think the Great Valley is now?"

"Not this way," said the harper, shaking his head. "I came to the Valley down the Dragon's Tail Pass. But I believe these hills curve southeastward to join the mountains they call the Dragon's Spine. This trail should bring us out a little north of there, but without a vantage point there's no way to tell how far it may be."

"Maybe we can ask at the settlement—" said Rana.

"What settlement?" exclaimed Frederic. "The priests at Awhai said no men lived here."

"Then perhaps it was another party of travelers," said Rana. "But we're not the only riders to come this way recently—see?" She pointed, and now Julian saw the trail suddenly broadened to a swath of trampled grass as if a large company had ridden toward them and turned around again. The horse droppings they had left behind were no more than a day old.

Julian straightened in his saddle and glanced warily around him, but saw only a buzzard making patient spirals in the sky. He bit his lip, uneasy for no reason that he could identify, but suddenly he wished that he had not sent Lady Madrone off to look for a camp with water.

"Hold up a little," he told Frederic. "I'm going to scout

ahead." He dug his heels into the bay mare's sides and set her at an easy canter up the slope of the hill. From the summit he saw another parklike vale, but there were no oak trees here—only haggled stumps like broken teeth and a litter of branches on the ground. Beyond the horizon an odd smudge stained the clear blue of the sky. Was it smoke, or only the Valley's ceiling of haze? After a moment's hesitation, Julian kicked the mare into motion once more.

Silverhair sat with his right leg resting on the high pommel of his saddle, whistling softly, while his dun horse nosed at the dry grass. The change in position should have relaxed him, but he felt the stiffness of tension in his shoulders despite the welcome heat of the sun. The tune of his walking song continued to echo in his head, and very softly he found words to another verse for it forming in his head.

> "But in this world, so vast and strange,
>   Have we not cause to fear,
> Lest dangers we have never dreamed
>   Should suddenly appear?
> We trudge ahead, denying dread,
>   And hope, before the end,
> To find each foe a friend,
>   To find each foe a friend!"

"You're right," said Frederic as Silverhair's singing faded to silence. "Julian should have been back by now!"

The harper stared at him, suddenly aware of the subconscious signals that had prompted his song. Now the emptiness of the land around them seemed sinister, and the circling of a buzzard overhead some portent of disaster. He was no surer of his feelings for his nephew than he had ever been, but something within him ached emptily at the possibility of Julian's loss. He swung his leg back over the pommel, feeling for the stirrup with his toe, and took up his reins.

"We'll follow, but carefully. Stay below the skyline until we know if the trail is clear."

They crossed the next two folds in the land and saw no

one, though at the sight of the ravaged oak trees Frederic
began swearing softly. The third vale was empty as well, but
halfway up the far hill the ground was trampled and torn for
a dozen feet on either side of the path. A broken sword
blade glinted in the dust, and a trail of droplets that were
already drying from red to brown led eastward. Without
need for consultation Silverhair and Frederic dismounted
and crept toward the rim of the hill. After a moment's
hesitation Rana followed them, and Eva and Piper came
after her.

Perhaps Julian could have made them stay in safety, but
Silverhair was too appalled by what he saw below him to
think of trying.

Before them the land fell suddenly away in long smooth
slopes to the Great Valley, covered with a pall of brown
haze. But though they had sought it, they had no eyes for it
now, for to the north rose the blue ridges of the Coast
Range, and where the spine of the mountains met the hills,
smoke was spiraling lazily from a stone tower.

The tower looked as if it had been there since the wizards'
wars, but new stone stood out white above the weathered
grey of its lower courses, and it was surrounded by a new
palisade of oak logs. A confusion of shanties clustered in its
shelter, and men moved like ants around them, dragging
loads of wood and stone. As they watched, the wind shifted,
bringing the smell of smoke and garbage, and the sound of
hammering.

"Bandits?" whispered Rana.

Silverhair shook his head. Raiders needed to be mobile.
They might have made the ruined tower their refuge, but
they would not have put this much energy into repairing it.
Despite its ugliness, this construction had an orderly quality that suggested a military discipline. But whose army?

The trail they had been following curved past the tower
and wound down the slope toward the valley. But now a
new road joined it, which led to the tower and around it, up
into the hills. Dimly he could make out the white line of the
valley road that curved around toward the Dragon's Tail
Pass. He nudged Frederic and pointed.

"This is Southern Shores territory, but hardly anyone
lives down here," said Frederic. "If the fort at the foot of

the pass were neutralized you could move men and supplies from Elaya up that road with no hindrance at all.''

They both turned to gaze at the line of peaks that separated the coastlands from the Great Valley. Even in the time of the Ancients those mountains had never been heavily populated, and the Convenant reserved them for the wild kindreds now. A man-made road there threatened the bond between humanity and nature, which was the essence of Westria, and worse still, that spine of mountains led straight to the Royal Domain and the heart of the land.

As they watched, a horseman rode out through the open gateway with two others trotting close behind him. Sunlight glittered on the rivets in his leather gambeson, but even without the armor, his bearing would have marked him as an officer. Silverhair's eyes narrowed, searching for the gleam of blue and silver that would mark the man as Elayan, but when he turned in the saddle, apparently to survey the progress of the walls, what Silverhair saw on his breast was a blood-red badge.

Back behind the next hill, the harper found that he was still shivering. Looking up, he saw grey clouds moving in from the west, and was obscurely relieved to think that his body's reactions might have a reason other than fear. *Those men belong to Caolin!* He fought to shut the thought away and found it replaced by a worse realization— *Julian is their prisoner. . . .*

"Do you think they've killed him?" asked Rana when they had pulled up beneath the shelter of one of the few uncut trees. Silverhair glared at her.

Frederic shook his head. "Not in the fight, anyway—I can't see them carrying a body away for decent burial.''

"More likely, they've taken him for their work force," said Eva grimly. Her eyes were haunted, and Silverhair remembered how she had lost her home. "The folk they had looked starved and scrawny, and Julian's a strong lad. If he makes no trouble, they'll keep him as long as he's of use to them.''

"Well, the Maker knows Julian's got more self-control than any six other men," said Frederic a little more hopefully, "and he's stronger."

"Is he?" snapped Silverhair. "He was before we came to

Awhai, but if you think he's recovered from that damned drug you let them give him you have no eyes!"

Frederic pulled back as if the harper had hit him, and Silverhair glared at them all. If he had been leading the party they would never have gotten into this mess, and by the Guardians, the others must obey him now!

"Let's not argue about what's already happened," said Rana sharply. "How are we going to get Julian free? We're too few to attack them, and if we ride up and ask politely they'll snap us up as well."

"The first thing is to find out what they have done with him," Silverhair answered more calmly. "A harper passes everywhere, and men who've had no amusement for weeks on end will be only too happy to welcome me!"

"Silverhair," said Frederic patiently, "aren't you forgetting whose men these are? You're pretty distinctive, and they must know Caolin is looking for you!"

"Then I'll give myself up in exchange for Julian's liberty!"

"Don't you know Julian better than that?" asked Rana disbelievingly. "Even if Caolin's men are willing, do you think Julian would be willing to trade your life for his own?" She looked disgusted, but Piper had drawn up his pony next to her and was staring at Silverhair with shocked eyes.

"He'll have no choice," muttered the harper, but it occurred to him that Julian could stop him by threatening to reveal his own identity. Would the boy be that foolish? He could not be sure. . . .

"At least wait until morning—" pleaded Frederic. "It's almost sunset now, and perhaps Lady Madrone will return. She should know what has happened before—"

"She's deserted us," said Silverhair. "Maybe not by intention, but how can you expect a tree to understand the needs of men? And even if she does come back, what do you expect her to do?" He looked westward, where the sinking sun gave the cloudbank a molten glow, and sighed. "Oh, very well, let's make camp here. But in the morning I'm going back." He suppressed another shiver, thinking of Caolin's men. He doubted he would sleep, but perhaps the night's grace would give him time to conquer his own fear.

* * *

Rana sat up in her blankets and took a deep breath of damp air. The cocooned forms of the others looked like fallen logs. She hoped they were sleeping like logs, too. It would be humiliating if they caught her now. Biting her lip to keep her teeth from chattering, she rearranged her blankets to make it less obvious that she was no longer inside them, and slipped the note she had prepared the night before beneath the pack that had been her pillow. The blankets would not fool anyone once it was full day, and then they would find the note. With the damage done, perhaps they would have the sense not to follow her. She gave the pack a farewell pat when she was finished, but it would not suit the part she had to play to come too well supplied.

As she picked her way down the hill she looked back and thought she saw movement against the greying sky. But there was no outcry. She hurried on, and it was only when a small, cold hand closed on her arm that she realized who had followed her.

"Piper, what are you doing here?" Rana glanced quickly behind her. Tree and rock shapes were separating themselves from the surrounding gloom—soon it would be light and the others would wake and come after her. She tried to detach her sleeve from Piper's fingers, but he only clung tighter. His thin face was a pallid blur.

"Piper, I'm going to the fort where the bad men are—you don't want to go there! Get back to the others now. Don't worry about me!" At least if the boy couldn't talk he would not be able to give her away! Rana took a step forward and Piper moved with her, still holding on to her sleeve.

She stopped, almost growling with exasperation. She had to get rid of the boy before he spoiled all her plans!

"Piper, let go of me! Look, if I don't go find out what's happened to Julian, Silverhair will go, and you know they'll kill him if he's recognized. So I'm going to save Silverhair too, all right?" She jerked her sleeve from his hand and began to run. On the other side of the hill she stopped, panting, and saw him just coming over the crest behind her. She started to run again, then stopped suddenly and waited for him to catch up with her.

"Do you want to come with me? Is that it?"

Wordlessly Piper nodded, and Rana tipped up his chin to look into the wide brown eyes.

"Will you follow directions if I let you come?" When he nodded, she let go of him and began to walk on. Piper trotted along at her side. "It might work even better this way," she said as much to herself as to him. "You look even more bedraggled than I do, and if I tell them we're orphaned and hungry they'll let us in. They need the labor, and I don't think they'll watch us too carefully—what harm could a pair of half-starved kids do?" She grinned and lengthened her stride.

When the guard of the little fortress changed at dawn, they found the two children huddled before the gateway, shivering.

Look cowed! Rana told herself as the big man finished his order with an obscenity. They wanted more kindling for the cookfires, and she scurried for the woodpile. There were comments from the men as she passed, and she wondered if perhaps she should have put more mud on her hair before they reached the gate. Compared to her sister she had never had much of a figure, and she had thought that three months of hard traveling had destroyed any curves that could attract a man's eye, but now she was not so sure. Maybe it was enough just to be female, and young.

By the time she came back with the wood the men were spooning up porridge noisily. Rana felt her stomach contract and wondered whether they would leave any for her and Piper. The gaunt faces of the other men and women who had been pressed into service were not encouraging.

"Aach, this is foul swill!" exclaimed one of the better armored soldiers. "I'll be glad to be heading northward again. At least the Blood Lord feeds us well!"

His companion grunted. "I'm just as happy to serve him at a distance. I've heard tales . . ." He looked uneasily around him. "I'd rather live rough and keep my blood in my body! Oh—I'm as loyal as any man, but if I have to die for the Blood Lord I'll do it with a weapon in my hand!"

Rana swallowed sickly and thrust another stick into the fire, trying to keep her features slack and witless, to look as if she would not have understood even if she had heard.

"Are you afraid? No wonder you're stuck in this hole!

You've heard true, but it was only the one time," said the first soldier. Rana thought his voice wavered a little, but he held his scornful grin.

"Then why are you taking that new prisoner north with you?" asked the garrison man. "The others I could understand, if you need more workers for Blood Gard, but I hear he's still half silly from that blow he got when we took him, so what use will he be? Better leave him here. We can use his labor too, y'know."

The first man shrugged. "Maybe when Captain Esteban has questioned him, he'll change his mind. So far, the man's not been in his senses long enough to answer questions. Maybe he'll die and save us all some trouble."

"Especially himself—the captain's *good* at questioning." The garrison man grinned nastily and began to lick the last bits of porridge from his bowl. His mate laughed, then saw Rana, who was swaying, lightheaded with the shock of what she had heard.

"Hey you, girl, go get us some more wood before you fall into the fire! Aach, they're all silly here."

Rana's head rang as he cuffed her on the ear, and she staggered to her feet, vaguely aware that shock and the pain of the blow had combined to make her look as half-witted as she could have wished. Julian was hurt and they were going to take him away! She had to do something!

When she reached the woodpile, someone shoved a hempen bag into her hands and shouted at her to go outside to gather more. By the time she reached the nearest trees she had got her wits together, but she still felt sick from the blow. No one seemed to be watching her. Quickly she ducked around behind a rock, thinking that perhaps she could rest for a moment and clear her head there.

"Hist! Rana!"

The whisper could have come from anywhere. Rana threw up her head like a startled hare, looking wildly around her.

"Get your head down, you fool! I'm over here!"

Heart pounding, Rana crouched again. She heard the man who had come out to supervise the woodgatherers calling, and shouted some reply. Then she blushed as she realized what he had thought she was doing behind the boulder and looked up to meet Frederic's blue gaze.

"I'm not a fool!" she whispered before he could speak again. "I've found out that Julian's still alive, but he got knocked on the head when they captured him. But we've got to do something right away, because Captain Esteban's going back to Blood Gard soon, and he's going to take Julian with him."

"Well, come away with me now, and we'll discuss it," Frederic began, but Rana shook her head.

"If I run off now, they'll search, and then they'll find you. Besides, Piper is still in there. We're loosely guarded, though, and it hasn't been bad so far. We'll escape tonight or tomorrow, I promise you, and maybe by then I'll have a plan. Just don't let Silverhair run his head into the noose —this Esteban is Caolin's right-hand man!"

"Don't worry about Silverhair. . . ." Frederic grinned.

"Why not?" She looked at him suspiciously. "Has he changed his mind?"

"No," said Frederic simply, "but Eva put an infusion of poppy in his tea. Silverhair will be asleep for quite a while."

It took Rana a moment to take that in, then her grin mirrored his. "I'll tell Piper," she said, "but don't let Eva go blaming me for him being here too—he followed me!" There was another shout, and she looked up nervously. "In the names of the four Jewels, stay hid!" she hissed at Frederic. She stood up and straightened her clothing, then marched back to pick up her bag of twigs with a confidence she did not feel.

That night it rained. Julian, turning restlessly on the inadequate heap of straw where they had thrown him, heard the pattering on the roof of the tower and thought he was back in the Ramparts. He began to cry out for the men he had fought beside on the border patrol.

"That's a mountain town he's babbling about—" came a rough voice from the other side of the stout door. "Up north. I've been that way. What's the lad doing down here?"

"You tell the captain to ask him that, all right? But shut up and let me get some sleep now! It's bad enough having to

guard a crazy who couldn't stir if he wanted to without
listening to your blathering!" The two voices contended for
a few moments longer, then died away into muttering.

Startled into a momentary awareness, Julian held his
breath until the two guards were still. Yes, he was in the
south, near—Awhai—with an effort he remembered the
name. He had been riding under a clear sky, but it was
October, and time enough for the rains to begin. More
memories shaped themselves out of his confusion—he had
seen smoke, and then he was surrounded by horsemen who
wore Caolin's badge.

He must have fought—logic told him that, and the pain
in his head told him how the fight had ended. He touched
the throbbing ache above his left ear and gasped as agony
speared his brain. When it subsided enough for him to
think again, he forced himself to think back from that
moment until he remembered who he was, and why he was
here.

Julian stifled a groan. He had never been so helpless, not
even when the slavers had taken him—at least he had been
able to move without passing out then. He was totally in his
captors' power, and a quick death would be the greatest
mercy he could expect from them. And what about his
companions? He could only hope they thought he was dead
—that was the only thing that would keep them from
getting themselves captured trying to rescue him. If they
were not prisoners already. Agony shook him at the magni-
tude of his failure. Julian rolled his head against the straw
and a wave of pain carried him into welcome oblivion.

For a time Julian wandered among webs of light through
which moved shapes that shimmered with geometric bands
or swirls of color. Somehow they were familiar, though he
could not remember where he was or what they were. But
there ought to be someone with him—a guide who knew
this realm as well as he knew—wherever it was that he had
been before. He began to move more quickly, seeking her.
Seeking *her?* For a moment impressions of leaf-dappled
sunlight overlaid the patterns around him. The leaves
whispered a name. . . .

He struggled and groaned aloud without knowing it, then
stilled as the confusion within him flickered into order and

he saw the pattern of brightness that was Lady Madrone.

"You have remembered!" Her tone held delight.

Julian stared at her, and then he did remember, and the wonder of his vision filled him again.

"Are you dreaming?" she asked then. *"I did not know you could reach this place without taking the drug again. Where is your body now?"*

Julian shook his head. The thought of his body made him uneasy. He had the impression that he had struggled hard to escape it, that there were reasons not to go back to it again.

"I don't know. Does it matter? I want to stay here with you. . . ." He saw her outline shimmer with some emotion. Then she drew close to him, and for a moment their energy patterns pulsed in unison. Julian felt an odd sorrow in her, and in himself a sense of loss when she withdrew again.

"Your body is hurt." Her gentle concern soothed him. *"You must go back to it so that I can help you—"*

"No!"

"You must, my prince—see, I will go with you." Lady Madrone swirled around him again, and in the delight of that union he forgot to resist as she forced him back along the slender silver cord that connected him to his body.

For one moment of dazzling agony Julian was aware of both worlds—bright patterns pulsed through the darkness around him; he saw Lady Madrone's body of light solidifying and knew her in both guises. Then vision left him. For a moment he felt the grip of hands smooth as polished wood holding his own.

"Lady Madrone—" he groaned, "you must get the others away!"

"Be easy, Prince of Men, and rest now!" came the answer, soft as wind whispering through leaves. Then those strange hands released his. Julian tried to open his eyes, but instead he felt himself sliding down, down, into a dreamless darkness beyond pain.

Julian was awakened by the trembling of the wooden floor beneath him. He blinked, found that the pain in his head had subsided to a dull ache that intensified but did not quite incapacitate him even when he struggled to sit up in the straw. From outside he heard confused cries, and a sound like the wind sweeping through the tops of many trees.

His first thoughts were of earthquakes, but no earth tremor could continue so long. The dry grass shifted beneath him—reason told him it had been dislodged by the shaking of the floor, but it had *felt* like the movement of a living thing. Swearing, he staggered to his feet. The sounds were louder now, all around him. If only he could *see!*

Julian groped for the stone wall, and snatched back his hand as it touched something that moved. From outside he heard a man's agonized scream. Then the floor shook beneath him, tilted, and with a grinding rumble part of the wall fell away. In the pale light of dawn he saw something green snake across the stone and tighten. Then the stone fell away, letting more light into the room. Wood groaned behind him—the door was shattering—no, expanding! Staggering to keep from falling, Julian stared in disbelief as oak planks rooted, sprouted new branches, and thrust through the arch of stones.

The floor heaved, Julian tripped over new branches and fell to his hands and knees; the horror that gibbered in his forebrain subordinated to the frantic need to reach the opening in the wall. The tower was three stories high, but death on the packed earth below would be better than remaining here.

He reached the gap that was growing greater with every moment as more stones were wrenched away. Then someone called his name.

Looking down, Julian saw Rana, riding a branch like a pony while the madrone tree to which it was attached stretched upward until it topped what was left of the tower. Rana reached out to him, and instinctively he leaped for the safety of the tree just as the floor gave way beneath him and the tower settled earthward in a cloud of dust and a thunderous rumble of falling stone.

"Lady of Earth, you're safe! Oh, Julian!"

Julian felt Rana's young arms hard around him as he felt the quivering of the branch to which he clung, but his eyes were on the heaving mass of stone and growing things that had been the tower. As the sun lifted above the distant eastern mountains, he saw green shoots forcing their way up between the fallen stones, bindweed and wild cucumber writhing over them to crack those that had not broken in the fall, grass hazing the rain-soaked earth of the courtyard with vibrant green. The logs of the palisade had already rooted, and the ruins of the fortress were ringed with young oak trees.

Beyond the ring a few men and horses fled wildly through the grass—pitifully few, if Julian had had any room for pity just now. Nearer at hand he saw the figures he had been searching for, five of them, on horses that were bunched and trembling on a little knoll. The sunlight struck gold from Frederic's bowed head, and silver from the harper's white hair. Julian sighed then and eased back, for the first time allowing his mind to focus on what had happened here.

Except for himself and Rana, no living human beings remained within the ring of trees. As for the dead—the vegetation that had been their death was providing a mercifully swift burial. Julian had killed men with his own hands, but he did not think he could have borne to look on those bodies. He felt sick, and did not know whether it was caused by revulsion or his head blow. Suddenly he understood what it must have been like during the Cataclysm, and why the College of the Wise enforced the Covenant so strictly. The unleashed wrath of the powers of nature was a terrible thing.

He shifted position to look at Rana and was abruptly aware of the smooth skin of the madrone tree beneath his hands.

"Lady Madrone?" It was not really a question, but Rana nodded. "She did this?" Rana nodded again. *She did this for me?* Julian did not voice that question. He swallowed, already knowing the answer, for he was remembering.

"My Lady—" Gently he stroked the thin red skin of bark that covered the branch that supported him. "My Lady, it is over. It is time for healing now."

They camped that night on the dry flats at the edge of the Great Valley. There was little water, and no greenery but the leathery clumps of chamise that drew a grudging nourishment from the alkaline soil. The haze of dust that always veiled the valley devoured the daylight. But Julian did not care. After what he had seen that day, he felt safer surrounded by this sterility.

Only Lady Madrone, transformed once more into a semblance of humanity with russet-skinned limbs limned redder by the light of the little fire, seemed unaffected by what had passed.

"The rain helped, but my people were already angry," she said in her soft voice. "Those men had wantonly destroyed good trees, and on protected land! They scarcely needed my pleading to rise in anger—they had a right to revenge."

Julian repressed a shudder, abruptly aware, despite all they had shared, of how different the Lady was from humankind.

"I'm glad of that—" he said aloud. "I would not like to bring down the wrath of the Guardians upon Westria for having broken the Covenant that keeps men from interfering with the other kindreds, and the powers of nature from attacking men!"

Julian frowned as he said that, but he could not think what else to say to her. Beyond an uneasy gratitude, which they all shared, he was not sure what his feelings for Lady Madrone were now. He only knew that his head still hurt, and he was very tired.

"I must sleep," he said finally. The others were already wrapped in their blankets, their movements hollowing out comfortable depressions in the sand.

"Yes. I will guard you. You may sleep without fear."

Perhaps, Julian thought dimly as consciousness faded. But what he hoped was that he would sleep without dreams.

⇛ FIFTEEN ⇚

Malin Scar came to the tower a week after its destruction, having tortured from a chance-caught Awhai hunter news of his prey. Caolin's last word to him had been clear. If need be he must let the harper go, he must sacrifice men, horses, anything. But the Blood Lord would find a death for him that even the Shadower might fear if he failed again. The Blood Lord wanted Julian. . . .

The Blood Lord's badge gave his servant the freedom of Elaya, and the Shadower had made good time through Saticoy and the Campos del Mar, pausing only long enough to buy fresh mounts for himself and his men. After the hard push through the Dragon's Spine and down the pass, the horses moved quickly across the lip of the valley, for the Shadower knew that whether those he sought had gone up the valley or foolishly decided to try Caolin's mountain road, they must have passed the last outpost tower.

What he found was a tiny encampment on a bare knoll just out of sight of the ruins of the tower, where Captain Esteban had gathered the mere dozen men that remained out of a garrison of twenty and the troop he had brought down from Blood Gard. Two men on good horses were on their way to Caolin now, but a wrenched knee had kept the captain in the south.

Perhaps it was just as well, for the nerve of even such men as served the Blood Lord had been thoroughly shaken by what had passed. Only a man as forceful as the captain could have kept them together. When Malin Scar rode in they were already beginning to build walls of loose stone and discussing where in the Valley they might find dead-wood to roof the place against the rain.

"Can you ride?" asked the Shadower when he had told the officer who he was following.

Captain Esteban's eyes were bright with a smouldering anger. "I will," he said shortly. "The pain in my knee is fading, but the sting of this dishonor smarts the worse for what you have told me. I thought we had to do with some sorcerer, but if these ragtag fugitives have found some trick to arouse the other kindreds they will not keep it long! I will come with you."

Since his last communication with Caolin, the Shadower had attempted to barrier his mind from the Blood Lord's wrath. But that night he consciously sought contact, straining with half-developed senses to span the miles to the Red Mountain. Perhaps the Blood Lord would understand what had happened here! However, Malin Scar's mind-touch with his master had always been at the other man's will, and the effort only wasted his energy. *So be it then,* he thought as he wrapped his blankets around him and sought sleep at last. He had always preferred to trust to his own skills anyway.

The next morning Captain Esteban and the four best swordsmen remaining to him rode out with Malin Scar and his pair. Soon enough they found where Julian's party had made camp that first night, and the clear trail they had left in the northern road's white sand. If the prints made by Lady Madrone's splayed toes and her long stride puzzled the Shadower, he said nothing to the others. Better mounted, and eager for revenge, the pursuers pushed after them.

The shortening days flowed one into another, featureless as the land through which Julian led his friends. To their left rose the dun folds of the coastal hills, broken now and again by a line of greenery where a spring surfaced briefly before disappearing into the Valley's bitter sands. To their right, the Great Valley curved away into featureless distance, covered by its dusty pall. At this season there seemed to be little life in it, though jackrabbits bounded from the shelter of leathery saltbush or sacaton as if they were racing the tumbleweeds that the wind rolled endlessly across the plain, and it was clear how it had earned the name of the Dragon Waste. Only twice during their journey did the wind lift the Valley's brown veil to reveal the great wall of the Snowy Mountains a hundred miles away.

As they rode northward, the land grew imperceptibly gentler, and the horses grazed eagerly on the sun-cured grasses that spread down from the hills. The good feed made up for the increasing chill in the weather. The protracted summer of the southlands had deceived them —though it did not rain again, clouds continued to threaten, and they moved deeper into autumn with every mile north.

They rode steadily along the level track, making perhaps twelve miles in a day. More than once they saw herds of elk or pronghorn in the distance, but they had neither the time nor energy to hunt them. Marshes spread out from the Darkwater, and Rana's bow brought down enough migrating waterfowl to eke out their dwindling supplies.

They had been a little over a week on the road when Lady Madrone, listening to the gossip of the grasses as she did every evening, learned that they were being followed. Then they began to push their pace, but it was hard to go any faster, for though their horses were willing beasts, they had never been bred for such punishing travel.

They lost another day when Frederic's grey strained a foreleg, and Piper had to ride double with Rana until they came to a holding where they could trade the big horse for a roan mare with a knowing eye that looked old enough to have carried her owner to the Battle of the Dragon Waste. She was no speedster either, but they found that she could keep up the same steady pace for miles, and gradually they began to make up ground.

But it was the last week of October before they reached the fork where the road to Laurelynn separated from the way into the Royal Domain.

Rana kept her eyes resolutely fixed on the double-humped peak that rose above the tangle of brown hills to the north, avoiding Julian's gaze. She had seen the tip of the Red Mountain many times, poking above the hills that edged the Bay, but she had never realized just how big it really was. Seen from this direction, the mountain dominated the landscape, even darkened by a cloud-covered sky. Somewhere on its summit, Caolin sat plotting his deviltries; somewhere at its roots lay the treasure that Julian must steal away.

"Rana, do you understand why I'm asking this of you?" Julian's voice was rough with strain. It was a far cry from the arrogance with which he had tried to order her home at the beginning of their journey, but what did that matter? His purpose was still to send her to safety while he went into danger with Frederic and Silverhair. And the worst of it was that this time she *did* understand why. . . .

"Malin Scar is barely two days behind us," Julian went on. "He *must* continue to believe we are running for Laurelynn. If all of the horse tracks go that way we may be able to fool him, and on foot the three of us will have a better chance of moving secretly through the Domain."

Reluctantly, Rana nodded her head. Finally she looked at him.

"Tell me one thing, Julian—" she said soberly. "If it were not for the need to mislead our Shadower and get Eva and Piper to safety would you take me with you? I'll do what you ask in any case, but I want the truth from you!"

She saw him color, and could not tell whether it was from shame or self-consciousness, but he did not look away. A few paces down the road the others were waiting with barely concealed impatience, except for Piper, who had pulled out the wooden flute they had given him in Awhai and was trying to imitate a red-winged blackbird's song.

"Rana, I still think you were wrong to run away with us, but certainly you have pulled your weight on this journey of ours."

He flushed again, and she thought with sudden insight that perhaps he himself had not quite lived up to his own expectations. She wanted to tell him that it did not matter, that perfection would not have compelled their loyalty as his self-critical integrity did now, but he had begun to speak again.

"Yes, I'd take you with me, if only to take care of the horses!" He grinned suddenly, and Rana felt something in her belly contract with an odd pain.

"Julian, please be careful!" she said stupidly.

He gave her a straight look. "Rana, I'll say the same to you. You're the bait to draw Malin Scar away from us, and you're in as much danger as we are until you get to Laurelynn."

She managed a grin. "We'll manage. Eva and I are the

sharp wits in this party, after all! I only wonder how you'll fare when we're not around to get you out of trouble again." She thought of the tower and the inn in Santibar. It was the breaking of their company. Whatever happened to them now, they would never again have the unique companionship that they had shared on the road.

His answering smile was a little twisted. "Lady Madrone will have to take care of us, I suppose—" He gave a quick glance toward the tree that had temporarily rooted itself at the crossroads.

"Julian, aren't you finished convincing her yet?" called Frederic. "It's almost noon!"

She saw him shrug the big muscles of his shoulders as he always did when he was worried and there was nothing he could do. Then Julian reached out and grasped her hand. For one appalled moment Rana wondered if he was going to kiss it, but that would have been silly. They were comrades, after all, and it was a comrade's grip that enveloped her own.

He let her go and she spun away from him. "Eva, Piper, get mounted—we have a race to win!" She would go—she had to, but she was not going to sit still while Julian and the others walked away from her. Let them breathe her dust and watch her dwindling down the road!

Rana's resolve carried her to her own saddle, and kept her from looking back as she and Eva and Piper lashed their horses to a lumbering canter and pulled the led mounts along behind. And after that, she could not have seen the three they were leaving even if she had looked behind her, for her eyes were blind with tears.

Julian stood in the shelter of a sycamore, gazing up at the shadow on the side of the mountain he had come so far to see. It cut across a red cliff face at the base of a pointed spur that jutted eastward from the lower peak, thickly forested with slender oak trees and pines. Behind it the main bulk of the Red Mountain loomed sheer above them, studded with irregular outcroppings of blackish stone. Topping its jagged rim he could just make out the smooth rampart of Blood Gard.

He shivered and eased back into the lee of the sycamore. It amazed him that they had been able to penetrate the heart of Caolin's power unobserved. They had been most exposed to danger as they wound among the open hills at the eastern end of the Domain, but there was a curious silence in this land. When they found the burned-out holding by the creek bed they had followed to reach this vantage point they began to understand why. Julian doubted now that there remained an untouched farmstead within twenty miles of the Red Mountain. Any place close enough to threaten the Blood Lord—or even to observe him—must have been destroyed or occupied by Caolin's men.

And on this side the Red Mountain needed no guarding. No one was going to come at Blood Gard from the east without wings. But Julian's purpose was not to attack the fortress but to steal from beneath it something that he hoped Caolin did not even know was there. He repressed a fear that his enemy had already found it; that even now Caolin was gloating over the Earthstone while his men waited to trap the seekers underground.

A buzzard circled lazily overhead, black against the grey sky. A damp wind whirled one of the sycamore's few remaining leaves rustling to the ground. At least where they were going they would not have to worry about rain!

Frederic was sorting into three equal piles the torches and tallow dips they had got at the holding where they traded horses. They had already divided up the food—if they were careful there was enough for three or four days. He hoped that it would be enough. Lady Madrone had found the entrance to the ancient mine for them without difficulty, but her people's domain ended at the subsoil, and she had no more idea than they did what lay underground. The slap of leather as Frederic closed their packs again sounded too loud. Julian took a deep breath, trying to calm his nerves.

"All ready—" Frederic said cheerfully.

"Let's get on with it then," grunted Silverhair. "Staring is not going to make it any easier!" He shrugged the harpcase a little forward on his shoulder and moved cautiously up the slope.

Julian hitched his own pack higher and went to the madrone tree that stood beside the creek.

"My Lady—" he whispered, "I thank you for standing watch here. If we do not return within five days, you must go back to your own people. You have done enough for the children of men."

He felt a tremor run through the sturdy trunk, but the tree form did not alter. During their journey northward the Lady had rooted herself whenever they paused, and he had been relieved not to have to talk to her. But now, as he touched the living wood, a pattern of brilliance flared in his inner awareness. Only for a moment—he suspected it was something from his vision that he had forgotten again —and he sighed. Then he heard Frederic and Silverhair calling, and hurried after them.

Two days after the three Westrians had entered the mine, six men on tired horses halted at the base of the Red Mountain.

"You see—" said Malin Scar triumphantly. "I told you that it was only a ruse with the horses! Look, there are the marks where they rested!" He poked in a drift of fallen leaves and uncovered something wrapped in a tattered blanket. "And here is where they stashed their extra gear!"

"Did they try to go up the mountain?" asked Captain Esteban, gazing in awe at the sheer slopes of stone.

"Maybe—or maybe they went into it—" The Shadower pointed to the cliff face. "You go on and warn our master while I follow them," he laughed. "Perhaps the men we sent to follow the horses will learn more, but it doesn't matter what they planned to do now—they have walked into the trap of their own will, and it is about to close!"

Rana could already see the lights of Laurelynn glimmering through river mist when four men rode out suddenly from behind an abandoned barn to block their path. She looked quickly around her, but there was no one else on the road. Eva brought her own horse close as Rana pulled up, muttering under her breath. Rana peered through the gloom, trying to see if the men who were approaching wore any badge, but all she could make out was their dark shapes against the dimming sky. Her bow was strapped behind her, and in any case, bird-arrows would have done little good against stout leathern jerkins. Her hand moved casually toward the dagger at her side.

"Oh sirs, good sirs—can ye tell us if this be the right road to Laurelynn?" Eva's voice cracked as she called out, and Rana shot her a quick glance, wondering if the other woman's voice was quavering by design or from fear. Then she felt the bright, almost mischievous touch of the older woman's mind. For a moment the only response from the men was deep laughter with an odd note in it that made the hair stand up on Rana's forearms. Then one of them rode out ahead of the rest.

"For thieves, all roads are wrong," he said coldly. "We've had word of some stolen horses. How did you come by the ones you're leading there?"

"Horse thieves! Well, I never! Do we look like desperadoes—an old woman, a half-grown girl, and a boy? We're honest hold-folk from down valley, and these beasts were given freely in exchange for our help by three wanderers who passed through." Eva's tone crackled with self-righteousness, and the muscles of Rana's face stiffened painfully as she fought laughter, for everything that Eva had said was true.

"Where were they going?" A second man urged his horse up beside the leader.

"Where—now what did they say, girl? You listened to their talk." Eva faced Rana, winking with the eye that was turned away from the men, and Rana, flustered by the sudden question, stammered like the green country girl she was supposed to be.

"The mountains? I think they said something about a mountain—" She stopped herself abruptly, afraid of giving too much away.

"They've headed for the Ramparts then," said the leader. "*He* said the leader came from some holding there—we should have thought of it before!" The other men began murmuring. Horses snorted and threw up their heads as men reined them around abruptly.

"Grandma, can't we be going? It's getting cold here." Rana's whine was not entirely assumed.

"Cold, aye, and my old bones are aching!" Eva answered her. "For pity's sake, sirs—only tell us if we're on the right road!"

"There's nothing more to be got from these hens," said the second man, "and our master will be wanting this word!"

The leader nodded. Without bothering to respond to Eva's last question, he signaled the others and the little troop clattered off down the road toward the Red Mountain.

By the time the wanderers crossed the bridge into Laurelynn-of-the-Waters, City of the Kings, it was full dark. But there were still people in the streets, and one of them told Rana the way to the palace, where the Regent of Westria stayed when he was here. The light streaming from the open doorway seemed very warm and comforting after the cold of the river mist, and Lady Rosemary's face, shining with welcome, more comforting still. It was only when she asked for news of her son that Rana felt the cold knot in her belly once more.

"He's with Silverhair and Julian," she said in a low voice. "They were going to try and make their way into the mines beneath the Red Mountain in search of the Earthstone. . . ."

The Gnome-King had his high seat in a lofty hall where long ago miners had bored two parallel tunnels and taken out the ore between them when they withdrew again. Mighty pillars of virgin stone twenty feet in diameter upheld it on either side, flanked by a series of rough anterooms. It was a fine palace. He did not want men to invade it again.

"Shall we let them come?" he asked the pisky who counseled him.

"They will never find their way this far. They cannot live long underground—they will give up and go back to the surface world."

"But if they leave they may spread tales of this place, and others will come!" the King objected querulously.

"We will rub out the signs with which they have marked their passage, and in a little while we shall make new pick handles from their bones!"

The pisky always had an answer, thought the Gnome-King, nodding happily. He was an excellent counselor. The gnomes were the elemental spirit of stone made manifest, eternal as earth itself, though they had gained in consciousness after the Cataclysm. But the imaginations of the Welsh miners who had delved here so long ago had given form to the raw stuff of spirit and produced the piskies, and the Gnome-King listened to them willingly when he had to do with men.

The tapping of hammers echoed hollowly through the cold stone. Silverhair sat up abruptly, blinking uselessly. His pulse was pounding like another hammer and he tried to steady it. It was all right—he was in a mine in Westria, not in the Caverns of Aztlan, and no ghosts waited to consume his soul. He pulled his cloak tighter around him, bones aching with the unchanging chill. Cavern or mine —that much was the same, and the cold was even harder to bear now than it had been eight years ago. This was the third time they had paused to rest. He thought they had been in the mine for at least two days, or maybe it was three—there was no way to calculate the passage of time underground.

He listened to the regular breathing of Frederic and Julian resentfully. This was a young man's adventure! He knew now that he should have gone to Laurelynn with Rana and the others. Julian had wanted him here because he had been underground before—but if he had only known it, that was just why the harper should not have come. As he sat here, old horrors gibbered in his memory, and his dry throat constricted with a sudden craving for wine.

Grit scraped as one of the others sat up. "Uncle, are you awake?" It was Julian's voice, and in a moment Julian's face that glimmered in the flicker of a struck light. The boy struck flint to steel again and thrust a taper into the tinder as soon as it began to burn. Julian jammed it into a cleft in the stone and sat back again.

The uneven light limned a roughly arched passageway about five feet wide and barely high enough for them to walk upright. So far they had kept to the larger haulage way, marking the turnings with charcoal to guide them out again, but he could see a narrow ore shaft angling upward from the main passage a few feet away, one of its old redwood pillars still visible, cured by the centuries until it was almost as hard as the stone.

"I thought I heard hammering. . . ."

Julian nodded. "Frederic says it isn't ghosts, for all these passages look as if the miners abandoned them only a little

while ago." At this season, only the deepest levels of the
cinnabar mine held water, and though the atmosphere was
dead, it was dry enough so that the rails on which the ore
carts had run and a miner's pick that they had found bore
only a surface layer of rust, which could be scraped away.
Julian had the pick thrust through his belt now, replacing
the sword that had been taken from him in the tower. It had
come in handy for tapping protruding slabs of stone to test
their stability. No one wanted to be brained by a piece of
falling rock after all they had been through.

"Gnomes—" Frederic's voice came muffled through his
blankets. "They like abandoned diggings—I told you." He
heaved himself upright and sat blinking owlishly at the little
flame.

"Well, if they enjoy living in men's workings so much, I
wish they'd show their gratitude by helping us!" complained Julian.

"I've tried," said Frederic defensively. "Not even the
Master of the Junipers could make them answer without
their will! If we had some dowsing rods, we might have tried
seeking the Jewel that way." He rummaged in his pack,
pulled out a piece of dried meat, and began to chew on it.

"What use is it to natter about what we can't do? I want
to know what we can!" muttered Julian. Then he saw that
Frederic was eating, and spoke more sharply— "Go easy
on the supplies—we don't know how long they will have to
last!"

"Oh, let the boy eat, Julian!" exclaimed Silverhair, wishing he could quench his craving for wine so easily. He knew
just how it would taste, at first tart, then mellowing on the
tongue and warming the belly with a slow fire. Red wine
from the vineyards near Bongarde, it would be, lucent as
garnet in the light of the sun.

He glared at his nephew. "The gnomes are probably
laughing their invisible heads off, watching us stumble
about in here, so why are we still wandering? Do you expect
to trip over the Earthstone in some passageway? Give it up,
lad—we've failed!"

"Turn back then!" flared Julian. "I never asked to bear-
lead a used-up harper and a half-trained priest on this
quest. You go on, and be grateful that you can! But I will
come out of here with the Earthstone, or not at all!"

As shocked by Julian's loss of control as by what he had said, both Frederic and Silverhair stared at him. Then the other boy edged around until the harper could hear his whisper.

"Let's go back to the entrance and get the rest of our supplies. Julian will be eager enough to follow us when he's spent some time alone in here!"

Julian had heard Frederic's whisper, but he did not care. Fury born of desperation blurred his vision, tired already from trying to focus in the wavering candlelight. This could not be the end of it! They could not fail after having struggled so hard and coming so far! And even if the others gave up, Julian's defiance had been no more than the truth. Without the Jewels he could not claim the Crown, and he knew now that life would have no meaning for him without the right to try and set right all that was wrong in the land.

Julian stared at the ragged surface of the wall, listening to the small sounds as the others crept away. Did they think that he could not endure without them? He wondered if they would really be able to abandon him. . . . Just now he was not sure if he cared.

After a time he blew out the candle. Perhaps he had been wrong to resist the darkness. Here at the roots of the mountain, light was an intrusion. How could he expect to win the cooperation of the powers who were native here if he clung to the daylight? As the glow faded from the taper's wick, Julian felt darkness smothering him, as if someone had dropped a velvet mantle over his head.

And it was so very still!

Julian's breathing rasped loud in his ears. He could hear the hiss of sand trickling down the wall, the moan of air drawn through the passage by changes in pressure and temperature many miles away, and underneath all those surface sounds a kind of subliminal creaking—the noise of rock surfaces slipping subtly back and forth along their fault lines, as if the mountain were stretching in its sleep.

Julian listened, imagining the Red Mountain breathing, sensing the respiration of the foothills that surrounded it, and beyond them the whole surface of the earth shifting imperceptibly to release stressed stone. He worked his own tight shoulders back and forth in sympathy and pressed his palm against the gritty rock of the passageway as if he could absorb the essence of stone through his bare skin.

Dimly he remembered the name his foster mother had given him. *I am Stone, I am in stone . . .* , he thought, and then let even that awareness fall away, trying to become as motionless as one of the fossils in the wall.

Silent, static, blind, Julian sat for a time that was measureless. Then, between one endless moment and the next, he realized that lines of pale light were dancing before his eyes. He blinked, but the patterns were still there. He supposed that this was some attempt by his body to deny light's deprivation, yet the patterns were teasingly familiar. Whatever their source, he knew that he had seen them before.

Once more, he forced his mental processes to slow. A band of greenish light flickered into being before him, became a circle, then an angular form dotted with white and red. For a moment another image overlaid it—the roof of a cavern upon which such figures had been painted in bewildering profusion. Julian's pulse raced suddenly—that had been the Earth Mother's cave!

Lady of Earth— he prayed silently, *I am here because of You. You could have killed me at any time on this journey—I must believe I am alive for some reason! Show me what I am supposed to do!*

Julian held his breath, thinking that surely there had never been such a good place for listening. But the silence was unbroken. Only after a moment he realized that the organic forms of his vision were transmuting into lattices of light that linked and angled around him. He blinked, but they were still there, and he realized that he was seeing the crystalline structure of the stone.

Joy sang in his veins, and for a moment the vision wavered. The Guardians had not deserted him after all, and that meant there must be some way to his goal! Julian took a deep breath and his sight steadied; he slipped the strap of his pack over his shoulder and got to his feet. The passageway curved around to the left. With a little effort he found that he could see through the surface structure into the stone.

Julian frowned a little, trying to call up the image of the one piece of stone he needed to see. The Master had

described it for him, but that was not the same as vision.
They said he had been blessed by the Jewels at his first
naming. Could he possibly recall something that had happened when he was only six weeks old?

"Mother, help me!" he whispered then.

*"In the Name of Earth I bless you, son of this land. Grow
strong as its bedrock, fertile as its soil, upright as the growing
things that seek the sun!"*

With his inner ear, Julian heard the rough-sweet voice of
the Master of the Junipers speaking those words and
jumped as if something heavy had been laid against his
belly. Then the pressure was eased, though a strange tingling passed through every limb. He glimpsed a belt clasped
with a stone that shimmered like an enchanted mud drop,
and beyond it, the pale face of a woman, crowned with a
mass of dark hair—the one face that through all the painful
years of his growing he had most longed to see.

"Earthstone! Earthstone, by my mother's grace I know
you!" Julian whispered. "I have come to reclaim you, Jewel
of Earth—reveal yourself to me!"

The Gnome-King heard those words, and cowered on his
cold throne, remembering the message that had come
through the earth at Midsummer. Was this the time fore-
told? Was this human the one? For eighteen years the Jewel
of Earth had been hidden in the mine, fairest of gems, a
focus for all the gnomes held dear despite that human
imprint, which he could never understand. Quick orders
sent his people scurrying through the passageways toward
the chamber where their treasure lay.

At the Red Mountain's summit, Caolin stopped suddenly
in the midst of listening to the men Malin Scar had sent
after the horses tell him that the fugitives were heading for
the Snowy Mountains. Leaving him staring, the Blood Lord
went to his temple. Some tremor of the spirit had shaken
him—it was like the power that had breached his warding
six weeks earlier, and like something else as well. Shaking,
he set his hands upon the raw stone of his altar and
projected his awareness outward in search of its source.

Julian felt as if some new sense had uncoiled in his
awareness. He moved surely through the passageways,

upward and inward toward the heart of the mountain, drawn by a force as powerful as the smell of food to a starving man. A color, a taste, a sound—it was like all of these, and he responded to it eagerly.

Now there was a glow in the secret chamber that even mortal eyes could see. Soft green and pale golden, russet and deep brown, color pulsed and shimmered across the rough walls. Julian's boots echoed on the stone floor. Hands trained to strength by years of cutting granite closed over the Jewel.

High he held it. Words rushed through his throat, resonated through the roots of the mountain and outward through all the land.

"By birthright do I take thee, my true inheritance! I am Julian Starbairn, the Earthstone's Lord, and by thy power will I claim Westria!"

The gnomes danced around him, appearing and disappearing in the forms of stone shapes oddly animated or matrices of light. Their King spun giddily. The imprint of the human will that had consecrated the Earthstone linked this human to it in a way he could not understand, and the mind of the man, joined to the Jewel, pulsed with a fearful power to which the elementals resonated. Compelled by a consciousness that was both less, and more, than his own, the Gnome-King bowed in an ecstasy of obedience.

But Caolin, clinging to his altar, recognized the uprush of a power he had held and lost a lifetime ago. His extended senses perceived Julian's proclamation, and he understood finally the flaw that had lain at the heart of his power, and cursed his enemy.

⊰⊱ SIXTEEN ⊰⊱

Their route marks were gone.

Silverhair stopped short at the end of the tunnel, gazing in disbelief at the unblemished arch of the entry to the larger passageway, so that Frederic, following too quickly down the steep slope, ran into him and nearly fell.

"You could have warned me—" Frederic began, but the words died in his throat as the harper pointed to the bare wall where their charcoaled arrow should have been. Retracing their steps downslope from where they had left Julian, they had covered half a day's march in little more than an hour, and each branching of their path had been marked by the signs they had made coming in. How could the marks suddenly have disappeared?

"Are you sure this is the right place?" asked Frederic.

Silverhair nodded. "The other side is blank too." Perhaps some kind of condensation in the tunnel walls had neutralized the charcoal. He shrank from the possibility that the signs had been deliberately rubbed away.

"I suppose we can always retrace our own footprints . . . ," said Frederic.

Silverhair grunted and held up his taper to illuminate the passage floor. The sand and rubble that covered it looked smooth. Almost as if it had been swept . . .

Frederic looked at him, swallowed, and found his voice again. "Can you sound out a way with your harp as you did in the Caverns of Aztlan?"

"It would be no use," said the harper. "There I knew how the passage outward ran, but could not see to find it, and the echoes from my harping let me hear my way. Here, we can see for as long as our tapers last, but all these passages look alike, so how will we know where to go?"

"We'll have to go back and tell Julian—" Frederic rubbed

his eyes tiredly. "At least I can remember the way we just came." He was turning to trudge back up the slope when a noise from the other direction made both men whirl.

Metal clanked on metal. Silverhair heard something like the rasp of leather boots on grit, but the sandstone walls of the passageway swallowed sound. Straining to listen, he swore as the noise faded, then stiffened as a mutter of voices came garbled from the darkness below.

"They'll see our light—take the tapers and hide behind that last bend," whispered the harper. "I'll wait here." His heart pounded, but he was wound like a spring with the tension of the past days. His sword came out of its sheath as if by its own will.

A bobbing glow highlighted the irregular surfaces below him. Silverhair pressed himself against the wall behind a swell of stone. The grate of footsteps came clearer now; he could hear hoarse breathing, and then a sneeze.

His own nostrils prickled at the dust in the air, and he shuddered. Lady Madrone had told them there was poison in this rock, though not enough to hurt them if they did not stay long. And if they were trapped here, Silverhair thought with a bitter humor, they would have worse things to worry about than cinnabar.

Light flared suddenly across the rising floor of the haulageway. Shapes moved behind it, at first dark and featureless, then thrown into abrupt relief that highlighted cruel faces and glittered on riveted jerkins and the hilts of swords. One face for a moment showed clearly, and Silverhair drew a quick breath as he recognized Malin Scar. His sword rose to the ready, quivering like a live thing.

They reached the fork in the passageways and Silverhair held his breath while they stood arguing. Then someone suggested that men who were seeking a secret way into Blood Gard would head upward, and they came on. The light flashed up the slope past Silverhair. They were beside him—the harper's sword stabbed at Malin Scar like a silver flame and he kicked the lantern from the Shadower's hand.

Someone cried out; metal crashed and burning oil snaked across stone. But there had been two lanterns—as the light of the second revealed him Silverhair launched himself up the dark tunnel with his foes in full cry behind.

Frederic was attempting a spell to confuse pursuit when

he reached him. Silverhair thought their own familiarity with the ground would be more use to them. He dragged the boy along behind him around the bend, heard curses as someone miscalculated the turn and slammed into the wall and a deeper cry as the shock brought down a loose slab of stone from the roof of the passageway.

The rumble of falling rock resounded back and forth through the tunnels as that first rockfall set off others. Silverhair and Frederic scrambled up and to the right. Light flared behind them and they leaped for the protecting shadow of a little bay. Then the others were filling the passageway; they could not get past, but there was an opening behind them—had that been there before? Silverhair had no time to wonder. Blood and dust only made Malin Scar's furious face more terrible; and somehow the harper had lost Frederic. He could only run, knowing neither where he was going nor where he had been.

As he staggered onward, the only thing that kept Silverhair going was the thought that once he gained enough lead on his enemies to stop and free his harp, he would play the chord whose vibrations could unknit the sinews of the mountain and bring it down upon them all.

The unshielded power of the Earthstone beat against Julian's senses as if an earthquake had its epicenter there. Equilibrium spun wildly. Gravity drew him equally toward ceiling and walls and floor, yet still he stood upright, rooted to the stone.

He tasted the richness of soil composted by the fallen leaves of centuries and the spicy flavors of minerals; he felt the enduring resistance of granite, the fluid silky flow of river mud; senses for which humans have no names brought him subtleties of form and structure and identity.

Julian had grown up in a quarry—he had thought he knew all the secrets of stone, but this knowledge was from within, and with every moment the Earthstone was drawing him deeper into its own world.

Flesh and bone exulted, yearning toward their element, but that part of him that was still human struggled, terrified at this loss of control. *I am Julian—Julian, not Stone! The Earthstone was made for the King, not the King for the Jewel!* Sense struggled with the senses, striving for sovereignty. And finally, with a movement that seemed far too slight for the struggle that had caused it, Julian opened his fingers and let go of the Stone.

The Earthstone clattered to the floor and Julian staggered. He could still feel it. Coruscations of color flared through the chamber, for in this place, surrounded by its own element, the Jewel had far greater power than in the open air. But at least while he did not touch it Julian could think again. The unleashed fury of the trees had frightened him, but the concentrated power of this primal element was terrifying. No wonder his father had feared to use the Jewels!

And yet he was going to have to find some way to carry the thing out of here. Julian cursed himself for not having considered that problem earlier—Frederic should have warned him, or what use was all that study at the College of the Wise? Maybe Frederic could think of some way to deal with the Earthstone now!

He looked up and saw the gnomes still capering around him. The Gnome-King stood close by, watching him warily. Some knowledge the Jewel had left within him told him the elemental's name.

"Ghob, your people know all that passes here—how far away are the other humans now?"

"Which ones?"

Julian had spoken aloud. The Gnome-King's response was communicated by some other sense, but the undertone of malicious glee was clear.

"The two who came in with me—" Julian began, then stiffened with realization. "Ghob—are there other men here?"

"Men chase, men flee! Rock falls—all will stay!"

"Bring my two companions here—" Julian began, but the gnome was shaking his misshapen head.

"Gnomes move rock, not men, can only open way!"

"Open it then! Tap out a rhythm along the passageways until they follow you—" Julian gritted his teeth in exasperation. He should go look for them, but he dared not pick up the Earthstone, or risk losing it by leaving the chamber.

"Frederic! Silverhair!" he shouted till the echoes rang painfully around the little room. "I'm here! Come this way!"

Racked by an eternity of frustration, Julian did not know how long it had been when he heard a step. Calling again, he saw Frederic bend a little to keep from grazing his head on the archway, and stagger into the chamber. The Earthstone radiated sufficient light for Frederic to see him. With a little sob Frederic let his pack slide to the floor and Julian grabbed him, holding fast until the shudders that shook Frederic's lean shoulders began to ease. Perhaps some new stability in Julian had become perceptible, because Frederic held on to him as a man being swept away by a mudslide will cling to a boulder in his path.

"Malin Scar followed us," Frederic gasped finally. "Rockfalls blocked the entrance. Thought I was trapped! Lost you . . . and I lost Silverhair!"

Julian gave him a little shake. "It's all right now. I'm here with you, and there are gnomes all around us. They'll show us the way!" He spoke with more confidence than he felt, but he had to get the other man calmed down.

Frederic lifted his head a little and stared around him, then blinked and sighed. "Is that what they were? I could tell there was something. Can you make them help us now?"

"I've found the Earthstone, Frederic. It commands them, but the Jewel is too powerful for me to hold."

Frederic turned and gave a low whistle. "I can see something, like a sunset shining through leaves. . . . Is that the Earthstone?"

Julian nodded. "Is there some way I can carry it without touching it with my bare hands?"

For a moment Frederic frowned, then he bent and began to rummage through his pack. "Silk's an insulator—just a minute, it's in here somewhere!" In a moment he had found the little basketry box where he kept his magical things and pulled out the silk cloth that covered his altar. "This should do it! And here—" He dumped several quartz crystals out of a leather pouch and handed it to Julian. "Put the Jewel in this pouch when you have wrapped it. The thong should go around your neck, so you won't have to worry about losing the thing."

Julian took a deep breath. Even while he was talking to Frederic, the Earthstone had tugged at his awareness. With eyes a little averted to avoid being trapped by its beauty, he reached out and covered it with the cloth. The light dimmed as if he had slipped the shutter of a lantern down, and the pressure that had beat against him abruptly eased. Carefully he poked the thin silk under the Jewel, folding until the stone was securely wrapped, then eased it into the pouch that Frederic had given him. He slipped the thong over his head and stood up with a deep sigh.

"Take these, too—" Frederic was holding out the crystals that had been in the pouch. Now that the Earthstone was shut away, they seemed to glow with their own clear light. As he looked at each stone, Julian's sensitized gaze saw clearly six planes defined by three equal axes and their length, the internal latticing of the crystal giving each its own identity. He could feel them resonating as the energy of the Earthstone awakened their own inherent power, and the hairs prickled along his arms.

"Put them where the Jewel was," Frederic went on. "We're taking the gnomes' dearest treasure. We should leave *something* in return. And now"—he latched shut his pack and shouldered it again—"don't you think we had better find Silverhair?"

Captain Esteban slammed back against the wall as the lash of Caolin's anger struck him again. The sorcerer scarcely moved from the temple doorway, but his fury had cleared a space around him. His men made a swaying circle just inside the blood-colored walls, afraid to come closer, even more frightened of breaking away. Even the massed clouds over the mountain rumbled apprehensively as flickers of lightning tried to discharge the overload of tension in the air.

Caolin was aware of it as he was aware of the terror of the men around him; channeling the force of emotions that would have destroyed the sorcerer's physical form if he had tried to hold them in. The Earthstone had captured his expanded consciousness in its own explosion of power, and Captain Esteban had arrived just in time to receive the backlash as that current was cut off.

"You should have come to me immediately, killed your horses, killed your men!" Caolin bound more power into the words as he flung them at Esteban and felt the pressure ease as they left him, ease even more as the man sagged and the energy that was passing through him grounded into the earth of the courtyard. The man's cheek was grazed where he had slammed against the stone, his skin pale and perspiring. Unable to speak, he gazed at his master with dilated eyes.

Caolin took a deep breath, awareness of his own body reasserting itself with a painful prickling like circulation returning to a numb limb. *Don't kill him*—the cold mastery of his reason spoke at last. *He may still be useful. . . .*

"Esteban, Esteban, you were defeated by unnatural arts—" The Blood Lord's voice was shockingly gentle now. "But you shall have your revenge!"

The fallen man shuddered and pushed himself upright, a little color returning to his skin. "The trees—it was horrible! But, Lord—how could I have known? And knowing, what else could I do but follow them? I sent messengers by the secret road, but horses have to pick their way through those hills."

The man was repeating himself, babbling. But Caolin let him continue and heard his voice strengthen as the repetition of his tale restored an illusion of control. And while he listened, the Blood Lord forced calm upon the turbulence within himself, letting the last ripples of passion die upon the still shores of his reason until there was only the dark mirror of his soul. Reflected within it he saw the words of the mantra from which he drew his mastery.

"Nothing may move me, for nothing is at the heart of all things. . . ."

"Malin Scar has trapped them, master," said Captain Esteban. "They will not escape again!"

If Caolin had communicated with Malin Scar since that last revelation near Awhai, Julian might have been in his hands long ago. With cold clarity Caolin judged himself as he had judged his servant, and knew that in his eagerness to corrupt the Council of Westria he had underestimated the boy.

He did not yet know how Julian had been able to compel the powers of nature to serve him—perhaps it had been a natural response to the desecration of protected land and no magic at all. Standing where Julian stood now, with the Earthstone in his hand, Caolin would have blown apart the top of the mountain and the fortress that crowned it and climbed over its ruins to freedom. The boy might possess the Earthstone, but he was not yet its master. Indeed, the abrupt cutting off of power might even mean that the Jewel had already killed him.

But this time he must be sure! He took a slow step toward his captain, saw the man flinch, and stopped again.

"Rest now," he said softly. "Eat and sleep. At dawn you will take me to the entrance of the mine. If the boy and the harper come out alive, they will be our prisoners!"

The distorted harmonies of the Chord of Unmaking shimmered in Silverhair's imagination. Soon, he would make it audible, and then he and his enemies would die in a thunder of disintegrating stone. His racing pulse began to steady as he caught his breath again. The chill of the air was beginning to settle into his bones, but it would not matter long. For the moment he had escaped his pursuers, and a few moments were all he would need for the last music he would ever play. He had begun to learn it when he heard Caolin's Song of Power on the shore of the Lake of the Sorcerers, and the man called Katiz had unwittingly taught him the rest in Awhai.

He had lost his light as well, but that did not matter. He had played Swangold through so many sleepless nights, he had no need to see. The worn sealskin of the harpcase was smooth to the touch, the silver buckles opened easily to his practiced fingers, and then his hands were caressing the smooth wood of the harp, and memory shook him as if a window had been opened to let in the wind.

Just so had he taken and tuned the harp in the Caverns of Aztlan. As he settled Swangold's familiar weight against his left shoulder he realized that the darkness in which he sat now had finally exorcised that nightmare.

And he had played in darkness through the night when all unknowing he had first met Julian. Silverhair's fingers tightened on the tuning key as anger, regret, and frustration stabbed him with a single pain. Julian was dead now, or doomed, and surely he, and Frederic, would prefer to crush out life quickly than to endure a slow starvation in the dark. Silverhair knew—he had faced that death before. He had sworn first to find Faris's child, and then, to serve him. Even in this moment, Silverhair did not know if what he felt for

Julian was love. But he knew that this was the only thing he could do for him now.

He plucked the lowest string, made a minute adjustment, and began to run up the scale. Even here, the harp's tone was sweet and resonant. The chord Silverhair meant to play would destroy the harp, too, but the ruins of the Red Mountain would be a fitting monument for Swangold to share with the boy who should have been King of Westria.

Julian—Julian! Silverhair's strong fingers drew from the harp the first notes of a song to Westria's golden hills. *All this should have been your own!* Sweet as memory, harpsong filled the little chamber where he had found refuge. One melody led to another, variation modulating into theme in a medley of rhythms and harmonies that distilled into one music, all that he loved in this land.

Enchanted by harpsong, he heard nothing but Swangold's music, and it was without surprise that he opened his eyes and saw Julian's spirit standing there.

From his breast shone a green and golden glow that limned his whole body in light, and a peace that matched the music was in his eyes. Silverhair bowed his head in homage, accepting this apparition as his authority to end it now. He took a last breath and poised his hands above Swangold's faintly glimmering strings.

Then boot soles crunched on stone, and suddenly Julian's arms were around him—hard, warm, *alive!*

Nerveless with shock, Silverhair let Julian bundle the harp back into its casing, understanding only fragments of what he was saying to him. He heard Frederic's voice too, then a shout and a flare of light behind them brought him to full awareness.

"They've found us!" whispered Julian. "Are you ready? Hang on to my belt so I don't lose you, and come on!"

Silverhair slipped the strap of the harpcase over his shoulder and struggled to his feet. He wanted to ask if Julian knew where he was going, but Frederic was close behind him and Julian was pulling him along.

There followed a nightmare journey through the dark. Aching muscles told him they were going upward, and it seemed to him that they turned right more often than left, but he could not be sure. Silverhair stumbled over obstacles he could not see, and winced at the hollow *bonk* he could hear even through the sealskin when the harpcase slammed against some rocky protrusion. Relentless as a hound, Malin Scar trailed them by the sound of their footsteps and their tracks on the sandy floor, never quite catching up to them, never so far behind that they could rest.

Once, Julian stopped to try and block the tunnel behind them with a few sure strokes of his pick against a bulge in the ceiling's stone. But even as the rock began to give way, the others were upon them. Swords stabbed in the narrow passageway and one of the Shadower's men screamed. Then Julian jerked them back as the rock crashed down. They slackened their pace a little as they went onward, but the rockfall had not completely blocked the tunnel, and too soon the flicker of light told them that they were followed once more.

The passages grew narrower. Panting, they paused where the tunnel branched, and Silverhair heard Julian talking to someone whose answers could not be heard.

"This way—" Julian whispered. "The air is bad down there."

They started up the new shaft, then a tug halted him.

"I've got an idea," said Julian. "Wait here for me."

Silverhair heard the diminishing whisper of Julian's footsteps, and gripped Frederic's arm.

"Who was Julian talking to?" he asked in a low voice. "How can he see?"

Frederic suppressed a small, triumphant laugh. "He found the Earthstone, didn't you guess? We're being personally guided by the King of the gnomes!"

Silverhair pursed his lips in a soundless whistle. The boy had actually done it! For the first time since he and Frederic had been separated, he began to hope again.

From the other tunnel he heard the sound of a hammer tap-tapping, as if someone was trying to break through, and then a rattle that could have been a thrown or falling stone. Malin Scar's light flared upward, and they heard a mutter of voices. In a moment Julian was back beside them, breathing quickly. The lantern glow passed the turnoff; Julian's grip on their shoulders froze them to stillness.

Then came a flare of blue light and the roar of falling stone. They heard men's screams as the echoes diminished, but by the time the afterimage of the explosion had faded,

there was no sound but the occasional rattle as the last
pebbles rolled to a final rest. Silverhair shuddered. If Malin
Scar still lived, shadowed and Shadower were equally in the
darkness now. But even for his enemy the harper would
have wished a quick ending. He knew what falling stone
could do.

Julian gave a long, shuddering sigh and spoke a word to
the darkness. Then he took Silverhair's hand. "This
way—" he said softly. "It's not far now."

By the time a circle of blue appeared in the darkness
above them, Silverhair was almost too exhausted by exer-
tion and emotion to care. With the mine entrance blocked,
it was clear that one of the ventilation shafts cut by the
Ancient miners was the only possible way out for them, but
he wondered where he could find the strength to make the
climb.

He slumped against cold rock while Frederic heaved
Julian high enough for him to brace his back and legs
against the sides of the chimney and work his way upward.
His struggling body blocked the cold light that streamed
down from the surface, then the opening was clear again
and the rope for which they had finally found a use snaked
down to them. Frederic tied their packs securely so that
Julian could haul them up, and then the harpcase, and
as Silverhair watched it swaying upward it was small
comfort to know that the harp would land on him if it
fell.

Then the rope was descending again. Frederic tied it
beneath Silverhair's armpits and gave him a boost that
shoved him into the shaft. Muscles screamed protest as the
harper struggled toward the light, but the pull of the rope
was steady and somehow he kept on. Dazzled, he shut his
eyes as his head reached the surface, and felt Julian's strong
hands closing on his arms and hauling him blind and
helpless as a hooked fish onto the dry grass.

"Uncle—look there—"

Julian's wondering voice recalled Silverhair to consciousness. He must have passed out for a few moments, for now
Frederic was there too, grazed and grimy, but grinning as if
his face would crack, and pointing down the hill.

They lay hidden in a tangle of brush on the northeastern
slope of the Red Mountain. Below they saw the long folds of

dry foothills, the blue gleam of the Dorada, and from the
island in the midst of it, a curl of grey smoke that came
from the cookfires of Laurelynn.

The sun had already dipped behind the Red Mountain by
the time Captain Esteban and his master reined in before
the entrance to the mine. There was a great stillness here.
No birds moved in the trees, but there was a lingering haze
of dust in the air. A barked order sent men climbing up to
the entrance, but they did not stay long.

"It's blocked, my lord." Captain Esteban turned to
Caolin. "Not even a mouse could get out of there now."

The Blood Lord nudged his gelding forward and sat
staring at the shadowed opening, trying to sense what had
happened here.

"I suppose it's a fitting tomb for your enemies," said
Esteban, "but I'm sorry about Malin Scar."

It occurred to Caolin that he should be sorry too, for the
Shadower had been a good tool, but he was too intent on
interpreting the traces of power that lingered in this place to
think about Malin Scar. Certainly there had been a great
explosion of energy, but it was fading fast. He sensed
neither Julian nor the Earthstone now. Julian's death could
account for that, but even untrained as the boy was, his
passing should have left some perturbation in the astral
which the Blood Lord could see.

But all he felt was emptiness. Reason told him that Julian
was dead, but his sorcerer's senses prickled. Wordless, he
reined around and headed the gelding back down the trail.
He would change nothing in his plans. He would send word
to the agent who was keeping watch on the Master of the
Junipers and to his people in Laurelynn.

He had to be sure.

When the Blood Lord and his men had gone, the vale at
the foot of the Red Mountain settled to silence once more.
A little breeze shook the bare branches of the sycamores,
but when they stilled, the madrone tree that stood among
them continued to tremble. After a few moments it shivered, dislimned, and re-formed in the shape of a woman,
red-skinned and clad in leaf green, who strode swiftly
westward.

* * *

The rosy blaze of the western sky was fading into a dim grey that made everything beyond the river a mystery as Julian and his companions trudged the last mile to Laurelynn. The dying light lent a deeper glow to the ruddy brick of its walls, rising sheer from the banks of the artificial island that men had built up from the mudflats of the delta where the Dorada and the Darkwater became one. Above the walls they could see the second stories and roofs of the houses, and in every window lights were flickering, as if to welcome them home.

Julian's boots clomped hollowly on the wood of the bridge. Men in the brick-colored jerkins of the city guard stood at attention along the rail, but the great gate was open, flanked by torches whose flickering light gilded the worn planks and glittered on the dark waters below. From inside the city they could hear sounds of singing, and children's laughter.

Julian cast a doubtful glance at Frederic, whose once fine clothes had been rendered unrecognizable by their passage through the mines, and the harper, whose identifying mane of silver hair was now a matted grey. Every muscle in his own body was aching, and as he fingered the tears in his tunic he wondered why the guards did not form ranks across the bridgeway and turn them away.

"This is not quite how I had imagined the return of the Prince to his city." Silverhair caught his breath on a laugh, as if his ribs were paining him. "But at least they're prepared to receive us."

"The welcome is not for us—" said Frederic in an awed voice. "In the mine we lost track of the days, but I have been counting. This must be Samaine Eve, and they have lighted candles in all the windows to welcome the spirits of the ancestors home."

Julian stared at him for a moment and then began to laugh. "Well, if we are not ghosts then surely we are the next thing to it. You should see yourself, Frederic! If we don't clean you up before we get to the palace your mother will think you a revenant!"

"And I have been given up for dead so many times half the country already thinks me a legend!" added Silverhair.

It was not really funny, but suddenly all three of them

were laughing. Half hysterical with exhaustion and the relief from intolerable strain, they reeled past the stony-faced guards. But as they lurched between the massive pillars of the south gate, Julian felt once more the weight of the Earthstone, and it seemed to him that he was the real ghost here, for the boy he had been the last time he passed this way was forever gone.

At some time during the hours of darkness, the brush of the Red Mountain stirred once more as something wriggled through a forgotten opening. Broken and gibbering, it had once been called Malin Scar. Through the cold of that night it lay whimpering, and there was only a little life left within it when Caolin's men found it on the following day and carried it to Blood Gard.

SEVENTEEN

"Well, Julian—I understand you have found yourself some fine parents indeed!" Lord Philip stood next to the Council table with his brother by his side.

Julian felt the greeting which he had been rehearsing for the past two weeks slip away like the raindrops that were sliding down the windows of the little Council chamber, leaving him mute and gaping. *He will think I've become half-witted as well as presumptuous!* Instinctively Julian stiffened the muscles of his face into an unrevealing mask. But he could not control the anxious cramping of his stomach. Would Philip accept him as King?

Philip's brother Robert had jumped up as Julian and Silverhair entered. His blue eyes were aglow, and he was grinning from ear to ear. It was a good sign, but not conclusive—Philip did not take his younger brother into his confidence.

The Lord Commander lifted an eyebrow at Julian's

silence. Then his gaze moved to the harper and he looked questioningly toward the head of the long table where Eric was sorting papers.

"I asked Sir Farin to join us, Philip, since he knows as much as any man about the dangers we face now." Lord Eric cleared his throat. "Do you remember him?"

Philip stared, and Julian took advantage of the respite to catch his breath. A gust of wind flung rain rattling against the windows, but the fire crackled valiantly, its ruddy light glowing on the arms of the Estates of Westria glazed into the tiles. Julian looked at the arms of the Ramparts, trying to figure out if he was feeling relief or despair. Lord Philip's right to the throne was as good as his own, and he had ruled a Province for nearly ten years. It made no sense that such a man would give it all up to a backwoods nobody who had been his own squire!

"You were only fourteen, my lord," said Silverhair, "and it was a long time ago. You have changed too." He smiled, and Julian looked curiously at the man who had been his commander, trying mentally to subtract the stoutness good humor had added to Philip's belly and replace the brown hair that responsibility had worn away, trying to understand. But Philip's face had become as unreadable as Julian's own.

"That was the year everything changed," said the Lord Commander soberly. "But I am not likely to forget your harping. I am glad to see you again, sir, for I have heard some rumors about your wanderings and would like to hear the full tale. Eric has told me how your quest ended—" His brown eyes fixed Julian's, and the younger man could not look away.

"And so—" Philip went on, "my squire becomes my lord and I add a cousin to my kin!" He shook his head in wonder.

Julian braced himself, and abruptly the power of speech returned. "I will accept the title of cousin gladly, my lord. But as for the other, King Alexander was grandfather to us both. When the Council comes to consider claims, yours or Robert's is as good as mine."

Philip gave him a long look. "Do you wish to be King?"

"I wish to justify my mother's agony . . . ," Julian said slowly, forcing out words he had memorized during long sleepless hours. "I wish to avenge those who have died by Caolin's treachery. I wish justice and prosperity for all the kindreds in Westria"—he thought of Lady Madrone and the broken tower—"so that the Covenant may be maintained. If this is to wish to be King . . . I do." His eyes met those of Lord Philip desperately. Some emotion changed Philip's face, and with dawning wonder Julian realized it was a smile.

"That is well then, cousin—for I do *not!*" said the Lord Commander. "I saw my father worn out by the weight of governing this land. You have turned up in the nick of time for me!"

Before Julian could stop him, Philip had gone down on one knee. He reached out to raise him, but the Lord Commander shook his head.

"No lad—I kneel not to my squire, but to the King you will be. And to that King I offer all my strength and wisdom, for as long as I shall live!"

Robert knelt beside his brother, his blue eyes luminous with unshed tears. Swallowing, Julian held out his other hand to his friend, knowing that Robert's answering grip was only the confirmation of a bond that had been made between them long ago. And that, more than anything else, gave him the courage to look at Lord Philip again.

"If I am in any way fitted for this task, it is because of what you have taught me, my lord. The Guardians know how I need your counsel! Now will you please get up again?"

Philip laughed. "Indeed I will!" Julian felt his weight for a moment as the Lord Commander pulled himself upright. "That floor is cold. But if we are going to sit in Council then I want some of that tea I see simmering over the fire!" He eased gratefully into a chair and Robert went over to get the mugs and teapot.

Julian felt himself finally relaxing as the hot liquid went down. He had not realized how much he had feared this day.

"So you have sent out the invitations for a Midwinter Council?" asked Philip, taking a long swallow of tea.

Eric nodded. "I would have acted sooner, but I could do nothing until Julian returned. Perhaps it is just as well—as the weather worsens, even the woodsrats must go to ground!

Men will be more willing to come to a Council if they believe their homes will still be standing when they return."

"We saw the work of sea wolves on our trip down the coast," said Silverhair. "Have you been suffering in the mountains as well?"

"Julian could tell you! If anything, they have been worse this year. If I thought such a rabble capable of organization I would say they were conspiring!"

"They can *be* organized," said Silverhair bitterly, "and, my lord, Caolin means to do just that!"

"While your attention was on the borders, he has wormed his way into the heart of Westria," echoed Julian. "He has built a stronghold on the summit of the Red Mountain, and his fortresses grip the spine of the coastal hills!"

"You have seen them?" asked Robert.

"I was a prisoner in one of them," said Julian. He broke off, remembering how the trees had torn apart the tower, and suddenly the Earthstone seemed to weigh more heavily. *I have it,* he thought grimly, *but will I dare to use its power?*

"We have seen the fortress on the Red Mountain as well," Lord Eric said heavily. "Caolin calls it Blood Gard. You will say I should have guarded against this—but how could I have guessed that even Caolin would do such a thing? Farin brought news of his attacks on our borders, and I went north to confer with Sandremun soon after Julian left Bongarde. I have only recently returned." For a moment the Regent massaged his forehead with his muscular fingers as if his head was paining him. Then he went on.

"They tell me that for months the Red Mountain has been swathed in shadow, but on Samaine the clouds cleared suddenly and we saw the fortress there. It is not yet widely known in the Kingdom—that is one of the matters we must bring before the Council. I do not know how the Estates will react to the news."

"To which news?" asked Robert suddenly. "We have found the Prince, and the Prince has found the Earthstone! Surely Julian will have the vote of Seagate and the Corona as well as of the Ramparts. That's three of the four Provinces. That leaves only Las Costas, the Free Cities, the administrators, and the College of the Wise."

"Whose vote is not at all certain—" said Eric. "And if

the land is not united behind the sovereign, we will waste our strength fighting each other—"

"And Caolin will be swift to take advantage of our divisions!" added Julian. "He's right, Robert. It would be different if I'd been raised in Laurelynn and everyone knew me. But some will call me upstart or imposter even if the Council is unanimous—"

"Well then, we need to catch the imagination of the crowd!" Robert grinned.

Lord Philip took a long swallow of tea, set his mug down and wiped his mouth with the back of his hand.

"You've been resisting my attempts to knight you for two years, Julian! But you can hardly protest your unworthiness now!"

Julian knew that his face must have betrayed him finally, for Philip began to laugh. Even Silverhair was smiling.

The Regent nodded, his face growing less troubled as he thought about it. "The Council cannot object to that. . . ."

"Do it just before the meeting," said Silverhair. "Set up a platform in the square before the Council Hall, so that everyone can see. The vote could be carried by the enthusiasm of the crowd!"

Lord Eric looked at him, and his eyes kindled suddenly. "You sing to them, Farin—as you did before. It was your music that turned the people against Caolin!"

For a moment Julian understood what Eric must have been like before the weight of ruling wore him down. Then he saw revealed in the harper's face in swift succession pride, and apprehension, and pain.

"Music certainly we must have, but I think we should ask Master Ras and the musicians of the city to provide it. No one here would even know who I am now."

From the top of the Red Mountain, Laurelynn was a grey jumble surrounded by a brown ribbon of river. But at the end of a winter day, the glass in its westward facing windows caught the light of the setting sun like a veining of gold in what had seemed a lump of worthless ore.

Caolin stood beside Malin Scar, looking at the city of his enemies. The sorcerer's spies had confirmed that Julian was there now. But he had not sensed the Earthstone. Without training, Julian could not use it. And the Blood Lord would make sure that the boy never had a chance to learn.

Caolin set his hand upon Malin Scar's shoulder, and the Shadower turned abruptly to face his master.

"You shall have your chance at the boy and at the harper as well." Caolin spoke slowly, clearly, for the Shadower had been partly deafened by the silence underground. His eyes seemed permanently dilated, as if he had looked too long upon darkness. Those eyes were not entirely sane, but that did not trouble Caolin. He understood madness.

"Now I have another task for you. There is a man called the Master of the Junipers, who lives on the slopes of the Lady Mountain. He is the boy's teacher. He must not be allowed to go to him in Laurelynn. . . ."

Malin Scar's reply was only a whisper, for his voice had been destroyed by screaming where no one could hear, but Caolin understood his meaning. And when the Shadower left him, the Blood Lord smiled.

Ordrey was waiting when Caolin returned to his chambers, and for him the Blood Lord had other orders.

"The Council of Westria will meet in the week before Midwinter. The lords of the Estates and all their holders will be there. The Red Mountain ought to be represented as well. . . ."

"Will you go to them?" Ordrey grinned like a hound.

"Not yet. You will be my delegate, Ordrey—" Caolin's voice deepened; a flicker of his fingers compelled Ordrey's attention, and as the man's eyes unfocused in trance, Caolin began to tell him what he must do.

Focus is everything, Julian told himself. *Aim your awareness like an arrow and your mind will bear you where you need to go.* The Master of the Junipers had taught him that. He wondered if the Master would be here tomorrow. He knew that Lord Eric had sent word to him, but there had been no reply.

He must not allow himself to worry about the old man—not now, during his vigil. The night of his knighthood—the pun made him smile and he thrust the thought away. He had seen men who took their knighting as lightly as going to a festival, and others who agonized over their fitness. Julian realized that somewhere during the past months his awe of the sword of knighthood had been put into perspective by fear of the mantle of the King. But his knighthood would be part of his Kingship. He must be the Defender—bearing the Sword of Justice through the land. Confused visions of battle and victory warred in his imagination.

Julian settled himself more comfortably on the thin cushion and took a deep breath. One of the candles on the altar flickered wildly as the flame came to an uneven place in the wick, then steadied again. The small temple in the foundations of the palace was a little damp because of the river. Redwood paneling kept out some of the chill, and there was matting on the floor, but Julian was glad of the cloak that Lady Rosemary had made for him.

He pulled it more closely around him and reached out to touch the glittering links of the mail shirt lying before the altar, the sheen of greaves and vambraces, and the burnished gleam of the steel helm. *But remember,* he told himself, *your real armor is within. . . .* He felt the beginning of that sinking sensation that heralded a change in consciousness when someone sneezed outside the temple door.

Julian's eyes flew open. "Is somebody there?" The door eased open and candlelight gleamed on copper hair.

"Rana—what are you doing here?" Julian's lips quirked as he remembered the first time he had asked her that question. He saw a quick flush stain her fair skin.

"I've a gift for you," she said quickly. She held out a folded piece of silky white wool and shoved it at him. "It's an undertunic," Rana hurried on. "I'm not good at embroidery, and I didn't want to give you something like a scarf where my mistakes would show. As it is I got blood on it when I pricked my finger, but you can't see it if you don't know where—" She paused for breath and gave a little laugh. Her hands were firmly clasped behind her back again as if she didn't know what to do with them.

"Thank you," Julian said gravely. "No one else thought of that, and the wool will absorb sweat and stay warm." And with Rana's blood on it, he thought that perhaps something of her bright courage would warm him as well. But she was still flushed, and he didn't want to embarrass her further by saying so. After a moment Julian realized that he was afraid of embarrassing himself as well.

"Well, it's the best I could do. I know I should have given

it to you before, but I just finished it. I hope your vigil goes well," Rana added with more composure.

"It's only because of you and the others that I'm here at all," he answered with an earnestness that surprised them both. "I owe you my thanks for that, too!"

Rana was blushing again, but her eyes were as bright as the candles now. She ducked her head in something that was not quite a bow, then wind fluttered the flames as the door opened and closed, and she was gone.

Smiling a little, Julian settled himself for meditation again.

Perhaps an hour had passed when he heard a step in the passageway and came back to full awareness. He was already watching the door when Frederic opened it. Moisture glittered on his wool cloak, and his fair hair was dark with rain. It seemed to Julian that his friend's face had the drained look that the passage of great emotion leaves behind.

"Are you all right?"

"I will be." Frederic managed something like his old sweet smile, then cast a practiced glance over Julian's piled arms. "That blade they gave you is good enough, but this one is better. Will you accept it from me?" he asked abruptly. From beneath his cloak he pulled a sheathed sword and offered it to Julian.

Wondering, Julian took it, then looked quickly up at his friend.

"Frederic, this is your sword!"

"I won't need it anymore. My father has given permission. I'm to return to the College of the Wise!" His face shone with a kind of fearful joy. Looking at him, Julian felt an odd sensation, as if there had been some subtle shift in the earth below.

When you return from Awahna, and I am King, you will be my Seneschal. . . .

For a moment Julian thought that he had spoken aloud, for Frederic was looking at him in wonder. How could he know such a thing, when he did not know if he would ever wear the Crown? But wherever that thought had come from, he supposed he should not be surprised that Frederic, who was already half a Master, had heard it—not after Awhai.

Trying to cover his confusion, Julian looked back at the blade. He had admired it often enough, but he had never held it before. Now it came sweetly out of its sheath and swung up like an extension of his hand, catching the candlelight as if it had been forged from flame. For a moment he held it that way, savoring the faint quiver in the flexible steel, like a live thing. Then he brought it around and down in a swift arc, and slipped it into the sheath again.

"This is a great gift!" Julian said wonderingly.

"My father bore it when he was a young man."

"Then the sword should go to your brother, not to me." He started to hand it back again.

Frederic shook his head. "My father said I could give it to you. He's not a man of words, Julian, but I think the sword will tell you what he wanted to say. . . ."

Julian pulled the blade a foot out of the sheath, watching the play of light on polished steel, and nodded, swallowing. He had known that the sword would bear the impress of Frederic's gallantry, but now he recognized the sheer delight in battle that came from the man who was Westria's most famous warrior, and he understood the loyalty that policy would not yet allow the Regent to offer him.

After Frederic had gone, Julian found it hard to concentrate again. He half-expected more visitors, but as the night drew on, the temple remained still. Fighting sleep, he rearranged his gear, contemplating the inner meaning of each item as he replaced it. The body armor was his protection from hatred as well as against more tangible blows, and he thought that Rana's undertunic would ward him as well as the mail. The helm guarded his head from blows to the reason. The sword was to strike down injustice and cut evil away. And the shield—remembering how Caolin's power had struck them at Registhorpe, Julian settled the shield on his knees and began to consider seriously what a shield ought to do.

Julian was not much of a horseman, and he had told them he would feel silly with a horseman's triangular shield. He had insisted he wanted a round shield, and the armorer had covered it with brown bull's hide, edged and cross-banded with strips of gilded bronze so that it looked suspiciously like the circled cross of Westria. Julian grinned, wondering whose idea that had been.

He slid the shield onto his left arm and hefted it, feeling the muscles in his upper arm and the top of his shoulder harden with strain. The grips were well-made, measured precisely to fit his arm, but the shield was a little heavier than he was used to, and it had been months since he had held one of any kind. He was going to have to do regular shield-lifts until his muscles became accustomed to it again. Still grinning, Julian took Frederic's sword in his other hand.

Sword and shield balanced each other—offense and defense—stern justice and the sheltering mercy that tempered it. Both were necessary. But as Julian thought about Caolin, his awareness focused on the shield again. The shield of the warrior was like the sphere of protection they had visualized around Sir Randal's hall, something that could ward off blows, or perhaps become a weapon itself to reflect them back again.

Julian drew a long, shuddering breath, remembering the cold touch of the sorcerer's attacking will, and his own deep reaching for earth force with which to power their protection. And as if the memory had awakened it, he felt an answering throb of power from the Earthstone. Frowning, he set down sword and shield and looked at them again. The cross of Westria was the Cross of Earth—the four elements made manifest. Clearly, this was an earth-shield. Julian's hand traced the pattern of the banding and paused on the golden boss. That roundel of metal was softer—real gold, perhaps, for it gave just a little when he pressed with the hilt of the sword.

Compelled by some instinct he did not wholly understand, Julian drew his dagger and began to haggle at the roundel, his horror at defacing the smith's work overwhelmed by need. Soon he had made a jagged hole, and with trembling fingers he undid the wrappings that protected the Earthstone.

Its unshielded power pulsed in the little room. Abruptly Julian was aware of the stone and wood around him, the roots of the island that the river tried ever to gnaw, the deep strength of the earth below. Handling the stone through the silk that had wrapped it, he jammed it into the gap in the shieldboss, working it under the torn flaps of metal and pressing them down again until it was tightly wedged. A smith could do it better—with a smith's tools, he himself could make a job of it that would be aesthetic as well as secure. But that did not matter now. Breathing hard, Julian slid the shield back onto his arm.

He could feel the power of the Earthstone throbbing through the layers of wood and leather and metal and vibrating in the flesh of his arm, but the cross-banding transmitted much of it outward to the rim, where it circled, radiating a mediated energy into the surrounding air, and he found that if he concentrated he could bear it. Indeed, it was more than simply bearing it, for as he sat with the shield on his arm, Julian sensed a current of energy linking him to the earth below.

"Earthstone—one day I will learn to use you to heal—but for now, may you shield my shield arm as my arm shields Westria! Thus in the name of my knighthood do I pray!" Julian cried aloud, and the words vibrated through his bones.

And as if that prayer had been a spell, abruptly Julian shifted into the tranced state for which he had been straining. And suddenly he realized that someone else was in the room, a tall, helmed figure cloaked in warrior scarlet who stood in silent vigil before the altar, holding a naked sword.

And in his vision Julian knew that this was the Champion, who had come to keep watch beside him until the dawn.

❯❯❯ EIGHTEEN ❮❮❮

Murmuring with a sound like the deep voice of the river that surrounded their city, the people of Laurelynn flowed into the great central square. Silverhair watched them from the platform that had been hammered together in front of the broad porch of the Council Hall, remembering the days when he had been Sir Farin Harper and a knight of Westria.

A fitful sunlight flickered from behind scattered clouds, glowing suddenly on the deep primary colors of wind-whipped banners and striking gleams of silver or gold from their embroidery. The wind that was breaking up the clouds had blown the dark mists of the Valley away, and the chill December air had a wintry clarity. The Council had been called for three days before the Feast of Sunreturn, and Julian's knighting was to be its prelude.

The cloaks of the warriors on the platform made a blaze of color beneath the grass green banner of Westria, whose golden circled cross seemed to blaze even when the sun was behind a cloud. The setting was perfect, thought Silverhair. Now they had only to bring off the ceremony.

The guildmasters and holders who had come to represent their districts at the Council had reserved seats in the bleachers in front of the chancery. Despite the weather and activities of the raiders, a surprisingly large number of them had managed to get here. He hoped that was a good sign. The music coming from the steps of the guildhall showed that Master Ras was doing his part. A shiver of movement rippled through the double line of city guardsmen who were keeping open the route between the palace and the Council Hall, and the dance tune shifted into a more stately, martial, air. Silverhair stiffened, knowing that Julian must be coming now.

As he moved, the folds of his cloak released the spicy

scent of the cedar chips in which Rosemary had packed it
away after he left Laurelynn so long ago. The soft touch of
the crimson velvet reminded him painfully of his own
knighting. Faris had made the cloak for him, setting his
device of a hawk alighting upon the curve of a harp upon its
back in exquisite embroidery. Silverhair's eyes stung as he
remembered the glory of that day, when everyone he loved
had still been living, and his only worry had been whether
to follow the way of the harp or of the sword!

In the end he had followed both ways, though neither in
any fashion he could have expected; he supposed that the
chronic ache in his bones came partly from that strain. And
now he was here, armed as a knight again, but bearing the
harp that had become his most useful weapon, as well as a
blade.

Silverhair felt a stir among the men around him in
response to the movement he glimpsed at the palace door.
Eric looked as hollow-eyed as if he had kept vigil along with
Julian. It could almost have been the first Regent, Robert of
the Ramparts, standing there. Silverhair remembered the
hotheaded boy who had been his friend and wondered if it
was the weight of responsibility or only time that had
changed him. Then he remembered his own white hair and
knew that they were all different now. Would the years do
the same thing to Julian? He suppressed a smile. Whether
through prenatal stress or temperament, Julian seemed to
have been born responsible.

The harper turned back to Eric, seeing as if for the first
time the grey that salted his old friend's brown hair. Staying
up all night was a young man's indulgence, though young
Alexander of Las Costas seemed scarcely more rested.
Philip, on the other hand, looked almost aggressively cheerful, and Sandremun, who had made it down from the north
in record time, had lost none of his old carefree air.

Drums rolled from across the square, and Silverhair
straightened, feeling his pulse quicken even though he knew
precisely how the effect was produced and why. There was a
flicker of green and gold as the Herald of Westria strode
down the lane between the guardsmen, then more movement as an honor guard formed by the heirs of the Provinces followed him. Robert of Rivered came first, wearing
Ramparts purple and gold, his beauty prompting more than

one countryman to wonder if this was the prince that everyone had sought for so long. Elinor of the Corona marched beside him, her golden hair hidden beneath a helm, and the white belt she had earned in the northern wars cinched tightly over the black and white surcoat of her House. Then came Alexander's heir, an older cousin in the red and black of House Battle, who peered around him as if he was wondering what he was doing there, and next to him Frederic, looking surprisingly austere in Seagate's loden green. As they drew closer, Silverhair realized that though he bore the white belt of knighthood, Frederic was neither armed nor wearing a sword, and he began to understand some of the pain he had perceived in Eric's eyes.

Then Silverhair's·breath caught as the big double doors opened again and another figure emerged from the shadows of the palace, dark-haired and cloaked in brilliant blue. The harper caught his breath, and heard a muffled groan from Eric, close by, and knew that for a moment both of them had thought they were seeing Jehan. . . .

But it was Julian—who else but Julian walked with that deliberate, heavy tread? And of course he was taller and broader through the shoulders than the King, who had been, despite his prowess, a lightly-built man. Julian was walking now as if he carried Westria, not just his round shield and his helm. The shield's canvas cover repeated the Starbairn arms.

Whispers ran through the crowd like the rustle of wind in a forest, cut off by a sudden blast of clarions, whose bittersweet braying soared into a march that was supported by the steady rumble of the drums. The procession paced forward, the city guardsmen peeling off two by two from their posts and falling in behind. As the lane was left unguarded the people flowed forward to fill the empty space, so that Julian's progress left a swirling wake as if half Westria were rushing to follow him.

The Herald mounted the steps. The Commanders adjusted their spacing to let their heirs take their places beside them. Then Julian began to climb the stairs, and it seemed to Silverhair that the entire platform trembled to his tread. The city guard fanned out behind him in a half circle around it.

Clarions blared. The Herald's staff crashed down. In the sudden silence his trained voice carried clearly.

"Hear me now, ye people of Laurelynn! We are gathered here to witness the making of a knight of Westria. The candidate who stands before you is Julian of Stanesvale, true son of Jehan Starbairn, King of Westria, and Faris of Hawkrest Hold, his Queen. Who will speak for him and attest his right to the honor he seeks here?"

The Herald paused to let the murmur of commentary on the first public proclamation of Julian's identity fade.

"I will speak for him!" Robert took a step forward, grinning broadly. "He has been my brother-in-arms since I took my name!"

"Sir Robert of Rivered speaks for the candidate!" The Herald's echo informed anyone who had missed Robert's ringing tones.

"I will speak for him!" The glow of Frederic's hair in the sunlight matched the radiance of his smile. "He has saved my life and more!"

"And I— He is worthy of his name!" Silverhair added suddenly. He had not intended to say anything, being such close kin, but it was this boy's father who had spoken for and knighted him, and as the words left his lips he realized that they were true.

"Sir Farin Silverhair speaks for the candidate!" the Herald repeated without the flicker of an eyelid to show that he knew precisely what he was doing by so linking the harper's old name with his new one. But the babble of question and answer among the people proved that though everyone might have forgotten Farin Harper, the legend of Silverhair was going strong. The harper felt his eyes sting.

"I'll speak for the boy too, if I may—" The shout from the crowd was loud enough to need no permission. "Last winter he saved my village from raiders and kept us going till spring." The burly speaker would have added more, but apparently the crowd included a number of Ramparts men, and his voice was lost in the uproar as they elaborated.

Julian's stone face shone suddenly with astonished delight, as if it had never occurred to him he could deserve such loyalty. Jehan had never quite believed it either, thought Silverhair. If Julian could win the kind of love his father had inspired, he would have no trouble gaining the

Crown. The harper remembered the passionate devotion he had offered the dead King—had that been only a boy's enthusiasm? He looked at Julian, standing in the pride of his youth before the nobility of Westria, and knew that though he had spoken for him, his heart did not hold that kind of love for his nephew now. Just what it was that he did feel he could not tell.

"Julian of Stanesvale has been presented to the people and spoken for—" The Herald had refocused the attention of the crowd at last. "Who will give him the accolade?"

"I will!" Lord Philip's voice rang across the square. "For the past two years Julian has been my squire, and I claim that right as his kinsman and his lord!"

The question of who should perform the ceremony had been debated through a long, wet night, but even if Julian had been raised as a prince the honor would probably have gone to the man who trained him. This way they need not worry about whether Eric's participation would imply the support of the Regency.

Lord Philip took from the hands of the marshal a shining blade, which also happened to be the Sword of Justice of Westria, and turned to face Julian.

"Julian, in recognition of the valor and skill in arms that you have displayed in the defense of the people of Westria, and the skill in all the accomplishments befitting a gentleman, which I have observed in you, I am minded to make you knight. Will you accept this from my hand?"

"My lord, I will."

"He who would take up the sword must abide its judgment. Strength must be restricted by its own severity. Do you accept that law?"

Julian knelt before him. His low voice carried clearly.

"As I bow my head beneath this sword, I bind me to that justice with my word."

The great blade trembled as Philip lifted it. "You are honorable, courteous, and brave." Sunlight flared from the falling sword once, and then again as its flat struck Julian on each shoulder. "Rise, Sir Julian of the Stones, Knight of Westria!"

As the cheering of the people beat against his ears, Silverhair reflected on the inspiration that had led Frederic to suggest that name. On the surface, it was a courteous reference to the holding where Julian had been raised and the milk name his foster parents had given him. But *the* Stones of Westria were the four Jewels, and with or without the Crown, Julian was their natural lord.

Philip pulled Julian to his feet and hugged him. Lord Alexander of Las Costas came forward to place around his neck the gold chain. Then it was Lady Elinor's turn to buckle on the white belt of knighthood, but it was Eric himself who knelt to bind the golden spurs to his booted feet.

"Julian," said Philip when they were done with the embracing, "you have been my squire, but that belt gains you your freedom. Where will you offer your service?"

Silverhair saw Julian take a deep breath and stiffened, wondering what the boy was up to now. If he had discussed this with Philip, it had not been when the harper was there, and Eric's startled expression suggested that it was unexpected to him as well.

"Philip, you have been a good Master, but I may not swear allegiance to any lord." Julian turned with a steady deliberation that compelled the attention until he could see the other three Provincial Lords and the people beyond them. His face might have been carved from granite, and when he spoke, his voice was calm and clear, but Silverhair saw that his hands were trembling. Julian waited until the stillness was almost tangible; then he bowed.

"Instead, I offer my service to all of you, and through you, to the land of Westria. This sword I dedicate to the destruction of her foes—" In one swift movement Julian unsheathed the shining blade and struck it point-first into the wood of the platform. While all eyes were still mesmerized by its quivering, he slipped the canvas covering from his shield.

"And with this shield I will ward her from her enemies! To this service I bind myself until the Lady of Westria releases me or my own life ends; this I swear in the name of the Guardian of Men!"

Straightening, Julian lifted the shield to face the sun and suddenly the air was all adazzle with coruscations of multicolored light. Silverhair could not tell if the platform trembled beneath his feet or if the shock had staggered him. Blinking, he realized that the light was coming from the shield. He heard Frederic's awed whisper.

"It's the Earthstone!"

In moments what Frederic had whispered was being said by others more loudly, as the rumor spread through the crowd. But this was too holy a thing for cheering, and in moments they were still again, waiting for the Lords to answer him.

"No one of us here has the right to accept that service—" Eric's voice was shaking, and Silverhair could not tell if it was with joy or anger at having been forced to take a stand. "You have sworn to the Lady of Westria in the name of the Guardian of Men. Let them receive your vow!"

"So be it," said Julian quietly. He slid the casing over the shield again.

Silverhair shook his head in pity. In any other oath-taking the new knight would get the support of his lord in return for the service he was offering. Even in a coronation, the people promised their support to the King. But Julian had bound himself to the land with no guarantees from anyone.

But as the procession formed up to move on into the Council Hall, the people began to chant Julian's name, and Silverhair realized that what Julian had said was perilously close to the oath a King took at his coronation, and neither speech nor silence could change the fact that Julian had just publicly claimed the Crown of Westria.

As the light of the unveiled Earthstone blazed over Laurelynn, its power pulsed also into the earth below. From particle to particle, across the strata the message passed— *"The Master of the Earthstone has come to his City."* Swifter than thought it traveled. In the Sacred Wood the trees trembled, though there was no wind, and in a sunny glade, a madrone tree shivered and suddenly dislimned, reappearing in the form of a woman, who passed swiftly through the forest and began to stride eastward.

In the hidden valley of Awahna, energy which had been potential everywhere in the land suddenly coalesced, and for a moment the form of a woman whose hair was the gold of the waving grain appeared.

"Did You hear?" she said to the sunlight that surrounded her.

"Before he lay in his mother's womb, I have heard," an-

swered the Guardian of Men. *"Will You receive his vow?"*

"He has already given Me his service, though he does not yet understand what that means." The Lady's voice held a smile.

"He still clings to the surface of meaning. He fears the power of the earth that bore him."

"He believes that his mother abandoned him. He has much to learn. . . ."

"But he has begun." At the words of the Guardian the sunlight intensified suddenly.

When it faded again the figure of the woman was gone, but Those Who Dwell in Awahna had recorded their words.

On the Red Mountain, Caolin felt the sudden wakening of the Earthstone's power, and lent the full force of his will to the man on the piebald horse who was even now riding through the open gates of Laurelynn.

Malin Scar reined in before the cottage, his trained awareness taking in the placement of doors and windows, the shed, the garden behind it, and the surrounding trees, without need for conscious analysis. He saw no fences, not even against pigs or deer. The men the Regent had sent to guard the Master of the Junipers lay dead on the road up the Lady Mountain. There should be no difficulty.

A hoarse order sent his men moving out to either side. When the cottage was surrounded, the Shadower touched spurs to his mount's sides and rode across the garden, treading down the last of the kale. As he approached, a side door opened and an old woman came out, carrying a basket. The horse snorted and pawed at the ground as his rider reined him in, and the woman seemed to become suddenly aware of him and straightened, her mouth opening in a soundless O.

Malin Scar neither knew nor cared how he appeared to her. His drawn sword told its own story. He gestured; refuse spilled as she dropped the basket and scurried inside. Once more he set the horse into motion.

They were almost to the door when the beast stopped suddenly, throwing up its head with a jingling of bits as if to avoid running into a wall. Malin Scar turned his mount and extended his weapon. The blade moved freely, but when his hand reached the point at which the horse had stopped, he felt an invisible resistance.

"So—" his voice creaked painfully. "He told me you might be shielded. Never mind. I serve a greater sorcerer than you are, and he has told me how to deal with you!" With no change in expression, the Shadower yanked the horse's head around and trotted back toward his men, trampling the rest of the garden.

When he reached them, whispered orders set them to gathering dry kindling and cutting down trees.

"Julian, why didn't you tell us you were going to do that?" exclaimed Frederic as they took their seats in the Council Hall. "I thought my father was going to have a fit. He may have been a bull on the battlefield when he was young, but he doesn't like surprises."

Julian sighed. The excitement that had carried him through the ceremony was draining away, and even though he no longer bore the shield and the Earthstone, he felt desperately tired. What was he doing here, anyway? He didn't really belong in the Seagate section, nor did he have the right to sit behind Lord Philip anymore. The Regent was taking his place in the chair that had been set before the empty thrones on the eighth side of the octagon. But the time had not yet come for Julian to sit there. His tired gaze followed the lazy curl of smoke from the central fire toward the sky-hole and the painted beams of the arched ceiling. Where he really wanted to be, Julian thought dully, was back in bed.

"Neither do I," he said quietly. "I was just going to say something general about wanting the guidance of the Lord Commanders, but it didn't come out that way."

Frederic laughed at the understatement.

Julian shrugged. "Last night, during my vigil, I thought I understood who I am and what I'm supposed to do. Sometimes that certainty comes on me, and it's always worked out all right before. This time I'm not so sure."

Frederic gave him a hard look. "Don't doubt yourself. That's just the body speaking—you need sleep, and probably food as well. Some kind of reaction was inevitable. Don't you think I know?"

Julian managed a smile as the clarions called for silence in the hall. "Well, for good or ill, it's done, and it's out of my hands now."

The first hours of the Council were consumed by administrative procedures and status reports from the Estates of Westria. Julian tried to keep awake by examining the four counselors whom he had met for the first time only a few days ago—Alexander of Las Costas, a stocky young man with thick reddish hair, who was only a few years older than he; Loysa Gilder, a woman in her fifties who ruled the Goldsmiths Guild and was representative for the Free Cities as well; a worn, nondescript man called Tanemun, whose lack of personality managed to dull the scarlet of the Seneschal's robe he wore; and crow black and bird thin with the wasting of years, the crone who was Mistress of the College of the Wise.

They would decide his fate soon, but Julian could read nothing in their eyes.

Then Tanemun rose, and in his dry, unemotional voice began to read the proposal to recognize the man called Julian of Stanesvale as heir of Jehan Starbairn, and candidate for the Crown of Westria.

Immediately there were objections. Mistress Loysa pointed out that before they could decide either question they must establish Julian's identity. She meant no disrespect by saying what everyone knew—that the late King had been generous with his favors. Julian might well be a son of the King and yet no son of the Queen.

In answer to this Lord Philip pointed out that despite his many love affairs, only the King's marriage had ever resulted in a child, and surely any woman with a child of Jehan's blood would have been quick to produce him after the disappearance of the Queen.

But was this young man in truth the same child that the Queen had taken away with her, asked the Seneschal?

For that, they needed the evidence of the Master of the Junipers, and though the testimony of Silverhair and Lady Rosemary resulted at last in a grudging acceptance, the Master's absence was damaging. The Regent had sent an escort to bring him to the Council. Men were murmuring that perhaps the Master had refused to come, but Julian's belly churned with darker fears. If the Master's health had worsened, surely there would have been some message. He fought the impulse to rush out of the Council Hall now and take the Seagate road.

"I will accept the boy as Jehan's get, but his fitness for the Crown is another matter—" said the Mistress of the College. "The King of Westria must be Master of the Jewels. Both his father and his mother feared them, and they both had been trained at the College of the Wise. The lad's quest for the Earthstone demonstrates his courage, if not his common sense—let him come to the College for training, and when he has the knowledge to find the other three Jewels we will consider his right to the Crown."

Julian stared at her. From a dark face black eyes glittered back at him, too much like those of the ravens he had seen in the south for his comfort, as if she saw through the calm with which he covered his feelings to every midnight fear. He chewed on his lip, wondering if she had the right of it. He knew his own lack of wisdom only too well. And Frederic was going back to the College—they could go together. . . .

"I would like to second that suggestion," said Alexander of Las Costas suddenly. "I find the burden of lordship heavy enough, and I have been trained to it from a child. Many times I have heard my mother tell the story of the Council that first decided on a Regency. You were on that Council—" He gestured toward Lord Eric and the Mistress of the College. "Was not the decision then to wait a full twenty years before choosing a new King? I have no fault to find with Lord Eric's stewardship—"

He bowed toward the Regent, but Eric was not listening. A man in the livery of the City Guard was whispering to him, gesturing toward the door. Alexander's voice faded. There was a sudden hush in the hall. Then Eric looked up.

"My lords and ladies, I beg leave to interrupt your deliberations. News of the Master of the Junipers has come." His face looked frozen. Julian felt a tremor go through Frederic, sitting beside him, and the knot in his own belly tightened painfully.

"There is a messenger outside who demands to speak to us. Is it the will of this Council that he come in?" Eric's face remained expressionless, but a smouldering anger glowed suddenly in his eyes.

"Demands to speak to us?" Philip raised one eyebrow. "Who is this messenger?"

"Ordrey the huntsman, and his message is from Caolin."

For a moment nothing moved. Sunlight made a static pattern of the intricate carving of the pillars; even the hearth-smoke hung motionless in the still air. Julian stared at the entrance as if he had been turned to stone.

There was a stirring at the door.

"That's the man who attacked us on the road to Registhorpe!" exclaimed Frederic. "The one who ran away!"

A short, round-faced man with sandy hair and eyebrows so fair they were nearly invisible came down the stairs carrying something shrouded in a red cloth. He moved with a leisurely step to the center of the Council floor, and stood insolently smiling back at them. Julian did not recognize him. He supposed he had been too busy fighting Ordrey's men to notice him when they had met before.

"Lords of Westria . . . ," he drawled. "My master has a bargain to propose. Something he has, for something you have." Suddenly he flicked the cloth away from the thing he carried and they saw what looked like a Master's staff. A murmur of horror swept through the hall, and Ordrey flung the cloth over it again. His smile broadened and he went on. "The Lord Regent should have given the Master better guards if he wished him to reach Laurelynn. . . ."

Julian felt the knot in his belly explode. The flame of certainty that had carried him through the ceremony that morning tingled through every limb and brought him upright. Once more his lips moved without his intending it.

"For the return of the Master, what does the Blood Lord demand?" he heard himself say. Ordrey turned to face him and Julian felt the full force of that malicious grin.

"The Earthstone . . ."

"No!" exclaimed the Mistress of the College. "The Master would offer his life to keep it from Caolin's hands!"

"My lady—it would appear that he already has—" said Julian quietly. "But I cannot leave him in the hands of his enemy. The Master of the Junipers received me from my mother's womb. He heard my oath when I took my name.

There is no one in this hall with a better right to fight for him than me! Still, I will not give Caolin the Earthstone. Let him take it from me if he can."

"You are only a fledgling—" Ordrey said scornfully, taunting him. "Your shoulders are still bruised from the accolade, and you think that you can challenge the Blood Lord?"

"I think that the Blood Lord is challenging me."

"You don't have the right—" the Mistress of the College began, but Julian's voice struck her words aside.

"You would not allow me to bind myself to your service." His gaze swept the white faces of the holders on their benches, and fixed each of the seven members of the Council in turn. "The Crown is in your gift, but by right of discovery and inheritance, the Earthstone belongs to me. I have the right to risk it and myself if I so choose." He waited a moment, and saw Eric's eyes glow, but the Regent said no word.

"I suppose your master has appointed a time and place for us to meet?" Julian said to Ordrey.

"Indeed." The little man grinned. "Be at Spear Island tomorrow at dawn. The Blood Lord will be waiting for you there. . . ."

❧ NINETEEN ❧

Rana felt the boat surge as it turned toward the island, and Julian put a hand to the rail to steady himself. Frederic was standing in the prow of the second boat, a few yards away, with Robert, the Regent and the Herald and a troop of picked men. The steersmen kept the longboats parallel to the long spit of land that formed the "shaft" of Spear Island, for the meeting place was very close now.

Rana swallowed and recognized the taste of fear. In the confusion that ended the Council, she had been the first to

swear she would follow Julian to his battle, and Frederic
and Silverhair and the rest of them had echoed her. Even
old Eva had insisted on coming, though Rana wasn't sure
whether it was from loyalty or because Piper refused to be
separated from Silverhair. In the excitement of evading her
father's watchful eye, Rana had forgotten they were going to
meet the power that had bruised her mind at Registhorpe.
She had forgotten that Julian was to face Caolin.

Nervously she looked back over her shoulder. The Red
Mountain loomed on their left, its summit swathed in dirty
clouds that were growing brighter with the rising of the
hidden sun. Laurelynn was upriver behind them, the Great
Bay somewhere in the darkness ahead, but as it emerged
from its screen of foothills, the mountain overshadowed the
river as its master's shadow darkened the lives of the puny
mortals who floated there.

"They say that evil cannot cross running water," said Eva
a little shakily.

Rana shivered. "Caolin can."

The stiff wind that always blew upriver from the Bay
tugged at her cloak and she pulled it closer around her. The
point of the island was nearing rapidly now. Too soon, she
felt the jarring of the keel on sand. For a moment no one
moved. Then the other two boats drew in beside them and
Julian stepped lightly out onto the land.

A narrow trail wound through the willows that edged the
shoreline. Terse orders formed the soldiers up behind the
Regent. Julian adjusted the strap that suspended his shield
from his shoulder and said something to Frederic, who
tried to smile. Eric glanced at the little group that included
Rana and Eva and Piper, and frowned, then strode down
the shore to Julian.

Rana thought the Regent looked younger. His movements had a new energy, as if this challenge by Caolin had
driven all his doubts about Julian away. If so, then all this
was accomplishing something useful, but the wind was very
cold, and she knew she was afraid.

"I would order you home if I could spare the men to take
you," growled Eric. "Since you are here, you may as well act
as witnesses. But I warn you—Caolin has never been an
honorable man. If there is trouble, get out of the way!"

Rana nodded, then glanced surreptitiously around her.

They were on an island. If things went badly wrong, it might be that none of them would escape from here.

They emerged from the willows at the edge of a meadow that formed a shallow bowl. New grass was already poking through the dead growth of the summer, and the cotton-woods and laurels that surrounded it were half strangled by vines. In the lee of the trees the air was close and chill.

In the center of the meadow stood Ordrey, caparisoned like a herald in a crimson tabard with a silver wolf's head on its breast. Behind him in close ranks stood the Blood Lord's men-at-arms. Rana heard Lord Eric counting them behind her.

"Thirty-five! At least I have the bastards outnumbered," he said finally, and began to order his own men into formation.

Rana pulled Eva and Piper out of the way as Silverhair stalked past them, his eyes fixed on a figure that glowed like a splash of blood against the trees on the far side of the field.

"Is that Caolin?" Eva asked softly.

"I think so," said Silverhair, holding his harpcase like a shield before him. "Though he clutches his illusions around him so that his shape is hard to see. My heart tells me it's him—"

The Herald of Westria marched determinedly down the slope to face Ordrey.

"I speak for Julian of the Stones, Champion of Westria, and for Eric of the Horn, Commander of Seagate and Regent of Westria!" His voice echoed around the bowl. "They come prepared for battle. Where is Caolin?"

Faced with a challenge, Eric had apparently decided that a united front was advisable, but Rana could hardly appreciate that victory now.

"The Lord of Blood Gard is here, soon *he* will be Lord of Westria! But he has agreed only to meet with Julian, who calls himself Master of the Earthstone." Ordrey spoke lazily, but his voice carried.

Eric's fingers plucked nervously at the peace-strings that bound his sword. The Herald stumped back up the hill and whispered to Julian, then returned to face Ordrey.

"Prince Julian will speak with Caolin, but claims the right to one companion."

"Let them come down then, so long as the Regent is not

with them. My master has instructed me to speak for him,"
Ordrey continued. The Herald began to protest, but Julian
had already laid a soothing hand on Eric's shoulder, and
motioned Silverhair to follow him down the hill.

"Before we talk I must be assured of the Master's safety,"
they heard Julian say.

Ordrey laughed. "He is as safe as man can ever be. By
now the fire will have made ashes of his bones."

Frederic cried out, and Ordrey looked at Julian's stricken
face and laughed again. "Your sentiments are admirable,
but they have betrayed you. My master thanks you for
bringing him the Earthstone."

"He does not yet hold it in his hand," said Julian
dangerously. "If I cannot have the Master living, I will have
justice on his murderer!"

There was a silence while they all stared at the red splash
on the hill. Rana rubbed at her eyes. The air seemed
thicker, and she felt a throbbing at her temples. Abruptly
she remembered the pressure that had beat against them at
Registhorpe, and the voice whose whisper had stained her
soul.

"Be careful, oh, be careful!" she moaned, not knowing for
what they should take care. Eva drew close to her, and
she felt the glow of the old woman's courage like a fire.
Piper clung to her skirts, staring down the hill at Silverhair.

"Fool!" The voice seemed to come from far away, but its
malice grated on their ears. "Fool, do you challenge me,
knowing that we must battle with the weapons *I* choose?
You have come here just as I planned—what need have I for
physical weapons now? I will take the Jewel, and I will take
you, and the harper, and that used-up mastiff who calls
himself Regent of Westria as well. I do not think the
Council will deny me anything then!"

"You may find that easier to say than to do!" said Julian
boldly, but his words sounded hollow.

"You are right, Caolin—we were fools to trust you, who
have been a liar since the beginning. . . ." Silverhair's voice
vibrated with strain.

"Liar? I?" The sorcerer's tone held just a hint of anger.
"No man can say that Caolin of Blood Gard has ever told a
lie!"

"What of your oath to serve the Queen and her child?" Silverhair's tone grew thin with rage.

"Why so I did—" Caolin's laugh was terrible. "And so I *must* destroy this prince or be forsworn! I swore to serve the Queen and her child *as I served the King.* . . ." For a moment no one breathed. "Did you believe Jehan died simply of his wound?" the cruel voice went on. "That was my doing. Even the Master of the Junipers could have cured a wound a natural beast had made. . . ."

"Oh, my dear lord! Jehan!" whispered Eric.

"Then I see that I have my father's death as well as that of my mother to pay you for." Julian had gone very pale, but he spoke steadily.

"Ah yes . . . poor Faris." The silky voice parodied sorrow. "For her I almost forgot my oath, for she was very fair. But foolish—too foolish. She rejected my love."

Something snapped, and Eric strode forward, the broken peace-strings fluttering from the hilt of his drawn sword.

"The only fools were those who let you leave the Council Hall alive all those years ago!" Signaling to his men, Eric began to run, but Ordrey and his soldiers were already retreating. "Cowards! Traitors and cowards too. Come back and fight!" screamed Eric. But the sorcerer had disappeared.

Laughter burst like thunder above their heads. "Tut, tut, Eric—who has broken truce now? I will have a fine tale of your deaths for the Council, and all true. I have told you—" And here his voice grew terrible. "I do not lie!"

Thunder rattled again, and a wave of shadow flowed toward them from the trees.

The fires that surrounded Juniper Cottage burned pale in the grey light of dawn. Since the afternoon before they had been burning, and no one had even tried to break through. Malin Scar stood and stretched, thinking with a dull satisfaction that his task was almost done. The Blood Lord would be pleased.

"Let the flames die now." His voice scratched the silence. "We will sift the ashes for some evidence to take to our master."

They took blankets to beat down the last flames and

began to stamp out the embers. Where the cottage had stood there was now a blackened shell. One might have expected such old wood to burn completely, but surely nothing could have lived inside such an inferno. As the dawn wind cleared the air one of the men took an ax and swung at the charred wall.

Charcoal scattered like black snow, but the ax bounced back and the man dropped it with a cry. Where he had knocked the burnt wood away they could see within, and something was moving there.

"His spirit waits for us!" whispered one of the men. "I will not fight the dead!"

"Back, get back and let's get out of here—" said another more loudly. "The old man's ghost won't follow us to Blood Gard!"

Malin Scar's ruined voice could not compel them, but his sword struck down two before they could reach their horses. The others scrambled onto their mounts, as frightened now by the wild eyes of their leader as they were of the ghost. For a few moments a thunder of hoofbeats echoed on the road. Then the Shadower was left alone with whatever remained of the men he had slain.

If this was a ghost, it did not matter that the armsmen had run away. Malin Scar smiled, knowing that the Blood Lord could deal with spirits or spiritless men with equal ease. If it was something else—well, he still had his sword. Holding it ready, the Shadower stalked toward the charred timbers that hid his prey.

"Man of shadow, why have you destroyed my home? If you had knocked on my door I would have come out to you. . . ." Smoke-grey, ghost-grey, a bent figure limped through the ashes toward him.

Staring, Malin Scar lifted his sword.

"Have you come to kill me?" The Master of the Junipers straightened. He was a small man. He had to look up to meet the Shadower's eyes. An ugly little man, thought Malin Scar, held by that gaze. But the brown eyes that fixed his were luminous, and they were not afraid.

"I came to stop you from leaving here. How did you escape the fire?" he croaked finally.

"You could only destroy the shell of my habitation."

"And what protects you now, old man—more magic?"

Malin Scar's blade hovered just over the Master's heart, and he did not know if it stopped there by the other man's will or his own.

"This body is already damaged, and old. But if you strike it down, still you will not kill *me*. Where then will be your victory?" The Master's voice grated, but there was a sound like distant trumpets behind it. The Shadower remembered long-ago battles, when his heart had still been clean.

"I was sent to keep you from aiding that boy Julian while Lord Sangrado deals with him, and I have done it. This defeat doesn't matter. At the end there is only darkness anyway . . . ," said Malin Scar. The Blood Lord understood that. It was why the Shadower served him.

For a moment the Master of the Junipers stilled, as if that had shaken him. Then he nodded. "I have seen that Darkness and gone through it. Beyond it, you will find Light."

Malin Scar shook his head. He could not argue with this man. The Blood Lord would know how to answer him —there was a darkness in Lord Sangrado like the pit at the heart of the world. The Shadower was still shaking his head when the Master reached out his hand.

"My child, let me show you—"

The sword slipped from Malin Scar's nerveless fingers as he realized that this man was speaking the truth—that killing him would change nothing at all. Heat radiated from the Master's body as if he had consumed the fire. Shaking, the Shadower backed away, but the old man came after him.

Then the Master of the Junipers touched him. Lightning shattered the Shadower's darkness, and he sank at the old man's feet, weeping like a little child.

Caolin gathered darkness in a great wave and loosed it upon his foes. The dimming of daylight did not trouble his vision—he sensed allies and enemies as spots of warmth upon the cold game board of the meadow. Some of those spots flickered brightly with terror; he tracked them easily as they broke and ran, and saw the little lights extinguished by the pulse of pure fear he rolled over them. Cloaking his blood-colored robes in shadow, he moved down the slope, seeking Julian.

Caolin could have arranged to acquire the Earthstone in many other ways. He had wanted to see with his own eyes this child of the two people he had loved and hated—when he still was capable of either emotion—more than any in the world. But there had been no aching resemblance to Jehan to test his control—he had killed men who looked more like the King than this boy.

A thought set his own men spreading out behind him, though he hardly needed them. Still, to see this would help them to appreciate his power, and if terror killed some of them, it would save Caolin the trouble of winnowing from his service those who lacked the requisite courage or despair.

His enemies had clustered in a tight flickering knot in the midst of the meadow. As the sorcerer sent another wave of terror toward them, green and amber light rippled uncertainly, then firmed into a bright barrier against which the Blood Lord's darkness beat in vain. From behind it he sensed triumph. He eased the pressure, letting them think they had beaten him.

The Blood Lord recognized the Earthstone's strength in that barrier, and was not surprised. He had felt its presence in Julian's shield, and had been waiting for the boy to use it. The linked symbolism of shield and stone had a logic that in an odd way pleased Caolin. It showed a natural sensitivity for the structure of magic, and although the lad would have no time to develop it, he had shown himself a worthy enemy. After so many years of struggle, it would have been almost a disappointment if the lordship of Westria had dropped like an overripe plum into Caolin's hand.

The earthshield arched over Julian and his companions, glowing like sunlight on a summer forest. It was very beautiful, but its strength came entirely from the focusing of Julian's will upon the Earthstone. And that, thought the Blood Lord, was its weakness. His attention completely on controlling the Jewel, Julian had none to spare for the other souls it was protecting. And too many of them had brought their fear with them into the circle.

Caolin could feel someone, possibly Frederic, trying to calm and bind them into a unit that could support Julian. But the initial terror had been too great, and Frederic did not have the authority the Master of the Junipers would have brought to this task. Maintaining the darkness around the sphere with enough pressure to keep Julian occupied, Caolin extended part of his awareness toward the sparks of life he sensed within.

He would not have dared this if Julian had been willing to attack him with the power locked in the Stone. But it was clear by now that the boy could not, or perhaps was afraid of not being able to control the consequences if he should try.

The Blood Lord was like a fisherman, delicately trolling his line, waiting for the invisible disturbance that would tell him something had taken the bait and could be reeled in. He touched a mind—read a fear of being taken advantage of and played on it, suggesting that it was being used to protect an adventurer who would abandon it to the darkness when he had won his own safety. Soon a speck of resentment shadowed the barrier, and Caolin felt the slightest of weakenings.

Again the sorcerer cast his lines, and again, avoiding the furious fire of Silverhair's hatred, the steadier flare of Rana's loyalty, Frederic's pure flame, and the other lights closest to Julian. Time enough to attack them when he had thinned their protection. And it was thinning. He could see figures behind it now.

A touch more would set many of them hurtling outward in terrified flight—onto the waiting swords of Caolin's men. But without the dead weight of those weaker souls, Julian and his companions could uphold a possibly impenetrable barrier. Their bright resolution must also be shaken somehow.

Subtly the Blood Lord began to shape the shadows. The great cat-creature that had attacked Registhorpe stalked again, slavering, but Frederic recognized it and named it illusion. Caolin folded darkness into wide wings and added the glitter of a black eye, sent the raven winging over the sphere, and was rewarded by a woman's cry. But Frederic's soft assurances steadied her, and in a moment he heard the liquid ripple of harp music and voices lifting in song. He considered singing his own power song. It had broken the harp before. But he had thought of a better use for his energy. It seemed they were proof against imaginary terrors. Caolin gathered his resources and set about creating something that would be more real.

Until now, he had veiled himself from their vision. Now they would see whatever face he chose to wear, with the physical force of the sorcerer behind it to give it reality. Using as his mirror memories that were vivid even after all these years, Caolin clothed himself in the lithe swordsman's body, the dark hair and brilliant blue eyes of Jehan the King.

With the swift, eager stride that Jehan had never lost, the sorcerer moved toward the shining barrier, stopped, and pushed back the hood of the blue cloak he seemed to wear. The harpsong soured suddenly and he heard the twang of a snapped string.

"Eric—" his voice throbbed with horror, "Farin—what are you doing? The Earthstone was never meant to be used this way! It will destroy you—you know its power. In the Names of the Guardians I beg you, get away from there before it is too late." There was a moment of shocked stillness, and he let his features assume the look of astonished hurt that Caolin remembered only too well. "O my brothers, will you betray me again? I am your King!"

From Eric came a cry of mingled pain and rage, and the strength that he had given to the barrier was suddenly withdrawn. Then the harp spoke suddenly in the melody of the lament that Farin had made for his dead King.

For one terrible moment nineteen years fell away. The music bypassed all the mind's barriers, and Caolin felt the full desolation of that moment when he understood that Jehan had left him alone.

His concentration shattered. Caolin felt the illusion dissolving and had just enough strength to turn and hide his own scarred features beneath the hood once more. Instinctively he restored the pressure of the darkness, then stood breathing harshly, waiting until the wild flutter of emotion exhausted itself against the cold walls of his will.

He could not use Jehan's face, even now. And surely the harper must die, for he had the gift of music that had been one of the links between Caolin and his King, and apparently that had the power to reach deep levels of feeling that the sorcerer had not known were still there.

But if Caolin could not wear the face of the man he had loved, he could bear that of the woman whom he had hated, and that might be the best weapon of all.

Marshaling his will, the sorcerer set a simulacrum of himself to glowing redly on the hillside. Then, remembering the night when he had transformed the woman Margit into the image of Faris for his first great sorcery, Caolin set about re-creating the slender body, the pale, fine-boned face with its huge brown eyes, and the masses of silver-shot dark hair that had belonged to the Queen.

"Please, won't you help me?" He added a soft, hoarse voice, a swift look over the shoulder as if she feared the sorcerer would follow her. "The Master lied to you —Caolin has held me prisoner all these years! Eric, you swore to act as my champion! Farin, will you run away again? You can save me now—give him the Stone and he will set me free!"

Eric was sobbing, but Silverhair's voice came distorted through the barrier. "My sister is dead. How dare you desecrate her memory?"

The image of Faris shook its head sadly. "You said you loved me, but I see it was a lie, and your legendary search for me was only a flight from responsibility. But I see one among you who will not desert me. Star, my baby—my son grown to a man—how I have longed for you!"

"The mariposa lilies grow upon my mother's grave," came the voice of Julian.

"Is that what they told you?" she asked sorrowfully. "I left you in safety at Stanesvale and fled, and Caolin caught me on the road. Oh, my arms ache to hold you—won't you come to me now?"

"My mother is dead." His voice was harsh with pain, but it did not falter.

The figure straightened with a terrible laugh. "Then she is dead to you! Did they tell you I wept when I learned I was with child? Your weight held me to a throne I never wanted! I abandoned you eagerly!"

Caolin knew that the illusion was turning into that of the Lady of Darkness, whose embrace had poisoned him. But that did not matter—it was the woman's true image —let her son see her dark face as he had seen it, and understand!

He let the Lady's searing laughter beat against the barrier, every sense alert to the changing emotions of those within. The warding wavered! Triumph leaped in the sorcerer like a flame. He let the illusion of Faris fall away, and spoke the Word that he had learned from the sorcerer of Awhai.

Light shattered and exploded outward, like leaves from a wind-tossed tree. Suffocating shadow rushed in to replace it, and Caolin's men closed in.

The sorcerer started after them, stumbled, recovered himself, and then tripped again. Startled, he looked down.

The grasses were trembling, but Caolin could feel no wind. He blinked, but the blurred movement continued. Something wound around his ankle and with a curse he jerked free. Lost concentration had let the darkness lessen; he saw a quiver run through the trees that ringed the meadow, an uneasy shuddering that intensified until suddenly they were in motion, lurching toward him down the hill.

Men cried out in a horror greater than anything produced by Caolin's illusions. His own men as well as the others were shrieking and throwing down their weapons as they fled from the trees. Some slipped through gaps where the woods had been; others blundered against hard trunks, were caught by whipping branches, crushed or strangled, trodden into the soil.

Caolin tried to stop a man who ran past him, but the fool cursed and pointed to a graceful madrone shape and staggered on. Shapes of tree and woman blurred together as it swept past him toward the center of the meadow —toward Julian. There was a glow about her; the sorcerer recognized the force that had motivated the trees, and, shriveling the grass around him with a pulse of darkness that disrupted not its physical substance but the pattern of energy that bound it, grasped for his own power.

"Julian!" Caolin cried. "You have challenged me! Will you hide behind a tree?"

Green light blazed as the earthshield was lifted. "Lady, this is my battle!" cried Julian. "Get out of the way!"

"The Lord of the Trees told me to serve you, but this is for love, Prince of Men!" The words came with a rush like wind in many leaves as the madrone tree rooted, broadened, and branched out into a thick canopy of shining foliage.

Caolin focused, perceived the matrix of light that was the Lady's true body, and projected a pulse of disrupting

power. Where he touched her, particles swirled meaningless
as sparks from a flame.

She screamed. Julian burst from behind the tree trunk,
thrusting his shield forward to deflect Caolin's power.
Amber flame flared from the Earthstone as the sorcerer's
energy touched it; then, adroitly as a swordsman slipping
over his opponent's parry, Caolin altered his aim and cast
the full force of his hatred at Julian's unprotected head.

As he collapsed, the sorcerer started toward him to take
the Earthstone, but the Madrone's agony had stimulated
the other plants to even greater frenzy, and all his power
barely kept them away. Step by hard-fought step, he was
forced to retreat, while all around him his men fought
Eric's, or the trees, or each other, and died. Only Ordrey
and one other who had fled at the beginning of the battle
had reached the boat drawn up on the shore, and they were
already pushing it back into the water when the sorcerer
came down the bank like a dark flame.

As the current whirled them away toward the Red Mountain, Caolin turned and saw a mad tangle of vegetation
heaving above the surface of the island. He shuddered, and
looked away.

When Silverhair opened his eyes, the cold grey light of a
winter afternoon revealed a storm-wracked landscape, and
every muscle in his body seemed to have been wrenched by
the same power. He put out a hand and felt the hard shape
of the harp frame—Swangold was probably in better shape
than he was. He tried to sit up, groaned, and fell back again,
shutting his eyes against the pain. He remembered the
fury of the trees and wondered why any of them were still
alive.

Silverhair could hear someone breathing close beside
him. Small cold hands stroked his forehead awkwardly and
he heard a whimper.

"No, Piper—" came a hoarse voice he hardly recognized
as Rana's. "Let him rest while he can. Soon enough he'll
have to know."

How long had Piper been watching beside him? How long
had he been unconscious, and what had happened while he
was taking refuge in oblivion? He could hear the sounds of
people moving and talking in low tones, of a body being

dragged, and a stifled sob. *Was it Eric?* he wondered grimly. *He would have wanted to die fighting Caolin. . . .*

"Shall we take him back to Laurelynn?" That was Eric's voice! Ice touched every nerve at once; then Silverhair was struggling upright, unaware of pain. He saw Eric's face ravaged by grief. The Regent was looking downward, where Frederic and Robert and Rana knelt beside the body of Julian.

On the left side of Julian's head the skin was bruised and a livid tracery branched from his temple to his cheekbone, as if the pattern of his veins had been stamped into the skin. The rest of his face had a waxy pallor, and for the first time Silverhair recognized in the structure of the boy's skull something of Jehan. He must have made some sound then, for Frederic looked up and said the words for them all.

"When I held a sword blade to his lips there was no mist there. I think he is gone."

Shivering, Silverhair knelt and took Julian's hand. It was cool already. How could anyone who had been so alive lie so still? He remembered how he had begun to mourn Julian's lost promise in the mines under the Red Mountain, but that had been self-indulgent posturing. This was the reality—not self-pity, or regret for the loss to Westria, or even anger that Caolin had won—but a grief like a hole in the heart of the world because he had only now recognized that what he felt for Julian was love.

I swore to find you and your mother, he thought. *I failed and did not find her—and you I found and have failed!* He took a deep breath and felt something give way in his chest. Something was very wrong there—he had suspected it before, but what did that matter now?

"The light is fading," said Eva. "I don't think we should be here when dark falls. The trees are quiet now, but I don't trust them."

"We have enough men for two of the longboats," said Eric. "If we leave now, by evening we can be in Laurelynn."

"Not Laurelynn!" said Silverhair harshly, standing up again. "You go back to the Council that rejected Julian and tell them how the hope of Westria fell! I will take him to the Sacred Wood! He deserves at least to be buried as a King of Westria!"

"To the Wood! Yes—he will grow a new body there!"

They all turned, and winced, seeing Lady Madrone, or part of her, anyway, for there was only a pattern of light where the sorcerer had blasted her side away.

"Lady, Julian was not one of your people, though he will lie among them," Frederic said very gently at last. "When men's bodies are slain, they do not rise again."

Lady Madrone did not answer, but something human in her expression told him that in a way that should have been impossible to her kind, the Lady had also loved Julian.

"Lay the Earthstone on his breast, for no one else has a right to it now," said Silverhair painfully, "and together we will take him home."

≫ TWENTY ≪

Julian fell into darkness forever, hurled downward by the force of the sorcerer's blow. He was swallowed by a serpent whose curled coils engulfed him, but no serpent had ever been so huge. Slick-sided, the slippery passageway sucked him deeper within. The memory of his battle with Caolin shattered; self-awareness was flayed away as rough walls scraped his skin. Rocks clashed like incisors, tearing at his flesh. Bleeding, head throbbing, he came to rest upon a cavern floor.

A bear shaped from shadow came padding toward him. Teeth gleamed out of lightlessness. Julian screamed, but no sound came! He dodged the fetid breath that fouled the air, but there was nowhere to run. And now another horror flapped black wings from the passage. Hemmed in, he struck at them. Jaws shut upon his arm, a sharp peck paralyzed thought, but still his body struggled. Terror passed, and he found himself strangely beyond fear.

Fangs tore through flesh as the creatures fed. Julian felt muscles ripped, and sinews snapped as the substance of his body was stripped from his bones. The beasts' cawing and growling rumbled like thunder; they burrowed in his belly, gorged on his genitals, pulled out his entrails, worrying at each morsel. And still, somehow he was living, though his bones were scattered without pattern.

Stones echoed with shouting. A woman came walking, black-skinned, white-haired, wearing skulls for a necklace. Laughing, she kicked her creatures from their carnage. She picked up Julian's head by its hair, tied it to her girdle, and letting it dangle, began to bundle up all of his bones. Singing, she gathered them, sorted and stacked them, and carried them away.

In another cavern a cauldron was bubbling. Hanging from the walls were many skulls. Their smooth planes were painted in patterns. They were adorned with feathers and beads; they watched with glassy crystal eyes. The woman cast the bones into the pot, plucked out Julian's eyes, and popped his head in with the rest. His boiling skull rang against the side of the pot. He could hear the woman singing—

> *"Toll the knell, hear my spell, time will tell*
> *What befell bones and skull, boil them well!"*

Over and over the words were repeated as the last flesh was boiled from his bones. And when every fragment was as clean as clamshell, the woman fished the fleshless bones out onto the floor.

In order she arrayed them, one by one she numbered them, naming them by form and by function. She set the skull above them and gave it eyes of crystal. Like a tracery of inset silver, the branched pattern of Julian's own life energy, which had been disrupted by the sorcerer's blast, gleamed from the bone. Julian saw his skeleton stretched out before him.

"Behold," said the woman, *"the holy and eternal bones."*

Then she went away. The skulls on the walls were singing. Dragon and deer, bear and buffalo, unicorn, horned cow, and eagle all began talking. The air shimmered with images of green grass and jungle, drought and icy winter, and the red death that had ended it all.

Time passed. A new singing silenced the spirits. Someone came walking, white as a lily, her hair like the fall of night streaked with bright silver. Sweet came her singing, sweeter than harpsong or bells in the evening heard over water. And Julian listened, lulled by the lullaby—

> *"If you are not sleepy—oh, hear the sweet sound—*
> *Bright spirits will dance for you on the dark ground,*
> *But when you grow weary, the music will slow,*
> *And under the earth all the spirits will go!"*

Surely he had heard it, not in his childhood, but earlier, somewhere. Surely he remembered the voice he heard singing, as he remembered the face of the lady who was bending over him now!

Her touch soothed the smooth planes of his skull.

"I created your first flesh from my own body," she said softly. *"Now I shall make you a spirit body, better than before!"*

Singing, she inserted into his breast a piece of pink quartz carved like a rose. She made him new lungs from a cloud, fashioned a stomach from a seashell, entrails from seaweed, a phallus out of a polished horn. She spun feathers with her fingers and stretched him new sinews, made muscles for him from the flesh of horses and bears. Then she covered the body with an elk's tough hide and to protect his head, from a coyote's brush she took the long hairs. Then she clapped her hands together and a spark sprang in through his nostrils to light the space within his skull.

Fire burned in his brain; in every vein life leaped. His new-made limbs belonged to him once more. He sat up and faced her, as a son he embraced her, and the long sorrow of losing her found healing at last.

An echo of sweet singing rang in Silverhair's memory. He stirred, felt the hard knob of a tree-root digging into his side, and as he realized where he was, the melody altered into the plaintive mellow notes of Piper's wooden flute. He groaned and ground his face against the harsh fibers of the blanket, still damp with dew, though the sun was already high. Another day had come to the Sacred Wood. He was still alive, and Julian was gone.

Turning over, Silverhair saw the mound that covered the shallow hole where they had laid the body, scattered with redwood needles for a pall. Beyond it, a grove of young redwoods extended down the hillside to the stream, but the ruddy limbs and shiny deep green leaves of the Madrone were stretched protectively over the grave. Dew pearled the haze of new grass in the clearing, though it was only the third week of December. Soon, he supposed, grass would cover the mound as well and there would be nothing to show that the last direct heir of House Starbairn had ever been.

The easy tears trickled from beneath Silverhair's eyelids and he rubbed them away. At his movement, Piper put down the flute, stirred up the embers of the fire, and put the kettle on, as if he had been waiting for the harper to wake. For two days they had kept the vigil here. At any other time during the past months, Piper's insistence on staying with him and his anxious care would have filled Silverhair with hope that the child was rejoining the human race at last, but now he was too numb to wonder. Eric should be returning with the other Lords of the Provinces sometime tomorrow for the formal farewell, and then it would be over.

And what would he do then? If Caolin had somehow escaped the madness of Spear Island, should the harper spend his life in a useless assault on the walls of Blood Gard? That would be preferable to dragging out a meaningless existence as Rosemary's pensioner, remembering his failure.

Silverhair found his fingers fumbling for the hilt of his dagger, felt Piper's mute, reproachful gaze upon him, and forced himself to reach instead for his harp. He had to endure until tomorrow. Piper and his own word denied him that way out, for even in this agony, Silverhair would not place the burden of his death upon the child, and he had promised to wait for the others here.

In the stillness of the morning the woods were achingly beautiful. He wondered how the forest could hold such serenity when such a grief gnawed his soul.

Sweet music poured from the golden strings like the sunlight streaming through the leaves of the Sacred Wood. The springs of music had dried up in him after Jehan died. At least this time the Lord of the Winds had not deserted him too. He let melody modulate to melody, not caring what he played, losing himself in the music until he found himself singing an old children's song.

> *"Oh, to the Greenwood let us go,*
> *Robin and you and I,*
> *And lay us down upon the grass*
> *And look up at the sky.*
> *Oh, let us take the little flowers*
> *That grow beneath the trees,*
> *And twine them into wreaths and chains*
> *And wear them as we please."*

The beginning of the next verse escaped him, and for a few moments he played variations until the words came to him again. Piper picked up his flute and began a halting descant on the tune.

> *"And you shall have a poppy crown,*
> *A lily wreath for me,*
> *But Robin shall wear ivy leaves*
> *As fresh as they can be.*
> *And we will make my brother king*
> *My sister shall be queen,*
> *But Robin, he shall rule the wood,*
> *Clothed all in green."*

Suddenly tensing fingers shortened the last chord, and Silverhair understood why he had not wanted to remember the rest of the song, for his sister had indeed been Queen, and through her he had been brother to the King, but this wood was all their child would ever rule, clad for his burial in the Wood Priest's extra robe of green.

He was trying to find another tune in Swangold's strings when he heard a stumbling footstep. Turning, he saw two strange figures approaching through the forest—a little man in a grey robe, leaning on the shoulder of a man in the worn black leathers of a hunter. Piper retreated to the protection of the redwoods as Silverhair set down the harp with elaborate care and got to his feet, staring.

"It *is* you!" he breathed as the Master of the Junipers came into the clearing, a little pale and careful with his breathing, but no ghost—not with mud stains on the hem of his robe and little beads of perspiration glittering on his brow.

"Ordrey said Caolin had you captive, and then that they

had burned—" Silverhair's words died in his throat as he
realized that what he had taken for mud stains were smears
of charcoal. His gaze moved slowly from the Master to the
man upon whom he still leaned, finding the black clothing
disturbingly familiar, but not recognizing the features.

Then the Master sighed, and as his companion turned to
help him sit down Silverhair remembered the mutilated
face of Malin Scar. He grabbed for the sheathed sword that
lay beside his blankets, and had it half drawn when he
realized that the other man had not moved. The harper
stood still with the sword in his hands.

"Did you bring him here or did he bring you?"

For a moment the old sweet smile flickered in the
Master's eyes. "A little of both, I suppose—" he said gently.
"You can put down your sword, Farin. He has no memory,
but his body is still strong, and I don't think he would leave
me if I ordered him to now."

"He was hunting me—" Silverhair began. The man who
had been Malin Scar looked up at him incuriously and then
away again.

"He found *me*. Too late—" he added, "or too soon . . ."
For the first time the Master's gaze rested on the mound
beneath the madrone tree and his eyes clouded with pain.

"It's the Eve of Sunreturn," said Silverhair harshly.
"Have you come to celebrate the anniversary of Jehan's
death or to mourn that of his son? You couldn't save the
King—couldn't you have done something to protect Julian? He was so young!"

"How did it happen?"

For a moment grief closed the harper's throat. Then
bitterness opened it again, and he recalled with all his
bard's skill the duel at Spear Island and how Julian had
taken the blow meant for Lady Madrone.

"The Earthstone was in the shield when Caolin struck at
him?" asked the Master.

"Yes," Silverhair answered dully. "But it fell out and the
Lady found it. We clasped it in Julian's hands when we
buried him. He was the hope of Westria!" The agony flamed
into life again. "Where is the reward for all your care now,
old man, and all my sufferings?"

"Where indeed?" murmured the Master, frowning.

Silverhair stared at him suspiciously. "You won't tempt

me to hope again—" he began, but the Master's look stopped him.

"I tempt no one!" His voice rang like a gong. "But you have sworn to watch here until Eric comes. Watch also over me!"

"What are you going to do?" Silverhair's voice faltered, for the Master was already maneuvering his half-crippled limbs into the position for meditation.

His eyes closed, his back straightened, and his empty hands rested open upon his knees. The harper heard a harsh breath drawn in, let slowly out again, in and out in a regular rhythm as the breaths grew steadily shallower, until it was hard to tell if the adept was breathing at all. The short hairs rose on Silverhair's arms as he realized he was going to have to pass the next twenty-four hours alone with the old man, who was now so deeply tranced he might have been as dead as Julian, and his companion, who was turning a fallen leaf over and over again and laughing at the play of light and shadow as it caught the sun.

Julian walked with his mother through the halls of Earth, and the spirits of his ancestors attended them. The bones of the bedrock were laid bare before him—strata of stone from ancient seabed to congealed rivers of fire, with the stone bones of creatures no longer known preserved forever within. And as he had understood the structure of his own skeleton, Julian comprehended earth from stone to soil. He saw the patterns of energy for everything living—the skeletons of the spirit—and seeing, remembered fully what had been revealed to him during his vision in Awhai.

His father the King walked with them, and he understood why men had loved him, and with him came other sovereigns of Westria, speaking of their deeds and days, even the first Jewel Lord, from whom Julian had taken his name.

But there was one spirit whom he missed. Ordrey had said the Master of the Junipers was dead, and he wondered if there was some other realm where the adepts walked when flesh had released them. But as they passed a dark river, Julian saw a figure robed in light approaching and recognized the Master, though he walked straight and uninjured, and the brightness of his spirit transformed his ugly features. For the first time, Julian saw unveiled the beauty that he had always sensed within.

"I see that you have found him—" the Master spoke to Faris. *"I guarded him for you until he was grown."*

Jehan smiled and answered, *"You have fulfilled your promise. He is more than worthy of the staff and the crown!"*

Julian looked at them in confusion. *"What are you saying? The body I wore is buried by now!"*

"Buried but not lifeless—" said the Master. *"The power of the Earthstone radiating from your shield filtered the force of Caolin's blow, and as it rests upon your body, it maintains a flicker of life there still. Your physical form lies now in trance with mine, awaiting your return. But the time allowed for it is almost done."*

"No—" For the first time Julian felt emotion. He could not even be glad that the Master was not dead after all. *"How can I go back to all of that pain?"*

"If you do not," said the Master, *"Westria will suffer. The Blood Lord lives as well, and the country's defenses will not protect her from him for long. Still, the choice is yours. If you drink from this river, you will forget your land and all that you have loved."*

Julian faltered, looking at the black waters, remembering the beauty of sunset upon golden hills. Words came to him then from his own self-binding. It appeared that death had not released him from it, and the Lady of Westria had not absolved him, nor had the Guardian of Men.

"The Lady of Westria belongs to the living. But the Guardian of Humankind has walked even here." At the Master's words, for a moment bright sunlight shone through the shadows and stirred Julian's soul with awareness of a Presence whose smile could set a world laughing.

"I will go back then. You must show me the pathway—"

"No. I will stay here. Is not my task finished?" In appeal, the Master stretched out his hand to Faris. *"Julian's feet are firmly on the path that leads to the throne. My body of earth bears me only with pain. Did not you promise that I should join you when all was done?"*

But Julian shook his head. *"I won't do it alone!"*

The Master sighed. *"There lies your road then."* He pointed, and Julian saw looming ahead of them the roots and the trunk of a towering tree. *"As for me, I must go back the way that I came."*

"That is the Worldtree, of all planes the axis, from the depths of the dark to the high place of heaven," said Faris softly. *"Climb, my beloved, and let our blessing go with you, for now you know that all the worlds are one."*

He would have stayed to embrace her again, but some power was already moving him toward the tree. Father and mother faded behind him. He climbed, and the darkness was transformed into day.

It was still dark when Rana sat up and threw aside her blankets, but already the household of Seahold was stirring. She heard the murmur of voices hushed by sleepiness and sorrow, and the glimmer of a lighted lamp as her father came toward her with a mug of tea.

"Thank you." Rana drank thirstily, feeling the hot liquid revive her as it went down. The air was damp and bitterly cold at this hour—as chill as the grave, she thought dismally. Light flickered on the strong planes of her father's face and struck red sparks from his beard, but his eyes were shadowed. Rana reached out and took his hand, drawing strength from its callused grip. At least she had made peace with her parents again, and when she came back from Spear Island she had needed the comfort of their arms around her.

"Are you going to go with us to the Wood?" she asked.

Sir Randal shook his head. "Julian was a fine young man, but he never had a chance to belong to all of us. This task is for the lords who should have served him."

"And for his companions . . ." Rana shivered.

Her father's hand was surprisingly soft on her hair. "Yes. Your mother and I agree that you should be there."

Rana felt tears stinging her eyelids and pressed her face suddenly against her father's side, trying to draw comfort from the familiar scent of tobacco and sweat on the leather jerkin he wore. What use was it to have won that admission now? She tried to tell herself that it was something to have shared Julian's adventures, but danger had lost its attraction early, and in the end they had all kept going for Julian's sake and for Westria.

Westria remained, and if there was now no joy in her

service, that did not lessen her need. But at least they could give Julian a proper farewell.

By the time Sir Austin pulled open the gates of Seahold to let the little procession depart, the sky was a dark grey that dimmed the stars without leaving enough light to see the road. Torches bobbed like red flowers above the dark figures of the riders. Eva brought her horse close beside Rana's, her lined face grim. *She has endured so much,* thought Rana. *Perhaps I can endure this too.* Eva's dour presence steadied her. She turned in the saddle to thank her for being there.

"I wish I had something to leave as an offering," said Eva unhappily.

Rana remembered their discussion at Ravensgate. "It's not our custom in the north, though sometimes a warrior's arms or a craftsman's tools will be burned with them on the pyre so that their spirits may go together. But not when a man is buried—the Ancients left too much entombed in the clean earth. And those who had lordship in their lives, like Commanders and Kings, go naked into the land they ruled."

And what would I offer if that were our way? Rana asked herself. When it came to gifts she had always asked for horse harness. The only treasure she possessed was the lovely basket with the earth cross woven into its pattern in gold and black, which she had carried in the festival at Awhai.

"But Julian never ruled Westria," said Eva then. Rana looked quickly away. It was not grief that made her eyes sting, but anger that it should all end this way.

The horses moved more quickly as their muscles warmed, winding up the trail and over the ridge between the Sacred Wood and the Bay. By the time they started down the canyon that led to the Wood's entrance the sky had a pearly sheen that was beginning to shimmer with opalescent color like the inside of a shell. Rana could make out the shape of Lord Eric's slumped shoulders and the pale gleam of Frederic's bowed head, with the less familiar silhouettes of the other lords behind them. The damp dawn wind brought a hint of spice from the trees, and beneath it, the tang of the distant sea. But no bird yet sang. The only sounds were the crackling of the torches and the dull rhythm of hooves on the soft earth of the road.

Rana realized that she was holding her breath, and let it out in a long sigh. She wondered if it was her own tension that was tightening the muscles across her shoulders, or the stillness around her, as if all the world were waiting for the sun to rise upon Midwinter Day? She shrugged her shoulders to ease them, and bit her lip as she remembered how often she had seen Julian do the same. Her temples throbbed as if a headache were coming on, and suddenly the slow pace of the ponies was unbearable.

The trail widened, and a slight pressure from Rana's heels moved her mount alongside Eva's. By the time they rode down into the meadow before the entrance, she was next to Frederic. The Warden of the Wood came out to meet them, his eyes reddened as if he had been weeping too. Rana got herself off her horse and out of her boots while the others were still sorting themselves out and stretching muscles that had grown stiff with riding, and she found herself moving closer to the shadow of the trees.

The tension in the air increased. Perhaps the trees were motionless because the slope of the mountain sheltered them from the wind, but Rana felt a waiting stillness in the forest before them. She saw Frederic lift his head and stare around him as if he too sensed something. Then his father spoke and Frederic had to answer him.

In the east the clouds had opened like the petals of a rose, color deepening from the palest of pinks to a coral that was suffused with gold as the sun lifted over the Snowy Mountains on the other side of Westria. A glimmer of light sparkled through the leaves of the nearest tree. Was it the sun? It had seemed to come from within. . . .

She tried to say something, but her throat would not obey. Only her feet had volition, and they bore her away from the others and into the shadow of the trees.

Julian woke in a darkness heavy with the rich scent of the soil. He felt pressure all around him; weight pressed him down into a softness that had molded itself to the shape of his body. His shallow breath barely stirred the redwood boughs that covered his face and kept whatever was holding him from pressing there too. He lay still, secure as a swaddled child in its cradle, for the moment feeling no need to move.

A sense of warmth came from between his hands, which were clasped above his solar plexus. The faintest contraction of finger muscles gave him the feel of something hard and smooth, whose heat seemed to gradually increase as he noticed it, tingling gently through his fingers and along his arms, penetrating his belly and radiating outward until he was fully aware of his body again.

—And not just of his own body. Consciousness expanded into the medium surrounding him, identifying the patterns of particles of stone and humus that made up the rich earth in which he lay. Its constriction caused him no fear, for his senses extended outward in every direction, following the roots of trees skyward until he fluttered with the leaves in the wind, tasting the sweetness of water seeping through the soil. Hearing received the rhythm of approaching hoofbeats, as if the earth had been a drum.

I thought I was dead. . . . The awareness of life within him came slow as the thoughts of trees. The earth around him communicated its own identity, and he understood that he was in the Sacred Wood. Dimly he remembered having once promised that its trees should feed on his bones, but for that, the flesh must be cold, and the pulse of life was beating ever more strongly in him now.

As Julian's mind began to function like that of a man once more, he knew that the hard thing he held was the Earthstone. But the power he had once feared was warm and comforting. His temple tingled faintly, but not unpleasantly, where he had received Caolin's blow. And now he remembered where he had been. For a moment that knowledge shook him, for his memory held every detail of his dismemberment and regeneration, and not only that, but the full content of his vision in Awhai. And he remembered also the face of his mother, and knew that she had been as close to him as shadow to sunlight all through those years when all comfort had seemed far away.

His body trembled with longing to return to her. But with every moment his spirit was anchoring itself more firmly in flesh. At least for now that way was shut to him. He felt the blood throbbing in his veins. Through his shut lids he could see an amber glow.

Julian's skin prickled with an unreasoning terror lest they should have buried him too deeply to get free, but his extended senses were already probing the soil above him, and in a moment he knew that he was held here by less than a foot of earth and a scattering of leaves. But for a little longer he lay without moving, reluctant to leave this peace.

Then Julian opened his fingers to free the power of the Earthstone, and the soil slid easily away from his body as he sat up, blinking at the light of the dawning day.

Clearing vision showed him that the sun was barely risen. Its light hardly penetrated the leaves. But it was enough to reveal Silverhair, who appeared to have fallen over with Swangold cradled in his arms as if he had played himself to sleep. Piper was curled close beside him, but not quite touching, like a dog who fears rebuff but cannot stay away. On the other side of the clearing the Master sat in tranced stillness, and beyond him Julian could glimpse another sleeping form.

But if the humans slept, the trees around him were shimmering with life. Julian recognized the patterns of those trees rooted there by nature, but there were more whose outlines wavered from tree to human to body of light—Laurel, Oaks of several kinds, Willow and Cottonwood, Spruce and Cypress and Pines, and brightest among them, Lady Madrone. All the Guardians of the Trees were here. As if his awareness had been a signal, light flared from tree to tree until the whole Wood sparkled, and a whisper of excitement rustled through the leaves.

Julian got to his feet, looking at them in delight.

"Hail, Prince of Men!" The Lord of the Trees and Lady Madrone stood before him. Julian saw the partly regenerated gap in her side and remembered how she had tried to protect him, and he held out his hand.

"Lady, if I am here, it is because of your loyalty!" he said in the speech of the heart.

"Only loyalty?" came her reply, and Julian remembered her words on the battlefield. He looked at her in wonder, for he had feared her alien power even as necessity forced him to make use of her. But now he had been reborn, like her, from Earth's dark womb.

"No—" His thought came slowly. *"Sister . . ."*

She moved toward him and he grasped her hand. Something passed between them then, fairer than a human's fears, stronger than a wood spirit's dreams.

"From this day all of my folk will fight for you as they have done for no other sovereign of Westria," said the Lord of the Trees. *"The People of the Wood hail the Master of the Earthstone!"*

And with those words the trees bowed before him as if beneath a mighty wind.

But there had been no wind, and in the distance Julian heard a shout. He felt the vibration of footsteps pounding the forest floor and looked around him in panic. In a moment the commotion would wake Silverhair. How could he face the harper's questions, or the knowledge in the Master of the Junipers' eyes? And now others were entering the Wood. He was a man, but he had been wrenched beyond the comfortable limitations of humanity. He had never been good with words. What could he say to them?

Swiftly he passed across the clearing and through the trees, his fear fading as the peace of the Wood enfolded him. The sky blazed with gold as the sun lifted over the mountain, and he felt the thin warmth of winter sunshine on his skin. Julian walked lightly upon the new grass, breathing deeply of the scented air without thought of past or future.

He came to the clearing where he had first met the Lord of the Trees, and for a moment the sudden dazzle of full sunlight blinded him. Blinking, he realized that someone was standing there—it was a woman cloaked in blue, crowned by the sun with a blaze of gold. Julian's pulse pounded heavily. His fist clenched around the Earthstone as he sought words to hail the Lady of Westria.

Then his vision finished adjusting and he realized it was only Rana, pulling her blue cloak around her sturdy shoulders as if she were still cold. But her copper hair was aflame in the sunlight. She looked at him, and all the glory of the new day seemed to glow in her wondering eyes.

"You're alive—" It was not quite a question.

Julian nodded wordlessly. Unable to offer any explanation, he opened his hand so that she could see the Jewel. But when she started toward him, he flinched away. *Alive*—he read her thought—*but changed. . . . There is a silver tracery like the root of a tree from temple to cheekbone now.*

Rana's fair skin had paled. Now she reddened again.

He saw a scattering of golden freckles across her nose, a smudge of dirt on her cheek as if a dirty hand had wiped tears away. Red horsehairs clung to her cloak; the faint scent of horse and woodsmoke opened the doors of his senses to all the physical awarenesses of humanity.

"We had better go find the others," Rana said practically, though her voice was unsteady. "They must be wondering what happened to you."

As if her words had completed some spell, his spirit settled completely into his body at last, and he was whole.

Julian laughed for sheer sudden joy. Then he worked his heavy shoulders back and forth a few times to loosen them and began to brush the dirt out of his hair.

THE BEST IN FANTASY

ANDRÉ NORTON

☐ 54738-1 THE CRYSTAL GRYPHON $2.95
54739-X Canada $3.50

☐ 48558-1 FORERUNNER $2.75

☐ 54747-0 FORERUNNER: THE SECOND $2.95
54748-9 VENTURE Canada $3.50

☐ 54736-5 GRYPHON'S EYRIE $2.95
54737-3 (with A. C. Crispin) Canada $3.50

☐ 54732-2 HERE ABIDE MONSTERS $2.95
54733-0 Canada $3.50

☐ 54743-8 HOUSE OF SHADOWS $2.95
54744-6 (with Phyllis Miller) Canada $3.50

☐ 54740-3 MAGIC IN ITHKAR (edited by
Andre Norton and Robert Adams) Trade $6.95
54741-1 Canada $7.95

☐ 54745-4 MAGIC IN ITHKAR 2 (edited by
Norton and Adams) Trade $6.95
54746-2 Canada $7.95

☐ 54734-9 MAGIC IN ITHKAR 3 (edited by
Norton and Adams) Trade $6.95
54735-7 Canada $8.95

☐ 54727-6 MOON CALLED $2.95
54728-4 Canada $3.50

☐ 54725-X WHEEL OF STARS $2.95
54726-8 Canada $3.50

Buy them at your local bookstore or use this handy coupon:
Clip and mail this page with your order

TOR BOOKS—Reader Service Dept.
49 W. 24 Street, 9th Floor, New York, NY 10010

Please send me the book(s) I have checked above. I am enclosing
$_____ (please add $1.00 to cover postage and handling).
Send check or money order only—no cash or C.O.D.'s.

Mr./Mrs./Miss _____

Address _____

City _____ State/Zip _____

Please allow six weeks for delivery. Prices subject to change without notice.